Star Tower

The Thirsting Forest

Zachary Michael Stivers

To Ben, for helping me craft this world and bring it to life. Without you, this book would never have been written.

And to my wife, for encouraging me from day one, and supporting me all along this journey. Thank you for all you do, every single day.

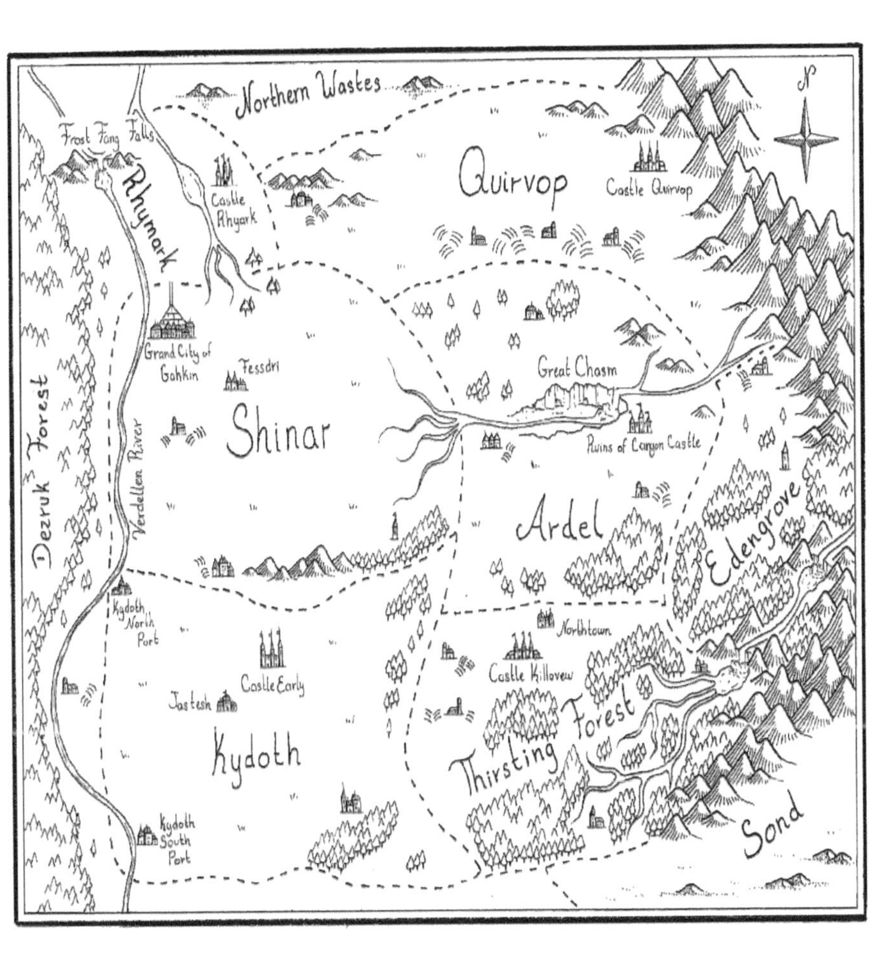

Northern Wastes
Frost Fang Falls
Rhymark
Castle Rhyark
Quirvop
Castle Quirvop
Dezruk Forest
Grand City of Gahkin
Fessdri
Shinar
Verdellen River
Great Chasm
Ruins of Canyon Castle
Ardel
Edengrove
Kydoth North Port
Northtown
Jastesh
Castle Early
Castle Killovew
Kydoth
Thirsting Forest
Kydoth South Port
Sond

"He will erase all sorrow, all pain, all tribulations. Those who suffer shall be granted peace. Those who hunger, satiation. Those who thirst shall have their thirst quenched. The God-King is the pure energy from which flows all life, from the stars unto the lands of men. The Great Flash of His sword will baptize the land, and purge evil from the realms of men and usher unto the faithful their star life."

-    The Habibrok, Disclosure 15

I

At first, just three wagons came.

The Sondite people, their faces gaunt, purple eyes shriveled, fled their home across the mountains only to get themselves lost in the Thirsting Forest. When they finally arrived at Castle Killovew, they told stories of the sun hovering on the desert horizon, never setting. Just sitting on the edge of the world, scorching their crops and charring ruination upon their ancestral lands.

The seasons were slowing, just as the Habibrok foretold.

The Great Flash neared.

Now at least fifteen wagons sat outside the castle, with more on the way.

Lord Jacob Killovew watched the starving refugees cross under the gate and onto the castle lawn. He squeezed the ancient stone railing of his castle's breezeway, steadying himself for the task to come.

Normally, Jacob adored the unobstructed view of the southeastern lawn and the sprawling forest. Beyond the torchlight, the forest faded from greenish-gray to black as it crept into the distant mountains. The twilight sky, an ever-deepening purple, refused to yield to the darkness. The few stars bright enough to stand out twinkled white and green.

Now Lord Killovew saw only a landscape of looming trouble and a horde of broken people he could not help.

Behind Jacob, two Acolytes from Shinar waited, arms crossed. The priest rulers of the capital city had arrived shortly after the first Sondites, and now they commanded Jacob to refuse sanctuary to the refugees and send them away.

"The First Hand has spoken with Gahkin. The God-King knows best," the Acolytes had said when Jacob pushed back against their message. Yet it was not Gahkin who he doubted, but the word of the Acolytes themselves.

Now they hovered behind him, watching him as he watched the Sondite refugees, awaiting his decision. Not that he really had any choice.

"Give me a flicker longer."

He left his vantage point and the two purple-robed priests and crossed the rest of the breezeway. He ascended a set of spiral stairs and entered a small bedroom. He walked over to the bed by the window and reached out his hand, pausing just before touching little James Killovew. He did not wake him, though he wanted to see the boy's cheerful eyes, to see the innocent twinkle of hope that pushed Lord Killovew to be the best ruler he could be. Instead, he watched his son's chest, rising and falling, rhythmic and gentle.

Lord Killovew smiled despite the struggles of the kingdom. One cycle, this son would lead the Thirsting Forest Realm, and he could ask for no better heir to the throne. No doubt little James would help his people achieve a bright future, brighter than any Killovew Lord before him. Jacob needed to ensure that the realm—and the whole kingdom—that he left behind for his son was safe and prosperous.

That task was beginning to seem... challenging.

He scooped up the gold signet resting on the wooden bedside table and left the room.

Lord Killovew adjusted his brown and green cloak over his shoulders. He pinned the bright gold signet of the God-King next to the smaller green sigil of the Thirsting Forest Realm. He tugged at the tight collar around his neck. He brushed the stone dust off his trousers.

As he crossed the breezeway for the second time, Jacob noticed a wispy patch of clouds to the north.

Perhaps the floods *will* come.

And perhaps the sun will set in Sond.

Jacob scoffed at his own sarcasm. The Sondites would not abandon their realm unless it was truly beyond salvation.

Sond sat on the far side of the Gilv Mountains, southeast of the Thirsting Forest, doomed to be swallowed up by the desert. They had endured drought for season after season, and finally, their will had broken. They had hoped and prayed the sun would sink further one season instead of less. But, of course, it never happened. Only drought, starvation, and never-ending sunlight awaited the refugees if he sent them back there. They had already tried that course for far too long.

If this is truly the God-King's will, he thought, head bowed, it is beyond man's reasoning.

As he came up to the Acolytes, no longer fidgeting, he spoke, "I would meet with you again, in the throne room, if you'll wait for me there."

"And our commandments, Lord Killovew? Will you follow them?"

"I am seeing to them now."

Jacob moved through the castle with haste and purpose after leaving the Acolytes behind in the breezeway.

He no longer tugged at his collar. He no longer brushed at his trousers nor fiddled with the ring on his finger. He smiled and nodded at his advisers, his cloak billowing behind him. He went from corridor to corridor, taking the shortest route possible down and out the ancient castle until he threw open the massive door leading into the southern yards.

The inner lawn bustled with a few hundred of the homeless Sondites. They flashed fleeting smiles at him, grateful to be within the strong walls of Castle Killovew, but their heads bent to the ground again as fast as their frowns returned to their faces.

As Lord Killovew walked through his trampled field, one of his youngest knights popped up from behind a makeshift tent.

"Sir, may I speak with you a moment?"

"Seems so."

"Ah, yes." The apprentice knight cleared his throat and continued, "Are we supposed to clear these Sondites out? I've heard talk that the Acolytes—well, it might take two or three candles before we can get them all outside the gates, and even then—"

"No, Trittion. Listen to orders, not rumors. The men who are within my walls are my men now, with a home, and do not fit the Acolyte's description of refugees. Those camped outside the castle must still be sent away, however." Jacob glanced up at the ramparts to the breezeway. The two Acolytes gazed down, looking directly at Lord Killovew and his knight. To Trittion he said, "But do not act on that yet. I want you to go find at least four elder knights and tell them to meet me in the throne room immediately."

"It shall be done. And…" Trittion looked up from the ground. "…Sir?"

"Yes?"

"Well, I'm not sure if this is my place to say…"

"It wasn't your place to have approached me at all." The boy's face flushed, but Jacob dropped his authoritative look. It was better to have thoughtful knights than mindless ones, although it was not always easier. "Come speak with me in my study later, Trittion, and we can discuss your thoughts further. But for now, go, follow your orders."

Trittion rubbed the back of his neck and then spoke anyway, "I—I just want you to know. I agree with you, sir." Trittion hustled to his task.

Lord Killovew walked out under his open castle gate, pushing past the incoming Sondites, and looked at the stone gatehouse to his right. Jacob found one of his old sword tutors, Sir Nestin Oak, stationed at the wheel. The old knight's face looked more aged now than ever, especially as the torchlight flicked deep, shifting shadows across his wrinkled brow. All his life, the man had seemed to be squinting, always looking out for danger far ahead. These cycles, the man could barely lift a shield, but he was still a sworn knight, and thus he still squinted into the dark, still watching for hungry bandits or chasm creatures or whatever else might emerge from the edge of the Thirsting Forest.

He noticed Lord Killovew in his peripherals and addressed him, "My lord? Do you have orders for me?" The knight had known Jacob when he was still in swaddling clothes and yet still maintained the formalities.

Jacob looked out at the near thousand Sondite refugees camped out around his castle, some still heading toward the gate. He sighed and then spoke, "I command the gate be shut, Sir Nestin."

The gate master nodded curtly. "As you say, sire. It shall be done."

"I wish you foul weather and fair health, Sir Nestin."

"I wish you muddy paths and clean health, as ever, Lord Killovew."

Jacob walked back inside the castle walls as the gate winched closed behind him. The guards stationed outside stepped in front of several Sondites, who dashed forward to try to get inside. One Sondite boy dodged past a guard and slid under the closing gate. The soldiers inside the walls quickly surrounded him. Despite the boy's youth, no older than young Prince James, some aimed spear and sword at him. Lord Killovew frowned.

From behind the circle of soldiers, someone shouted, "Wait. Lower your weapons." Trittion pushed through the crowd. "He is just a boy, not a Vistonex, for Gahkin's sake. Is your family within the walls, son?"

"My family?" The boy blinked up at the young knight. "Well, my dad and sis, they didn't make it over the mountains."

"And your mother?"

The boy shrugged his shoulders. "Stayed behind in the forest. Couldn't keep going."

"Your sorrow is now mine, young one." Trittion placed a hand on the boy's shoulder.

Lord Killovew waved to the boy and the young knight, "Come with me, the both of you."

"Sir, this boy—"

"I heard, Trittion. Everyone else, do not point your weapons at any youngsters, Sondite or otherwise." Jacob took the child's hand, and the three of them walked back toward the castle interior. "You may stay within my walls, son. What is your name?"

"Kamau, sir, and thanks. The last thing my mother told me was to make it here. Just make it to Castle Killovew, and I'll be safe, she said. She said the Killovews are good people. And I did. I made it." He grinned. "But just barely." His head swiveled back and forth, the purple Sondite eyes flashing between the shadowy stone walls and the tall towers barely visible in the dusky torchlight.

Lord Killovew said to Trittion, "You are to find a family who has lost a child around his age, at least more than a season ago. If there is not one here at the castle, check the village censuses. Bring them the boy and tell them it is a gift from

Gahkin to raise him."

"If they refuse him, my lord?" Trittion took the hand of the Sondite boy from Jacob Killovew.

"If the family takes the God-King's gift so lightly, tell them it is also a command from me."

"Yes, my lord."

"Try to find a woman whom you would trust to raise your own son."

"Yes, my lord."

"Are the others waiting for me in council?"

"Yes, my lord." The young man nodded. "Four of your elder knights should be there already. And plenty of councilors too, I'm sure."

"I'm sure." Jacob knelt and put a hand on the Sondite's shoulder. "Kamau."

"Yes?"

"You are a citizen of the Thirsting Forest now. That is as much a responsibility as it is a privilege. May your future be long and wet."

"Okay…"

"It's a saying we use here. You can use it too, now." Jacob stood up and said to Trittion, "Go find this boy a home."

"Right away, my lord." The apprentice knight and the younger Sondite turned away and disappeared back into the crowded yard.

Jacob watched them as they slipped through the people, eventually losing them among the rest of the folks trying to get settled. Some Sondite had boiled a kettle full of soup, or maybe broth, and was ladling it out to whoever stopped and asked. One of the Killovew guards was hammering in iron stakes, instructing a refugee woman to hold her tent lines taut. She wiped tears from her eyes but pulled on the rope, and the tent lifted into existence.

He watched people without any real hope at all, hoping anyway.

He watched his citizens helping the Sondites, and he watched the Sondites helping each other. He watched, and he ground his jaw tight. He watched, and his eyes grew hard, and his resolve strengthened.

He watched their resilience for a while longer. When he left the yard, he took some of that resilience with him, fists clenched.

Jacob met his elder knights in the throne room, along with a smattering of his other advisers and some of the chieftains of the realm. The Acolytes from Shinar were also there, waiting off to the side. Jacob Killovew, Lord of the Thirsting Forest, sat in the highest chair. His throne was carved of pliable wood found in the thick of the forest, known as Squidroot. Squidroot was a common and well-known tree in the swamplands of the rainforest. Each piece of the chair had been specifically sun-bleached to ensure a different shade of gray. The gray-scale rainbow of Squidroot stood as a symbol for the people and their Lord, and Jacob tried to weigh its unspoken advice with every decision he made.

Just like Jacob's ancestors, when he spoke in front of his men, the Killovew voice reverberated with authority and confidence across the room.

Jacob spoke to his elder knights first. "Split the Sondites outside the gates into four different groups. Lead them toward Kydoth, and to Canyon Castle… and to the Edengrove. The final group, if any choose to go, can go back toward Sond. We will *not* be forcing anyone who is now within my castle walls to leave." Lord Killovew glared at the Acolytes standing by the doors before continuing, "The fact of the matter, though, is that we can't support the rest of the refugees on our own."

Two of the Acolytes leaned together, whispering.

Jacob waited for the whispers to end and then continued, "Bring however many riders you see fit. Whoever leads the trip to Sond, bring twice as many of your men as you think you may need. It will not be an easy journey, and I want to avoid as much hardship as possible. Drought waits on the far side of the mountains. Do not harm any of the Sondites, even if they prove disobedient. Detain them if you must and escort them all the way out of our realm but do your best to avoid unnecessary violence." Jacob chewed at his tongue for a second. "And bring plenty of food and water. Do not send the Sondites off at the border without a decent stock of supplies. You can take from the royal reserves if necessary. That is all for now. See to it."

The knights left the room to divvy up their roles without questioning the order.

His other councilors and chieftains were not always as quick to act or to accept his decisions without suggestions or arguments. They were wise men, though, and they had earned the right to argue with their Lord on behalf of the people of the realm.

An adviser lifted two of his fingers and inclined his head. Jacob nodded at him.

"My lord, mercy and selflessness are great qualities. But they are not traits that help feed our people. How do we intend to take care of the Sondites still here on the castle grounds? You just sent off half the castle surplus with the departing Sondites, and now we have three hundred new mouths to feed right here."

"Griff, there are barely two hundred Sondites within the walls, and we both know it. The castle will make do for a while. I intend to divide them up and send them to our villages. With many of our young men"—Jacob cast another hard glance toward the Acolytes—"dutifully serving in the God-King's army, we could use them. Over the next two cycles, we need to continue the census and find out what these folks did for a living in Sond. Most of them will be useful in some fashion or another."

"Very good, my lord."

A second adviser spoke, two fingers in the air, not waiting for a nod of acknowledgment, "Lord, we've heard word from our merchants that some of the Quirvop northern villages have been attacked by… well… by cannibals, sir."

Murmurs broke out across the hall.

Lord Killovew raised his hands, "We will not react rashly to rumors from half a kingdom away. The Quirvop realm has not asked for aid, and we have enough issues within our realm to deal with."

Another adviser raised two fingers, and Lord Killovew gestured to him.

"Some of our forest villages have asked to hunt off permitted land, deeper into the wild forest. The game is disappearing from their safer hunting grounds. And we will need to raise quotas based on our new… guests. The men think it is the dwellers, sir. The longer light seasons are pushing them south, it seems."

"There are new caves found every dark season, Lord," another added.

Jacob thought for a moment before answering. Sighing, he said, "Send an envoy with a knight to each of the villages filing the requests and assessing their individual needs. Tell them they will soon have more able men sweeping the forests. If they cannot wait, then ensure only the most capable of hunters are given permission. In fact, I'll sign some warrants that—"

"My lord, requiring *more* warrants is the opposite of—"

"I *do not* want children or women out in the deep forest. If the dwellers are hunting the dwindling boar or deer population, so be it. Better than hunting some poor widow's only son. I'll sign a thousand warrants if needed but hunting in the wild forest will not happen without them. There is a reason we stay out of the deep forest; I don't feel I need to remind you all of that."

Silence settled in the hall, thick as the forest fog.

"Honored Acolytes, do you have anything you'd like to add?"

A surprisingly youthful man walked forward, his deep purple robe shimmering in the torchlight. His footsteps echoed in the hall. The men all watched as he stepped up to Jacob's throne.

He leaned over and whispered in Jacob's ear with hot breath. *They all need to go back to Sond, they will be welcome nowhere else. Including those you've… saved.*

"Leave us," Jacob commanded of his councilors. They gathered their things and shuffled out of the room. Some took longer than was necessary and cast questioning looks toward Lord Killovew, but he simply smiled back at them. Griff seemed to stall at the door, lingering until Lord Killovew flicked his hand at him, waving him away. Eventually, they all left, and the thick doors slammed shut.

The Acolyte leader did not step back from Jacob's seat, and now his hawkish eyes peered downward at the Lord of the Thirsting Forest. Lord Killovew would have been made uncomfortable by the move, but he had been uncomfortable ever since their arrival.

Jacob was on the edge of anger, and it would not be wise to unleash it upon the Acolytes. He needed to be clever in which words he used. He spoke slow and quiet, each word intentional.

"When you first arrived, Isaac, you made no mention of where to send the Sondites. You only said they all could not stay on my land. I can understand that… in a way. My people are growing lean of food, same as any other realm, and they are perhaps more *faithful* than these refugees, so… they deserve the bounty of the forest Gahkin has provided, and the Sondites do not. I did as I was commanded. Yet now you say I should send them *all* back to Sond, where only starvation awaits. Why must that be? This seems unlike Gahkin, who provides for all, and keeps the sun rising and setting in the southeast…" Though a few candles slower each season.

At the current rate, every few seasons, a whole cycle was dropped from the dark season in the Thirsting Forest. It would be even worse in the far southeast where Sond lay. Jacob would have left Sond seasons ago if he had been the ruler there. But Jacob could not mention *that* to the Acolyte.

"The Ruler of Rulers does not give a people a home so they might choose to leave it on a whim. Perhaps their realm is being punished for lack of faith. When was the last Sondite in Shinar? When did the last Sondite set eyes upon His glory?"

Jacob sat in silence. *He* had never been to Shinar, he doubted a Sondite had made the trip anytime recently. The westernmost realm in the kingdom, merchants from the Thirsting Forest spent half a season to get to the capital city of Shinar. If a man rode all ten candles of each cycle, switching horses and sleeping on horseback, he would still be hard-pressed to make the round-trip journey before the seasons changed.

Generally, only the rare trip to present tithes or witness the commencement of a new First Hand demanded the realm lords' attendance. When the merchants did return, they were always full of religious fervor, filling Killovew's peoples' heads with their chance at the star life and the miracles raised in Shinar. The Star Tower, of course, was a miraculous building certainly worthy of admiration but the infinite twisting metal was a relic from a different era. The purpose of these ancient relics was long forgotten if ever known at all.

Jacob bit his tongue and replied in a measured voice, "Perhaps I should send them to Shinar. They could regain their faith and beg for a new home from the Ten Hand Council, or at least be told the proper direction to go in search of one."

"They know where their home is! But let them grovel to the Ten Hand Council if they desire. It is no sin to seek them out. There is always forgiveness from Gahkin, but only for the faithful. Perhaps they need a sign of his presence?" Isaac cocked his head and smirked. "Perhaps Castle Killovew could do with a sign as well?"

That was too bold. Jacob knew to give a quick answer this time. "I think I speak for all my people when I say we would always welcome a sign from Gahkin, though we shall never need one."

"And if one did come, my lord?" The Acolyte leader asked. "Would the Realm of the Thirsting Forest answer the call?"

"We would answer it, of course."

Isaac smiled, but his eyes did not change. He turned away from Jacob and retreated down the steps. From there, he said, as much to the other priests as to Lord Killovew, "I shall tell the council the Killovew realm remains… how did you say it earlier? *Faithful.*"

They took their leave, purple robes shuffling down the hall to the far doorway, whispering all the way out. At the doorstep, the leader stopped and turned back.

"Ah, I almost forgot, my lord. we have something for you." He walked all the way back down the hall and up the stairs to the throne. He withdrew a small package wrapped in thick hemp paper and tossed it in Killovew's lap. "Open it."

Jacob unpeeled the wrapping and pulled out some sort of thick bread loaf. "What is this?"

"It's food, my lord. And we have three thousand more bars outside in our wagons."

"I don't understand."

"It's food from the Ten Hand Council. Blessed by Gahkin. It provides enough sustenance to keep a man healthy and energized for two cycles, no other food needed. We are not asking for anything in return."

Jacob hefted the small loaf in his hand. It was certainly dense.

"Would you like the other three thousand loaves, Lord Killovew?"

Jacob frowned. "Why are you offering these to me?"

"Why wouldn't we? We are here to help all the realms in the kingdom. It's our surplus. We give it freely."

Jacob stared at the bar and then up at the Acolyte. "You'll make us all dependent on this," he spoke softly. A declaration, not a question.

Isaac smirked again and stepped backward to leave. "Gahkin provides, Lord Killovew. If you simply accept our gift, we can help feed your people. Sounds like you've chosen to feed more than expected… A heavy burden in these trying times."

Jacob did not speak. Almost imperceptibly, after a long moment, he nodded.

Isaac said, "I did not hear you, my lord."

"Yes, I accept Gahkin's gift, Isaac."

"Distribute your three thousand however you want," the Acolyte said coldly. "They will last a full season before they rot. More will be available in future seasons. Keep the faith…"

Jacob wearily stood from his throne. He watched the Acolytes leave and then went to fetch his son.

He reached the breezeway leading to his chambers and found his son already awake, staring out at the very same spot where Lord Killovew had been gazing earlier in the cycle.

He pulled him back from the dangerous ledge and asked, "What do you see, my son?"

The boy looked up at his father, eyes still sleepy. "There are eighteen stars out that I can count."

"Indeed?" Jacob stood alongside his little heir, looking up to count the stars himself.

"Two more than the past cycle."

"What does that tell us?"

"That it is still getting darker and that the rains may still come and that the sun is still setting." James looked back out toward the yard and the forest. "Are you sending the Sonds away?"

"Sondites, son."

"Are you sending the Sondites away?"

Already, the knights and their riders moved about among the refugees, lanterns in hand, organizing the chaos outside the castle walls.

"Only the ones we can't keep here at the castle or in the villages nearby. We cannot feed them forever, and the Acolytes said Gahkin demanded it."

Little James was silent for a while, watching the knights try to organize and divide the refugees. Finally, he said, "They look like wolves, splitting up a herd, but they are just dogs, doing what you commanded. If Gahkin commands that *we* do something, are we just like dogs to him?"

Lord Killovew frowned. "You ask tough questions. I don't know the answers to most of them, and this one is complicated." The Lord of the Thirsting Forest shook his head and raised his shoulders. "I don't think of my men as dogs, son. I think of them like people, like you and me. So… I think we are both less and more than dogs to the God-King. They say he looks like one of us and gave us this life, these lands, this home. That he united the realms and built a civilized kingdom, and returned to the stars in the Star Tower.

"Men use dogs because they are loyal, and take to man's side naturally, and can be helpful allies… But on a cold night in the deep forest, man and dog have similar needs. Warmth, food, shelter. I'd guess Gahkin probably needs little of what we need. Gahkin is… more… than we can understand."

Both father and son stared out toward the dark forest, eyes glazed over, silent for a long while. The men outside the gate milled around, grouped into a few different clumps. One clump began to march off down the road in the direction of Kydoth and Ardel. In the darkening twilight above the forest, a little star appeared, twinkled, and then dropped out of the sky.

James asked, "Do you hear that?"

The boy raised his hands and covered his ears. Lord Killovew heard nothing at first. He tilted his head and detected a distant, high-pitched whine coming from deep within the Thirsting Forest. Or maybe… from above the forest.

It grew louder, and soon Jacob had to cover his ears as well. A small flock of birds alighted from the canopy of the forest, their black shapes scattering in every direction, unorganized. They looked chaotic. Frenzied.

A thick beam of light flashed downward from the sky. This was no strike of lightning but a solid ray of burning gold. All those inside and out at Castle Killovew looked up, shielding their eyes from the sudden brightness. It ignited the forest, trees splintering and disintegrating as the beam crossed over them. Jacob gripped his son's shoulder tightly. The beam grew wider as it traveled closer and illuminated the castle as if the season of the sun were at its peak. The Acolytes, mounted on their matching silver steeds, watched transfixed with the rest of the people. Jacob was about to run with his son, sure the pillar of light had come to lay ruin to his castle when the beam paused… and then abruptly disappeared.

At first, he could see nothing but blackness. His eyesight returned after a few moments of blinking and rubbing away the remaining echoes of light still floating in his vision.

The forest cracked and popped. A thick line of gray smoke rose from the gap carved through the trees. Wonder and fear lingered over the people, nearly as palpable as the smoke over the forest.

"Are you okay, James?"

The boy nodded his head, but his whole body trembled. Jacob put a hand on his son's shoulder, steadying him.

Lord Killovew shouted out from the open breezeway down into the yard below.

"Acolytes of the West, Priests of Shinar! I shall ride with you to the Grand

City of Gahkin, if you will allow my company."

A moment of silence hung over the stunned and blinded crowd. Then someone shouted back, "They agree, my lord!"

Little James's eyes widened as he looked up at his father, his hands clutching onto the loose garment of Lord Killovew's robe. "Father, what... Why are you leaving? What was that?"

Jacob Killovew knelt and looked at his boy.

"Son," he said, "I think that is how Gahkin summons his dogs."

II

White light surrounded a naked body. For the briefest moment, or perhaps for ten thousand centuries, all was still.

Then two fingers on the right hand twitched.

Gray-blue eyes flicked open, and the man drew a gasping breath. He turned his head slowly, looking right and then left. Empty white space surrounded him an infinite distance in all directions. He had a peculiar sensation that he couldn't tell if he was standing up or lying down, for he felt no tug of gravity in any specific direction but rather felt a strong pressure squeezing across the entirety of his skin.

He struggled to raise his arm. He concentrated, and his arm slowly lifted, but after rising a few inches, the pale limb bumped against an invisible surface. He strained and thrust his other arm up in a panicked rush, and it slammed against the same invisible surface. Everywhere his frantic hands searched, they found only a white wall, mere inches from his body. His arms dropped back to his sides. His chest heaved.

He called out, his voice hoarse, his words indistinct. There was no response. He was trapped. He was alone. Beating his palms against the flat white surface, he called out again.

The whiteness—the complete, empty, suffocating, silent, monstrous whiteness—swallowed up the noise. No echo replied.

A woman did, though.

"Good morning, Adam," she said, her voice silken soft. The words were accompanied by the moist breath of a whisper in his ear, "You woke up ahead of schedule."

He turned his head, but there was nothing there, no woman to be found.

"What's happen—where am I?" The man she called Adam struggled to articulate his words. His tongue was dry and sluggish.

"In a moment, you will begin to remember," the voice murmured. "Please lay back and try to relax. All your questions will be answered."

"Wait! What's happened to me?"

"In time, Adam. Please, do not worry."

He tried to lift his head, but the pressure was too strong. He felt a tiny vibration at the back of his skull, relaxing his knotted neck muscles. The squeezing sensation across the surface of his skin subsided.

The sensuous voice continued, "It's a common side effect. A lot of the crew experience disorientation and memory loss. Everything should be a little clearer now."

He closed his eyes and smiled. Adam felt his hibernation tomb move and it did not startle him in the slightest.

"You're being transported to your new quarters. You may notice you have already regained much of your strength."

Adam looked down at his arms. They seemed larger. The skin was tighter. When he lifted them, they felt much lighter than before.

"In a few minutes, you will be free to meet the current team. Your new teammates are excited for you to join. They'll fill you in with their progress and the specificities of your role on the crew. They will be awaiting your arrival. Good luck, Adam. Remember our commitment. Remember our vow."

The lid of the coffin cracked open, lifting away from him. Adam sprung fully out of his crypt-bed. He touched his toes and twisted his back. He rolled his shoulders and cracked his neck. He felt refreshed. He took a deep, contented breath.

A picture of his family sat on the corner of his desk. On the back, his mother had written: *we love you.* His father had written: *good luck, son, we're so proud of you.*

Adam touched his finger to the glossy face of his mother and stared at it for a long moment. He placed the picture back on the corner of his desk and moved to the closet. Three one-piece jumpers hung alongside a couple of white lab coats. After dressing, he walked to the only door in the room. The door itself had no knob, just a little recessed button where a doorknob should be.

He pressed the button with his thumb; it emitted a soft orange light and beeped warningly at him.

That didn't sound quite right.

The door glided open with a soft, near silent *swoosh.*

Most of the hallway outside his room was dark. The few bulbs still lit flickered in the ceiling. Little red lights blinked on several different doors further down the hall.

He took two hesitant steps into the hallway and looked in both directions. One way faded into complete darkness. Dusty light from an open door illuminated the other end of the hallway. Adam began walking in that direction, his pace slow and wary.

He noticed a palm-sized screen pad on one of the doors with blinking lights. The rolling text said, 'OCCUPANT ABSENT.'

Adam crept on.

He crossed the bright threshold at the end of the hall and stepped into an enormous cargo bay. The roof was at least two hundred yards high, and the warehouse stretched back further than Adam could see. Crates and boxes and shipping containers, color-coded and stacked, in some places to the roof, lined the walls.

Adam walked up to the closest shipping container, marked with a blue stamp that read, 'INITIAL FR. RLC.14 P# 610, 611, 613, 621.'

The door was closed. He gripped the big handle, built like an iron steering wheel, and tried to twist it upward. It did not give. It felt as though it weighed a thousand pounds. Adam spread his feet and tried again. His arms bulged, and his core tightened. The wheel rotated a little. He twisted it a final time, feeling an unnatural pressure in his muscles, but he found the strength, and the wheel cranked upward, popping the two big pins that locked the door in place. Adam heaved backward, his boots digging into the hard floor. The door swung open.

The crate was empty.

Adam pushed the door shut and twisted the wheel back into the locked position. He walked deeper into the middle of the warehouse. Each crate Adam opened was empty; each new aisle he turned down was as quiet and motionless as the last.

After snaking his way through every single aisle in the warehouse, Adam finally found the back wall. Composed of three massive sections of shuttered steel, the sections were marked 'DOCKING ZONE 1,' 'DOCKING ZONE 2,' and 'DOCKING ZONE 3.' In the back corner sat a forklift and a micro-crane.

As Adam got closer to the back of the warehouse, he saw a speaker box mounted on the wall. He reached the box and examined it closely. One of the buttons was labeled, 'BROADCAST.' He pressed it down and spoke into the vented metal gills.

"This is Dr. Adam Scott. Does anyone copy?" His voice sounded stronger than before, and he had no trouble with his tongue. There was a long silence. Adam held the button down again and said, "Is there anyone on board? Please respond. Over."

A moment passed, and then another. Adam pressed the button to speak again but was cut off.

The middle steel door marked 'DOCKING ZONE 2' began grinding upward. Adam flinched at the sudden noise. The sound of the turning gears and creaking steel echoed off the large walls of the warehouse. The door halted after raising up about ten feet. The noise of metal churning and scraping ceased.

Adam stared into the gap. Nothing more happened.

He walked closer and then stopped at the foot of the opening. He scratched his head. He waited. He craned his neck over his shoulder. All was silent. He waited some more. He took a deep breath, cracked both of his middle knuckles, squeezed his hands into fists, and strode into the dim garage.

The room was almost empty. A handful of small crates were scattered near the entrance, and a couple larger boxes were stacked along the walls. An unrecognizable shape sat in the back corner, and Adam's curiosity drew him toward it.

Tan and gray, it was a vehicle Adam had never seen before. In fact, he had never even heard of such an… aircraft.

The body was half tank and half school bus, gifted with wings and a rotor and a rocket engine tail. The two stunted wings on each side formed an X shape, and thin silver cylinders hung at the end of each wing. The cargo doors were closed, and the cockpit windows were dark. There was no movement.

Adam stepped up onto a footstool near the cockpit. He peered inside, his hands cupped around his eyes. Nothing moved within. He reached down, popped the handle, and pulled open the door. Leaning in, he scanned the empty cockpit.

With a snap and a heavy metallic crash, the steel wall behind him fell shut. Adam was thrown off balance and into complete darkness. He heard the hissing rush of air, sealing the room for what was to come next.

A wide steel door at the back of the docking room snapped open, revealing the vast, glittering blackness of space.

Everything loose in the bay was ripped out into the vacuum. The pressure wrenched Adam's breath out of his lungs and yanked him forward into the cockpit. A footstool slammed into the door, knocking it closed before bouncing off and zooming out into space. The small aircraft maintained its position for only a moment before it rolled over twice and then flipped out over the cusp. The tank-copter plummeted down, barrel-rolling as it plunged. G-forces pinned Adam to the far side of the cockpit. Only green was visible through the front window, and the ship shook violently.

A shimmering beam of light shattered the cockpit window and sliced through the hull, eating its way through steel and iron, through a control panel spitting sparks, through a pilot's chair and a sphere of tightly weaved wiring and microscopic computer chips. Arcs of electric energy danced through the air. The wind, rushing through the gashes in the ship, screamed as loud as a thousand train engines. Everything not strapped down was ripped out, mostly in pieces. Shearing apart, the ship lost its spin, and Adam was sucked out into the sky. The gold beam ate its way through the thick-walled ship like a chainsaw through butter.

The beam touched the fuel tank.

A sudden explosion consumed the vehicle, sending wreckage in a hundred directions.

The beam disappeared.

Debris and dust fell through the air and into a dark forest canopy, landing in mossy trees, tangled vines, and on the occasional hooting creature. Adam splashed into a cold black river, steam rising from his charred body.

One

Jason and Jinala faced each other in the dim light of dawn, swords in their hands, panting. The young sun filtered light through the trees to the southeast. Brother and sister circled each other. The girl wept but did not bother to wipe away her tears. Her pale emerald eyes, wet and glistening, stayed locked on the deep, dry jade of her brother's.

A white horse grazed a few yards away, ignorant to the fighting. Behind Jinala, Castle Killovew rose out of the low mist. The highest towers basked in sunlight, but the rest of the castle was dark gray, still in the shade of the mountains. Behind Jason, the fronds of a Royal Palm, wrapped by a Strangler Fig and bent toward the ground by seasons of gentle influence, fluttered as the wind picked up.

The older brother charged his little sister, and steel met steel. The sister held her ground, twisting her shoulders to deflect the blow wide to her left. The brother, officially a man now at his sixth sunrise, whipped his sword back at her. She deflected it again, but this time stumbled backward at the strength of the blow.

"Come on, Gina. I'm disappointed." He smirked and, with one finger, beckoned her closer.

She pointed the sword at his chest and lunged forward. He flicked his wrists, her sword glanced off his, and Jinala's thrust missed his body by half a fist. She felt cold steel against her neck. She froze. She lowered her blade to the ground.

"You're dead, little sister." Jason lowered his sparring blade and speared it down into the wet grass. Jinala tossed hers next to it.

"I can't focus." She looked at him, and her lower lip trembled. "I don't want you to go to Shinar."

Jason shook down his left sleeve, revealing a sparkling strip of leather tied around his wrist. He untied it and dropped the Heir's bracelet into his little sister's palm, smiling without parting his lips.

"I'm sad too, princess. That's yours now, until I get back."

He flicked Jinala's ear when she looked down at the jewelry. She didn't even look up. In the dark season, when they were both children, she might have retaliated with a punch in the stomach or tried to push him over. Not anymore. It was dawn now. The seasons were changing, and Jason was no longer a child. She gazed at the shards of emerald and diamond embedded in the leather.

He reached out toward her shoulder, but she turned away from him, bracelet clenched in her fist. She moved a few paces away and scratched at the neck of

Rara Silva Nix. The white horse nickered back and turned its head closer. Jason did not follow her; he stood alone.

She said, "You don't have to go, Jason. You don't have to join them."

"Yes, Gina, I do. I must go because I have chosen to go, and I will not betray my words. And because Father has... well, Father has need for me to go."

In the direction of the distant castle, a dark line of men on horseback trotted toward them, small gray shadows in the meadow mist but drawing ever closer. Lord James Killovew, their father, led the procession. They followed the edge of the Thirsting Forest, as Jason and Jinala had a candle or so earlier. Jinala's time with her older brother was running out.

"Thanks for... this. And all the practice." Jinala pulled a strand of cloth from her skirt's front pocket. Dangling in the center was a tiny fish scale, grayish-green, glimmering in the sunlight. She handed it to her older brother. "This is my lucky necklace. You have it. It's a trade, until you come back for the bracelet."

The yellow sunbeams shone through the green canopy and bathed them both in soft, fog-filtered light. Jason's eyes told her the truth his mouth would not. He did not believe he would be back to claim the Heir's bracelet. Jinala knew he did not believe it. Jason took the necklace and tucked it into his robe with a tenderness she had never seen from her brother. She ripped her eyes away again as a fresh batch of tears threatened to fall.

Above them, for the first time in many cycles, the pale blue sky was empty of stars. The bright green one, first to show up at dusk and last to disappear at dawn, was gone. Wispy pink clouds, the last vestiges of the dark season storms, blew away from the forest toward the northwest.

"Could we ride just a little further? One last time? There's no horse as fast as Rara in the whole realm. I'll miss her." *And you.*

"Delaying the inevitable, eh?" Jason walked over and helped her into Rara's saddle. After she was seated, Jason grabbed the pommel and pulled himself up behind her. They circled around in the meadow and trotted along the tree line away from the men and the castle.

Jinala held the leather reigns, but Jason's heels nudged Rara Silva Nix onward. The princess smacked her lips together, but the horse trotted along, ignoring Jinala's command to gallop.

Jason laughed. "She'll run for no one except me." Jason reached forward and scratched the horse behind her ears.

"Then you tell—"

Rara Silva Nix snorted and twisted her head, looking toward the trees at the forest edge. A shadow in the upper branches moved against the wind and disappeared into a thicker part of the canopy. Jason squinted, instinctively putting his hand on his sword hilt. He found nothing but air; his sparring sword was lying on the ground thirty yards back. Rara stepped away from the forest a few paces.

Jinala said, "It was just a bird, Jason. Grown-up or not, you're still twitchy."

The young man leaned back, still tense. The horse snorted again, listened, and then trotted on. Jason relaxed.

"Maybe," he said, still scanning the tree line for more movement. "Okay, I guess we can run her a little. Squeeze your left leg against her side." Jason made fast-paced kissing noises. The horse sped up.

"It's just..." Jason continued looking into the trees, "I still remember when we were attacked, Gina..."

****

During the most recent dark season, they had traveled with their father and his men deep into the forest.

Darkness hung thick outside the caravan's small oval of torchlight. A single rider at the front shouldered a large flag, which hung flat and unrecognizable in the humidity and stillness of the Thirsting Forest. The front and back wagons were loaded with heavy bags of miracle bars from the west and letters from beyond the Verdelen River. The middle wagon carried Jason, Jinala, and their father, James Killovew. Jinala peered out the open window, watching the whole procession amble along the overgrown forest road.

They were traveling toward the village Creek, situated at the intersection of two creeks. Her brother had told her the villagers were not as smart as the people who lived at the castle and thus were not too clever with naming things. He had also told her that the village was starving, and they had become cannibals whose favorite meal was grilled princess, but she had not believed him for two flickers. She glanced over at her older brother, shining his new sword with the corner of his cloak. He was about to spit on it when Jinala shoved him. His saliva splatted onto his pants instead.

"Gina!" Jason pushed her back hard, and she knocked into the side of the wagon.

Their father turned around from the front bench and peered in under the roof. He looked manlier than usual. He had thick stubble and had stopped wearing his crown. He spent time setting up camp and keeping watch like the rest of the knights and riders. Soot and dirt smudged his tanned forehead and whiskered cheeks. His dark red hair tumbled over his light green eyes, and most of the time, he smelled of smoke. Jinala liked the less-than-royal look.

"Knock it off," James Killovew said. "Son, sheathe your sword, or I'll take it and won't give it back until the light season. Revealing your sword all the time makes you look fresh, not formidable. Do you think Sir Damian walks around shining his all cycle?"

Jason was silent for a moment. "No," he mumbled eventually, sliding his sword back in its leather scabbard. Jason was almost a man, and she knew he hated being talked to like a boy. She smiled.

"The gleam of dwellers' eye stalks in the dark is the only gleam you need to be worried about," her father said, turning around.

Jason looked over at his sister and frowned at her. Jinala stuck her tongue out at him. He tried to grab it, but she slipped it back in her mouth and smiled.

"Too slow," she said and stuck her tongue out again. Jason had his father's dark red hair, but it was pulled back into a long ponytail. Sir Damian wore his hair the same way.

Jason stared at Jinala, his eyes looking darker than usual. Almost as dark as the cycle she caught him down in the dungeons. She didn't think Jason did that kind of stuff anymore, now that he was older, but still… she did not like playing with him when he got that… *look*.

Jinala crossed her arms and looked back out the window at the thinning tree line. There was a glimmer of a light shining through the brush from around the next bend. She stuck her head out the window and glanced upward. She could see more stars, red and green and white, blinking above her. The canopy of the forest was receding.

Open skies in the night season were rare. The old folks said they did not like them because they needed all the rain they could get during the dark season, but Jinala loved the little lights which hung so low. When she was younger, she climbed up the east tower to the very top to be closer to them. Her nanny told her the stars were Gahkin's fairy warriors who flew too high and were frozen in the great black. They flashed their lights for help, so one cycle, a fairy prince might fly up and cut them free. He would only do so, though, when the Vistonex war was won. And then the warriors would earn their star life and disappear from the sky, signaling evil had been defeated, and the heroes of the realm were returning home.

"Flagbearer! Ride onward and make known our arrival," her father shouted. The three men at the front of the pack urged their horses into a gallop, the flag unfurling behind them. The brown fabric, shaded in warm torchlight, revealed the Killovew insignia: an all-green oak tree, thick and wide. Their father turned back to face his children. "Remember, Jinala, these people will show a lot of deference to us, and they may be thinner than you are used to seeing, but that does not mean we should treat them with less respect. Jason, I *shouldn't* have to remind you of anything, so watch your sister. Don't let her go out of sight of the wagons once we stop. Oh, and don't—"

"Leave 'em be, my lord." Sir Trittion chuckled from behind the reigns. "They won't bother nobody in Creek. I've spent enough time playing politics with the village chiefs this trip. I'll keep an eye on both of 'em." He looked back and wiggled his thick gray mustache at Jinala, which, like always, made her laugh. Lord Killovew turned around, apparently content.

The wagons curved around a final turn, clattered over a small wooden bridge, and then the forest trees parted. A large meadow, twinkling with torches, sat under the jeweled black sky. Huts and cabins and larger buildings with no real walls adorned the forest clearing. The biggest structures were raised up on wooden stilts, had triangle-shaped roofs, and were much longer than they were wide. Skinny villagers stood on either side of the wagon trail, watching as the entourage passed them by. They were not shouting unintelligible languages or wearing especially dirty clothes and reminded Jinala more of the people she had seen near Castle Killovew at Northtown than of cannibals. They might be hungrier than was healthy, but they weren't barbaric animals. The village looked more civilized than Jinala had expected.

The whole ensemble stopped in front of one of the long buildings, and almost instantly, the villagers crowded around the wagons. The Killovew riders jumped out and formed a defensive perimeter. They did not have to draw their swords at this village; the citizens obediently gave them space. Some of the guards began unloading the cargo. They rolled the barrels off in a few different directions and stacked the heavy burlap bags full of the miracle bars in front of the biggest building in the village. One guard climbed on top of the front wagon. He shuffled through the letter bag, calling out family names.

A well-fed man with broad shoulders and wearing a fox skin cap, complete with intact fox head, stood at the top of the stairs of the big building and gave a halfhearted smile. He had thick brown sideburns that ran all the way to his chin, almost touching each other. He wore traditional Killovew colors and had two more fox skins tied around his waist.

James Killovew hopped out onto the ground and swung open the door for Jinala and Jason to exit. The fox man walked forward and shook James's hand. He cuffed Prince Jason on the shoulder and said, "Growing tall like your father, lad."

Prince Jason responded with a curt bow and said, "Thank you, Chieftain Fox. We appreciate the hospitality of your village this cycle."

"Listen to that deep, regal voice! You are indeed a Killovew, Jason, through and through! Speeches will echo through Castle Killovew long after your father and I are gone, and that is a great thing." The chieftain bowed back to Jason. "You are always welcome, Prince Jason, to my village and my hospitality, as required and as desired."

He stepped over in front of Jinala, and she was afraid he was going to hit her on the arm too, but he took it in a gentle, callused hand and inclined his head.

Her father stepped over and put his hand on the man's shoulder. "Chieftain," he said, "This is my daughter, Jinala Killovew. I don't believe you've met her in person before."

"I have not had the pleasure. Princess Killovew, thank you for gracing our village with your beauty and your grace. We are proud to have you as a visitor."

Jinala was still not very good at speaking with strangers, or speaking in front of others at all, for that matter. "I... uh, thank you," she said meekly, then added, "It's, um, a pleasure to meet you too."

Chieftain Fox bowed even lower and then turned back to her father. "Is she...?" He raised an eyebrow, but James shook his head. "Ah, of course, of course. We are not barbarians anymore. She'll make her own choices one cycle. Still though, a beautiful little thing." He spoke like she wasn't still standing right there.

He walked over to the burlap bags, which were stacked as high as his shoulder. The guards continued pulling more from the wagon, stacking a second pile. "Thank Gahkin," he said, and leaning closer to James, added, "and thank you, Lord Killovew."

He spread his hands toward the villagers who were waiting in a large circle around the bags and the Killovew guards. "Line up over here behind the wagon and go ahead and take three bars each. Don't worry about the rations tonight. Eat all three if you want. Then we will count and divvy up the rest after the resting candles on the morrow. Thank you all for your patience. As I said it would, it has been rewarded."

Chieftain Fox and Lord Killovew handed out the bars, three to each man, woman, and child. No one rushed or fought for extras, and most offered thanks and praise to Gahkin for the sustenance. Jason and Jinala stood at the steps and watched the handouts. Jinala was impressed. These folks looked hungrier than the other villagers they had visited before. She could see it in their eyes, something... *desperate*. Still, they all behaved.

Lord Killovew greeted each villager and spoke humbly as he handed out the food, but when they all had departed, he turned to Chieftain Fox and asked gravely, "How close did you come?"

"Closer than we'd like, my lord. I have the hidden surplus, of course, and we didn't have to dip into that. And a few of my rangers with warrants for the deep woods have brought back some meat that we are salting and stashing aside, but James, almost all of the crops failed this past season."

James pinched the bridge of his nose. "Bury me… bury me deep," he muttered. Then he noticed Jason and Jinala still standing off to the side. "Trittion, take them away from here. I'm sorry for my language, Jinala."

As they walked away from the two leaders Jinala heard her father ask about the crayfish and the coconuts. "Almost no crayfish left in the streams, my lord, but we did harvest many coconuts. Thank Gahkin for the coconuts."

Sir Trittion, Jason, and Jinala walked back toward a darker section of the village to look up at the stars. The old knight shared Jinala's fascination with the lights in the black sky, but she suspected he went with them as much to get away from the other adults as to look at the stars. The three of them lay on their backs, Trittion pulling from his wineskin now and again.

"Sir Trit, do you think Gahkin can see us right now?" Jinala asked.

"Gina, if he's looking down here, he's too busy to be looking at us," Jason replied, even though Jinala had deliberately not asked him. "He is probably watching the war. I know I would be. When I'm there, I'll show them a new side of the Killovews. No Vistonex will stop me."

"Jason," Trittion said, speaking slowly, choosing each word with care, "it would be better to be a little… humble. You are more skilled than most with a blade, and you learn fast. You are smart, and quick and handsome… but you are not a boy anymore. You'll be a man by the next sunrise. Boasts like that could get you enlisted if the right ears overhear."

"It's not a boast! I really do want to fight. I want to be more than just another Killovew, I mean, not… be given things, I want to take things for myself and earn a place in the scrolls because of, well—not because of who I am but because of what I can do. Because I'm a Killovew, I never have to worry over thirst or starvation, and most people aren't so lucky… I get that. But I also can't carve my own path. There is so much more to life than just passing out food and lounging in the castle, you know? I want to march and stare out at the howling grass from Castle Early. I want to train under the Sky Tower in Shinar, I want to go beyond the river, and I want to see the Great Chasm and the Ice Mountains and the Frozen Daggers. I want to see city streets crawling with people like an anthill, and… and… I mean, I know life is going to be a lot worse than I make it out to be, but how can I know, how can I learn to value this realm if I've never seen any of the others in the kingdom?"

I want all that too! At least Jason could enlist and travel and fight if that is what he ended up choosing when he became a man. Jinala did not have a choice. Lord Killovew had barely allowed her on this little trip into the forest, and that had taken convincing, and it was right in the middle of their own realm. She would never be allowed to go to any of those other exciting places.

Sir Trittion sat up and looked at Jason, who was still lying on his back in the grass, looking up at the bright stars in the sky. Jinala watched them from her side. Jason continued, "I know I'm not a boy anymore, Trit. That's a part of why I feel this way, I guess. Enlisting might be risky, but so what? What's so great about staying here and living the same life as everybody else? I have so many questions. I want to go out into the world and find some answers for myself."

"What about your little sister? Or your father?" Trittion asked.

Jason sighed. "I would miss them, I suppose." He looked over at Jinala, and she smirked. "Father, I mean. I would miss Father, I suppose. I would definitely not miss my annoying little sister." His face was too dark to interpret, but she knew he was pulling her leg.

Sir Trittion lay back into the grass. "Jason, whatever path you choose next season, and all those that follow, you will be remembered for both who you are and what you do. That's just the way it is. Odds are you will end up far from here while you're a young man. You are a whole lot like your father, and that's... that's what he chose. And what your grandfather Jacob chose as well." Trittion was quiet for a long while. Blades of tall grass occasionally blew into Jinala's view, pitch black compared to the faded purple-black of the sky. "I guess I'm saying I understand, Jason."

Jinala stretched. She was tired, and the tall meadow grass was quite cozy. Trittion continued, "But from an old man to a young one, just remember you have a lot of life left, and rushing off from one place to another might keep you from ever truly knowing any single one of them. Your grandfather once told me seeking fame will kill you before you are ever wise enough to know fame's not something worth seeking."

When Jinala awoke, she found herself blanketed by Trittion's thick cloak. She rolled over, wrapping the cloak around her, intending to go back to sleep, but she couldn't.

Trittion and Jason had what seemed to be a snoring contest. Right after Trittion's deep snore, like a saw grinding over an oak trunk, Jason would snore. Her brother's snore sounded like an explosion, a cough combined with a sneeze followed by a gentle whistle. And then Trittion would argue back with another sawing snore of his own. It was never-ending.

Jinala covered her ears and rolled over in the other direction.

She spotted her father, illuminated by only the flickering stars, walking away from the village.

Creeping toward the edge of the dark forest, carrying two wicker baskets, Lord James Killovew was alone. Her father was never alone, whether he wanted to be or not. Jinala tossed Trittion's cloak off, and quietly stood up. It was a little chilly, but she did not mind. This was a real mystery that needed her investigating.

She considered waking her brother but did not want to risk rousing Sir Trittion, so she snuck off after Lord Killovew by herself, staying low to the ground and behind the highest clumps of tall grass. She stubbed her toe on a rock and bit down on her tongue to keep from groaning.

I'm as tough as Jason.

She stalked on. Her father disappeared into the shadow of a bushy tree like a mongoose into the ferns. She crept closer, but with more caution and at a slower pace. She did not want to risk running up onto him if he was waiting within the tree line.

I'm as sneaky as Jason.

She lowered herself even further into the grass and crawled on all fours forward into the darkness. Under the canopy, with the starlit sky blocked from view, she could not see more than a few yards into the blackness around her. She squinted, looking for movement when a bluish light ignited—right out of thin air.

Jinala had never seen anything like it before.

The light illuminated the surrounding trees like a torch but did not flicker, nor cast everything in an orange glow. She could vaguely compare it to the spark of flint when starting a campfire, but the spark never extinguished. It just... glowed. Continuously.

Magically.

As her eyes adjusted to the new light, she saw something even odder. The light was atop a rusty silver staff, held by a man in a dirty white cloak, unbuttoned, with no hood. He had a long brown beard, knotted and muddy, down to the middle of his chest. Stranger still, standing right next to him, squeezing his shoulder familiarly, stood her father. At their feet, two large baskets of m-bars.

James Killovew was unshaken by the magical blue torch, but Jinala was not. Whatever she had gotten herself into was clearly well beyond her understanding. She would crawl back to Trittion and Jason and then, maybe, ask her father about it when they got back to the castle. She turned to go but then set her jaw tight and forced herself to face the forest again.

I'm as brave as Jason.

Before she lost her courage, she darted in-between the nearest trees and circled the two figures at the fringe of the light, keeping in the dark ferns and stepping softly.

The light vanished. Everything went black. She could not see the trees, let alone her father or the stranger. She sat still. There was no rustling, no muttering. Behind her, a few lanterns from the village flickered dimly. She turned and crept as quickly as she could out of the forest, back toward the comforting light of civilization.

I'm not as brave as Father.

The stars were bright, just as bright as when she first sat down in the meadow. Sir Trittion was still snoring when a tall, muscular knight who had come back from the war last season shook Jason and Jinala awake. They stood and stretched and then meandered back to the wagons. Almost everyone was aboard or mounted on their horses.

Her father shook hands with Chieftain Fox and said, "You'll need to do no more forest food drops unless you hear otherwise from one of my pigeons. That should help bolster your rations through the rest of the dark season. I will see you again after the sun rises at Castle Killovew."

Chieftain Fox bowed his head, "May your journey back be safe and wet, my lord."

A short time later, they were underway, watching Fox and the other villagers disappear around the corner. Jinala had not yet wiped all the sleep from her eyes nor stopped to look at her father up close before they were back in the dark forest. The canopy closed in over the top of them, thunder rumbled to the north, and the jungle grew denser and denser along either side. The caravan wound its way through the Thirsting Forest, heading northwest toward the grumbling clouds.

The wagon wheels turned, and the horses clopped along in front and behind. The noises of the journey settled into a hypnotic rhythm. Jinala sat, not tired but pensive, and could not trick herself into believing she dreamed the magical blue light and the wizard in the forest. Her father had met the wizard, walked off with him. Yet he was still here, directing knights and chatting casually with Sir Trittion at the front of the wagon as if nothing special had happened. He seemed to be no worse for wear from his encounter.

Jason picked at a small imperfection in the wooden door, where the grain ran backward and had frayed out. He stripped away a large splinter, stuck it in his mouth to chew on, and continued to pry away at the gouge in the otherwise smooth surface. *Should I tell Jason?* She scooted toward him and then laid her hand on his arm.

"Jason?" she whispered.

He shrugged her off. "Go away, Gina. It's too hot." He went back to picking at the wood. She would not tell him. Not now, anyway.

Rain fell.

Trittion instructed them to close the drapes as it strengthened. Thunder and lightning followed. The wind grew fierce; the horses whinnied; their calls muffled by the hammering water on the roof. Jinala pulled back the thick drapes, and slanting rain sprayed inside, soaking her hand and half her face. It was darker than usual. The torches were dimmed. Some might have even gone out. Another bolt of lightning struck; a handful of eyes shined in the flash, just off the edge of the forest path.

"Jason!" she shouted over the accompanying thunderclap. She pointed into the trees where she had seen the glowing dots. He peered out the window, another bolt of lightning struck, and they gleamed again. Jason laughed and turned away from the window, pulling his sister away with him.

"Jinala, that's probably a raccoon or something. Dwellers have eight eyes." He had to raise his voice to be heard over the swelling drumbeat of rain on the carriage roof.

"I could have sworn I saw more than two."

The front drapes swished open, and James Killovew leaned his head in, soaking wet. "We may stop to shelter the horses, Jason, so I need you to—"

A crash, loud and deep and much different from the sound of thunder, shook the wagon. The roar came from further up the road, not above their heads.

"Whoa!" shouted Sir Trittion from outside. "Whoa!"

James withdrew his head back into the storm outside, and the drapes fell shut. Jason leaned forward.

"Stay with me, Jason!"

The prince threw open the thick curtains.

Through the falling sheets of water, they saw the lead wagon's back wheels lift into the air. It hung precariously for an instant, and then the whole wagon fell forward into the open earth. Jinala knew what that meant.

Cave-in.

Dweller.

Jinala leaned back and squeezed her hands together.

"Jinala!" Her brother shook her. "Take this and stay here!"

He had placed his own helmet in her hands.

Lord Killovew crashed through the front window into the back with them.

"Move, Jinala!"

She jumped up, and James flipped up the bench she had been sitting on. He ripped out a steel chest piece and swung it around onto his shoulders. Jason helped him tie the plates together while he dug out his steel half-helm and slammed it onto his head.

Thunder roared overhead, and someone screamed from outside. Jason reached under the other seat and pulled out another set of armor. "I'm coming with you!" he shouted at his father.

"No!" James Killovew slid up the visor on his helmet and locked eyes with his son. "Put that on and guard your sister. That's an order from your Lord and from your father." He kicked open the door and jumped out, drawing his sword and slamming shut the door behind him in one single motion. Another scream, dulled by the pouring rain, ended abruptly with a distant thud.

Jason shrugged on his armor. Jinala watched from the corner of the wagon, her knees drawn up to her chest and her arms wrapped around her knees, the big helmet wobbling loosely on her small head. Her face was wet, but she did not know if it was from tears or the rain. Jason stopped bothering with his armor greaves. He held his sword, breathing heavily, and waited at the door. All was silent, aside from the pounding rain.

"I'm going to go out there," he whispered.

"Don't leave me, Jason," she whispered back. "Please."

Jason ignored her and reached for the door.

Jinala heard a scraping sound along the roof. Jason paused and looked up, tilting his ear toward the noise. It sounded like a jagged plow dragging against the grain of the wood.

Something slammed into the wagon, knocking it up onto two wheels for a moment before it fell back down into the mud. Jason lost his balance and toppled into the bench. He grunted and stood back up. Another blow jolted the wagon. It rocked upward again—*it must surely turn over!*—and landed back on four wheels. Jason collapsed to his knees, holding onto the bench to keep from hitting his head. He locked eyes with his sister and reached for her hand. "Jinala!"

Four long claws, white as bone, slashed through the roof, inches away from their heads.

Jinala shrieked.

****

"Jinala," her brother said.

The sun had overpowered most of the mist, and she could clearly see her father and his men riding toward them. Rara Silva Nix trotted toward the other horses. She neighed and a few of the horses echoed back her call.

"Our last gallop is over, little sister, and I really must go now."

She turned around sideways and hugged her brother. He held her in strong arms, but after too short a time he lifted her out of the front of his saddle and dropped her onto the ground. James Killovew and the others circled up around her and her brother. She felt even smaller than usual as she looked up at everyone else seated on their horses.

Jason and James shared quiet words. They shook hands, both of James's clasped around the younger man's single hand. Neither father nor son cried. Jason looked past James Killovew and asked, "Sir Breigo, I assume this is everyone?"

One hundred men from across the realm had left nearly forty cycles ago, before the sun had even crested the mountain ridge, fulfilling the realm's quota. Jason and his team of knights and sworn swords were going as *extra* support. Royal volunteers to help lead the campaigns and to show that the Thirsting Forest was committed to protecting the whole kingdom from the Vistonex. Committed enough that even Prince Killovew, heir to Lord Killovew, was going. Jinala didn't fully understand, and she wondered why any other men would sign up willingly to go to war now that the realm had met their requirements.

"Yes, Prince Jason. We are the final group for the season. We are ready whenever you are."

"Sir Trittion, keep the old man in check while I'm away."

Trittion said with a sad smile, "I'll do my best. You know how well he listens to me. Take care of yourself, Jason."

"And you, yourself." Jason shifted in his horse and looked down at his sister. "Don't forget your sword on your way back to the castle."

"I won't."

"You'll need to find a new sparring partner."

I have, but they aren't the same. "I will."

"Okay. Goodbye, sis."

"Goodbye. Don't be dumb, Jason."

Jason chuckled but then frowned at his sister. His smile turned serious, "I'll see you before you know it."

He turned his gaze to his father. Rara Silva Nix shuffled backward. Above the trees of the Thirsting Forest and the distant ridge of the Gilv Mountains the top half of the sun peeked out. Its light skimmed across the rain forest canopy, casting the figures as dark silhouettes. A pair of ospreys alighted from the trees, screeching at each other in the distance. "I won't let you down, Father," Jason said.

"I know."

"I'll see you soon."

"I know. Good luck." Father and son shook hands again. James put his other hand on Jason's shoulder.

"A bit sappy, isn't it?" One of the other riders said out of the corner of his mouth. Jinala frowned at him.

A man that must have been the rider's twin, pretending to wipe tears away from his cheeks, added, "Oh come now, it's very touching, brother."

"I'll touch you," the first rider said, swinging a big fist at the other. He missed.

Jason noticed the outburst and gave his father a final head nod and a smile.

The Prince of the Thirsting Forest pulled the reigns on Rara Silva Nix, and she circled around, facing away from the castle. "To Shinar."

He put his heel into the horse, and they galloped off, followed by the four others. Jinala watched them ride along the side of the forest until they curved away to the north. She and her father and old Sir Trittion were the only three left in the meadow.

"They won't keep such a brisk pace up for long." Trittion chuckled. "Your son will do well, my lord," he added.

"My father left me for Shinar, too, Trittion, as you well know. It felt much like this."

He reached down and tapped Jinala on the shoulder. She grabbed his hand, and he helped her up onto his large stallion. "We'll miss him, won't we?" His voice was hesitant and a little hoarse. She'd never heard her father on the verge of tears before.

"Yeah," Jinala answered. Old Sir Trittion clicked his teeth, and they started off toward the castle. The knight wiggled his mustache at Jinala, and she forced a small smile in return. The Princess of the Thirsting Forest looked behind her. Her brother's entourage raced onward, away from home.

Two

Jinala dropped out of the stable loft window and snuck alone into the rainforest, as she did after all her calligraphy lessons.

In the Thirsting Forest, the oak trees and the ceiba trees and the tall coconut palms grew thick, knotted together by strangler figs and all varieties of winding vines. In the deepest parts of the forest, the sunlight never reached the forest floor at all. All varieties of moss and ferns and bushes grew in the shade of the big trees. Jinala had been told the forest was once all swamp and moist mud and home to a mighty river, but with each season, it sucked up more and more of the moisture, earning its namesake as the wide river that tumbled down from the glacial headwaters in the northeast shrunk into a series of creeks and streams. Nevertheless, the forest was hot and humid this far south.

Though much sparser at the foot of Castle Killovew, it did not take Jinala long to find herself knee-deep in clumps of thorny briar and searching for sunlight through the shadows of the thick branches overhead.

Somewhere around this area, Jinala would usually find the Sondite brothers— or rather—they would find her.

She heard a young voice call out, "Gina!"

The princess rose from behind a leafy fern and there they stood, right in front of her. Skinny as stick bugs, both brothers were tall for their age. The little one was near as tall as Jinala, even though she was a full season older than him. Yet, young as they were, they were masters of their home in the forest. Even when the season of the sun was at its blazing peak, like it had been for the last hundred or so cycles, they could slip into the trees and disappear into the deepest shadows.

Like all Sondites, their eyes were a glistening purple, and their skin much darker than Jinala's. The younger brother had a smooth, round face coupled with light purple eyes. The older brother's face had already developed hard lines around the corners of his darker purple eyes. Orphaned and forced to take responsibility for both himself and his younger brother, he had aged faster than most boys.

To Jinala, the brothers were as much a part of this forest as were the trees and the birds and the carpet of dead leaves spread across the ground. She was their connection to the civilized world, and they were her only outlet into something wild and exciting and forbidden. But that wasn't fair. They were outlaws, and they were only a part of the forest because they were not allowed to find a home anywhere else.

She was breaking her father's rule of going into the forest alone, but by spending time with the orphans, Jinala was breaking the law of her God-King. Sondites were forbidden from all the free realms of the kingdom, except Shinar. Though the princess was young, she knew enough that as a subject of Gahkin she should turn them in, and she also knew she would never do it because these two orphan outlaws were her best and only friends.

"I'll catch you guys, one cycle. I'll find you, and you won't even know I'm there," Jinala said, grinning.

"Not if you keep rustling," the younger one named Martin said, "and don't hide your weird hair from flashing in the sunlight."

"I do not have weird hair."

Jinala had curly blond hair, in fact, and it was the envy of most women in the castle. She had not gone a cycle of her life without a compliment on her hair, and to hear it called 'weird' was rather refreshing. She ran her hands through it.

"You're just jealous," she said, shaking it back behind her shoulders in an exaggerated motion, where it did indeed catch a thin sunbeam and glint through the shadows.

"Jealous? No way, you're just crazy. Can you imagine us, with hair like that?" Martin said. The older brother chuckled. He turned around and faced away from the others, watching their backs.

Martin walked up beside Jinala and tossed her hair across his own head.

"Crichton, look," Martin said. Jinala giggled. Out of the corner of her eye, she could see Martin draped in her own golden curls. Martin was wearing a ridiculous smile, batting his eyelashes and clasping his hands together under his chin. In a girly voice, he said, "Oh gosh, just look at my hair. I will have to have it washed three times before the ball."

"I don't sound like that!" Jinala whacked Martin in the arm and stepped back, removing his wig. Crichton snorted but still shifted nervously, looking back and forth between the castle walls and the denser foliage behind them. He was never comfortable this close to civilization.

"We should go this way," he said, pointing into the thick jungle.

They set out into the deeper parts of the forest, crossing over and leaving behind the small paths and game trails the hunters used.

The Mud Wizard would never be found this close to the castle.

The brothers seemed to have a good sense of direction in the forest, even after long sessions of searching that left the children surrounded by never-before-seen branches and thick moss. They could always lead Jinala straight back home. She was only mildly impressed.

It's not hard to know your way around your own home. She could have just as easily gotten them lost in the halls and secret passageways of her father's castle.

Coming onto a dense patch of thorny brush, the three scaled up a tall strangler and climbed over the thick vegetation below. Not too long ago, the princess would have turned back, unwilling and unable to climb something lacking so many handholds. But over the last season she had spent plenty of time exploring the forest with the outlaw brothers. Now she moved through the trees with ease, rarely needing help and asking for it even less. They climbed up into the higher limbs, where the branches intertwined with other large trees. They stuck to the canopy from then on, crossing from tree to tree and dodging much of the non-traversable tangled greenery below. In some places there were knotted vines tied together that the brothers had placed to help cross larger gaps.

They were soon in unexplored country. The convenience of linked rope swings disappeared. The younger brother led the pack, racing along the branches and leaping into the air, floating momentarily, and then landing deftly on another branch. The princess always hesitated when she jumped, catching herself with her hands. She didn't have the balance of the Sondites. The older brother followed along behind her, on the lookout for the Mud Wizard or for predators like tree snakes or water dragons. He switched trees with ease, though less headlong than his younger brother. The princess grew tired after about a candle length, so they stopped to rest in the crux of a massive ceiba tree.

"I don't think we have ever been this far east before, Crichton," Martin said.

The older brother shrugged Jinala's pack off his shoulders and hung it over a convenient limb.

"No, we have not. Never this far…" He looked around at the tightly packed trees, twisting and throwing large branches toward the sun. Dark shadows swayed across the ground far below. Moss and dead brown muck were clumped in the knots and crannies between the immense variety of green leaves and sharp thorns and flowers and hanging vines that walled them in.

"…into this much thick," he finished.

"I thought you guys had been everywhere out here," Jinala said.

"You thought we were evil too, Gina. And in cahoots with the Mud Wizard. Shows what you know." Martin climbed up higher into the tree, heading for the top. Crichton pulled a mango out of the pack and took a bite.

"Mmm," he said. "We haven't found any healthy mango trees in a long time."

"There aren't many left," Jinala said, "but I brought some special for you. You can only eat so many m-bars, you know?"

Crichton nodded and passed the pack over to Jinala but stopped mid-reach. Something had caught his eye. He stared down past the Killovew princess.

"Look," he said, dropping onto the branch and peering closer, the half-eaten mango in his other hand forgotten. A rectangular black box hung below a thick branch, connected by strong metallic strapping. The tiny box, not quite the size of Jinala's smallest finger, had a circular glass surface on one side, aimed east, deeper into the forest. Crichton brushed his fingers against it and then leaned down and smelled it.

"What does it smell like?" Jinala asked.

"I don't know. Doesn't really have a smell. Like steel, I guess. Like a sword."

"Hmm," Jinala said, climbing down to get a closer look.

Martin made it to the top of the tree. "Guys, this is one of the tallest trees out here! I can see everything... even the castle, Gina!"

"Look southeast, Mart," Crichton yelled up, positioning Martin in the same direction as the black box. "What do you see out there?"

Martin adjusted in the flimsy branches, turning around. "There is a weird gap in the trees! It leads to like a swamp or something!" He climbed back down. He dropped onto the branch above Gina and Crichton. "Well, are we going to go out there or what?"

"I've got to go back; we have already been gone too long."

"We have not been gone too long, Gina. We stay longer than this all the time." Martin frowned at her.

"On the morrow's cycle, I have to be at the reception feast."

"Gina," Martin said, "how can you have a feast when people are starving all over the kingdom?"

"The feast is all the food we have saved and rationed for the season. Everyone eats below their rations, and we earn the feast once a season to share with the Edengrove realm. It gives everyone something to look forward to. It helps people!"

Martin looked at her dubiously, then asked, "Well, how are we going to find the Mud Wizard if you are stuck at the feast?"

"I'll be back on the cycle after tomorrow. I promise. We just can't go now because it will take almost two candles to get home from here, so who knows how many it will take from all the way out there." Jinala looked around, unsure if she could navigate the way home.

Martin glared at her. "I hate feasts."

"You have never been to a feast."

"I still hate them." Martin turned away from Jinala. "Or do you command my feelings now too?"

"You can't hate something you don't even know about."

"I hate feasts," he repeated.

Crichton ended the argument, as he usually did. "We will head back, but we will come straight here cycle after the morrow. You will have more candles to burn then, right Jinala?" he asked. He was still rubbing the metallic rectangle hanging from the tree, peering through the leaves in the direction it was pointed.

"Yes," she said, glaring back at Martin.

Crichton nodded. He wrapped Jinala's pack around his shoulders, adjusted his leather spear strapping, and then took off running. He bounded along the thick branch, then leaped lightly off his right foot, launched himself off a higher branch with his left, and disappeared through the wall of leaves surrounding the tree. Gina ran after him, followed begrudgingly by Martin.

When they could see the castle through the trees, they stopped within a small grove, where the ground was mostly dirt and dead leaves and lacked the usual thorny bramble. They could see the massive castle's burning algae candle in the fifth candle-hole along the rampart, from the top of the trees, and Jinala figured she had half a candle left to burn before she needed to return to the castle.

Martin's anger had been building all along their journey back.

He shouted at Jinala, "I challenge you to *shodullen!*"

In Sondite culture, Crichton had explained once, a shodullen was a battle between knights or members of royalty. It was an alternative to full-out battle between large groups, or even armies, where one or two champions would face off. The victor of the shodullen would represent the victor of the battle, and the leaders would be able to negotiate as if the armies had already done battle. A shodullen was an ancient tradition, and always to the death, Crichton said, and must always be granted when requested.

Jinala smiled at Martin, "Okay then, I accept."

It would be good for the boy to blow off some steam.

The Sondites weren't practiced swordsmen, outside of whacking birds and squirrels or stabbing fish. Jinala trained with her older brother before he went off to war, so Crichton and Martin liked to practice their swordsmanship with her. She did not mind. She missed practicing with Jason, but the boys were better swordsmen than a tree, which was her only other option.

When she first trained with them, she was able to dodge most of their unbalanced strikes and poke them with her own stick easily enough. They were fast but unsophisticated. As they had gotten older over this last season, though, she had to admit, they tested her more and more. Crichton had even beaten her a few times.

Crichton watched the fight from an outstretching low tree branch while his younger brother and the Princess of the Thirsting Forest squared off. They each raised their practice swords high, bowed in the typical Sondite fashion, one knee touching the ground, and then began.

Martin was no strategist, but his balance and speed more than made up for it.

Jinala was the opposite. She had learned how little effort it takes to deflect a blow, how only the smallest motion was needed to send a strike away harmlessly. She twirled in place, her brown skirts lifting in the wind. Martin was still angry. He had never beaten her, and it was clear he wanted to end his losing streak. He dashed in, spinning his stick to confuse her.

He did not twirl it nearly fast enough to deceive her. Jinala only had to watch for when the stick shot out in her direction and twitch to deflect it. Time and again, she deflected him, but he kept coming on, scaring her a bit with his wide open purple eyes that never seemed to blink.

"Take it easy, Mart," Crichton said.

Martin came at Jinala faster than ever.

Time to end this.

Jinala switched to a two-handed grip and deflected Martin's stick out wide to the left.

He never learns.

She had him spinning the wrong direction, and her stick was closer to his body than his; she thrust at his shoulder with her hilt.

But Martin was ready. He lurched away from her, avoiding the full force of the blow, making Jinala trip toward him with her unexpected momentum. Still falling away from her he kicked out his trailing foot and managed to catch her leg.

They both tumbled to the ground, Martin in a controlled backward plop and Jinala in a much less controlled face-first crash.

Martin grabbed his stick-sword up off the ground and poked her in the back as she scrambled to grab her own sword. She rolled over, and he stood above her, his stick aimed at her chest, triumphant.

"Nice job, Mart!" Crichton shouted.

Jinala tried to get up, but Martin's stick prodded her back to the ground.

"You win, let me up!"

Martin stepped back and raised his weapon. "Cancel the feast," he said.

"Mart, you know I can't do that."

"It's shodullen, you have to do as I command."

"It was just practice, Mart," Crichton chirped from above.

"I still don't understand how you can have a feast. You should give away your extra food," he said, anger still in his eyes.

"It's for an important occasion, I told you!" Jinala shoved herself up from the ground... and then Martin swung, hard.

Jinala jumped backward but was not able to dodge the cheap shot. The tip of the wooden stick smacked into her arm as she fell backward into a pile of brown leaves.

Martin aimed his sword down at her again. "You can't order us around, Jinala. You are not *our* princess. I beat you in shodullen. And so, as the winner, I demand you skip your feast."

"You can hit me all you want. I will do no such thing."

"I hate you!" Martin threw his sword into the underbrush and ran away from Jinala and his brother and the castle walls into the dark shadows of the forest.

"Martin!" Crichton yelled. He did not chase after him.

Jinala felt tears in her eyes, and she quickly blinked them away. She wouldn't in a thousand suns give the boy the satisfaction. She knew Martin was probably watching from the brush, just out of sight. She held out her arm while Crichton examined it. A small scrap sat at the center of a thick red welt on her forearm. It was barely bleeding, but it would probably turn into a nasty bruise.

"I'll be okay, Crichton," Jinala said, pulling her arm away from him.

"He didn't mean to hurt you. I mean, he didn't really mean it." Crichton's face did not look as convinced as his words sounded, though.

"It's fine," Jinala said, taking her eyes from her arm and looking at Crichton. She noticed the dirty rag wrapped around his upper body, pretending to be a shirt. "I'll bring you both some new clothes next time."

"He's so young, Gina. I know he seems old and tough, but this is only his third sun. And I can't... I can't always know what—what my parents would have done. I don't want us to just... become common bandits. Or barbarians." His head dropped to his feet as he murmured the last word.

Jinala lifted her hand, hesitated, and then lowered it again. With her friends, she didn't normally trip over her words, but now, with the stress of the moment, she couldn't quite organize her thoughts.

"I... I don't know how to find your father. But... maybe... maybe the Mud Wizard will know. After the morrow's feast, we'll follow the black box we found. And, well, maybe it will lead us to him."

Crichton raised his head. He met her gaze, and Jinala could see her own emerald eyes reflected in his dark purple ones. But then his eyes flicked away, reflecting only the green of the forest, and he became the distant older brother again, the boy who had to be a father but who had never known his own.

She lifted her hand, confidently this time, and placed it under Crichton's chin, aiming his eyes back at hers. She was the Princess of the Thirsting Forest. And she wanted to help her friends.

"Don't forget, Crichton, this new sun is only your fifth. You can't expect to be perfect. I'm going to help." She smiled at him, despite the pain in her arm. "And tell Mart, he's wrong. I *am* your princess, and that means I'm going to take care of you both. I promise." She stood up on her toes and kissed him on the cheek, smiling despite herself as she turned back to the castle. Her cheeks flushed red.

The princess remembered when she had befriended them in the first place. They had found her alone and lost in the woods. They had reunited her with her father, and Jinala had sworn silently she would return the favor. Yet, as the dark season faded into dawn and then the season of the sun, despite all the candles spent exploring the wild regions of the forest, they had not seen the Mud Wizard again. The only adult who had ever taken care of them, after their mother died, had disappeared. This cycle they had found their first clue, and after the feast on the morrow she would spend all ten candles of each cycle searching if she must. They would find him.

Jinala slipped through the wooden struts of the window and stepped into the second floor of the stables. She changed quickly out of her brown skirt and leathers and into the yellow sundress she had worn when she left the castle. She swung her brown cloak over her shoulders, leaving the hood down but sliding her arms inside the long sleeves. *There.* The cut was hidden, and she looked the same as when she left the castle. Motion outside the window drew her eye.

A scout rider galloped down the southwestern road at an alarming pace. It made her think the Ardellian raiders had finally organized, had broken into the realm, and stormed Northtown!

But a scout rider from Northtown would come from the *northern* road not the southwest. And they would probably send a hawk or a dove, not a scout rider. Jinala twirled her finger through her hair.

This was an interesting mystery.

She jumped into a pile of hay on the first level, kissed the pony she startled, and left the stable in a rush.

She hustled across the lawn as the rider cut around the corner of the road and galloped through the gate, not even acknowledging the befuddled older man sitting next to the winch. The scout woman was in some hurry. Curiosity peaked even more, Jinala sped up. That must be some news to blow past the gatekeeper.

"Whoa there, princess," the watchmen said. "What's *your* hurry?

"Hi-gotta-go-sorry-bye!" she said, hurrying through the open gate, chasing after the messenger woman.

"Come back here, princess! I'm the gatekeeper!" the old man shouted, now behind her, half angry and half sad. "Doesn't that mean anything anymore?" Jinala looked back. The old gatekeeper shook his fist in the air. She laughed and ran on into the castle grounds.

The mysterious rider had already dismounted from her horse and was walking toward the castle doors. Jinala rushed across the inner lawn and slowed to a walk at the doorstep. She stepped inside and looked around. The scout woman was at the far side of the atrium, heading up a flight of stairs that would take her to the breezeway toward her father's offices and chamber.

Maybe she has a letter from Jason. A letter he couldn't trust to any hawk.

A handful of other people milled about in the atrium, talking idly while passing through on their way from one side of the castle to the other. Jinala walked as fast as she could without drawing attention. A Killovew adviser and arithmetician named Finch waved her over, but she feigned ignorance and just waved back and moved past him and a boy who must have been-

"Jinala, come over here. You must meet my new apprentice." Jinala sighed and turned around. She couldn't just ignore everyone she passed by. She would probably never learn what secret message the scout woman was carrying. Like a good little princess, she trotted over and curtsied to Finch and then to the boy and then gave a deep curtsy to them both.

Finch said, "This is Mikder. He is your age, I believe…" The boy was clearly younger than Jinala. Finch frowned, suddenly unsure of himself. "Wait, how old are you now, princess?"

"Uh… this is my fourth sun, Mr. Finch. But, um, I was a dark season child."

"Speak up, dear; I can't hear you when you murmur like that."

Jinala sighed and stepped closer, speaking louder. "My third sun! But I was born during the dark season!"

"Oh, of course! The seasons all blur together for me now. So, you're… just half a season older than Mikder."

Half a season can make a big difference.

Finch placed a hand on the boy's shoulder. "Mikder has come highly recommended from Elkwood. He's Chief Kevin's nephew!" The last apprentice Finch tutored ended up swiping coconuts and making fenny. He got caught selling the drink to young ones in the Northtown villages, in the very shadow of Castle Killovew. After a short stint in the cells, he now stood guard at the realm border, last she heard. Keeping an eye out for food bandits coming from other realms. Finch felt partially responsible, Jinala knew, and now he went about trying to convince everyone his next apprentice would be more credible.

Finch went on, "He's very bright, princess, just like you, but he also struggles with his articulation and speaking, like you as well. You two can work together now to overcome your… issues with conversation. I'm sure you'll get along great." Finch walked away, smiling to himself as if he had accomplished something remarkable.

They stared at each other for an awkward moment before the boy recovered and bowed low. "It's very beaut—I mean, it's very nice to meet you, prin—prin—prin- princess." The boy's chubby cheeks grew very red. Jinala did not laugh at him. She smiled.

"And it's nice to meet you too, Mikder. But, uh, I am on my way to my chambers, so… I'll see you around the castle, okay? I've got to go. Bye."

Jinala waved and walked off before the boy could respond. She made it to the stairs and then quickly turned onto the breezeway. The scout woman was leisurely meandering toward Jinala, gazing out toward the mountains.

Her message had been delivered.

Jinala slouched in defeat and walked on toward her father's offices, sure she had missed her chance to catch the secret message.

Around the next corner, she heard hushed but angry voices coming from behind the closed doors of the commanding elder knight's office. Her father's voice was among them. Jinala spun around, looking for anyone else in the hallway. She saw no one and moved quickly to the door. She put her ear to the crease in the door and the wall.

"—as if unannounced Acolytes on our roads aren't bad enough."

"Yes, but"—her father's voice—"at least she knew enough to come to warn us anyway, even if she trusts them wholeheartedly. Just to be curious of Acolytes movements, even trespassing Acolytes, is a rarity these cycles."

"Why do you think they are here? Do you think it's related to—"

"It can't be, Trittion. They won't be even a third of the way there yet."

"But what if one of them-"

"They won't have."

"Even the dragon wrangler?"

"He'll only know if Jason sees fit to tell him. And I trust Jason." There was a short silence and the drumming of fingers on wood before he continued. "They must be here for some alternative reason. But I admit, I did not predict them to come around this soon, regardless of why."

"Well, we can't rightly postpone the meeting and feast with Lord Eden."

"We don't need to do that. The feast can carry on. There is nothing suspicious about two border realms' lords having a meeting together. We've worked all season to be able to afford this. But I'm still worried. They want to catch us by surprise but bury it if I can figure out why!"

"So… carry on and do nothing?"

"Yes, just like I told Scout Lana. Tell no one—"

"Of course. But I might mention to the gate master on duty to forget he ever saw her ride in, especially since she came in such a hurry."

"No, no, don't ask him to forget. He doesn't like to be kept out of the loop. Feed him some innocent reason as to why and he won't have to keep any secrets. As for you and me, let us hope we are prepared to dodge whatever unknown trap they plan to spring on us."

"And Eric? Should we warn him?"

"He's smart enough to piece everything together, if necessary."

A finger tapped Jinala's shoulder. Jinala jumped nearly out of her clothes. She had closed her eyes to hear within the door and did not sense anyone sneak up on her. She turned and saw Mikder staring at her.

"What are you do… do… do…" He shook his head, unable to get past that word. "Why are you li… li… listening to a door?" he asked, finishing speaking rather loudly.

"Mikder!" She hissed. "Get out of here. You are standing in my father's royal office."

The boy looked up and down the hallway. "I th… th… th… isn't this juh… juh… just a hallway?"

"Well," Jinala said, "Okay, yes, it is just a hallway. But it is connected to the royal offices and chambers and has nothing to do with you."

"Oh," Mikder said, dejected. He hung his head and turned to go.

Jinala heard the knob twist, and she bolted over next to Mikder, slinging her arm around the boy.

Sir Trittion stepped out, followed by Lord Killovew.

"Hel—hel—hello," Mikder squeaked out.

"Hello, Mikder," Trittion said. "I see you have met the famous eavesdropping princess of Castle Killovew."

Jinala removed her arm, realizing it was a lame attempt at camouflaging her behavior. Lord Killovew looked at his daughter from under raised eyebrows.

The two adults walked past the two children and toward the breezeway, heading to the main floors of the castle. Jinala's father turned back and said, "Would you like to accompany us back to Mr. Finch, Mikder?"

"Uh… yuh… yuh… yuh… yes sir, my lord, sir… yes. Lord," Mikder answered, leaving Jinala and moving toward the adults.

"One sir or one lord is plenty, Mikder. You'll find I'm not quite as stern as Chief Kevin." Lord Killovew added to Jinala in an afterthought, "Please don't go sneaking around for the next couple of cycles, Gina dear."

Something sneaky is going on all right, but I'm not the only one doing the sneaking.

Jinala crossed her arms and watched them leave. Her father even gave Mikder more attention than her, whether she was sneaking around or not.

Three

Taroke and Ratoke Greenfoot scowled across the greasy wooden bar at the two bartenders. Seated beside them, Sir Breigo Aldev tapped a copper square on the counter, loudly. It was ignored.

A large handwritten sign above the bar read:

NO meat
NO grain
NO M-bars

Despite the lack of food, the tavern was crawling with thirsty men and a few women. Unfortunately, neither employee behind the bar seemed in any rush to take any alcohol orders.

One bartender, staggering and hiccoughing, jabbed wildly with his pointer finger while ranting about something. Jason Killovew was too far away to make out the words, and besides, the bartender seemed far too drunk to be able to use words in any comprehensible way. The other bartender leaned against the counter, engaged in rapt discussion with a chubby woman in a low-cut dress.

Jason Killovew watched his companions from a sticky table in the back corner of the inn with his other journeymen, Mako Black. The man from the Water Dragon Keep gulped heavily from his mug. Mako did not drink Spice, like the Greenfoots, but he drank more than enough algae ale to make up for the difference in potency. So far on their journey, he had proven to be an intensely quiet man, and even if you filled him full of ale, he spoke only a little.

Behind them, the fireplace was empty. The sun had followed Jason and his men as they rode northwest, and as it climbed high enough to put a wide stripe of sky underneath it, it brought warmth back to the middle of the kingdom. There would be no need of fire until the sun sank below the horizon, many cycles from now.

Jason turned away from the bar. He needed to stay focused. Anyone with a dagger and a foul mood could make a name for himself. The Prince of the Thirsting Forest shouldn't be in a place like this.

He scanned the inn for the third time. The main door was about thirty paces away, the back door probably double that. Thick curtains hung outside, covering the southern windows, shading the room in dim, dusty light, and repelling the heat as much as possible. A window behind the bar and a window next to the front entrance were wide open, begging for a cross breeze that refused to come. Candles sat in their mantles, but none were lit, save the sixth algae candle of the cycle above the fireplace. Twenty or so tables were haphazardly scattered across the Mid-Kingdom Cross, and almost all were full of people.

At the nearest table, some older fellows—cattlemen by the look of them—played a drinking game. They went around in a circle and yelled out random numbers, although there seemed to be a hidden pattern known to them. They were shooting straight Spice whenever one of them shouted the wrong number. The men were already drunk and getting worse. They were not the only ones, either. Most of the room was in some state of intoxication. That was the nature of these dire cycles, Jason concluded. The worse it got, the more some folks drank to forget, even for just a little while.

One table started singing, drowning out the old skinny flutist on stage. He hopped down and crossed the room, changing his tune mid-song and joining the crowd to their delight. A few men tossed copper coins into his case, but most everyone else added nothing when he came around collecting. Two yellow-colored men, bare-chested and wearing furs around their legs, sat at the bar drinking mead, ignoring everyone else and speaking among themselves.

A lumpy-looking woman approached them, but they waved her off. She wandered through the crowd, sat down on some man's lap, and was immediately tossed off onto the ground. Another man, bottle of Spice in hand, helped her up and together, they staggered toward the stairs at the far side of the room. At the foot of the staircase two short, heavy-set men, thick hair sprouting out of their half-buttoned shirts, eyed the crowd. Now and again, they would point at a table and lean together, whispering.

Another woman, sickly skinny and pale, drew Jason's eyes up the staircase. She perched for a moment at the landing, looking down at the dining room with hollow eyes. She saw Jason and descended. She wore black leather heels. Her long legs wobbled just a little, and her small calf muscles drew tight and hard. A dark red dress, ornamented with strips of black cloth, clung tightly down her thin body. Wiry black hair tumbled over her shoulders down to her naval. Well-fed, she might have been pretty, but as it was, she was almost a skeleton with a thin layer of flesh stretched across her bones. With golden hoops in her ears, thin lips and sharp, high cheekbones, Jason thought of a vulture floating toward them. She smiled at Jason from across the room. He looked away.

Mako Black, a few mugs deep, turned to Jason and said, "The woman smiled at you."

"I do not want her coming over here." Jason looked up and accidentally made eye contact again as she weaved her way toward their table.

"Too bad, bub. You should have worn dirtier clothes."

Her strut broke as her heel found a hole in the ground. She stumbled forward and, with unexpected deftness, pulled out a chair and sat down instead of falling. She stared across the table at Jason, her sunken black eyes sizzling, unblinking.

"I'm Diana." She gave an immodest look downward before looking back up and biting her lower lip.

"We are not interested."

She reached for him under the table, but he pushed her hands away. She smiled and grabbed at him again, causing anger to surge through Jason's veins. He grabbed her hands and held them still. With a few deep breaths, he calmed himself. It seemed more and more of a struggle every cycle to contain his anger. Sometimes it felt almost as if his temper had a mind of its own.

"I said we are not interested. Sorry."

"How do you know, pretty boy, if you've never tried it?"

Jason looked at Mako for back-up, but the water dragon wrangler just snorted and continued to watch. Jason nudged her seat away from the table with his boot. "No offense, lady, but you are not my type."

"I'm everyone's type, pretty boy."

The prince felt a sudden rush in his chest, but he fought it aside.

Take it easy, Jason.

"Sorry, but not this cycle." Jason pushed her chair further away. It stuck on the grimy floor and tipped backward.

She tumbled out and rolled over onto the ground. She coughed on the dusty floor for a few flickers, writhing rather dramatically, and then gathered herself and stood up.

Looking over her shoulder at Jason, she said, "I'll be waiting." She walked away, dodging the grabs of drunken men, and disappeared back up the staircase. Jason rubbed his thumb along his knife's hilt under the table.

Mako Black looked at Jason. "*Have* you been with any women before?"

That is not something that a bodyguard should ask his prince.

Sir Breigo Aldev, as an elder knight of the Thirsting Forest, had sworn to protect the royal Killovew family anywhere in the kingdom and would be loyal to Jason no matter where they traveled. Ratoke and Taroke were allied to Jason in both conspiracy and coin. But Mako Black had made no such vows nor knew of no conspiracy, so instead, food and bed and a large sum of gold was exchanged for his agreement to continue to serve Jason during their journey. Now that they were outside the Realm of the Thirsting Forest, Jason was not technically royalty, just an employer. Mako Black seemed to think that changed the rules of their relationship.

"I have," Jason answered, knowing himself a liar. It was not the first lie he had told Mako Black.

Mako took another drink and then said, "You don't drink, neither."

"I drink plenty. Water and coconut juice and goat's milk…" Jason admitted with a smile, "but if you mean the stuff that dulls men's senses? No, I don't; you are right."

Strangely, Mako Black continued the conversation. "I think you should go get yourself a real drink. Some cycle you may have a need to dull your senses or your memory, boy, and you don't want to be a virgin to *that* stuff when you really need it. Men don't trust men who don't drink."

"Do you trust me, Mako?"

Mako turned his head and looked at the prince. Jason looked back at Black, right in the eyes. The man's scarred ear and forehead were gruesome up so close.

Mako Black did not blink… but after a moment, he smirked and turned away. He swallowed back more of the golden-brown ale. Trails of the liquid dripped through his thick beard.

"I don't think you're out to rob anybody, boy, nor do I think you have the balls or the conscious to put a dagger in some man's chest as he sleeps. I don't have a problem playing bodyguard, but to be honest, no, I don't trust you. You got schemes or a secret or… something." He drank the rest of his mug, burped, and wiped his mouth with the back of his hand, "I don't much care, mind, since your father paid me plenty of gold to help keep you out of trouble, but sure as a dweller digs, you got schemes. I trust you about as much as I trust a water dragon to guard a pig."

Jason shrugged and stood up from the table.

Cleverer than he looks.

He walked toward his other companions seated at the bar, scanning the room again. He saw nothing new and sat down on the stool next to Sir Breigo. Ratoke and Taroke had finally got their hands on a bottle of Spice and were in deep conversation with a wrinkly old shepherd.

Sir Breigo didn't look over at Jason when he sat down but said to him, "It's getting testy in here."

The first bartender, still chubby somehow despite the tighter rations and seemingly drunker than the second, put a finger into the other bartender's chest. As he spoke, he grabbed hold of the man's shirt to steady himself.

"This isn't your inn—*hic*—and I'll be damned if you are going to—*hic*—change the prices." He took a deep breath. "Soldiers or Acolytes or whoever. Same price."

The thinner barman slapped the hand away. "This *is* my inn now, you drunk lunatic. Get out of my way." The barman knocked his colleague aside; the man stumbled and splayed out across the bar and spilled a mug of ale down the wrinkled shepherd's robe. The old man shouted and jumped up.

"This place has gone to the dwellers," he said. "The both of you idiots have ruined your family's tavern!" The shepherd flapped out his robe, splattering drops of ale all over the place.

"Watch it!" another man said, leaping up from his chair.

Here we go.

The splashed man shoved the shepherd backward. The shepherd turned around and squeezed his robe out onto his feet. The Greenfoot brothers roared with laughter.

The shepherd laughed as well, and then he got punched square in the jaw. Taroke and Ratoke stared for a moment and then launched at the man, but not before about six of his friends had leaped up from their table. The two brothers met them all with drunken fists.

The rest of the bar erupted. Some men ran toward the brawl and some women darted upstairs, but most everyone just snuck outside with drinks in hand. The flutist, cursing, jumped back on stage, grabbed his gear and few coins, and then fled out the back door.

Ratoke and Taroke, outnumbered as they were, handled themselves fine. They were built to throw fists. Short but strong and heavy, they had long arms for their size and had spent their youth running lumber and precious metal across the realm. Their hands were all calluses, and they had clobbered each other too often for anyone else to trouble them. They knocked most men down in one blow if they made solid contact. Jason and Sir Breigo stood off to the side, unsure if the strange set of brothers needed help or not.

The fighting grew chaotic, transforming into an every-man-for-themselves affair. The thin, less drunk bartender pulled a crossbow from under the counter and shouted a warning, but no one was listening. The fat bartender recovered from his stupor and lurched upward, an empty mug in hand. The thick glass connected with the thin barman's forehead, toppling him into a couple of empty barrels.

"Gahkin's wands!" Sir Breigo shouted, "Enough!"

Taroke extracted himself from the brawling crowd, winked at Jason, and took a pull from the bottle of Spice sitting on the counter. He turned back, ducked a punch, and threw a fist into another man's stomach, doubling him over. Someone else grabbed him around the neck, and Taroke fell into the mess of people again, spilling Spice everywhere.

The fat bartender shattered a bottle and cocked his arm back, aiming to throw the dangerous glass into the crowd. Sir Breigo jumped the counter; the drunk bartender swung the bottle.

Breigo caught his arm in one hand and broke his nose with the other. He squeezed the bartender's forearm, the bottle dropped, and Breigo snapped the man's arm before the bottle hit the floor. He squealed.

The thin bartender pulled himself from under the barrels and scooped up the crossbow on the ground. He aimed it at Sir Breigo.

"That's my cousin!" he shouted.

Jason lunged over the bar and tackled him. The arrow fired and lodged itself in the ceiling. A woman shrieked from the floor above.

Jason yanked the crossbow away from the bartender, twisted his arm behind his back, and pounded his face into the ground. Blood sprayed out from his mouth and nose. Some twisted part inside Jason swelled with pleasure at the sight of the gushing blood. He lifted his skull into the air, aiming to smash it back down a second time.

Someone grabbed him on the shoulder, and the Prince of the Thirsting Forest whipped around, throwing a blind punch at whoever it was. His knuckles collided with the palm of Mako Black, calm as ever.

"That's enough, *Prince* Killovew."

Jason's men sat around the large table in the back corner. The bar did not completely empty out after the brawl, but it was subdued. Between Jason, Sir Breigo Aldev, Mako Black, and the Greenfoot brothers, the other drunken men were settled down quickly. Outnumbered and outclassed, they left with half-muttered curses and relative peace. Jason had caught an elbow in the jaw when he tackled the bartender, and Ratoke had a black eye he swore Taroke gave him, but aside from that, they were all unharmed.

As was tradition after a rousing bar fight, the group reveled in the retelling, passing the bottle of Spice around, pulling straight from the bottle. Taroke handed it to Jason. He looked at it for a moment, and then he passed it off without taking a swig.

"Mako," Taroke asked, "when did you decide to hop in?"

Ratoke added, "Because normally you just watch our shenanigans."

"I honestly thought he was mute the first couple cycles we rode with him."

"I thought a water dragon bit his tongue off."

"How would that be possible, huh? Four-inch-long teeth, bite off someone's tongue, and nothing else?"

Mako sipped the Spice bottle and watched the brothers bickering. Under his thick beard, Jason thought he saw a tiny smile.

Sir Breigo said, cutting in, "I now understand why twins are considered a curse among the soldiers on the other side of the river. They must have met you two."

The brothers stopped arguing, and both laughed heartily.

"Not twins, actually, Breigo," Taroke said.

"Not even full brothers," Ratoke added.

The knight said, "But you look almost exactly the same."

"Complicated bit of family history—"

"Yeah, you see, our mothers are twins—"

"Dad always claimed he got them confused—"

"That it was just a one-time mistake—"

"That he loved whichever one he was talking—"

"But I think we all know what game Pops was playing."

"Anyhow, nothing comes between our mothers so, despite being knocked up by the same lying bloke, they both gave him up and kept the two of us—"

"So here we are, looking like twins—"

"But barely brothers!"

Mako shook his head, chuckling. Ratoke and Taroke rose from the table, almost in unison.

Taroke said, "The resting candles are burning, Jason, so if you don't mind, I'm off to bed. Come on, brother."

"Don't stay up too late, boys, huh?" Ratoke added.

Taroke said, "We've got to be responsible with the apocalypse around the corner, eh?"

Ratoke clapped Sir Breigo on the shoulder and then they both left toward the stairs.

Jason watched them go, spying Diana standing at the top step. Taroke dodged around the skinny woman, laughing as she reached out for him. She shot Jason another venomous look and then chased after the half brothers.

Sir Breigo Aldev rolled his eyes after they left. He turned and said to Mako in a subdued voice, "I do thank you, Mr. Black, for your assistance with the unruly patrons… and for… helping Prince Killovew remain calm."

Mako just nodded and took another sip.

Sir Breigo shot Jason a meaningful look. It was about time, Jason thought, to reveal the true nature of their journey to Shinar to Mako, though he knew Sir Breigo felt otherwise.

Up to this point, he had not yet decided whether he was going to reveal his father's plot to the water dragon wrangler, who had joined the group late in the planning. His intentions for going to Shinar were far less traitorous than Jason and the rest of his men. But he had no option now. Mako knew they were up to something.

Mako Black rubbed his hand through his beard, as was his habit, and leaned back in his seat. He stared into the distance for a while, and then he spoke, his eyes still glazed over, thinking.

"I've heard you are the best swordsman from the Thirsting Forest Realm, Sir Breigo. Maybe in the whole kingdom. I heard you won the Shinar single combat tournament your first season. Heard you withstood a Vistonex raid that took out the rest of your battalion. I even heard you put the final sword in that big dweller last season." He turned toward the knight, looking him in the eyes. "All that true?"

Sir Breigo didn't hesitate to respond. "I wouldn't phrase it all that way, and I don't know about being the best in the kingdom. But yeah." Breigo scratched his chin. "That other stuff is all true, I suppose. Why do you ask?"

Jason felt a hidden edge in Breigo's voice, despite the knight trying to speak casually.

Mako Black nodded. "Maybe I believe all that." He took a slow breath then asked, "You know what my profession was, before now?"

Sir Breigo responded, "Yes, Mr. Black, I do. A dangerous way to earn a living."

Mako grunted.

Jason cut in, hoping to end the tension. "Why do you ask about this, Mako?"

Mako smiled and turned his dark eyes toward Jason, as if he had been waiting to respond to Jason.

"In my line of work, it's not the big ones that you have to worry about, even though they have fangs as big as your head. The ones that know they are dangerous, they are confident, predictable… easy to handle. Give them what they want, and they'll leave you be. Nothing to prove, so to speak." Mako looked at Breigo for a long moment, before turning back to Prince Jason. "No… not the big ones I'm worried about. It's the young ones. The upstarts. They are aggressive and unpredictable and want to prove themselves. If you underestimate them because they are smaller, they'll grab you by the ankle while you aren't looking, pull you into the brown water, and they'll drown you."

Mako went on. "I don't care how good a swordsman you are, Sir Breigo. And I've decided I don't care how much gold your father gave me, Prince Jason. You two aren't good secret-keepers. I can read it in your eyes. I know you two have plans. Plans beyond what is written on our enlistment papers. So, before I get dragged any deeper into this swamp, I need to know why the best knight in the kingdom and the heir to the Thirsting Forest throne are *volunteering* to go to war.

And don't tell me it's for Gahkin or gold or glory, because I know it ain't."

Breigo said loudly to Jason, "Do not say anything you don't want to, Jason. He has no right to question you or be suspicious of your desire to enlist. He can come with us and keep *our* gold, or he can go home."

Jason looked between the two men.

"Pass me that bottle."

Mako Black smiled, grabbed the Spice bottle, and slid it across the table to Jason. The Prince of the Thirsting Forest snagged it in his open palm, raised it to his lips, and drank the remainder in two gulps. It tasted like nasty algae medicine, smelt like the stuff you might put on wounds, and burned his throat. He almost gagged but choked back the impulse. He shivered, shook his head, and exhaled slowly.

He met the dragon wrangler's eyes. "I'm willing to trust you. But if I'm to tell you this, I'm going to need you to trust us, too."

Mako Black nodded slowly.

With low whispers and furtive glances thrown at the few surrounding tables still occupied, Jason explained their heretical plot to him.

After the conversation, Mako said nothing for a long while. He stroked his beard and sat in silence. Sir Breigo fiddled nervously in his seat, but Jason waited. He did not want to rush the man who could now get them all thrown into the dungeons below Shinar. Below the table, Jason fingered the hilt of his dagger.

"Bury it all," Mako said. "I'm in."

Four

The Princess of the Thirsting Forest sat below her father, admiring the decorations in the great hall. Two flags dangled from the high ceiling. The Thirsting Forest flag hung next to a pale cerulean flag. Bordered with mint green, it had a cluster of pink mulberries at its center. The flag of the Edengrove.

Freshly picked bouquets of blue and white oleander and purple stork's-bill sat in baskets along each table. Cream-colored orchids with rippling green roots clutched the arms of goldenglass chandeliers. It was the peak of the light season, and the room was more than bright enough, but the maids had decided to burn torches too. The wide open windows ushered a distant mountain breeze into the room, but a bead of sweat still trickled down the princess' spine. She sipped from her cup of chilled mango and coconut juice brought up from the deep cellars, stirring goosebumps on Jinala's warm, fair skin. The scent of cinnamon apple pastries wafted through the cracks of the ancient kitchen doors hidden behind the throne's platform. Sir Trittion caught Jinala's eye and rubbed his belly. She nodded in agreement with a smile. They hadn't been allowed to indulge in deserts since the dark season. Some of the crowd had already arrived and couldn't resist raising their heads and sniffing at the pungent air. Their eyes danced across the room, from the flowers to the open windows- even to her and her father. Lord James Killovew looked far more regal this cycle than when he was out on the road, his golden crown resting gently upon his trimmed and parted dark red hair.

The folks at the castle were well-fed but mostly on just essentials. M-bars and a little meat and vegetables were about all anyone had eaten in the past season, and now they had pastries and pies cooling downstairs, waiting to be shared among the crowd.

Jinala thought it was going to be the most beautiful reception and the most delicious meal she might ever eat.

She couldn't wait to leave.

The Killovew girl shifted in her chair and slid the silken sleeve of her green dress up just enough to peek at the scrape and bruise on her forearm. It had grown larger and darker, now a blotchy dark brown and purple that ran from her elbow halfway to her wrist. She shook her sleeve back down and then glanced up at her father sitting in the gray-scale throne. His eyes flicked downward and met hers.

"What's wrong, sweetheart?"

"Nothing," Jinala lied, squirming again in her chair and looking away from him. The doors at the far end of the hall swung open, thankfully distracting Lord Killovew from whispering any further questions.

A young page stepped through the door and bowed before speaking. "My Lord, I present Lord Eric Eden and Lady Barbara Eden of the Thousand River Realm."

The youth stepped aside, and the royal couple strode through the doors, followed by about twenty men and women. The crowd was a mix of those the Edens had brought with them and the envoy of Killovew knights and ladies that had met them at the realm border.

Lord and Lady Eden drew all Jinala's attention.

The fringes of a cape fluttered behind Lord Eden, buckled at the shoulder of his high-collared cloak. The cape was the inverse of his flag. A border of silky, icy cerulean fringed the otherwise solid mint green fabric. He wore brown trousers held up with a leather belt accented with light blue gems to match the flair on his cape. Sparkling silver wire, coiled in beautiful spirals and loops, circled around his short, black-haired head.

If his fashion was shockingly bright compared to the rest of the dull couples behind him, his wife was that much more brilliant than he.

Her dress was all shimmering blues. Strapless, the top half of the dress fit snugly around her torso. The fabric stretched taught around the hips and then billowed out in an uneven fashion down her legs. The right side skimmed along the floor, but the left cut so short that her leg was visible all the way up her thigh. A mint green ribbon wound up her left leg until it disappeared into the folds of the dress. An aquamarine jewel hung around her neck. The transparent jewel reflected the sun from the windows, sending a thousand little shards of light across the walls and turning the lady into the focal point of the whole room. Her tiara was thin like her husband's crown but contained many jewels nestled within the silver wire. She wore her long brown hair loose and wavy, cascading down well past her shoulders.

Jinala loved the lady's look, but she would not be allowed to wear clothes so… suggestive for at least a few more seasons. And, she had to admit, she was too young and skinny to fill out the shape of the fabric's curves, *allowed* or not.

The procession reached the steps leading to the throne. Lord Eden held out his hand, and Lady Eden took it and curtsied to Lord Killovew. Then Lord Eden bowed, back straight, hands tucked behind his back. Her father stood and bowed in return.

Equals.

The crowd of knights and citizens followed suit, some more elegantly than others. It was only then, as everyone else bowed, that Jinala noticed the two

Acolytes standing behind the guests.

Cloaked and hooded, they stood still as statues, flanking the large doors like purple phantoms. Her father must have noticed them, but he ignored them and addressed the guests from Castle Eden.

"My friends, welcome to Castle Killovew. I am truly glad to host this gathering again. Most of you know this already, but—for those shameful few who do not—this is the tenth Killovew-Eden banquet. It is a fact I am proud to celebrate." The crowd cheered and clapped.

Lord Eden said, "I hope we can have a hundred more." The crowd cheered again.

Jinala was proud of her father for his realm diplomacy. Not all the border realms got along like the Killovews and the Edens. In fact, almost none did. With worrisome news from the Quirvop realm that their northern fields were flooded with locusts, and the Grayson knights and workers abandoning their chasm outposts, the kingdom was beginning to feel too crowded for comfort. Very many more would go hungry soon, and too many were already on the verge of starvation, like the Ardellian raiders who probed both the Eden's and the Killovew's borders. The need for strong allies with fertile lands, like the Edengrove, was more important now than ever before.

Her father continued, "We have much to celebrate and share, and the chiefs and councilors will have business with Lord Eden and myself to review. But! Like many of you, who have been doing your part to make the food stretch longer all season, I think it is far overdue that we eat a good and proper meal. To our guests and my citizens, I say, let this meal remind us of the good times before rations and m-bars."

"Aye!" An apparently hungry knight cheered from the middle of the pack. Lord Killovew's eyes wrinkled at the edges, and he cracked a knowing smile. With a whistle and the double clap of his hands, serving women appeared from recessed passageways, arms laden with trays of food and jugs of chilled wine and mead.

"Lord and Lady Eden, it would be my pleasure if you would join Jinala and me at our table."

The crowd seated themselves and dug in at once. Jinala noticed most of the knights from both realms sat together, the councilors and chiefs together, and the ladies together. All the groups fell into conversation quickly enough, swapping news and stories and jests from the villages and cities across both the Edengrove and the Thirsting Forest.

Jinala rose when her father beckoned and went straight to Lord Eden. She gave him a big hug which he returned.

"Uncle Eric, I've missed you."

"I wish I could visit you more, sweet one." Eric pulled out a seat for Lady Eden and for Princess Jinala. Jinala bowed gracefully to Lady Barbara, who smiled and bowed back. Jinala did not really know Eric's wife, but she tried to be nice to her.

"It's nice to see you again too, Lady Eden."

"Thank you for welcoming us into your home, Princess Jinala."

They all sat down, and their first dish was served before them. Unlike the other tables where the people helped themselves to their portions from large serving dishes, each entrée was brought individually to their small table at the front of the hall.

The first dish was roasted boar with steaming onions and gravy and a sweet cranberry slaw. She savored every bite, trying to slow down and not look too ravenous.

Before she was finished, the Acolytes at the back of the hall began to make their way toward their table.

Her father mumbled, "Of course they couldn't even wait until we finished our food." He threw his small cloth over his plate. "Excuse me," he said, standing.

Lord and Lady Eden exchanged looks but said nothing. Barbara smiled at Jinala, but the princess was not paying much attention to her. Her eyes were half-closed, and she was straining her ears to hear the words her father was exchanging with the God-King's priests. James had only stepped a few yards away before inclining his head and listening to what they had to say, but Jinala only picked up one small phrase out of the whole conversation due to the din in the hall. It was less than half a sentence, but it made her shiver and near stopped her heart.

"... outlaws in the forest..."

Jinala reached for a fork to try to disguise her obvious flinch. Her sleeve slipped down and revealed her scraped and bruised forearm to Lord and Lady Eden. She quickly hid it again, but it was too late. Lady Eden had seen.

"Jinala, what did you do to your arm? That looks serious," Barbara said. Eric Eden looked down at her, eyebrows raised.

"I... tripped earlier, and I didn't want to ruin the feast for Father. Don't tell him; I will get it looked at later... I guess it's worse than I thought, huh?" She tried to smile, but her heart was racing. She needed to make sure her orphan friends were safe. But Lady Eden would not let it go.

"Oh, silly girl, your father will not be mad because you hurt yourself," she said, "let me see that now. How did you manage to scrape the *top* of your forearm falling to the ground?"

Lord Eden waved his hand, "Barbara, relax, she'll live."

"She'll live. Hmph. Gahkin's wands, Eric, you and James never cease to amaze me. This is Princess Jinala Killovew; I think we can do better than just barely keeping her alive, don't you think?" Lady Barbara stood and reached out for Jinala's hand. "Come, child, lead me to a room where I can help you get this washed up and properly bandaged."

Her father turned and saw Barbara standing and Jinala's outstretched arm. He had a deep frown on his face, and it deepened.

"Barbara, thank you, but Jinala needs to learn to take care of these things herself. Jinala, go get that washed and wrapped so that you look like a princess, not some wild orphan. And then go to your room. Go. Nowhere. Else." His eyes were locked with hers, and he let them linger there longer than seemed necessary. She nodded, mumbled farewell to Lord and Lady Eden, and quickly walked out of the hall.

As soon as she turned the corner, out of everyone's line of sight, she took off running.

Does he want me to go warn them? Or was he just mad at me?

She knew he was trying to say more than his words would allow, but what? Her heart and her feet were racing, yet she did not even know where she should go. She was headed toward her chambers but decided against it and made a right into a descending stairwell. It dropped down to some servant passages that would take her toward the back side of the castle. She could go through there and make her way into the kitchen cellars, then climb out into the spice gardens.

No other brilliant idea came to her, so she pressed on, jumping the last four steps and tearing off around the next corner. A few castle cats hissed and ducked out of her way, but she saw no one else. Luckily the servants were all attending the feast. It would not be this easy once she got outside. It was the season of the sun, and it would be as bright as Sond out there. She put her shoulder into an inconspicuous section of stone wall between two hanging tapestries. The wall rotated, and she slipped into the dim corridor. She needed a way to cross out through the castle lawns and make it to the forest unnoticed. Anyone who happened to glance out the windows at the wrong moment would see her running like a crazy girl for the woods. It was one thing to save her friends, but she would do them no good if the Acolytes knew she was helping them. She might accidentally give them away.

Would the Acolytes already be searching for the boys? Did they know where they were? What if they already caught them? She shook her head as she leaped down another flight of stairs in two bounds.

No, they can't have found them. I won't believe it.

She arrived in the kitchen cellars. She crossed to the corner where the spices were stored. A small, recessed stair would lead her up into the gardens. Out of the corner of her eye, she saw an apron hanging by a stack of wooden crates full of coconuts. That gave her an idea.

She sidestepped a table and made her way over to it. The apron was too big for her, which was good because it wrapped all the way around her, covering her elegant dress. She tore the sparkling green sleeves off, though it would cost her a lecture from her father's tailor, and now she just looked like some serving girl wearing a huge apron. Now she just needed to hide her hair.

She spun around looking for something, but it was dim in the cellars, and there were only fruit and vegetables and boxes lying around. She looked down and saw her green sleeves. She scooped them up, pulled her hair into a tight ponytail, and wound the sleeves around her hair. It wasn't exactly the height of fashion, but it would work to camouflage her enough.

She darted to the stairs, ran up, and then stopped at the foot of the door, breathing heavily. She inhaled deeply and pushed open the stone door.

Bright light almost blinded her. She stepped out into the gardens, shielding her eyes from the sun. She walked since it would not look very natural for some kitchen girl to be dashing away from the castle and because she did not think she could run anymore until she caught her breath anyway.

Thyme, rosemary, and mint, then oregano and cilantro filled her nostrils, accented with the ever-present smell of rich, manured earth. In these times, Castle Killovew, thanks to the master gardeners, was one of the few places left in the realm with a prospering garden, and yet even the castle had had to make cutbacks and adjustments. Every other row of herbs had been ripped out and were now replaced with potatoes to help provide excess food to the castle. Jinala hated potatoes, but the gardeners claimed it was the best food to grow to provide sustenance to the villages.

She walked along the northeast side of the castle all the way to the smaller wall that enclosed the potato-spice garden. She put her little fingers into the cracks in the stone and climbed up. It was not too high, and she was over in a flash.

She went across the yard, which separated the inner walls of the castle from the massive secondary perimeter walls. A small stone door, which would be sealed if war or bandits ever came to the castle gates, allowed easy passage in and out of the northeast side. Jinala put her shoulder to the heavy door, leaned into it, and opened it wide enough to walk through. She made sure to leave the door open since it was always locked from the outside. She looked out across the large field toward the forest. All she had to do was walk out there. A mere five hundred yards away.

It was the longest, slowest walk of all time. Out in the open, she realized the danger she was putting herself into. When she slipped into the forest, she would be as culpable as the Sondite boys. She had not felt this fear, this nauseous fear, since the dark season when the dweller ambushed their wagons.

Focused on fulfilling her promise to help them, as they had once helped her, Jinala made it into the Thirsting Forest. Her disappearance seemed unnoticed for the moment.

Now to find them. They weren't expecting her for at least half a cycle or maybe more. As she skirted the edge of the forest and swung around to the eastern side of the castle, she came into view of the front gate. It was open, as was usual these cycles, and a knight sat in the gatehouse, but she did not see her father or the Acolytes. She prayed they had not beaten her into the forest. She was confident the brothers could hide from the Acolytes, but only if they knew they needed to hide. Jinala had to find them and find them fast. She turned and peered into the forest, which quickly grew thick and dense and dark. The task seemed impossible, it was something she had never been able to do even when she knew where they were, and now she was just one girl with miles of forest to search.

Why did I come out here? What help am I?

"Are those creatures really necessary?" Lord Killovew's voice echoed off the castle walls. Jinala looked back toward the gate.

She crouched in the bushes and watched as her father, a handful of Acolytes, and a small entourage of knights and servants crossed out onto the open lawn between the castle and the forest. Two massive cats, buckled and leashed with gray chains, walked alongside the men. Jinala had heard of one, which was jet black, long, and lean. It was called a 'panther.' The other was tan, taller, and much thicker. Two massive fangs jutted out of its closed mouth. Jinala did not know the name of the panther's larger cousin. The tan cat turned its head and snarled at her father, but it made no move to attack him. The big cat's head was as high as a man's shoulder. One other Acolyte was carrying a hawk on his arm. Jinala saw her father gesturing and speaking more, but she could not hear his words.

The Acolytes did not heed whatever her father said and kept walking. They followed the southwest path toward the surrounding forest, thankfully away from Jinala.

Lord Killovew stopped and shouted after them, "You will not maim any of the *authorized* men out there, I hope!"

The Acolytes said nothing, walking onwards to the forest edge. A breeze from Jinala's back tickled her neck, disturbing the few loose hairs not tied down by her torn sleeves. The black panther stopped abruptly, sniffing the air. It turned around and looked at Jinala from across the lawn, despite her hiding in the bushes at the eastern edge of the forest nearly three hundred yards away. The panther lowered its head and pawed at the ground, seemingly staring straight at her. She gasped and fell backward. The other monstrous cat lowered its head and shoulders, and now both creatures were snarling in her direction. She scrambled up off her knees and ran deeper into the forest.

Her heart in her throat, Jinala flew through the undergrowth, and as soon as the forest grew too dense, she scampered up the nearest tree. She pushed and climbed her way through the intertwining branches as fast as she could, thinking of how fast Mart and Crichton could make their way through the jungle canopy.

Those beasts are hunting me right now.

A hawk screeched from above and dive-bombed through a gap in the canopy. She dropped onto a lower branch, and the bird pulled up before crashing through the denser leaf coverage. The hawk was on her, which meant the cats could not be far behind.

She jumped for the next branch, but her foot slipped on a patch of damp moss. She fell, tumbling down and crashing on her back halfway through a rotted log. She groaned, barely restraining herself from shouting out loud in pain.

She gritted her teeth and rolled off, her back throbbing and her fists clenched. She pounded the ground with one hand and stood up. She fought off another shout with just a groan and took off running, but she stumbled ten yards further on and fell. The pain was too much. Little pinpricks of white light sparked in and out of her narrowed field of vision. She felt light-headed. She strained just to keep her eyes open. A black shadow dropped in front of her, followed by another. Jinala screamed.

Crichton knelt and quickly covered her mouth with one hand. "Shhh."

"Are you okay?" Martin asked quietly at her other side. He seemed unsure of what to do, so he just patted her on the back. She groaned against Crichton's hand.

"Sorry, sorry, sorry," Martin muttered. "And I'm sorry for hitting you earlier, too," he said, his eyes aimed at the ground.

Crichton scoffed. "Now is not the time, sloth brain. What happened, Gina?" He removed his hand from her mouth.

"We've got to get out of here. They're after you." Jinala groaned. "They have a hawk and a panther and something… bigger. The Acolytes—" She groaned again and then continued, "The Acolytes are after you."

"Who are Acolytes?" Martin asked, his eyes flashing between Jinala and Crichton.

"They are the God-King's priests," Jinala said. "The ones who decided Sondites are not allowed here anymore. We've got to get out of here. Help me stand." Crichton and Martin gently stood her up. She looked at the tree branches above her and felt dizzy.

"Can you climb?" Crichton asked, following her eyes.

"I don't know. But, Crichton, listen. I think they know you and Mart are out here." She stifled a sob. "Why can't they just leave you alone?"

"How can they know we are out here? How do you know they know?"

"They just know, all right! And we have to get out of here or else they are going to catch us all."

"Okay, well, *you* have to get back to the castle, or else *you* will get caught. But we can avoid them. The Acolytes and their animals."

A crack in the underbrush snapped their heads around. The black panther emerged from a clump of ferns, the thin black slits in its yellow eyes narrowed at the sight of people. It held its body low, close to the ground.

Jinala was frozen in fear.

I'm not as brave as Jason.

Crichton shoved Jinala and Martin behind him and aimed his stick-spear at the panther.

He whispered, "Go. Both of you. I'll meet up with you later."

Jinala wanted to flee, to make it back to the castle and just be inside and away from the monster, but her legs were locked. Martin seemed to have the same problem. His wide eyes stared in disbelief at the animal, which in one pounce could be on top of them. The black fur did not hide the taught leg muscles nor the paws that were bigger than their heads. Crichton waved his spear menacingly at the panther, but it didn't flinch; its eyes just followed the stick wherever it went. He glanced back at them for just a flicker, his lips tight and sweat lining his brow. Jinala trembled. She thought her knees might buckle.

"Please, princess," Crichton whispered. "Save my brother."

Jinala jerked out of her paralysis, grabbed Martin's hand, and yanked him along as she sprinted off into the forest. She heard the panther snarl, but it didn't land on her. Tears blurred her eyes, but she blinked them away. She ran hard, knocking moss and vines out of the way with her free hand.

She squeezed Martin's hand tighter and kept running, sprinting as fast as she could, as fast as she ever had. She felt detached from the fire in her legs, to the stitch in her side, and to the throbbing across her back. She almost felt like she was watching herself run in a dream. She felt only two things, and they consumed her entirely. A strong guilt for leaving Crichton, but an even stronger fear that those evil yellow eyes watched her, still tracking her from the darkest shadows of the Thirsting Forest.

She kept running. Martin pulled on her hand, taking her to the left, shouting, "This way!"

Jinala kept up with Martin for about half a mile before her body began to fail despite her desperate spirit. Her legs burned with every stride, barely catching her fall with each step and tug from Martin. Yet she somehow kept on her feet for another few hundred yards as they dodged around tree trunk after tree trunk. Martin skidded to a stop in a swamp clearing. The trees looked the same in every direction. Squidroot was here and there, rising above the ferns and prickly bushes and brown leaf rot carpeting the forest.

"We're lost!"

"No. Crichton knows this area. Which means… so do I!" Martin spun around. "We are taking you to the castle… This way!"

He pulled her off in a new direction. A loud roar, deeper and longer than the panther's, reverberated off the trees ahead of them. Jinala jerked to a stop when she heard it, but Martin yanked on her arm, and they continued forward. He veered off his path a little, and soon they were struggling through a thick tangle of plants and bushes, knotted together with streamers and vines, too dense to run through. Martin and Jinala pushed through them, Martin using his little stick-sword and Jinala following right behind his path, her hands on his back, too afraid to cast a glance backward. The moving was slow going. Martin was struggling. The vines he couldn't swipe out of the way were dragging their thorns across his arms and face, tracing thin red lines on his skin. Jinala heard rustling behind her. They had to stop and cut him free from the vines before they could move on. They lingered in the dense foliage. Again, she had to help Martin cut himself free from the imprisoning greenery. The rustling grew ever closer.

Martin ripped his arm out of another tangle, drawing blood in several spots where the thorns had dug into his skin. They pushed farther through the foliage, coming to a big log leading up and out of the thorny bushes.

They clambered up onto the dead palm, which had fallen and gotten caught up in the thick branches of an old oak tree. They ran along it, and Martin helped Jinala pull herself into the gnarled wooden branches. They climbed through the tree and then out onto a long limb that led to clearer ground. They dropped down, and there, through the trees, Jinala could finally see the gray castle walls. They jogged through the sparser section of the woods and knelt at the cusp of the clearing. Glancing back, Jinala saw nothing behind them. For the moment.

Martin looked at Jinala. "Where should I meet Crichton after you go to the castle?"

"You're coming with me. We can meet Crichton later."

"What? To the castle?" Martin scanned the stone walls as if seeing them for the first time. "I don't want to go in there."

"Just while those cats are still out here. Father will never let them inside. And I know lots of good places to hide you." She looked toward the castle gates, and then scanned the grounds. There was no one. She glanced to the closest windows. She didn't see anybody looking out. A deep breath filled her lungs, and she held it, thinking of Crichton and his last request and some calm returned to her.

After one last glance around, she grabbed Martin's hand, and they burst out of the bushes and ran for the far side of the castle.

Before they reached the midway point, a hawk screeched from behind them. She looked over her shoulder, and there it was, gathering speed and height above the treetops, heading straight toward them. They were in the open, and in a matter of flickers its cries would draw countless eyes down upon the princess and the forbidden outlaw she was clearly trying to help.

Jinala stopped, looking around for cover, but there was nothing. She squeezed Martin's hand and faced the bird. In a moment, it would clear the trees and lead her pursuers straight to them.

A bolt of pure blue light shot through the treetops and struck the bird. It burst into a cloud of feathers and tumbled out of sight into the woods.

Pure blue light.

Jinala had an idea of what had happened, but they did not have time to think about that. They took off running again, a deep roar spurring them on toward the castle wall. They rushed through the open outer door, and together pulled it shut behind them. Jinala and Martin raced across the yard to the corner where the small garden wall met the secondary castle walls. Martin climbed it and Jinala followed quickly after. They dropped down into the garden, ran through the rows of potatoes and spices, and made it to the cellar door. She reached for the handle and pulled. The door swung open.

"Go on!" She motioned Martin down the stairs and then followed, making sure to close the door behind her and re-lock it.

She ran down the stairs three at a time and, before she could stop, found herself crashing into a big, round-bellied knight. He was already holding Martin, who was futilely kicking the knight in his steel greaves. He grabbed Jinala in his other arm before she could change direction. The knight's ornate oak visor was lowered, and Jinala had no idea who had grabbed her.

"I'm the princess! Let me go!"

The knight chuckled glumly, "I know who you are, Gina, so stop kicking me. We have to get Martin hidden and fast, or I'll be in as much trouble as the both of you."

Five

Crichton Raak wiped his eyes and sat upright. Footsteps echoed down the dungeon halls. Someone was coming, and judging by the shuffling double-step rhythm, it sounded like someone human. For the last few candles, all Crichton had heard was the sound of claws clicking on stone. The four-limbed shadow pacing outside and occasionally sniffing under his door had been his sole companion since he was locked in this cell. The man-steps grew closer, and Crichton squeezed the edge of the bed to keep his fingers from trembling. His cell door was pushed open about a foot or so; a tray of bread and half a coconut and a bowl of water slid inside.

"Wait!" he said as the door closed, but it shut without an answer. He moved to the tray, crumpling down onto the ground to try to eat. The bread was fresh, still warm in the middle. Under normal circumstances, he would have scarfed it down, yet it was dull and tasteless in Crichton's mouth.

Where is my brother?

Crichton was not hungry; he had lost any appetite he might have had, but his belly was empty, and so he tried to eat because it was better than laying on his splintery wooden bed and brooding. He could not even chew the food, let alone swallow it. His mouth was dry, and his stomach threatened to turn over. He choked down a tiny nibble of bread, his eyes blankly staring at the ground.

Crichton had last seen Martin as he fled with Jinala deeper into the jungle. They disappeared hand in hand over a small ridge, thick with bramble, leaving Crichton alone with the big predator. Just as he had wanted. The panther's gaze had never shifted from Crichton as they escaped. The older Sondite was its only interest. It had taken one slow half-step out of the bushes, narrow yellow eyes locked with his purple ones, both predator and prey frozen. The stare could not be broken, Crichton had thought. If he blinked, he would be dead. His right eye started to water. The panther pounced.

Crichton ripped the loaf of bread in two.

He had pricked the cat with his spear, but the big animal had collided with him anyway. Before he knew his jab had failed, he was on his back in the dirt. The panther stood above him and stepped atop his chest with a surprisingly gentle paw. If it had wanted to eat him, it would have been as easy as leaning down and taking a bite. Crichton had struggled to try to move, but it was useless.

He squished a chunk of bread in his fist when he remembered peeing himself.

He had begged the cat, pleading as if it could or would listen to him. Luckily the panther was content just sniffing Crichton's face and laying down next to him, its heavy paw still draped across his chest. Only then did the predator notice the thin spear sticking out of its shoulder, wobbling up and down. It turned its huge head and licked the few drops of blood away, knocking the stick out with its bristly tongue. The spear had barely pierced the panther's skin.

Crichton groaned. He was useless. And harmless. While he lay there, pinned down in his own pee, he heard the roars of another cat. It sounded, if possible, bigger than the cat that had captured him. The sound of its roar vibrated deep in Crichton's chest, echoing off the forest trees. Even the black panther looked around and pulled back its ears.

Still sitting on the floor of his cell, Crichton drank from the bowl of water and then gazed into the puddle that remained, staring at his pathetic reflection. He sobbed and then tried to stifle his tears.

The roar of the tan cat bounced around the inside of his skull, and all he could picture was his little brother, broken and bleeding, lying underneath that awful monster. While Crichton was being led back into the castle, the big cat had come bounding up to the group, dark red blood smeared across its muzzle.

Crichton slung the wooden bowl against the door. It bounced off and clattered in the corner, upside down. Now he had no water to share if Martin showed up. Crichton crawled back toward his bed but instead of climbing up into it he wrapped his arms around his knees and slept on the cold stone ground.

****

Home.

His mother lay dying on their one small bed, his toddler brother asleep in her arms. A small amount of blood had dribbled from her nose and had caked onto her upper lip while he was away. He put down the basket of eggs and bars he had stolen and grabbed a small cloth by the bedside. It was bone dry. He tossed it over his shoulder and left the cabin for the creek. The Mud Wizard was nowhere to be seen.

It was near sunrise, which meant Crichton could see, but he could not see *far*. Such twilight was perfect for stealing eggs, yet not perfect when trying to negotiate the prickly path that led to the creek. He walked on his heels, avoiding clumps of weeds that looked like they might have sharp pricker seeds growing in them. If one of those lodged itself in his foot, only Mother could get—*not anymore, Crichton. If you step on a pricker, you've got to take it out yourself.* Crichton slowed down and stepped even more gingerly through the tall grass. He didn't know if he was old enough and brave enough to take one out himself, and he had to get to the creek, which meant he had to avoid them at all costs. Perhaps he could cut toe holes in his old shoes and fit into them again. That would give him a little protection the next time he had to go walking through the weeds.

Squinting hard in the gloom, Crichton made it to their little creek and pulled up the bucket of water. He tossed the cloth into the bucket and then untied the bucket from the rope that held it on the edge of the creek. He took a few steps, but the bucket was much too heavy. He splashed a good amount of water out to lighten the load and then walked back toward home, stepping with care through the weeds. A candle burned in the cabin's window, guiding him back. The roof looked worse than ever, and Crichton had no idea if he could ever go about fixing that.

Their rotting cabin had not always been rotten nor overgrown with thick vines and shrubbery. Once, it stood away from the Thirsting Forest, in an anonymous meadow, hidden from villagers who might spot them and turn them in for the color of their eyes. Crichton did not remember this time, but when his mother was healthier, she often spoke of it. She would tell him stories of Father from before he was taken prisoner. And of her parents, who had been young when they fled Sond and came under the mountain pass and fled into the jungle. How her father, Crichton's grandfather, had built the cabin with his bare hands, all by himself. Well, all by himself except for Shelly the ox. Crichton's mother would smile wide when she told that story. Grandmother never let Grandfather claim he did it all by himself; she'd always say, 'It was Shelly that did the most of it, and you never give her any credit.' But his mother would sigh, and an all too familiar dark shadow would cloud her face; she would sigh and end her story, 'Well, it *was* a beautiful home once.'

He walked back inside and put the bucket beside the fireplace. He would have to get a fire going soon, too. It always took him ages to get a fire going, even with the candle that he left burning all the time. Making fire without flame was something he'd never done. Usually, Mother would do that too. Maybe the Mud Wizard could teach him… if he ever came back.

Crichton pulled out the soaking cloth and wrung it out over the bucket. With gentle hands, he dabbed at his mother's face, cleaning the blood from her upper lip. He used a clean corner to wipe her brow and her cheeks, under her eyes, and around the fold of her jawline, where the sweat usually ran down to her chin. He cleaned in and behind her ears and down her neck. He paused to inhale through his nose. The smell of her hair was still tinged with the sweet scent of lilac and lavender. He used to fall asleep with her hair draped over him, nearly suffocated by the aroma of his mother.

As he rubbed at a smudged spot on the front part of her frail throat, his hands stopped moving. He stared at the small circle of skin next to her star-shaped freckle. Usually, that spot of skin bumped up and down.

It was not bumping.

Crichton put his cheek right up to his mother's mouth. No air warmed his face. No sound at all. He shook her a little and pressed his cheek right against his mother's lips. She didn't pucker them together and kiss him. They didn't even twitch. They didn't even try to draw breath.

No, not yet. I'm not ready yet, Mother. Please. Please, Mother, come back.

Crichton should not have grabbed at her and shook her, but he did. His brother Martin woke up and looked over at his older brother, shaking Mother up and down.

"Mama seeps?" Martin asked.

Crichton let her go. He rubbed at his face and eyes before he answered his little brother. "Yes, Mart, she's just sleeping. You can go back to sleep too."

"KraKra?" Martin asked. He was getting good with his words, but he had yet to say a complete sentence, and he struggled with Crichton's name.

"Yes, Mart?"

"KraKra seeps?"

"No, I'm not sleepy yet. I'll make some food, so when you wake up you can eat."

"Eat now? Eat now, pease." Martin sat up. "Foo now, KraKra."

"Food soon. You want eggs?"

Martin crossed his arms. "No eggs. Yucky. No eggs, pease, KraKra."

Crichton sighed and laid his head down on his mother's still breast.

Please, Mother. Not yet. I'm not ready yet.

For the millionth time in his dreams, the memory of her death returned with breathtaking pain. He buried his own mother at two suns old. And now she had died again, like always, leaving him far before he was ready.

****

His eyes snapped open.

A man knelt on the ground next to him with a hand on his shoulder. Crichton hung onto the arm, thinking he was still with his family for a flicker, but the man smelled of old steel and rancid sweet-wine and raw fish. Crichton pulled away and backed into the corner. He turned and looked up into the face of the man who had awoken him.

It was a pale old man with a thick silver mustache and a round belly stretching out underneath a brown and green painted breastplate.

"It's okay, my boy," he said. "I'm on your side."

Crichton was silent.

"Look, I have something important to tell you, but you must keep it to yourself. It's a very, very dangerous secret, and you must promise not to tell the Acolytes—the purple-robed men—no matter what they might say or do to convince you otherwise."

Crichton nodded slowly.

"You are in great peril, but you have friends that want to help you. The Acolytes, they don't know you have any allies or a younger brother."

"Is he safe—"

"He and the princess are both safe, yes. He is well hidden, and if all goes to plan, you and Martin will be together soon. But listen. If they ask you, you live alone out there in the forest. Alone. And if they make you say someone helped you, tell them food was delivered to the edge of the forest, but you never saw who did it. Follow along with whatever Lord Killovew says when you go before him. The Acolytes will be back soon, so I must go. I can't be seen here."

The old man stopped to listen, and the room was quiet. The claws of the black panther were silent, but Crichton could hear the creature breathing heavily outside the door, sniffing and snorting and licking at something on the ground. The knight- at least, Crichton thought he was a knight- saw the Sondite boy looking at the shadow of the panther in the gap under the cell door.

"Lucky for us, the monster guarding you is more bark than bite. Or more purr than pounce, in this case, I'd say." The knight chuckled at his own wit and extended a hand to the boy. "Come over here and sit up on your bed. Come on."

Crichton clenched his jaw. *He thinks I'm a baby.* He swallowed and stood up.

"Thank you for"—his voice cracked, but he cleared his throat and continued—"hiding my brother... but why?"

The old man smiled at him, but his eyes were far from happy. "I can't tell you now, but I suppose... Well, soon, we will explain everything to you." The knight stood, pushing himself off the bench with a little grunt. "For now, you just sit patiently, hard as it is. And remember what I told you. Those purple men mean you and your brother no good, despite what they may tell you. Trust Lord Killovew, Jinala's father, no matter what. Oh, and here."

The knight pulled something out of his dagger sheath that was not a dagger and handed it to Crichton. He took it but looked up at the knight, confused. Whatever it was, it was wrapped in a white cloth and felt lumpy and soft in his hands.

"Mango-lime tart. We get these maybe once a season, and it is my favorite, and just baked. Some people might pay a full gold bar for one of these. You have got to eat it too, or else they will know someone else has been here. Now give me back the napkin. Okay, goodbye for now, Crichton."

"Wait! What's your name?"

"Sir Trittion Oak, my boy. Farewell for now."

The knight shuffled out of the doorway, closing it quietly behind him until it latched. Crichton heard a low snarl, but it was cut short by a whispering voice.

"Shh, shh, shh. Look, more fish. Mmm, raw trout. Nothing tastier than stinky, raw trout for a big, spoiled kitty. That's all you are, huh, a bi—ow! Okay, okay, shh, shh. Have it all, have it all; I'm not saving any of that stinking fish for myself. There's a good kitty."

Crichton's lips twitched upward. He ate the tart with a fresh appetite, thinking how his new allies might be plotting his and Martin's escape. After finishing his food, he tried to go back to sleep.

He lay awake, his eyes closed, and fought to recall the image of his parents. He barely remembered the face of his mother, and he had never known his father. But the smell of his mother's hair... if he focused hard enough, he could still remember its fragrance. Almost as if a waft of lilac and lavender pollen had found its way into the dungeon. He turned over and remembered the feel of her arm wrapped around him, his baby brother laying on her chest by his side. Martin would just stare at him with those big, dark purple eyes, and they would fall asleep, all three of them in the same bed, curled up and cozy and happy in their solitary cabin in the woods.

Six

The heavy door swung open and crashed against the wall. Two men stepped inside, robed in purple with their hoods drawn, one holding a jagged knife. He raised it up, and Crichton squirmed backward against the wall—but it was just an iron key—and the Acolyte tucked it into his robe.

"Come with us," the man said.

The other Acolyte tossed a lumpy shirt, thick brown leggings, and leather boots on the ground at Crichton's feet. He changed quickly out of his dirty rags and into the wrinkly clothes and then left the cell.

As he stepped into the dungeon hallway, the panther flicked a paw out at his ankle.

"Emushéré," one of the Acolytes commanded. The panther stepped back, sat down, and was silent.

Crichton looked up the dim hall, lit by a sparse torch here and there, and found a third man in purple waiting for him. Crichton walked up toward him, keeping his head straight and trying not to look at the dingy cell doors on either side of him. The man turned around and stepped into a side passageway, leading further upward. Crichton followed.

Looking back to see if the two other Acolytes were following behind him, Crichton saw the big cat. Just feet behind the whole party, the black panther stalked, alert, the narrowed eyes reflecting in the torchlight an intensity as fierce and focused as when it was hunting Crichton in the Thirsting Forest. It padded along, stopping to sniff at the other cell doors occasionally. Crichton swallowed and faced forward again.

After taking many turns and ascending four different flights of stairs, they emerged into a bright hallway full of sunlight. One of the Acolytes shut the dungeon doors before the panther could cross over the threshold.

They moved on through the brighter walkways of the castle proper, and at one point, Crichton thought he saw curly blond hair disappear around a corner, but he could not be sure. He held his chin high from then on just in case anyone was watching. He would not let Martin or Jinala think he was afraid or in any danger.

They marched down a final hallway that emptied into a giant reception hall. The room had a high domed ceiling, spotted with wide open windows that flooded the whole area with sunlight. Many passageways, big and small, converged here.

To one side, the double doors were thick and reinforced with vertical strips of iron. Three horizontal stone beams slid halfway into their iron brackets, braced one of the doors shut. The other could be opened at will. Crichton doubted anything could knock down those doors if the stone beams were locked all the way in place.

The double doors at the opposite side were as ornate as the others were hardy. A wide oak tree and two tall coconut palms were carved in relief onto the wood. Crichton had never seen anything he could call art before, but this *was* art. It was beautiful. Looking closer, he saw little monkeys hanging and scampering in the tree limbs.

As he and his captors walked toward it, he could make out individual twigs and leaves. It was all wooden brown, and yet every detail was sharp and distinct. The relief was flanked by a pair of Killovew knights. They did not speak but swung open the mystical Oak tree doors. Crichton was nudged inside, followed by the three Acolytes.

About fifteen men had gathered at the far end of the great hall, most of them assembled in a semi-circle on a wide staircase. Sitting higher on the stairs than any of the rest was Lord Killovew, ruler of the castle and all the villages in the Realm of the Thirsting Forest.

Sunlight streamed in through the windows, glinting off the golden crown atop James Killovew's head. The fact that most of the men in the room wore green and brown cloaks and shining steel armor as opposed to the dark purple robes of the Acolytes heightened Crichton's cautious optimism.

They are on my side.

To the right of Lord Killovew sat another important-looking man, a tangle of glittering silver circling his head. He was the only one in the room wearing a light blue cloak with mint green edges. His cloak was different in another way too. It had a tight, high collar and a strange cape that hung around one shoulder and billowed out from behind his chair.

The caped man and James Killovew stood when Crichton walked closer, and the others followed suit. Lord Killovew nodded toward Crichton, or perhaps to the Acolyte behind Crichton. The men all sat back down, and the Lord of the Thirsting Forest spoke.

"Isaac, you know you are, as required and as desired, always welcome to join me here in the Realm of the Thirsting Forest. But... my word... a boy? You disrupt my feast, my guests, and myself, release dangerous beasts into my backyard, keep everyone in lockdown, just to hunt down and capture a Sondite boy hiding out in the forest? It looks like he lives on squirrel meat. What does Gahkin need him for?"

The leader of the Acolytes, who was a hunched old man, stood in front of the semi-circle. Crichton and the other Acolytes walked forward through the long hall and stood beside him. He was smaller and feebler looking than the Acolytes who had retrieved Crichton from the dungeons.

He pulled back his hood to reveal a wrinkled, bald head. Brown age spots dotted his skin down to his neck, which disappeared into the cloak. When he spoke, his voice wavered now and again, as if his throat didn't always cooperate with his mind. But his voice was also deep, and his words conveyed a sense of control and command that his body did not suggest. He annunciated more crisply than most men and yet still spoke with slow precision.

"The council decided to come to Castle Killovew for two reasons. The first reason was to search and then rid the nearby forest of any illegal residents. This boy is a Sondite; thus he lives illegally upon your land; thus we have captured the very suspect Gahkin told us to remove. If the boy does not measure up to your standards, Realm Lord, find comfort he measures up to your God-King's."

Lord Killovew, stroking his chin, looked at Crichton.

"What is your name, Sondite?"

Crichton cleared his throat, a little unsure of the steadiness of his voice. "Crichton, sir," he said.

Lord Killovew leaned toward the man with the silver wreath in his hair and spoke loud enough for the whole hall to hear.

"I do need a servant boy, come to think of it." He tapped his fingers in quick rhythm along the armrest of the Squidroot throne. He turned back to the Acolytes. "Since this trespasser is living illegally on *my* land, I think I can make use of him. I'll send him along for his salvation when he's older and fit to fight the Vistonex. Gahkin surely isn't in desperate need of a *boy* for his army, I'm sure."

"You can ask Him yourself; we will summon Him so He might speak with you. This is the second reason why we are here. The outlaw was not our primary concern," the hunched man said. He turned back toward another of the Acolytes standing by the door. "Go get the summoning block." The robed consort left the room.

"What do you mean, Isaac? Are we going to pray to Gahkin together?" Lord Killovew asked, genuine confusion etched underneath his golden crown.

"You will see, my lord."

"I've heard of this… miracle, James," said the man in the cape to Lord Killovew's right. "Some sort of magic orb that lets anyone on the Ten Hand Council speak directly to the God-King."

"Is that so, Eric?" James Killovew raised his eyebrows and leaned back in his seat, turning his head toward Crichton from time to time. The Acolyte returned from gathering the summoning block. He carried the heavy-looking thing in a large burlap sack.

"If we are to use the globe, we need to go somewhere dark, Realm Lord, so if you will accompany—"

"No need to go anywhere, Isaac, I can dim the hall," Lord Killovew said and then clapped his hands twice. A few people emerged from the side passages, and James flicked his hands toward the windows. "I've had enough of the sun, thank you."

Grasping the dangling ropes, using an exhaustive twisting and tugging motion, the servants drew up sets of heavy fabric from below the windows. Once the openings were covered, the men pulled the ropes taught and wrapped them around recessed rungs at the bottom of the wall. The carved doors leading to the atrium were closed. The sunlight was entirely shut out from the great hall, but it was still only dim, not dark. The chandeliers and torches on the walls kept most of the shadows back in the deepest cracks and corners of the room.

"Too much light still, Lord Killovew. It would be best if we left—"

"Darker, please," James commanded.

The servants began putting out the flames until only a handful of torches were left. Two of the remaining burned behind the shoulders of Lord Killovew, who was transformed into a blackened shadow on an all-black throne. The man who had been called Eric was but half a silhouette, and the other men of the council were as good as invisible. Flickering, the torches cast deformed shapes onto the dark orange walls of the hall.

"I suppose that will be sufficient enough for our purposes."

"You are dismissed," James said to the servants.

The lower-ranking Acolyte, groaning with the effort, bent and placed the heavy block down onto the ground in front of the old Acolyte named Isaac. He knelt, and with the dramatic flourish of a stage actor, tossed aside the sack and revealed a square black stone.

Crichton was reminded of the black rectangle he had found in the forest with Jinala and Martin. The color and texture—metallic smoothness without the shine—looked almost identical. Instead of a rectangle, though, this new object was a perfect square save a curved divot in the top. The divot looked like a spot one might rest a ball, so it would not roll around.

Crichton stood near the old man, but he could barely see his face through the darkness. Isaac reached into one of the many folds of his purple cloak and pulled out a bulky leather bag. A bulky leather bag that smelled of smoke and bird droppings. Isaac reached inside for the object, but then hesitated and looked up toward James and Eric and the rest of the council.

"You should dismiss your knights and chieftains, Killovew. If they stay and witness what is about to pass, you will be responsible for those who lose their minds. Speaking with Gahkin is a miraculous experience and worthy of great worship, but His voice can often disconnect the meek from reality and thus, disconnect them from their sanity."

James replied, "I am sure they are just as capable of—"

"My lord," one of the men squeaked from the darkness. "I can—or, uh, I am capable of—I handle food shortage and surplus distribution and cellar inventorying and village tutoring when need be and well, I mean, you all know what I do, but I'm… well, I'd rather not stay, to be honest. I'd like to just stick to arithmetic if it's all the same to you."

"Of course, Finch. Go ahead. That's quite all right."

The man stood and walked with short, quick steps down the stairs, past the handful of Acolyte priests, and all the way down the empty hall. He slipped out the door, letting only a momentary ray of sunlight slice inside. The door shut with a heavy thud, and the room was sealed in darkness once again.

"Anyone else feel the need to leave?" James Killovew asked.

"The little math rat is the only one of us afraid of the dark, my lord. I'm itching to see why this Ten Hand Council *Acolyte* turned our great hall into a Gahkin-cursed shadow temple. Place reminds me more of a dweller dungeon than a holy site. The God-King I worship don't need to hide from the light. Let's get this snake show over and done with."

One of the Acolytes snapped back, "You will be hum—"

"Silence, Sarpho," the leader of the Acolytes snapped.

Lord Killovew said, "Excuse Sir Damian, Isaac. He runs the Killovew Fort at the chasm and deals more with dwellers and other dangerous creatures than with priests such as yourself. The darkness is no ally of his."

"His faith is apparent, at least. Ignorant and barbaric but apparent, nonetheless. We *should* respect that." Isaac looked at the Acolyte who spoke up earlier. The old man took a deep breath and then spoke on. "Now, come closer, those who would stay."

James strode down the few steps from his throne, followed by Eric. The dark shapes of Killovew's chiefs and elder knights rose and joined them, forming a much closer circle around Isaac.

"You will need to kneel. We must humbly ask Him to join us." The men all knelt. The Acolyte noticed Crichton standing off to the side. "You too, Sondite. Just because your people once abandoned their Creator does not mean you shall disrespect Him also. As it stands now, I find Sondites to be some of the most capable and faithful citizens of Gahkin, given an opportunity. Now is as good of a time as any for you to start establishing your faith."

Crichton knelt.

Content at last, Isaac reached back into his bag and pulled out a dark blue sphere, the size of a man's fist. The top was flat and sunken seeming, and a pale blue color swirled across the darker blue of the sphere. Crichton squinted. The pale blue came from inside, giving off a faint glow.

Eric Eden and James Killovew both stared at the globe as well, unblinking. The others knelt too far away for Crichton to make out their expression, but he imagined they were as mystified as the two realm lords.

"Shut your eyes and repeat after me, realm lords," Isaac said.

A few of the Acolytes behind Isaac began to chant in hushed tones, "Hear us... Speak with us... Hear us... Speak with us..."

The old man continued, "Gahkin, I am your ever-servant, and I, Isaac, Third Hand of the Ten Hand Council, desire your wisdom."

"Gahkin, I am your ever-servant, and I, James, Lord of the Thirsting Forest Realm, desire your wisdom."

"Gahkin, I am your ever-servant, and I, Eric, Lord of the Thousand River Realm, desire your wisdom."

The old man lowed the sphere, inch by slow inch, until it sunk perfectly into the divot at the top of the black stone block. It locked itself into place with a metallic *clink*.

What was within the globe was set free.

It rushed outward in every direction as if a sudden, silent sandstorm had erupted in the hall.

Pale fog whirled through the room, painting the men and the walls behind them in a blueish glow. Only James and Eric kept their eyes open like Crichton, but many of the men would peek open an eye just to snap it shut again upon seeing the blinding globe and the mystical swirling mist. Crichton would have found their reactions amusing if he had not been so enraptured in the glowing fog himself. He had no idea how it was happening, but it must have been some sort of magic that unleashed the mist and light into the hall. His chest pounded.

"Hear us... Speak with us... Hear us... Speak with us..." The Acolytes chanting grew ever louder.

Isaac raised his voice again, struggling to be heard, "We are weak men, and beg for your presence, God-King!"

Eric and James repeated, "We are weak men, and beg for your presence, God-King."

"Come to us and tell us your will, Gahkin!"

"Come to us and tell us your will, Gahkin!"

"Hear us... Speak with us... Hear us... Speak with us..."

The shouting could not be spoken over any longer. Tears leaked out of Isaac's tightly closed eyelids. Crichton could not believe the old man was acting any longer. His passion leaked like his tears, true and plentiful, streaming down his face and onto the ground below.

The blue fog grew thicker and brighter until Crichton shut his eyes for fear of going blind.

"I am here."

A somehow familiar and frightful baritone voice rung out over the raucous chanting, quieting the Acolytes. It did not bounce off the walls like the other voices. The sound could be coming from any direction, or perhaps every direction.

"James Killovew. There is an unwanted being in your land. Do you know of him?"

Crichton squeezed closed his eyes as tight as he could. His whole body was trembling. The light was almost blinding, even with his eyes closed and his head aimed away from the globe. He felt ill.

"I... do, Gahkin. He is..." Lord Killovew inhaled sharply, and his voice steadied. "He is but a boy, a Sondite boy—"

"How dare you open your eyes and try to look upon me?" the voice roared. Crichton covered his ears, and still, the volume did not dim. *"I would not show myself to such as you! My voice is more gift than you deserve. I do not speak of the boy. The boy is nothing, and the boy is mine. Do not defend him, and do not give him another thought. There is another illegal presence, Killovew. And it is not a Sondite child. Where?"*

Crichton could barely hear James's stammering over the ringing in his ears. "I... I do not know, Gahkin. I did not... I did not know of this boy, and I do not know of others. Outlaws may linger in the far southern forests—"

"You lie! You lie, James Killovew; you lie to the one who gave you all you've ever known. Everything that is yours was once and is still mine. I built the Killovews' this great castle in my kingdom, gave you land rich with men and the means to keep them. I carved the very rivers of this world and, with my own clenched fists, broke them into creeks to wet the lips of all those who thirst. I plowed all your soil with my bare fingers and planted the seeds of your strongest oaks. I rose the forest, green and thick, stocked it with birds and deer and fox so that you might clothe and feed yourselves. I taught the palms to drop their fruit when it was ripe and the bees to raise their young on sweet, nourishing nectar. I visited your world as a man, united the warring realms and created a kingdom so you might defend each other, established trade so you might enrich yourselves, wrote the very truth of the universe into your primitive language so you might find the eternity after death you call the star life. And yet, after I give you this realm of milk and honey, after I map for you the path to civilization and etch the road to immortality, you shelter my enemies from me in my own forest."

"No, Gahkin, no. I am not sheltering anyone."

"Know this, Killovew. Your castle will crumble, your secret allies will fail, and your lands will burn if you lie to me now. Where is Evrost?"

"I… I don't know who Evrost is. I don't know." James's mutterings dissolved, and he fell silent.

Crichton felt as if a chain was tightened across his chest. His breath came in quick, shallow pants. The bright light was dimming, and the ringing sound was fading. The smell of burning hair was in his nostrils, the taste of copper in his mouth. *I didn't do anything wrong. I'm sorry, I'm sorry, don't kill me, I'm sorry.*

It took all of Crichton's strength to murmur, "Help me." He could not hear his own voice. It felt as if his lungs were broken.

"Domray, Second Finger of the Third Hand, take the Sondite boy outside. He is important to me. Bring him to Shinar." Crichton felt hands under his arms, and then he was being dragged away from the hallowed light. He could still hear the Voice as he left the hall.

"James Killovew, you are a brave man, and you have shown me the truth of your realm to come. So be it. You have withstood my tests. I admire your honesty."

Crichton could not breathe. His lungs were locked closed. The bright light transformed from blueish to yellowish, and Crichton dropped onto the ground, ringing still in his ears.

He needed to breathe, had to breathe. He lifted his head up, heavy as it was. Wild fear consumed his mind. Fear of the Voice, fear of the Light, fear of losing his brother, fear of death.

His neck could no longer support the weight of his head. His face smacked the stone floor. He still could not inhale.

His lungs were locked closed.

Run, Martin. Run away from here.

A black warmth enveloped Crichton from the inside out.

Seven

The lock turned over.

A man with a golden crown atop his head opened the door but paused in the doorway. The scuffed floor was covered with junk and pools of wine. The broken wine bag had soaked most of the other wine skins, the letters, and some of the candlesticks while the candles themselves had rolled all over the stone-gray floor from wall to wall. Martin sat next to the overturned cabinet, marred with scratches and ground-down corners.

In retrospect, he probably should not have decimated the room they put him in.

"Gahkin's wands…" the man whispered, scanning the room.

He had Jinala's eyes, but not her hair. His was dark red and fell just over his ears, parted right in the middle. The man shook his head and shuffled across the room, stepping over the mess toward a small bench. He sat down.

"Come over here, Martin."

Martin squinted at him. He stood up and walked over, one suspicious step at a time. Once he drew even with the man, he darted past him and ran for the open door.

Two men stepped right into his path. One Martin recognized, the old knight Trittion, but the other was a stranger with a pale blue and mint green cape. Martin tried to juke past them, but the stranger grabbed his arm. Martin threw an elbow at his groin, but he blocked it.

"Violent little thing!" The stranger said in the direction of the man, who was probably Jinala's father.

"Where is my brother?" Martin blurted out. The room grew silent. The two men at the doorstep exchanged looks.

"Martin, your brother is on his way to Shinar, and he won't be coming back," said the man with the golden crown after a long pause. "I'm sorry," he added.

He took off his crown and rotated it around his pointer finger, examining each jewel and etching thoroughly, avoiding looking up at Martin. The stranger holding Martin's arm walked him back into the room and gently pushed him down on the bench.

Martin did not resist. He looked at the floor while he spoke. "Crichton would not leave me. You're a liar."

The man with the crown dragged a big hand down his face and then said, "It is not Crichton's fault. He's not *leaving* you; he's being *taken* from you… You are the second person to call me a liar in the last candle, Martin, but the first to be wrong. I... I did everything I could think of, but I guess I trusted the wrong man. And I know much less than I thought I did." The Sondite boy said nothing. He did not look up. The man turned away from him and joined him in the inspection of the ground. Lord Killovew spoke to the stranger in the cape without looking up. "What if we were wrong about all of this, Eric? What have I done to my son?"

The man with the blue and green cape said, "I should have gone in your boy's place."

"You and I both know that would not have worked. You're too old, friend. I do not blame you for this."

"I'm guessing I wasn't the only one tossing and turning in my sleep the past few seasons. We both knew it was time, James. We had to do it. If Jason had never left, we would be even worse off. At least he still has a chance."

"Does he?"

Martin was still turning the idea of Crichton being taken from the forest over in his mind. Telling the truth or not, these adults did *not* know Crichton like Martin knew him. Crichton will come back. Martin did not doubt it for a moment.

"Crichton will come back!" he shouted, angry tears welling up in his eyes.

Trittion scratched at his shoulder, tugged at an armor neck plate. After a long moment, after opening and shutting his mouth a few times, he finally spoke.

"I hope he tries," was all he said.

Martin hated crying, and he tried to never let any scrape or fall bring a tear to his cheeks because Crichton never did. But Martin's will to hold them back failed. His red eyes surrendered.

He sobbed, and in-between sobs, he asked, "Could you just please tell me why this is happening? I just want to go home to Crichton." Martin looked over at Jinala's father. "Is he really gone?"

No one answered him. His hope that they were lying or tricking him was evaporating fast. He wiped away his tears and looked up at the old knight. Trittion was blinking as fast as a hummingbird beats its wings, his eyes misty.

Between the two men, Martin saw a single golden curl blow in and out of sight at the edge of the doorway. Then half of Jinala's face peeked around the corner.

She ran into the room. Her little nose was red and wet streaks ran down her cheeks. Her arm had been bandaged, and she had changed out of her torn, silky dress into a cotton green and brown sundress. She ran between Trittion and the man named Eric and stopped short in front of Martin. She looked at her father, who had cocked his head to watch her come in but otherwise hadn't moved. He looked back down at the floor again. Jinala reached her arms out for Martin and hugged him.

"Get off, Gina."

"I'm so sorry, Martin."

"You think Crichton is gone too, huh?"

"They took him away. I saw them take him away. He fell on the ground because of that... that... voice coming from the great hall. And they just picked him up and walked him right out. He—they—I mean, they just—he was... it was like he was asleep, Mart, he had no choice or chance or anything. They took him away, Martin. I'm sorry, but they took him away."

Martin looked at every long face; their eyebrows were tilted back, and their lips pressed tight.

"Do you think we should, perhaps, shut the door before this conversation drifts into the ears of someone a little more reverent than us, my lord?" Sir Trittion asked.

"I'm not sure anyone is going to be more of a believer than me right now, Trit." Lord Killovew said to the ground.

"Are you serious, James?" The man with the cape looked over his shoulder after his outburst, then continued, quieter, "After everything we've been through, you're just going to buy into that performance? I mean, it was an impressive show, and maybe we must admit now the Acolytes have power or magic—like Evrost. We thought they might. We just don't understand it yet, something we will have to figure out. It didn't prove—"

"Didn't prove? Some other-worldly voice called me out by name, just like they said he would, knew things no one aside from the three of us in this very room knows, and lit up my hall like—like that beam lit up the dark sky fifteen seasons ago when I was just a boy. He brought fog indoors, spoke from nowhere, and threatened... threatened horrible things to people I care about. He knew about Evrost, Eric! How doesn't that prove anything? It proves we have been woefully wrong and planning a conspiracy even more impossible than we originally thought, and the people closest to us are in a lot of danger, no matter what we've tried to do to protect them. It proves..." James cast a glance at Jinala before continuing, "It proves Sir Breigo is in way over his head! I may have sent him to his death. And it has just shown we can't protect Kamau's sons, even though I secretly swore I would."

"I'll go ahead and shut the door, then," Trittion said quietly, a few moments after Lord Killovew finished speaking.

"No one's up here, Trit; that's why you moved all the way up to this tower in the first place. So that you could drink yourself to death all alone..."

Trittion stared back at James, unblinking.

"I'm sorry," James added, "I shouldn't have said that."

"If these Acolytes can do what you say they can, we better watch our words around even the birds and the mice."

Martin looked over at Jinala, but she was just as confused as he was, even though they both were listening to every detail. The knight sat down on his bed after shutting the door and began untying the laces holding his armor plates in place.

The man with the golden crown in his hands said, "Martin, I'm Jinala's father, if you haven't already figured that out. My name is James Killovew. This is my most trusted friend, Eric Eden, Lord of the Edengrove and the Thousand River Realm. And that old man over there is Sir Trittion Oak, once an elder knight of the Thirsting Forest—"

"Still an elder knight, my lord. Don't you take your anger out on this old man. You know who is to blame for what happened this cycle."

"Yeah. You're right. It's me," James said, running his hands through his hair.

"You know who he meant, James," Eric said. "Don't blame yourself for this. You kept your mouth shut even while that voice was accosting you about Crichton and Evrost. You lied, and it seems you got away with it, so even if that really was—somehow, magically—Gahkin, we know he cannot read minds, which means—"

"Which means he or they discovered Evrost some other way..." James Killovew finished.

"Perhaps from someone else..." Eric said, looking over at Trittion, who had picked up a wineskin. "You know, if I betrayed my lord and my friends, I'd probably become quite the drunk too."

Trittion just sighed. "Eric Eden, you are the same thoughtless boy you were when we met you on the way to Shinar eight seasons ago. I won't hold your words against you because I'm an old man and have few friends and only a few suns left, I think. I drink, Eric, because of you and James' secret plot, not because I revealed it to the Acolytes."

James agreed. "Leave Trit alone, Eric. He's no traitor."

Eric went on, "You're right, of course, but that doesn't mean I'm wrong. What if it was one of the other conspirators? What if it was Tegan?"

James shook his head, "He risked his life and career the night he unlocked the tunnels for us. Besides, he has no knowledge of Evrost. As far as he knew, what we were planning then was just a dream, and yet it came to fruition, after all these seasons. No. It's impossible. We can't think that while there is still one man left unaccounted for. The one man we know who failed *his* job."

James sighed and looked to his daughter before looking back to Eric Eden.

"Look, why don't we all go downstairs to my office and talk this out. The children have heard too much already. They are too young for this to be on their shoulders too."

"No!" Jinala and Martin said at once.

Jinala looked over at her father, "Father, what is going on? You can tell us. Who is Evrost?"

Eric walked over and sat down next to Trittion, slapping a hand on his back. "Sorry, old man." He looked over at James. "Go on, you should at least tell poor Martin why he is losing his brother. Both those boys should have known about their father."

"My father?" Martin piped up, looking between Lord Eden and Lord Killovew.

"They would have when they were older, Eric. Bury me! Don't you think you should go find your wife? Surely you have some explaining to do to Barbara."

"She stopped worrying about my mysteries a while ago, James."

James Killovew stared at Eric for a moment and then moved in front of Jinala and Martin. He took a knee. "Let's see if I can string all this together for you. There are things that we—Trit, Eric, and I—know are going on we will not be telling you." He shot a warning look toward Eric. "But I'll try to fill you in on what's gone on over the last fifteen seasons or so. Jinala knows most of this already, although I might put it a little more bluntly than old Mrs. Bard did."

He took a deep breath and looked at Martin. "You and your brother are considered outlaws in the Kingdom of Gahkin, which you already know. Your forefathers abandoned their home in Sond, losing their faith in Gahkin when the Eternal desert consumed their crops and then their city at the foot of the Gilv Mountains. The Acolytes claim they lost faith, *and then* the eternal desert destroyed their home in some sort of divine punishment. Either way, over the next few seasons, the Sondites wandered north over the mountains, forced to look for a new home. They came here, to the Thirsting Forest Realm, first. You know this?"

"Yes, Crichton told me our people left Sond, and we are not allowed to be in any of the realms of the kingdom, except Shinar."

"Well... yes... sort of. The Sondites were deemed infidels and outlawed—"

"Infidels?"

"Non-believers. They were outlawed from every civilized realm in the kingdom, but according to the Acolytes, Gahkin would forgive them and offer them a chance at salvation if they went to Shinar. The Sondite men were forced to join His army. When the decree was issued, most of the Sondites went to fulfill their obligations and earn a peaceful star life, but some of the people, those with families or lovers, were opposed to the enlistment and decided not to go, to hideout elsewhere. Still with me?"

Martin nodded.

"My father was on his way to Shinar, and I was just a boy. The advisers in charge of my father's realm enforced the decree. A few of our villages tried to shelter and hide them, but most gave up when they learned what happened at the Great Gorge. That's where a large resistance of Sondites were being hidden. At Chasm—well, back then, it was called Canyon Castle. The whole city, castle and all, was razed to the ground."

"Razed?" Martin asked.

"It was completely wiped off the map. It was prophesied—predicted by the Acolytes—that Gahkin's beam of light would destroy any rebels or heretics—which means the same as infidels or non-believers. Well, that's exactly what happened. Gahkin's sword of golden light shot from the sky for a whole candle length. Melting metal, burning brick, cleaving stone walls straight in two, gouging—"

Eric Eden interjected, "Just to point out, for the sake of intellectual integrity, in those cycles there were hundreds of Sondite hideouts and only in retrospect did people say Gahkin had made pro—"

"Enough, Eric, that's over their head. After the beam disappeared, the city and castle were just rubble and ash and mud. While the survivors tried to salvage what they could, the canyon and small caverns shook, and the earth split open wider and wider, swallowing down the people, and the soil and the castle ruins in a massive cave-in. All that's left now is a wide crater in the middle of the gorge, wider around than even Shinar, deeper than a thousand of the deepest wells. A couple forts and rope bridges have been strung up to connect the pillars and encircle the chasm, so the algae mining can continue. That is all that remains of what was once a great, wealthy city in Gahkin's kingdom and the capital of the Ardel Realm. The remaining royal Grayson family was executed by the Acolytes, and now the Acolytes have assumed the rule of the realm."

Lord Killovew took a breath and continued, "The only people living at the gorge itself now are the miners, a few other stubborn families of the survivors, and the guardsmen that dedicate their lives to keeping the dwellers from rising up out of the darkness of the mines."

"Dwellers are the cave monsters that live underground, right?" Martin asked.

"Well, they're only animals, really, not monsters. But yes, strange, dangerous animals. You don't have to worry too much about them though, they live underground, and only come out around cave-ins. They are territorial, and it just so happens the big one that lived under the forest nearby here, well—it's dead as of just last season. But that's not important. The important part is the people learned quickly not to disobey the Acolytes' law. I was just a boy, but my father, the Lord of the Thirsting Forest at the time, had not yet returned from Shinar, the City of Gahkin. Plus, one of my best friends was a Sondite. So naturally, I distrusted—no, I suppose the word is, I doubted the God-King. You see, as Eric was saying, we believe the golden beam is just a weather occurrence. Not some divine punishment. The fact it destroyed Canyon Castle and Canyon Castle was holding Sondites was probably just a coincidence. Gahkin may or may not have built this world, he may or may not be immortal, he may or may not be omnipotent—"

"Omnipotent?"

"Now who's going over their heads?" Eric asked, eyebrows raised and a smirk on his lips.

"It means all-powerful, all-seeing, all-knowing. But… look, forget all about that last bit. The important part is this, despite what I doubted about Gahkin, I *did* know that what was happening to the people from Sond was wrong. I knew that the Acolytes, who claim to commune with the God-King, were ruling unjustly and, in my eyes, using the weather anomalies to fill in the generic prophesies that they laid out long ago, after observing similar weather anomalies."

Martin and Jinala blinked. "Huh?" Jinala said.

Eric Eden waved a hand over his head, his eyebrows cocked up.

"Right," James said. "Anyway, Martin, up until this very cycle, I doubted the Acolytes had any real relationship with something supernatural, let alone a true line of communication with the divinity that we call Gahkin."

Eric spoke, half agitated, half exasperated, "James! Evrost is magical, but it doesn't mean he is Gahkin, or he is another version of Gahkin or anything like that. Just because that old bastard Isaac showed us some magic trick and revealed a little more knowledge than we'd like them to know, that *voice* could not read your mind. Either that voice is Gahkin and Gahkin is not omniscient or that voice wasn't Gahkin at all. I'm assuming the latter."

James stood up. "You're assuming because you don't have a son's life at stake!"

Eric grimaced. Then, calmly, he said, "You're right. I don't have a son. His life is not at stake."

James looked ashamed, "I'm—I'm sorry, Eric, I didn't mean it like that… Jason has so much riding on his shoulders, and he's just half a season a man."

"He has a lot of great help, James, and he wants to be a part of this," The old knight said. "We sent the best knight in the realm, and Jason is smart and careful, and ever since you brought him into the fold, he has been passionate and willing. He knew the dangers. He cares about the people of this world, just as his grandfather did. Just as you do... That's just my opinion, anyway." Trittion took his eyes away from James.

James nodded in slow, hopeful agreement. He turned back to Martin. "Look, I'm sorry, Martin. You wanted to know about your father. My best friend when I was a younger man—my Sondite best friend—his name was Kamau, and he was your father. He was a real hero. You should be very proud of him."

"What happened to him?" Martin asked.

"He moved into the forest when things started to go bad for the Sondites. I visited him often. As the season of the sun set into twilight, I grew more and more uneasy about my missing father and more and more passionate about the unjust rule of the Acolytes. After we became young men, Kamau and I could put it off no longer. We traveled to Shinar by the back roads, through the forests and woods, and investigated what happened to my father. That's where Kamau met your mother. Unfortunately, Mart, it was a more dangerous journey than any of us expected and took much longer than we planned, and neither my father nor your father made it back alive."

"He's dead?" Martin's eyes filled with tears. "Crichton told me that Mother used to say Father would come back."

Trittion and Eric looked toward each other. Eric smiled a sad smile.

"Your mother always wanted to hang onto that hope, Mart, but we know he's dead, son. I'm very sorry. Kamau saved seven lives when he died, though."

"Who?" Martin demanded. Whoever it was, they certainly were not worth it.

"Well." James raised his fingers as he counted off. "Your brother, your mother, Jinala, Trittion, Eric, me, and a strange man named Evrost." Then, with a sad smile, he added, "And you, in a sense, though we didn't know it yet. So, eight, actually."

The room dissolved into silence. James watched Martin and Jinala try to grasp it all. Trittion drank from his wineskin while Eric picked crumbs and flecks of dirt from his robe. Martin assumed the adults were lost in their memories of Kamau, while he was stuck thinking of his father in some imaginative fantasy.

Trittion squeezed the last drops out of the wineskin. Eric looked over at him and broke the quiet reverie.

"What is that? Your third this cycle?" he asked. "You better ween yourself off the stuff, Trittion. Even my private vineyards in the Edengrove are being replaced for more food crops. The wine's going extinct. It'll be algae ale, Spice, or sobriety for you soon."

"So, the apocalypse is coming, after all." Sir Trittion murmured.

James said, "We have a lot of work ahead of us. Eric and I have letters to write and scrolls to adjust. Roles to play and advisers to speak with. As do you.

But once our *guests* from Shinar are many miles away, we will go out into the forest. Evrost better have a good reason for letting Crichton get captured."

"That man has no reason at all," Eden said under his breath.

"Who *is* Evrost?" Jinala asked, reaching out and tugging on her father's sleeve. "You still haven't told us about him yet."

"I think you two have taken to calling him the Mud Wizard." Jinala's mouth fell open. "And we are going to go pay him a visit."

Eight

After leaving the Mid-Kingdom Cross, Jason and his companions traveled northwest along Old King's Road, winding their way toward Shinar. Nearly half the season of the sun had passed since they left Castle Killovew, and they had avoided any real problems or delays.

The group spoke with trade caravans and local townsmen along the way, sharing general courtesies and frivolous news from their home realms. As they reached the northern stretch of the road, they began to ask if it was possible to cross to Shinar without following the road, to cross as the bird flies. The consensus of the locals and the traveling merchants was that they would probably find no food in the flood plains along the way and certainly no people.

They would be on their own for many cycles. A shortened distance to Shinar was worth the risk of leaving the road in Jason's mind, but he would consider the other's opinions before making his decision. It was what his father would do.

The sun was still high in the southeast, though no longer quite at its zenith, and it was hot, even this far northwest, but they built a fire to pass the resting candles. A campsite without a fire, no matter the season, just didn't seem appropriate.

A dusty wagon rolled toward them from the horizon. As it got closer, Jason could make out a single rider driving the wagon.

The skeletal rider was near death. Jason had seen starving men before when food raiders made it past the realm perimeter guards and tried to break into the castle gardens, or more recently, where a few folks were begging for m-bars outside of a tavern. But this man was different. His eyes were sunken and hollow looking, and the skin across his body looked pulled too thin across nothing but bones. His body was eating itself alive. Somehow, he still managed to climb up and down out of his wagon, and he asked to share Jason and his men's fire.

Sir Breigo reached into his saddlebag and pulled out a handful of m-bars, and tossed them at the feet of the rider. He snapped them up out of the dirt but did not open any of them. He stashed them all into his cloak.

"Oh my, thank you," he croaked. "I don't have anything to give you in return, I'm afraid. I gave all my gold and silver for a case of m-bars just two cycles ago. All I've got left is this old girl," he gestured to the skinny mule pulling his wagon. "And I need her to get me home."

Sir Breigo said, rather bluntly, "Have you eaten any of those bars? I wouldn't have given you some of mine if I knew you were hauling a whole case already."

The skeleton man smiled a haunting smile and said, "You can have yours back if you want, sir knight, but I'd be ever grateful if you didn't. They aren't for me." He squeezed his eyes shut and spoke without opening them. "I'm taking them back to my family. The crops all failed this season, raiders stole our cows, so we didn't have no manure, and the rains never really came during twilight." He opened his eyes and looked around at Prince Jason and the rest of his men. "I think it's too late for me, at this point, anyway. I haven't had a single thing to eat in a long… long time. I'm just making it back to my family first before I'm taken to my star life. Oh, don't pity me, I've lived a good life. I'll be setting the lady and the boy off all right with these bars."

Jason sat in thought, wondering how it could be coming to this in the civilized portions of the kingdom. The Thirsting Forest Realm and the Thousand River Realm, along with portions of Kydoth, still managed to sustain fertile farms, able to grow crops and raise some livestock. The forest itself still supported a healthy population of game, though it dwindled each season. And Shinar, of course, maintained the eastern and western banks of the Verdelen, growing the special crops that went into the m-bars.

Yet here, in the open territory west of the chasm, folks were not just food insecure; they were straight up starving. And no one was doing anything about it.

"You all look well-fed," the poor man said. "Do you need a squire, by chance? My boy is almost of age. He can do anything, and he's quick, too. And smart."

Jason shook his head. "No," he said. "I'm sorry."

"Oh, it's all right. What are you all doing here, anyway? Shouldn't you be at home, to prepare for the end of the world?"

Jason spoke quickly to change the topic away from the apocalyptic rumors. "Actually, we are headed to Shinar to enlist. And we're more concerned with encounters with Vistonex out in the floodplains as we get closer to Shinar than the potential apocalypse. Have you heard about them crossing out there?"

"Ain't no potential about it, friend," he said. "As sure as the sun rises and sets in the southeast."

"Vistonex crossings?" Jason asked.

"No, the apocalypse. There isn't any potential about it; it is guaranteed by the Habibrok, same as the sun rises and sets, like I said."

Sir Breigo asked, "Right, but what about the Vistonex?"

The man thought for a moment and then spoke, "Vistonex are crossing the river more up north than ever before. Plus, bugs ate up all the grain in Quirvop, I heard." He stared at the grass beside the fire for a long time and then added. "And I heard rumors from some hemp merchants that the Frost Fangs are dripping. The northernmost ice… melting. They get more sun than ever before, even if it is so faint up there."

He looked around, expecting a response, but got nothing but pitiful stares from his campfire brethren. "You know… they've never melted before." He stared into the fire again. "Ignore it all you want; it's easy to ignore it when you got bags of gold and a sword and saddlebags full of food… but the end is coming. The Great Flash is coming."

Sir Breigo steered the conversation back toward Jason's earlier question. The knight had already made up his mind, it seemed. "Jason, tripling our chances for a run-in with Vistonex is not worth saving an extra fourteen cycles in travel. No matter how unlikely it is near Shinar, it's a lot safer to stay on the God-King's Road."

Jason estimated they were shaving closer to twenty cycles off their journey and that they had only marginally increased their chance for a run-in with Vistonex. This was not the first time Breigo had spoken openly against leaving the road.

"You don't need to be worried about the Vistonex," the dusty skeleton whispered. "Shinar is protected by the God-King's spirit. No way they can cross those borders. Like I said, up north round the Frost Fangs they'll cross the river. But not in the Acolytes' realm. Too much firelight in the dark season, and too many soldiers in any season, and then Gahkin himself still watches."

"They cross down south, too," Taroke said, aiming a thumb back down the road.

"And I don't think they've got much reasoning power," Ratoke added.

"But you're not the first to tell us that Shinar and the realm of the Acolytes is spared from the raids."

"See there, Breigo," Ratoke finished, speaking over the knight's grumbling retort, "Nothing to be afraid of."

Sir Breigo held up his hand and said, "I'm not *afraid*. I'm risk-averse. What of the dwellers, sir? Have you heard any mention of new cave-ins?"

Jason suppressed a shiver that ran down his spine. The Greenfoot brothers shared a look.

Must not have suppressed it well enough, eh, Jason?

"Oh, now they are a different story? Only Gahkin knows where they've been burrowing since Canyon Castle collapsed… I suppose your chances of an ambush are about as good out in the plains as on the road. Haven't heard of any fresh cave-ins, but there is a lot of empty plains between here and the realm borders of Shinar. And then a long way further to go before you reach the actual city, Shinar proper. And you can't be expecting any help in the wild. Folks here can barely take care of themselves." The man added in a sad whisper, "No, you all would be doomed if a dweller grabbed you." His eyelids flickered a little. "But we are all doomed anyway, so I don't suppose it matters too much how the end comes."

Jason ran the dweller ambush through his head enough while he slept; he didn't like being reminded of it during the waking times too. When he closed his eyes, he did not sleep. He thought of the dark season and the ambush.

****

Four dweller claws had slashed through the carriage ceiling.

Jason crashed to his knees, flailing his sword over his head. The blade lodged in the carriage roof. As he struggled to pry it free, another rake of the claws tore much of the roof clear off, unlodging his sword. He saw a huge, clawed tentacle, larger than he thought any dweller tentacle could grow, thrashing above the wagon in the falling rain.

Jinala, peeking through her hands over her eyes, whimpered.

Jason heaved and swung his sword at the tentacle as it whipped above the wagon. He missed.

Another tentacle struck the wagon, rocking it halfway into the air. The right axle snapped, and the carriage crashed to the ground, tossing Jason and his sister into the mud. The prince landed on his right ankle, felt it twist, and tumbled onto his back. His sword came tumbling out of the wagon behind him, seeming to hover for a moment above his head before it plunged into the wet muck an inch from his face.

Jinala scrambled into the forest, which Jason figured was the safest place she could go. Away from the cave-in.

Good.

Jason looked back to the road. The storm soaked everything, and it was too dark to see the cave where the lead wagon fell, nor where the back wagon may yet sit. The dweller tentacle was out of sight. One man lay unmoving, and another lay at the fringe of the torchlight, holding his stomach and rolling back and forth on his back.

Ankle be damned, Jason needed to act. He hesitated only to think how strange it was that he wasn't scared. Another *consciousness*, deeper down, seemed to engulf him. It urged him to act. And it released a blast of energy and excitement. Almost enjoyment. Jason didn't overthink it.

He pushed himself up onto his knees. And then, groaning, stood up on his tender ankle.

The Prince of the Thirsting Forest, not quite yet a man, wrapped his fingers around the sword hilt. He drew his blade from the wet soil. The rain lashed across his face, and a few locks of his drenched hair blew over his eyes. Slicking them back, he squinted into the dark, looking for a sign of the creature from the deep. He cautiously jogged to the toppled wagon and lifted out a burning torch with his free hand. He rushed to the nearest guard, but he was unconscious… or maybe dead. Jason moved on to the man holding his stomach, illuminating the darkness beyond the fallen rider.

"I'm all right, I'm all right." The guard groaned, sounding far from all right. "The spikes missed me." He coughed, and a little blood seeped out of his mouth. "Pretty lucky, huh?"

Another man lay on the ground ahead, but the rest were missing. Where could everyone be?

The cave-in.

Jason looked up into the darkness further down the road. The shape of another man, running toward Jason, materialized out of the black rain. Sir Breigo ran into Jason's torchlight and slid to a stop in front of the prince. His left arm was bloody, but he ignored it and acted fine, focusing on his prince.

He said, "Prince Jason. Gilgan and Sir Trittion, I think, got snagged and pulled in. Your father, Argo, and Peptone went after them. Sent me back to take command up here and keep you and Jinala safe."

The injured guard had risen onto one knee. "I can look for the princess with Jason, Sir Breigo."

Sir Breigo grabbed his wrist and helped him off the ground. He stood straight for a moment, then groaned and bent over, arms around his torso.

"You can go lay down somewhere dry and stay there. That's an order." The newly appointed elder knight gently pushed him down the road and then looked at Jason. "Where's your sister?"

"Jinala's hiding in the trees. Let's go after my father." Jason brushed past Breigo, but the knight grabbed his arm.

"No, you stay with me."

Jason shook Breigo's hand off. Rain slashed down onto the two men, thin rivers of water running down the blood grooves of their blades. Sir Breigo may have fought in the Vistonex war, and arguably was the highest-ranking knight in the realm while Sir Damian was away guarding the Great Chasm, and Sir Trittion was missing in the cave-in, but Jason was the prince, and he would not be taking orders from a knight. Any knight.

"My father is currently hunting a dweller in a cave-in, underground. In other words—he is incapable of leading. That means I am technically the realm lord now, Sir Breigo. You can stay here or go find my sister." Thunder rumbled but further off than before. Jason finished, "I'm going to help Father rescue the rest of our men. That's *my* order."

Jason pushed past Breigo again and walked toward the cave-in. Sir Breigo caught up to Jason and grabbed his shoulder.

"Bravely spoken, Prince Killovew." Breigo said, trying to hide a small smirk from cracking his visage, "but, when I came back from the Dezruk, I swore to your father to guard the Killovews with my life for the rest of my cycles as an elder knight. So, we can go rescue your father, but I'll be taking the lead."

Sir Breigo leaped into the cave-in without awaiting a response. He slid down the steep incline and hit the muddy cave ground on his feet.

Jason leaped after him, but while he negotiated the slippery descent, he tumbled onto his hands and knees and splattered face down when he hit the bottom. Breigo helped him up and then slapped him on the shoulder.

"I fell the first time, too, Prince Killovew. Honest."

Jason nodded, and together, they ran down into the darkness of the cave. There was only one tunnel to follow... so far.

Breigo dragged his sword tip through the dirt behind them, leaving a trail to follow to get back out. Jason stayed right alongside, holding his torch high. As they jogged, glimmers of pink and blue shined along the walls, rich algae veins flashing in the firelight. No wonder the dweller had dug so far south. The tunnel was dank, and an unpleasant smell lingered ahead, but it was ripe with algae.

They ran on, Jason's ankle somehow cooperating. More veins of pink and blue streaked through the dirt walls before disappearing. It was a rich cave. A light appeared in the distance. They skidded to a stop when they reached it. They saw a burning torch on the ground, with half an arm still clinging onto the handle.

"Bury me…" Jason whispered. *That could be my father's arm.*

Breigo walked ahead. "Jason, come look at this."

Jason caught up with Breigo. The tunnel opened into a wide cavern. Hundreds of veins, glittering pink and blue and even yellow, twisted and spiraled through the walls. That much algae oil could provide Castle Killovew with enough pure Ten Candle fuel to burn until Jason's grandchildren were ruling *and* enough Spice to last until his grandchildren were old enough to be getting drunk. Under different circumstances, Jason might have noted its beauty and wealth. Instead, he dropped down off the small ledge and walked into the middle, looking for a path to follow. Three more tunnels connected with the cavern. Jason heard Breigo land softly behind him. Jason moved to the nearest tunnel, which aimed… Jason did not know. He had lost sense of north and south. His torch sputtered in his hands.

"This way!" Sir Breigo whispered, pointing at a faint set of footprints leading into one of the side tunnels.

They ran on, less and less algae appearing as they descended further. Jason turned a corner and heard a loud crash of falling rocks, shattering the quiet. The echoes reverberated off the walls, and then silence returned, broken only by the sound of their rushing footsteps and heavy breathing.

The tunnel sloped steeply downward out of nowhere. Jason half slid, and half fell to the bottom. Again, Breigo negotiated the slope with a bit more grace. Together they moved around the next few bends, more cautious than before. They came upon a man-sized shadow in the middle of the tunnel. They moved closer. It was the shadow of a fat-bellied, wheezing old man. Jason sprinted to him.

"Sir Trittion? Where are the others?"

The old knight pointed further down the tunnel. "Your father cut me free. The thing is wounded. But still bloody fast. I've never heard of one that big. I didn't think they could—ugh…" Trittion held his upper arm, groaning. Jason lowered the torch closer. Trittion still had both his arms, but a small claw had snapped off in his shoulder.

Sir Breigo said, "We found an… arm. Back about 250 yards."

"It's Gilgan's. The poor scribe bastard. He's gone," Trittion said. "I'll take Jason out of here, Breigo; you go after the others."

Jason didn't even bother to argue. He dashed further down the tunnel. The smell of mold and ripe fruit grew stronger as he went deeper.

The cries of fighting men and screams of pain bounced off the cave walls. They were close.

Jason and Breigo rounded another corner. The tunnel widened into another large cavern, lit by swirls of glowing pink and blue algae in the ceiling.

The pale gray body of the dweller had collapsed into the dirt, its many legs bleeding or broken off entirely. The huge dweller body, shaped like a fat snake and longer than five cargo wagons end to end, was armored with thousands of thick scales. The eight tentacles that it hunted with, jutting out of its back, whipped around the room, claw-tipped ends whistling through the putrid air. One tentacle was a bloody stump and another writhed with a limp human body still impaled on the end. Jason recoiled in disgust, but only for a moment. He pushed forward, sword at the ready.

The eyestalks at the forefront of the creature's body were focused on the men at the other side of the cavern. They hid from the barrage of tentacles behind a jutting rock face. The Lord of the Thirsting Forest slashed at the tentacles when they crashed close to the boulder, seemingly no worse for wear.

Sir Breigo sprinted forward at the dweller's body without hesitation, his presence unnoticed by the creature. Jason chased after him.

Two of the eyestalks twisted around and spotted them. The thing was half-blind as it was, and probably fully blind from all the torchlight, but it could still sense Jason's and Breigo's moving bodies. Jason threw his torch at the eyes but, sensitive as they were, they stayed focused on Sir Breigo. A long tentacle whistled downward. Breigo lunged forward, and Jason jumped back, the tentacle smashing into the ground between them. Jason sliced deep into the beast's appendage, and dweller blood-foam burst onto his chest and arms.

Breigo continued his sprint and then leaped into the air, plunging his sword into the dweller's body- into a crease between its scales. His blade caught and dug in-between the armored plates. One hand slipped, but he held on, grabbing onto the edge of another scale with his loose hand. The agile knight climbed upward. The dweller body wriggled and squirmed, but Breigo hung on.

Jason sliced again at the tentacle as it pulled itself out of the ground, gushing even more blood-foam over his head. The clawed appendage slapped the sword from his hands, knocking him backward in the process. Jason wiped the blood from his eyes and fumbled to find his sword on the shadowy cavern floor.

The dweller writhed and fought but could not push itself forward on its remaining stubby legs, nor throw Breigo off. The pursuit had run it almost to death, but its tentacles were still dangerous for as long as the beast clung to life.

Lord Killovew tried to exit from behind his cover in-between the pounding wrath of the long tentacles, but even while distracted, the dweller did not lighten up its attack. Jason found and grasped his sword hilt and pulled it to him.

A small scale flaked off from under Breigo's foot, but the knight pulled himself up and rolled on top of the beast. Breigo waved down to Jason, shouting something.

Jason leaped up and sprinted toward the creature. He needed to get closer.

Lord Killovew shouted from across the cavern. "Roll!"

Jason threw himself to the ground as a tentacle soared past just overhead. The prince popped back up, and in three strides, he was there, leaning up against the ample sized body of the dweller. He looked up and saw Breigo leaning over the creature's back. With all his strength, he heaved his sword up to Sir Breigo on top of the beast.

Jason stumbled back away from the creature. He turned and looked up and saw an eyestalk twist around just as Sir Breigo chopped it clean off. He decapitated four more of the fragile antennae in his second swing and stabbed the final one as it retreated into its body. He left the sword impaled in the eye hole and leaped from the very front of the giant beast as its tentacles slammed down on itself.

Breigo hit the ground and crawled away frantically, not hesitating to watch the blinded dweller lash out, striking blows on itself and the cavern at random. A tentacle stump crashed down onto the sword hilt and drove it like a nail into its own head. The tentacles fell limp, and the creature exhaled one last rancid breath from its gill vents. It moved no more.

"Ow," Breigo said, smiling slightly, lying in the dirt.

Lord Killovew helped Jason stand, and they watched Sir Argo pull Gilgan's dead body from the end of a limp tentacle.

Jason's ankle throbbed with dizzying pain, seemingly catching up for lost time.

Lord Killovew hugged his son and then helped him leave the cavern, arm slung over his shoulder. They found Sir Trittion along the way, still bleeding a little but now relatively bandaged up. They followed the thin trail line Breigo left with his sword all the way back to the cave-in entrance by the wagons. James sent the two least injured men ahead to make sure Jinala had been found safe. James Killovew paused to review Jason with proud eyes.

After everyone else left the cave, James Killovew told his son that he would grant him his request to go to Shinar and then to war with the Vistonex. But first, they had a long talk about faith and the responsibilities of leadership. Later, in James's private candlelit office, Jason learned of his father's political secrets and his treasonous plot. He also learned the true fate of his late grandfather, Lord Jacob Killovew, who visited Shinar and the Ten Hand Temple and never returned.

****

Now Jason rode to Shinar, and the great burden of his knowledge urged him and his companions onward. After the men all slept, they packed up their gear and bade farewell to the starving man who had shared their camp. He crawled into his wagon and slowly waved farewell. The mule trudged forward, and the man went on toward his home.

Jason felt a pang of something in his stomach. He was not royalty in this realm, and his mission was more important than a starving family at a failing farm. But still.

"We can't save them all, one at a time, Prince Killovew." Sir Breigo tightened a strap on his horse and then hopped up into the saddle. "Come on, let's keep to our task."

Mako Black rubbed his hands through his beard. "No."

"No?"

Mako hadn't spoken a word at the campsite and had made no arguments since Jason and Breigo had brought him into the fold back at the tavern.

"I can ride down with him. Make sure he makes it to his family," Mako said. "I've got the lightest packs right now. And I have water dragon jerky. I can catch up to you all in the next town. I won't let it slow us down."

Sir Breigo frowned, but Prince Jason nodded at Mako. "All right, take Taroke with you. The rest of us will go into the next town and speak with the locals. We will have a decision on if we leave the road by the time you return."

The team parted ways; Mako and Taroke clopping along quickly after the disappearing wagon, Jason and Sir Breigo and Ratoke following the road further north.

The next town was barely a town at all, but thankfully the people did have some small amounts of food.

Over the next few cycles, Jason scoured their maps, weighed the advice of the locals, and tried to determine whether the extra time was worth the risk of the floodplains. If they continued further north into the larger town of Yittii, the road would fork, splitting east toward the locust infested plains at the foot of Quirvop mountain range and north into the upper plains of Shinar. Instead, if they abandoned the main road south of Yittii, heading more west than north, they would intercept Fessdri on the far side of the flood plains. They would navigate by putting the sun straight to their backs and heading toward the massive Star Tower. They would meet their contact from Shinar in Fessdri and then together they would all enter the capital city of Shinar, the Grand City of Gahkin.

The full team would be assembled and ready *well* before the Sundown Ceremony.

Mako and Taroke returned, and they had a full case of m-bars with them.

The water dragon wrangler looked at Jason. "The boy and the wife were gone. A little blood in the house. Overturned table. Door had been bashed in by an ax."

Jason turned to Taroke. Taroke added, "Cannibals, probably."

"Bury me." Sir Breigo murmured.

"What did you do with the father?"

Mako just shook his head. Taroke kicked at the dirt. After a long pause, Mako asked, "Did you figure out what we are going to do?"

"Yes," Jason said. "We're going to leave the road and cross through the wild floodplains."

They packed their gear, distributing the extra m-bars they couldn't carry to be shared evenly among the poor townsfolk. Jason made sure to leave behind as much food as was feasible.

As they rode, Sir Breigo asked, "The father, you didn't make it clear, what happened?"

Taroke responded, "We didn't make it clear on purpose, knight."

Jason frowned. He thought of the full case of m-bars they had brought back. "How are you going to be able to sleep next time we rest?"

"It's not like I've been sleeping all that well before now. We did him a kindness." Taroke scratched his neck. "I think we did, anyway."

Mako nodded and rubbed his beard, staring at the horizon. His eyes were distant. He asked, "What we're doing… what we're trying to do… it's going to help fix all this, right?"

"Yes," Jason said.

You don't know for sure, Jason.

"Yes," Jason said, more firmly, "we're going to fix it."

Nine

Jinala sat with her legs crossed and her hand laced around Martin's hand. He did not squeeze it back, but he did not pry it off, either. Trittion Oak sat in the front of the wagon, tugging gently at the reins now and again. Martin and Jinala sat behind him, under the roof. The outlaw and the princess were hidden from prying eyes behind closed velvet drapes. Jinala leaned her head to the window and pulled them back enough to peek outside.

Eric Eden and James Killovew rode ahead, leading the way toward the forest path. They had changed out of their royal garb into thick brown clothes and leather jackets, though Eric continued to wear his cape. They sat atop two of the prized Killovew palfreys. Trained deep in the Thirsting Forest, the horses could traverse the thick brush without too much jostling or bumping.

The leafy canopy reached out over the path, creating a tunnel of greenery. Soon the riders and the wagon were enveloped in the shadowy woods. The trees and vegetation grew denser around the road. As they picked up speed, the shaded trunks and dark green bushes began to blend. Jinala leaned back inside and let the drapes fall closed. She looked at Martin. The silence stretched on unbroken inside the wagon.

Martin wore a blank stare; he gave subtle, unconscious twitches. His chest lifted with slow sighing. Jinala knew his mind was far from his immediate surroundings.

Martin avoided looking at her, so she looked elsewhere. The interior of their carriage was light brown, lit by a small candle. The floor was marked with the dark stains of old blood where the edge of the green and yellow rug ended. The roof had been patched recently. A few of the old beams still showed splintered edges. Jinala was glad it was the season of the sun.

****

Four long claws had slashed through that same roof during the past dark season.

Jinala had shrieked when it happened. Jason fell to the ground, swiping his sword at the empty air above him with one hand and covering his head from the debris with the other. His sword's edge sliced just inches from Jinala's toes. Another swipe of the claws gouged the roof wide open. A long tentacle, armored with thick, white scales, whipped across the open hole in the top. Rain poured inside. Jason thrashed with his sword, but it was useless. Another tentacle slammed into the side and tipped the wagon up into the air. The right axle snapped; the wagon crashed sideways into the mud, landing cock-eyed, the door blown open and aimed at the ground. Jinala's grip on the bench failed, and she tumbled out of the wagon and straight into the wet dirt. She heard her brother shout. Wood splintered and then snapped behind her.

Her feet slipped as she tried to gain traction. She slid forward in the mud, all four limbs churning, stood, fell, stood again. She ran into the black forest without looking back.

With her hands outstretched, she darted past tree trunk after tree trunk. She tripped and gasped, afraid the scary tentacle had followed her and was slithering around her ankles. It was just a root. She kept going.

The storm thrashed on.

She slowed down when she came to a wide oak with limbs so thick and leaves so dense only a few raindrops landed on her. She wedged herself back into a nook at the base of the trunk and looked out at the storm. Branches shook back and forth in the strong wind. Everything around her was just a black mass of eerie forest. She looked in all directions, but nothing stood out, no clue to guide her back. A thick raindrop splattered right on her head.

I'm not tougher than Jason, and I'm not braver than Jason.

She cried in the rain for a while. She screamed at the thunder, begged for Gahkin to show her the way back, cried for her father and brother, cried for her dead mother. The storm blew itself out eventually, and still, Jinala sat in the dark. The wet tree limbs dropped less and less water down around her. She forced herself to crawl out from her nook and look up to the sky, but the jungle was too thick. She crawled a little further from the trunk. She felt unsafe out in the open forest. She could see only varying shades of black. The ceiling of leaves blotted out the stars above, and the torches from the wagons, if they still burned at all, were too far off to be visible.

Something heavy dropped to the ground a few yards to her left. She froze. Another thump came from the right. Then silence. Then, barely louder than the patter of dripping rainwater, a footstep.

"Hello?" she whispered, desperate to hear a familiar voice. The moment she spoke, she knew it was a bad idea. The thumps could have been anything. A big snake, a pair of baboons… even starving raiders from the north.

"Hello," a high-pitched voice said to her left.

"Martin!" Another voice, a little deeper, whispered back from her right.

The first voice called again, "Are you a lost princess?"

Jinala was frightened.

"Or are you just a lost unimportant person?"

"She is obviously the girl they are looking for—but be quiet. The Mud Wizard is around here, and if so, he's probably looking for her too."

The quiet footsteps moved closer from either side.

"Don't hurt me," Jinala whimpered, unsure if she spoke loud enough to be heard.

"Shh," the deeper voice said, "we won't hurt you. We'll take you back to the wagons."

In the distance, maybe thirty or forty yards away, a blue ball of light flickered into existence. A strange, long-bearded man stood under it, the same as when she first saw the blue light.

His silver staff tilted toward Jinala and the two mysterious characters that surrounded her. The blue glow bathed them all in light.

They were Sondites.

Both voices belonged to boys, not any older than Jinala. They had dark skin and purple eyes. One was very young; he'd seen three seasons at best, while the other was probably only a season older than Jinala, if that. Each carried a white cloth pack tied around their back, and the older boy carried a sharpened stick. Jinala tried to inch backward, but the older Sondite boy grabbed her shoulder, applying firm but not rough pressure.

"We have to stick together, princess. That is the Mud Wizard, and we think he might want to kidnap you."

Jinala remembered seeing the man with her father in the forest at Creek, so she couldn't imagine he was evil-minded *and* friends with Lord James Killovew. Yet the Sondite boys seemed convinced and willing to help her. Did they think she needed them to protect her? She remembered how her father had thrown on his armor and fought the dweller without hesitation. How her brother had stood against the onslaught on the wagon to protect his little sister. She was a Killovew too!

I'm as brave as Jason.

She shrugged the Sondite's hand off her shoulder and stood up to her full height, short as it was. She brushed her sopping hair out of her face and behind her ears.

She held up her hand to block the blinding light and shouted across the jungle, "I am Jinala Killovew, daughter of Lord James Killovew, ruler of the Thirsting Forest Realm! Take this light out of my face and speak your name."

I'm as brave as Father.

The light vanished. They were all cast into blackness. She felt the Sondites moving beside her. They were waiting for her to say something.

"Do you know the way-"

"Shh. He is still watching us," the deeper voice whispered. Jinala tried to blink her eyes to help adjust to the darkness, but she could not see anything. She reached out her left hand.

"Ow," the little one said as her hand collided with his nose.

"Sorry," she whispered.

They stood in silence for a long time before the older boy said, "Okay, let's go back to the wagon road." The boy put his hand on her shoulder, this time more gently, guiding her toward the path. She hoped.

"What are your names?" she asked. She did not have to ask why they lived in the forest. They were outlaws.

"My name is Martin, and this is my brother, Crichton."

"Where are your parents?"

The older brother's fingers flexed against her upper arm.

"We don't have parents anymore." The high-pitched voice didn't sound upset.

"Who takes care of you?"

"No one. The Mud Wizard used to help us—"

"Martin. Enough." The older brother named Crichton sounded stern. They walked around a big tree trunk.

Blue light blinded them again.

The Mud Wizard's staff was held out in front of his face, and at this distance, it was clear to see that the tip glowed with blue-white sparks, like those that jump from a flint. He squinted with one eye and leaned down to look at them, murmuring things under his breath that Jinala could not understand. His face was normal, aside from the muddy tipped beard and his glowing eyes. His hair was dirty blond, tangled and knotted, falling down his back. He did not look very old. Just dirty. He lowered his staff and made a loud *harrumph* sound.

"Hello, boys. Hello, princess. You are going back to the road. Good!"

Crichton and Martin exchanged a look, stepping back from him. Jinala held her ground.

He continued, "You three are a strange group, aren't you? So are we!" He reached into his tattered cloak and brought out two frogs. One stayed in his hand and just stared vacantly, but the other lunged for freedom. The wizard yelped and grabbed it in midair, then tucked them both back into his pocket.

"Nice try, Croak," he said, patting the pocket where he had tucked them away. He turned his eyes back to the children. He leaned closer, pointing at each of them in turn, and whispered, "Jinala Killovew. Crichton Raak. Martin Raak. This isn't your home."

He gestured at the forest all around him, waving his arms above his head. His sleeves dropped, and in the blue glow of his staff, the children saw his arms riddled with zigzagging scars. He stepped backward and straightened up. "Tell your dads hello for me." He walked off into the dark muttering, "Help them more? Protocol? That's not protocol! You're one crazy frog!"

The three of them were in silence for a long while before little Martin spoke, "Crichton, it sure sounds like he knows our father."

Jinala's fear had been replaced by a deep sadness then; the desperate hope in the voice of the little boy was unlike anything she'd ever heard. These two Sondite brothers, these outlaws, these godless men, were just two starving boys with no real family aside from each other. These two boys needed Jinala's help as much as she needed them to find her way back in the dark. Why would Gahkin abandon them?

Crichton said, after a long pause, "I think so, Mart. We'll find him again and figure it out. First, we take Princess Killovew back to the wagons."

They walked on, Crichton somehow leading them through the black forest. Soon she saw the burning lights from two wagons through the trees. The boys stopped walking.

"Here you go, princess," Crichton said.

"Thank you. But I don't understand. Why did you help me if you're not coming with me?"

"What else should we have done?" Crichton asked.

"Crichton says we have to be good even though people don't think Sondites are good," Martin added.

"No, Mart. We have to be good *because* people don't think Sondites are good."

Jinala pondered that thought for a flicker and then asked, "But... if you come with me, outlaws or not, I'm sure Father would give you some—"

"We can't join you in the wagon, princess." Crichton said. He spoke with a finality that Jinala could not argue against. "But we will follow you back to your castle."

****

Hand in hand with Martin, coming back to the present, she still couldn't understand the connection between the orphan boys, her father, and the Mud Wizard. James Killovew's friendship with Mart and Crichton's father, the man he called Kamau. He had known about them longer than she had. Why the effort to keep Jinala in the dark? If he had told her the full truth or told the boys the full truth, they wouldn't have been so susceptible to the Acolytes. Crichton wouldn't be in chains on his way to Shinar.

The wagon rolled to a stop. Trittion hopped down from the front and opened the door for Jinala and Martin. They climbed out, Martin with his head down, dodging Trittion's and Jinala's eyes. Ahead, Eric and James dismounted, tying their horses on a long rope to the wagon. James Killovew waved the rest of them to join him at the edge of the road. They walked over, nudging Martin along with them.

James raised his fingers to his lips, Martin and Jinala nodded, and they set off. Right when they stepped into the forest, Martin's head rose. He stepped with pace and meaning, a little off to the side, but clearly invested in the hunt as much as the rest of them. The Mud Wizard, Jinala guessed, represented Martin's last and only hope.

James led the way, using his long sword to clear the creepers and thick brush out of their path. Sir Trittion and Jinala walked side by side, followed by Martin and Eric Eden. Eric drew his sword when they heard the low grunts of some animal in the tree above them and did not sheathe it as they continued. They pushed through the higher forest ground, through thick brush with less trees, and emerged on the banks of a swamp.

Squidroot and saw palmettos dotted the otherwise flat landscape surrounding the swamp. Cattails and long blades of grass rose from the blackish muck. A few logs—or maybe water dragons—floated at the surface of the shallow water. James turned right, which Jinala guessed was west, and began circling the water.

Jinala had been excited when they left the trail, but by the time they were halfway around the swamp, she was bored. At one point, she thought she saw a human figure in the brushes alongside them, but when she looked back, it was just a clump of purple orchid flowers blowing in the wind. Her legs were tired, her feet hurt, and she had seen nothing moving except buzzing insects for the last candle. Martin had grown sad and listless again. Sir Trittion was sweating and breathing heavy but had not yet whined.

"Gahkin's wands, it's hot." Sir Trittion whined under his breath. "Why that man chooses to live in the middle of this Gahkin-cursed swamp, I'll never understand."

Jinala stomped along after her father. She tried to stay in his footsteps, where the mud was pressed down already, so her boots wouldn't get stuck. He had a long stride, but she managed to hop along after him. She turned around and saw Martin doing the same technique, followed by Eric.

"It's not a bad idea," Eric Eden said with a smile. He waited patiently for Mart to hop out of one boot print before he stepped in it.

As they slugged onward, James said, "Wasn't there something you wanted to tell me away from our advisers, Eric?"

"Oh, yes. Well, let me ask you this, first. The Ardellian raiders from the chasm, I assume they've given you trouble along your northern border, probably near Northtown?"

"Yes, but they've been pretty sporadic this season, sneaking in to steal from our gardens and farms and leaving just as quickly. Our patrols mostly just find the evidence of their theft, few have been foolhardy enough to stick around or try to come deeper into the realm."

"For a while, we had the same issue along our northwestern border. But they've drawn back some. Have you seen an increase or a decrease lately?"

"Actually, they've drawn back from my borders, as well, yes."

"We both have a lot of miles along our border to patrol. Keeps the men spread out. Not to mention, you have to watch your western flank."

"Aye, but Lord Early and I are on good terms. I assist where I can in guarding his ports. We have no qualms. What are you digging at, Eric?"

"Well, in large part, they were *successful* raids. And those people are starving in that realm. Worse maybe than anywhere else in the kingdom."

"I've heard…"

"Why would starving bandits stop successfully stealing food?"

Lord Killovew stopped walking. "That is a good question."

"I've heard that one of Lord Grayson's nephews survived the purge. And I've heard he has been rallying the Ardellian raiders to his cause."

"Sir Damian has made no mention of this. And I think he would hear this at the chasm."

"No, it's only whispers, James. And he is working the very outskirts of the realm. The folks who are the most desperate. Lady Barbara has connections that she swears would not give her false testimony, and she is confident he is more than just some optimistic rumor. That the boy is gathering a real following."

"That would be treason," Sir Trittion said. "If he tried to wrest back control of the realm. Especially if he is planning on using those outlaws to gain back his realm."

Eric gave him a patronizing look. "Those *outlaws* are just the starving children of the realm citizens who his family was sworn to protect and serve. They are his people."

James said, "You think he may be receptive to meeting with us?"

"Maybe. But I think he would be very suspicious of us. And I also think he is just as likely to be gathering his most loyal people for an all-out attack on one of *our* realms. If he's rallying them, he needs a plan to feed them. He'll need a more habitable realm than the one his family once ruled. Their farms are in much worse shape than either of ours, James."

James thought for a moment. "Starving bandits would stop stealing food only if they were planning something bigger. If an even better heist was available." He looked at Eric. "We need to get in contact with him, somehow, and quickly. He could be a powerful ally."

"Or a disruptive enemy…"

James sighed. "We waited and waited, all these seasons, with relative peace and quiet. And now that we've finally put our plans in motion, we can't keep up with all the new hurdles that threaten to trip us up."

"So it goes. I'll tell Barbara and see what strings she can pull."

During the conversation, Martin had wandered closer to the bank of the swamp water and was picking at the cattails that stuck up out of the water. After he plucked one, he was able to see all the way across the swamp to a bank further around the next bend.

There was a large gap in the foliage there. He could see the figure of a man with untamed hair and a muddy beard. His staff was stuck upright in the wet ground next to him. He was holding a thinner brown stick, flicking it with his wrists.

"Um," Martin said. "I think I found him."

Martin pushed aside the rest of the reeds so the others could see more clearly. Somehow, the movement must have drawn the Mud Wizard's attention. He looked up and flinched when he spotted them among the greenery. He tossed his stick to the ground, grabbed his staff, and started to run away.

"Halt!" James shouted. "Come on, Eric! Trit, stay with the children." James Killovew sprinted off after the wizard.

Martin, ignoring his orders, ran behind James, jumping with each stride to stay in his footsteps. Jinala glanced up at Eric, who realized too late what she was about to do. He grabbed at thin air as she dashed after Martin. Trittion groaned, Eric chuckled, and they ran after her.

The five companions ran in single file, two hundred yards behind the wild man named Evrost. As the Mud Wizard ran, he shouted back across the swamp, "Ollie, ollie, oxen free!"

James, Martin, and Eric overtook the Mud Wizard as the bank of the swamp bent back to the north. Jinala jumped from mud print to mud print, just as Martin stayed in the firm mud prints of James. Eric had blazed past them both at great speed. Her father drew his sword, just a few paces ahead.

The Mud Wizard spun around, bringing his silver staff crashing toward James Killovew, the tip sizzling blue. Jinala shrieked. James parried the staff, then with another strong swing knocked it clear out of Evrost's hands. The sparks extinguished the moment the staff lost contact with Evrost's fingers. It tumbled away and dropped into the wet dirt. James kicked the Mud Wizard behind his knee. The man yelped and crumpled to the ground, ensuring the chase was at a definite end.

"You would raise your staff against me?" James asked, eyes narrowed. Martin bent to pick up the staff, but when his finger touched the metal, he was knocked backward, almost off his feet. "Don't touch that, Martin," James said, much too late.

"Sharp steel, unsheathed, scared me into staff style self-defense," Evrost said, standing up and brushing off his robe. The loose dirt that fell off revealed more caked-on dirt underneath. If the inside of the sleeves didn't show a few patches of white, Jinala would have guessed the fabric had always been brown.

"You have good reason to fear me, wizard," James said, looking up at the tall man. "How did the Acolytes get in contact with you? Why would you betray Kamau's children? Have you lost the last shred of your sanity?"

"I'm no Benedict Arnold."

Sir Trittion finally caught up. Eric Eden circled around behind Evrost.

"James… Gahkin's wands… he hasn't aged at all," Eric said, scratching his head and squinting at the Mud Wizard. Trittion placed himself between the Mud Wizard and the forest. Martin saw what they were doing, so he stood between Evrost and the swamp water. Jinala stepped toward the staff.

"Don't touch it, Gina. It hurts," Martin said.

"No riddles, Evrost, and no games," James said. "Not this cycle. I will tolerate nothing but straight talk. I know you're capable. What happened? I trusted you. What else did you tell them?"

Evrost spoke in a drawn-out, overly articulate manner, using real words and made-up words interchangeably, as if he was speaking to a group of children. "I told them zilch. Nothing. I did not speak nor sign nor write nor fax nor text. I was close to the boys, but not too close, like a good Mud Wizard should be, not breaking protocol or promises, when I saw the little princess fleeing through the forest. She went away from something, so I went toward it, hoping to comprehend the conundrum. Then, next thing I know, a sabretooth tiger crawls out of the bushes, snarling and roaring and trying to turn me into lunch. Distracting, to say the least. I stunned it a few times and whacked it in the snout and the thing finally collapsed and then, by the time I got my bearings, I was able to find your girl and Martin standing in the middle of the castle lawn. I blasted the hawk on their tail then searched for Crichton. The older Sondite was already in chains on his way through the gate when I located him. A nuisance, not helpful at all, I would be at that point. So, I went back home." Evrost placed his hands over his eyes. "That hurt my head."

A blue bird chattered from the treetops behind Sir Trittion. There was no wind. The insects by the swamp buzzed and zoomed past Martin's face, but he did not swat or bother them. Jinala wasn't as accustomed to the bugs and kept tossing her hair and waving her hands around her face, but that only got their attention. James noticed them too, twitching his nose as they flew near him.

"Whether that is true or not, we are going to need to have a long discussion, and this is not the place to have it. You are coming back with us to the castle."

Eric Eden frowned. "James, I'm not sure that's such a good idea. I mean, he wasn't ever exactly… sane. And it looks like he's gotten worse. If the Acolytes—"

"We waited all this while before we searched him out for a reason, Eric. They are far from here and heading further away. The Thirsting Forest has proven to be an unsafe hideout already. Our hand may be forced sooner than we expect, but we must try to give Jason as much time as possible. They can't question his motives. They've taken Crichton, but they will not take Martin nor my daughter. We need to get a grasp of things, and fast, and plan our next move. We both must continue to rule our realms as if nothing has changed. The castle is our best bet for now. We will move him and Martin somewhere more permanent soon."

Eric looked like he was going to argue some more, but he sighed, and then said, "Fair enough."

James directed Sir Trittion Oak and Evrost to walk in front, and the others followed. Lord Killovew allowed Evrost to pick up his staff but did not take his eyes from him the entire way back.

It took over a full candle length to return to the wagon that they abandoned at the foot of the trail. The horses not strapped onto the carriage harnesses had moved into deeper shade as far as their leads would let them, their tails swishing through the air at the flies. Jinala felt tired, and Martin had gone from sad to hopeful and was now angry. He stripped his borrowed boots off and threw them into the jungle, complaining of blisters and the benefits of going barefoot. Sir Trittion grunted and retrieved the boots.

Jinala's eyes were half-closed, and she barely lifted her feet off the ground as she walked to the wagon. Despite the sporadic rushes of adrenaline fueling her, her lack of proper sleep was catching up.

After Eric corralled Martin and the Mud Wizard into the carriage, he tracked down his horse. "We are going to tie the horses onto the back; that way, we can all sit with Evrost. Trit, can you guide us back?"

"Indeed, Lord Eden," Trittion agreed, his head buried under the front seat of the wagon, digging for something.

Lord James and daughter Jinala stepped into the crowded carriage, followed by Eric Eden. He shut the door and dropped the drapes. Martin, Jinala, and Eric faced James and Evrost. A lone candle burned on the small table between them. Sir Trittion spoke to the horses, the wheels turned, and the wagon set off down the path back toward Castle Killovew. Everyone sat in flickering shadows, but only the Mud Wizard's eyes shone through the dark with a faint white glow.

Ten

The journey off the trade roads and across the wild flood plains began without problem. Many cycles passed without notable occurrence at all. The Greenfoot brothers broke up the monotony of the long journey with the occasional boastful story or frivolous argument, but for the most part, the group rode in watchful silence.

On the sixth cycle after leaving Old King's Road, they traveled into a low valley where a shady grove of acacia and hawthorn trees grew among thick brush. They chose a campsite five hundred yards or so downwind from the small pond at the center of the grove. Ratoke and Jason set off to try to hunt, despite the low odds, while the others remained behind to make ready the camp.

Jason carried a war bow while Ratoke carried a small jungle bow. Smaller than the long bows used in warfare, they were more accurate and less burdensome. The bow would kill few animals on its own, but once the arrow punctured flesh, the venom tip did the rest.

The Greenfoots had brought several different vials of concentrated water-snake venom and poisonous flower sap and other toxic serums from their swamp home. Dipping an arrow tip into a diluted mixture of the venom was enough to send an elk into a deep sleep that led to death or make a bull buffalo dizzy enough to fall over. Too little venom, and the creature would run off before any of the symptoms set in. Only the 'twins' diluted the venom serum, claiming the mixture must be exact. Neither Ratoke nor Taroke measured their portions, though—they just eyed it.

Jason crouched atop a fallen log, avoiding dry twigs underfoot. The grass grew tall in the grove, surrounding him on every side. He drew and nocked an arrow, then used its tip to gently brush aside a clump of the thick weeds. Nothing. He parted the grass in a few different directions, but all was still. He dropped down from the log and stepped through the grass into a small clearing. Ratoke emerged from nearby. Jason wondered if their horseback approach into the grove may have triggered any other creatures here to flee.

Just as Ratoke pushed through a scrub bush, a young antelope leaped from the bramble just in front of them. Before Ratoke could even turn and aim his bow, Jason snapped back his string and then loosed his arrow. He caught the adolescent between the rib and the shoulder, and it fell to the ground.

Jason hustled to the kill and pulled the arrow from the animal. The creature didn't even struggle or kick with any last gasps of breath. Jason stuck his finger in the hole and felt inside the wound. Being a prince, he practiced archery regularly growing up at Castle Killovew. Being competitive and arrogant, he did it well more than he was required to by his knight mentors.

He pulled his bloody finger out of the creature and looked at Ratoke. "Got it in the heart. Death with little pain. No venom needed this time, huh?"

Ratoke rolled his eyes. "I'm very impressed."

They carried the carcass to camp, and Mako cleaned it with fast precision. Taroke sprinkled a pinch of salt and jungle spices over the meat and cooked it over a slow fire.

The antelope meat crisped up on the outside and proved to be moist and only slightly gamy. It tasted like pure indulgence compared to the monotony of m-bars and potato stew. Sir Breigo took the first watch while the others fell into a contented sleep under the moderate shade of the Baboa canopy. It wasn't a dark shade like in the rainforest at Jason's home, but it was comfortable, and the temperature was cool. A warm breeze blew from the southeast through the trees. The ground was soft. Jason yawned. They were lucky that the traveling so far had been comfortable and safe. Sooner or later, they would run into trouble.

Jason sighed and rubbed the fish scale tied around his neck. Maybe their luck would hold all the way to Shinar and back.

The knight of the Thirsting Forest roused his prince far sooner than normal, a single finger held over his mouth. "Come look at this," he said.

Jason crept away from camp, following Sir Breigo Aldev toward a small boulder at the edge of the grove. He climbed up halfway and peered over the top. His eyes opened wide, and his hand slipped to his dagger.

A contingent of about fifty men on horseback galloped across the flood plains at high speeds, less than a mile away. They were curving down toward the grove. Most wore unstained brown leather armor, though Jason picked out a handful of purple robes billowing within the group.

Acolyte paladins, leading a platoon of soldiers. And not a Sondite among them, from what the prince could see.

Whatever a battalion of soldiers, led by a handful of Acolytes, was doing in the middle of the wild lands *east* of Shinar, Jason did not know. But it could not be good.

The men fanned out of single file and turned in a wide wave. They would wash into the small clump of trees and vegetation all at once. Jason dropped back behind the boulder, fingers pressed against his temples.

"What do you think, Sir Breigo?"

"Looks like a party of soldiers, sir, with Acolytes mixed among them. On the hunt for something, I'd guess. Or someone."

Brilliant insight.

Jason and his companions were not doing anything wrong technically, even though foreigners were encouraged to stay on the roads. They could be picked up as deserters, maybe, if the Acolytes thought they were abandoning their plans for enlisting in the God-King's army. That didn't explain why the soldiers were bearing down on the grove at unsustainable speeds, but it was enough to force Jason into a fast decision.

"Okay. Go wake the others, bring them here. And bring our warrants for crossing realms. Allies do not hide from allies."

"Yes, sir." Sir Breigo turned and ran back to the camp without argument, slumped low to stay out of sight.

Jason took a couple quick breaths, rubbed a hand across his face, and stood up. He walked from behind the boulder into plain sight, shouting and waving his arms toward the men on horseback.

The wide line of horsemen grew tighter as they all adjusted to ride straight at Jason. One of the men in purple rode to the front and led the rest of the horsemen down on the prince. He pulled up just in front of Jason, his silver stallion snorting and breathing heavily. The Acolyte drew a one-handed flamberge and pointed the rippling blade at Jason's face. Jason did not flinch nor step back, but his heart raced. The sword was a relatively useless weapon on the battlefield, but it was carried by high-ranking Acolytes, and Jason did not wish to confront any of his secret enemies this far from Shinar.

"I am Zedaff, First Finger of the Fourth Hand. Identify yourself and your purpose in the realm of Shinar." Three more Acolytes drew up beside the first, though none of them drew their weapons. The soldiers stayed just behind, awaiting orders. A couple pulled arrows from their quivers and nocked their bows. They did not aim but held them ready at their sides. The rest just milled about, looking at Jason with confused eyes.

They are not looking for a man like me.

"My name is Jason Killovew. I am the Prince of the Thirsting Forest, and my companions and I make for Shinar to join the war effort."

The man did not lower his sword. "Where are these companions? Why do you travel through Gahkin's flood plains instead of along the trade roads, supposed prince? Our Creator has granted me little patience this cycle. Speak straight and honest, citizen."

"Priests of the West, I saw you in the plains and sent my knight to rouse our sleeping companions. Four men travel with me, and they shall join us soon, in peace. We camped here to rest and fill our supplies. We mean to find Shinar long before the sun sets, so we chose to brave the wilds in order to expedite our arrival. What brings you into the plains with such a force, Zedaff?"

The Acolyte ignored his question. "Do you have the authorization to cross realms, and does the council know of your coming?"

"Yes, we have warrants from my father, James Killovew, Lord of the Thirsting Forest, to cross through the realms of Kydoth and the Great Gorge into Shinar. Each realm lord has approved our passage, and the Ten Hand Council knows of our imminent arrival." Jason hesitated, looking again at the eyes of each Acolyte.

The Acolyte grunted and sheathed his sword. His angry manner softened but did not disappear. "I will need to see those warrants, Prince Jason."

"I have them all at our campsite. I'm sure the others will bring them along with them."

"With the apocalyptic omens spreading across the kingdom, I wouldn't think anybody would test their fate by traveling through these wild lands." Zedaff was prying at Jason, trying to catch him in a lie. It angered Jason that Zedaff was so distrustful. Did the Killovew name still have negative connotations in Shinar?

"The way I understand the apocalypse, Zedaff, is that its very definition implies it doesn't matter where you are when it happens. Whole world gone in an instant. Wild lands and civilized both. An Acolyte, one much like yourself, once told me the Great Flash spares none."

Why are you saying this? Take it easy, Jason.

The Prince of the Thirsting Forest and the First Finger of the Fourth Hand stared at one another, eyes unwavering.

Zedaff glanced at another Acolyte, a pale man scarred along both sides of his jaw. The man nodded a fraction of an inch. Zedaff leaped off his horse and strode through the tall grass right up to Jason.

"I agree, Prince Killovew." He extended his hand.

Sir Breigo and Mako emerged from behind the boulder, hands held away from their weapons.

Breigo held the burlap sack carrying the royal letters. "I've brought all of the warrants, Prince Jason."

"Stay where you are," a second Acolyte said. He rode to them, took the offered bag, and brought it back to Zedaff.

The First Finger eyed the men before he turned his attention to the bag. As he rummaged, the Greenfoots walked into the open from the shade of the trees. Zedaff looked up, squinted at the two brothers, and then looked back down to the bag. He pulled out each scroll, unrolled them, and examined them. After a couple anxious moments, he stuffed them back in the bag, save one. Without raising his eyes from the parchment, he said, "Mako Black, your warrant is inconsistent with the rest." The bearded wrangler looked up at Zedaff but did not answer. "You are not authorized to travel into the Kydoth realm."

Mako scratched his nose. "Nope." He looked at Jason with a raised eyebrow.

The Acolyte scanned Jason's men, as Jason did the same from the corner of his eye. Sir Breigo still stood at attention, being a knight with the most political experience and patience. Ratoke folded his arms across his chest, placing his hands on the hidden pockets where he stored his poisoned daggers. Taroke fingered his bow string, ready to slip it off his shoulder and nock an arrow in half a flicker. Mako's hand rested on his belt, inching closer to his hilt. No one was smiling. The Acolytes and soldiers watched for a single move that would trigger a storm of arrows loosed at Jason's men. The standoff would not last much longer.

Jason said, "Mako Black joined our party late in the planning. We departed and took a longer, more northern route just to avoid crossing into the Kydoth realm."

Zedaff glanced back at the pale man, scarred along both sides of his jaw. He nodded his head again.

"Fine." Zedaff rolled Mako's scroll up and placed it with the rest. "I have a handful of Sondite deserters to track down if you might share your campsite with us. Make sure to mention your inconsistencies beforehand, Prince Jason, or someone may think you're hiding something."

"Thank you, Zedaff. I shall. And you may."

"Have you seen any sandmen cross your path recently?"

"We haven't seen anyone at all other than you and your men since we left the road."

"And you're unlikely to see anyone again until you return to the road. We will water the horses and search the trees for the Sondites before moving on. They may be in hiding, unbeknownst to you." He extended his hand again, and this time, Jason reached out and took it. "Welcome to the realm of Shinar, Jason Killovew."

"Thank you. A few Sondite deserters require a whole battalion of soldiers to hunt them down?"

"I will not speak further on the matter."

The men did not stay long. The soldiers searched every bush and tree and clump of grass in the grove. The prince and the Acolytes sat near the pond. The Acolytes ate the remaining antelope without an invitation. They offered Jason a sack of red wine. He squirted a few swallows into his mouth, winked at Mako, and then passed it off to the others. Zedaff spoke on their troubles with the band of Sondites.

"Their tracks from the river were clear until they mixed up with a cattle stampede. The ground was trampled beyond even Ty's ability to track." Zedaff nodded to the Acolyte with the scarred jaws sitting at his side. "If they are not here, we will continue east perhaps and catch them on the other side of the fork."

"No," Ty said, lifting his head from a bone, mouth shining with grease. His scars stretched and shrunk as he spoke, as if his mouth could unhinge at his neck like a snake. "We saw only a thin trail of tracks that led into the grove, which came from the east and belonged to these Thirsting Forest men. They left the road five or six cycles ago. The gully descends into this grove, which means the sandmen would have funneled here and passed Jason Killovew's men after leaving here. They would have had two options. Kill them or turn back. These men aren't dead. Either the Sondites came this way and turned back west—doubtful—or they knew they were being tracked and doubled back southwest earlier when they found the stampede trail. That is my guess. We go back to the cattle tracks. It's as I thought, and now we can be sure. They are doubling back, heading southwest with the herd. Looking for a hideout, not a direct escape. They will need to be close enough to negotiate the return of their hostage." He bent back to his food and gnawed at the remaining meat still clinging on the bone. Zedaff did not argue.

"Hey, how did you know we left the road six cycles ago?" Ratoke asked.

"Look at the bottom of your horses' legs. The sun is still above the horizon, though not by much, and when a horse walks through these flood plains, it hides the lower fifth or so of its leg in dark shade, in the moisture of the tall grass. It takes about five cycles for the mud and shade and water to start to discolor the horsehair. They grow darker and greener than the top of the legs. Now look at our horses. They have run through these plains for seasons."

Jason thought Rara Silva Nix's coat still looked all the same color. "Rara," he said, clicking his teeth. The horse trotted in his direction, but she was tied to a tree away from the pond and could not come much closer. Jason leaned toward her and squinted at her legs. He noticed an almost imperceptible darkening of her pure white hair starting halfway down her knee. Jason could see the ankles of the horses that the Acolytes rode were dark brown, the rest of their coat still silver.

"That's clever," Taroke said.

"Oh, thank you." Ty walked toward the foot of the pond, stroking his forefinger and thumb through the scar grooves on both sides of his face. He looked to his right at the horses and then back to the small pond. He spat his last mouthful of water into the dirt.

A soldier walked up and reported that the grove was empty. Zedaff instructed him and the others to prepare to ride. Ty turned from the pond and helped Jason to his feet with a strong grip. "I hope we meet again, Killovew."

The Acolytes shook Jason's hand and then took their leave.

Jason turned to his men once the contingent was riding away into the distance. Ratoke and Taroke smirked at each other. Breigo looked at Jason and then quickly looked away.

"Bury me, Sir Breigo, just say what's on your mind."

"It's just—well, Prince Jason, that Acolyte tracker knew something was off about us. I mean, this is a hunch, but I think—well, we don't want *any* suspicion lingering over us in Shinar."

"The knight is right." Mako Black sat down on a small boulder. "He knew something."

Sir Breigo continued. "We must be soldiers only, and you the royal prince, nothing more until the time is right. Any doubt in our legitimacy could spell failure. Already there are signs of rebellion within the city. Deserters leaving the city and a whole band of soldiers chasing them down? If the Ten Hand Council thinks we have anything to do with this… Our plot could be ruined. We can't allow for any distrust, and we must ensure the Sundown Ceremony happens."

"There won't be any distrust," Ratoke said, snickering.

"Why won't there be any distrust?" Breigo asked.

"Rat and I poisoned the water," Taroke said. "We tied our horses out of drinking distance, and the rest just slurped it up."

Ratoke and Taroke held a grudge against the Acolytes, but their positions were only soldiers. They came from a village that specialized in felling trees and milking snakes, not playing espionage. They should not have done that without direction from Jason.

"Wouldn't the pond dilute the venom?" Mako asked, confused.

"Not venom. I put a whole vial of the toad poison in there before we came out to meet you. Their horses will collapse in four, five cycles at most. The men won't last near that long."

Sir Breigo tilted his head. "You poison men's drink, they die. You shoot poison into animals, they die. You eat poisoned meat, but live."

"We *poisoned* their drink. We shoot *venom* into the animals. Ingestion versus injection," Ratoke said. Breigo scratched his head, perhaps not understanding the two different words.

Taroke flashed a vile smile. "We're good with all manner of nasty things, knight. Leave it at that."

"What if they were our allies?" Jason asked. "Those men weren't important leaders; they didn't start the war; they were just following orders."

"If they were allies, we would just tell them that the water was poisonous. We already filled our supplies. And they weren't leaders, but they *were* Acolyte paladins, hunting our old allies, weren't they?" Taroke said.

Ratoke added, "So we killed them, big deal. If they were suspicious of us, good riddance." Mako blinked in the sunlight, apathetic to the assassination of over fifty men. Sir Breigo's training kept him silent. Jason could see he disapproved, but not enough to speak up. The Greenfoots looked awfully smug about murdering over fifty men.

Do you feel guilty, Jason, or jealous that it was not your idea?

"This is war, boy," Mako said after a long while.

Jason detested being called 'boy.' The Prince of the Thirsting Forest rubbed his hand through his hair, pulling it back behind his ears.

"Our mission is not to fight the war, Mako. It's to bring forced enlistment and pseudo-religious rule to an end. To stop unjust violence, not engage in it. To—"

"Look here." Mako stood up with sudden anger, pointing his finger at Jason. "Your father's scheme is honorable as the star life, it really is, but don't you dare preach to me. I told you once—I'm in. I won't say it again. Nor stand for sermons because we killed a couple of men in the wrong place at the wrong time."

Ratoke said, "My brother and I signed on to this because the Sondites—"

Taroke cut him off, "—shared a border with us—"

"—their grandfathers traded gold for our grandfather's lumber—"

"—they were good men, no better or worse than any others in the kingdom—"

"They certainly don't deserve to be outlawed and enlisted because the sun doesn't set in their realm anymore."

"And you can bet that when we get a free shot to kill some of those purple priests-"

"We are going to take it," Ratoke finished.

Jason looked to his knight. Loyal Breigo would agree with him. Sir Breigo sighed. "They are right, Prince Jason. The blood of many Acolytes may be on our hands before we are done if we succeed. Now is as good a time as any to get used to it." Sir Breigo turned to the Greenfoot brothers. "You are positive they will die?"

"Oh, absolutely," Taroke said.

"And it will be agonizing."

The Prince of the Thirsting Forest gazed into the western sky, away from the setting sun. "Well, let's follow them just to be sure, then move on to Shinar. At least the hunted Sondites may live."

He walked past his men and began to break down the camp.

Eleven

Someone whispered unintelligible words into his ear, their breath sticky and smelling of squirrel blood. An unknown human wrapped in a tan pelt stood before him. The claws at the bottom of the pelt raked the loose dirt as the stranger walked closer. Dead eyes and a leathery nose adorned the hood that shrouded the mysterious man's face. Two great fangs hung aside his ears, long enough that they scratched into the shoulders and sharp enough that they dug out a little bit of bloody flesh each time they swung back and forth in the wind. He reached out a hand, intent on steadying the incisors, but the dead fangs came alive, the hood flared like a purple cobra, and the dark face morphed into something inhuman, something nightmarish, and the snake-man struck at him, again and again and again. He could not breathe. He punched out his arms, holding off the hungry face but for a flicker. His defense failed, and the sharp teeth bit into his lips. Acid burned his throat, and spit flooded his mouth.

One eye creased open. He lay doubled over a warm branch, rising and falling in the wind.

The sunlight brought pain and a rush of dizziness. He vomited into a river of green. The water rushed past, steadier than any creek in the woods. The branch he lay on must stretch out above a wide river. He bumped up and down. Up and down. Such a strong wind. It felt good on his face. He turned his head. Strange silver and brown ships, with sails of rippling royal purple and long silver and brown oars rose above the water, floating toward a blurry horizon at the top of an olive-colored hill. He did not understand. His eyes closed shut again.

Frigid winds skated down a mountainside. He stood at the base of the mountain, shivering. He took one step and fell through a thin layer of ice, plunging into freezing water below. Pale blue razors cut his palms as he splashed and tried to keep his nostrils above the frozen froth. Shivering in cold delirium, he climbed out onto the tundra and toward a glowing warmth not too far away. A ten-foot tongue with sandpaper skin coiled up his ankles and around his thighs. He ripped and tore himself free. On hands and knees, he hauled himself closer to the heat, calling for help with a broken voice.

Crichton awoke. A nightmare scream lingered in his throat, and an itchy burlap blanket lay tangled about his legs. His body was coated in a cold sweat, his head throbbed, and his insides hurt. He lay sprawled in front of a warm fireplace. No flames leaped, but the embers still glowed warm and red.

He rolled over. Dark timber walls wrapped around him. Once again, he was being kept in a dark jail, but it was an upgrade from the dungeons. He had a bed with a lumpy-looking mattress, and one chair with a tiny table. He smelled some roasting meat wafting up between the floorboards. His stomach rumbled.

He remembered the old knight and his promise that Martin and Jinala were safe. He remembered the Acolytes escorting him through the castle to his trial. He remembered an ominous voice and a blinding light, but was that a dream or reality? His most recent memories seemed distant. How long had he slept?

Crichton propped himself up, exhaling sharply as the throbbing in his head grew worse. Crichton tried to stand, but his right arm gave out, and he fell back onto the rug.

"How are you feeling?" A voice from the darkness.

Crichton did not respond. The voice did not ask again.

Silence.

Crichton shut his eyes. A while later, he opened them. A man in purple sat on the floor, only a few feet away. It was the same man who had retrieved him from the dungeons.

"Crichton. That is your name, isn't it?"

Crichton nodded.

"You lived alone in the forest?"

'The purple men mean you and your brother no good.' The knight's voice echoed in Crichton's mind. Better to not say anything about Martin. Crichton nodded again to the Acolyte.

"Don't you miss your friends?"

"I don't have any friends." Crichton coughed. His throat hurt. The stranger passed Crichton a skin of water, which Crichton did not hesitate to drink.

The man spoke, "Well, Crichton. I will be your first friend. And I will introduce you to the greatest friend of all. Your forefathers abandoned Gahkin, but He is merciful enough to accept their sons back into His service."

Crichton was silent, but his mind was racing. He needed to escape and find his brother. If they could go back to the forest, deeper than ever, they could find true safety. He would not trust anyone. Not Sir Trittion, not Lord Killovew, not even Jinala—and surely not this man.

"Crichton? Look at me. No doubt you are fearful. You have come out of a deadly fever that we were not sure you would survive. Gahkin be praised! Your life, like ours, has great value in His eyes. I want to save you. He wants to save you. Your eternal spirit shines with destiny!"

He smiled wide, both affection and concern plastered across his face. His eyes were unreadable. They unnerved Crichton. The man was either a virtuoso liar or terribly affectionate toward young strangers.

He continued, batting his eyelashes, maintaining the well-crafted grin, "But of course, I'm getting ahead of myself. I understand you may not trust me. I want to change that. I am Domray." He stood from the ground and asked, "Are you hungry? I'll send up some of the lamb and give you some time to think on the new changes coming in your life."

Crichton's head hurt. He did not want to deal with all of this. He thought of his brother, though, hiding away somewhere, scared and lost. "Where am I, Domray? I can't think trapped inside the castle like this."

"Crichton, the castle is far behind us."

"Behind us?"

"You have been in a fevered sleep for many cycles. We are on our way to Shinar, stopped at a tiny village, east of Jastesh."

Crichton did not know where any of those places were, but he knew it meant that he had been separated from Martin long ago and that they were far apart.

Domray continued, "I'll be your tutor, as well as a guardian for the rest of our journey. We will stay here to let you rest. We would like to be in Shinar before the sun sets, though, so we cannot dawdle."

Crichton swallowed down his sorrow and anger, trying to keep his mind focused on the important things. "So... so am I going to go home after... Shinar?"

"To the Thirsting Forest? No, that is a home for animals, not for men. No, you will have a new home. You will become a man by my teaching and under the eyes of the ever-watching God-King. We will shape your soul. Mold it. Your life will no longer be a daily struggle for food. You will forget all about your old life and home when we get to Shinar. You will join in the war against the Vistonex. You will earn immortality!"

Crichton had only heard rumors of the Vistonex war, and now he was going to fight in it to save his soul. He had never really thought about his soul before.

"Trust me, Crichton, your life is undergoing drastic change, but it will be for the better. Drastic change is emotionally challenging and physically weary, but you will overcome and be better for it, I promise."

Crichton just nodded, his eyes blank.

Domray added a handful of twigs and then a log to the fireplace. "Now, do me a favor and stir up that fire."

Crichton turned around and reached for a dull iron poker. He glanced at it, then back toward Domray.

"That would be unsuccessful... and a bad start to our friendship, I think."

Crichton lowered his eyes and proceeded to prod at the dead fire, reviving a bright red underbelly beneath the cooler coals. He blew into the fireplace, the tender caught, hot flames leaped into the air, and Crichton sighed.

Crichton's health returned at a quick pace, considering the many cycles he had fought the fever. The small portions of food he got down helped revive his senses, and a spicy broth he drank fortified his strength and soothed his throat. Domray opened the windows in his jail, bringing in fresh air and sunlight and the stomach-sinking feeling of being completely lost. There were no trees outside. Only a small wooden fence, beyond which stretched empty rolling hills. He was far from any forest.

He tossed and turned, and whenever he slept, he dreamed of Martin. He had never been away from his little brother since the cycle he was born.

Crichton's sleep was short-lived, however, for the Acolyte named Domray barged in almost every candle of the cycle, asking Crichton if he needed anything. Since he had no desire to speak with the overly enthused Acolyte, Crichton lay in bed and pretended to stay asleep. He awaited the cycle he'd be strong enough to climb out the open window and run away.

Though only Domray came to his room while he recovered, Crichton deduced that there were others about. Multiple voices drifted up the staircase now and again.

On the third cycle of rest and sleep, a stranger ripped open the door and entered the room, followed by an agitated Domray. A big finger, jabbed into Domray's chest, silenced the Acolyte.

The stranger did not speak at first. He stayed at a distance, leaning against the brick of the chimney, examining Crichton from afar. He wore a leather cloak, as opposed to a purple robe. Arms folded across his chest, Crichton could tell this was a man who spent most of his life in the wilderness. He dwarfed Domray, both in height and through the width of his shoulder. The calluses on his hands were visible from across the room, thicker even than Crichton's own. His hair was very short, but he maintained a trimmed beard, wore leather bracers and grieves, and carried a sword and knife at his hips. His dark eyes sat deep under his forehead in shadow, yet when he glanced out the window, they flashed with a sharp, cold edge.

"Stand up," the man said. Crichton stood. His vision blurred for just a moment.

Domray blurted out, "Now, Sarpho, I must insist. As the official lea—" The big man turned and frowned at Domray, which was enough to silence him.

The stranger strode closer to Crichton and drew his sword. Crichton clenched his jaw and closed his eyes.

"No, keep your eyes open." Crichton opened his eyes. Sarpho put the blunt edge of his sword against his cheek and applied a little pressure. Crichton turned his head left and then, when the sword was placed on the other cheek, back to the right. "Walk to the door and come back." Crichton walked past the men to the open door. He felt no desire to run. Fear held him in place. His head throbbed, but he forced himself to be steady and walked back to his starting point. "How do you feel?"

Crichton did not know the right answer, so he answered truthfully. He did not stutter. Even in his weakened state, Crichton knew he should not show this man just how afraid he was. "Better… but not great. Not normal."

"Good enough. We will leave on the morrow." With that Sarpho turned and moved toward the door.

"Come now," Domray said. "Intimidation isn't the way Gahkin would want us to treat the Sondite. You scared him into answering that way. He needs more cycles, Sarpho. At least, give him two more cycles."

Crichton's stomach tightened. He was not an injured animal who could not speak for itself. He was almost a man who had learned to live in the woods and raised a brother. He would not be treated like an infant. "I am ready to leave on the morrow's cycle. But I want to go home. Not to Shinar, or wherever it is you are taking me."

Sarpho cocked his head from Domray to Crichton and smiled. He asked, "Which way is home, I wonder?" and then walked out the door and shut it.

Crichton sat down on the bed, exhausted from his efforts. He did not know the answer. Domray poured a glass of broth and handed it to him. The mug steamed, and Crichton drank it back, hot enough that it burned his tongue. But he felt better.

Domray said, "Rest while you can. Riding will be painful on the morrow. I will pray for you."

He lay back in his bed, rolled over, and fell asleep, wishing he was with his little brother more than anything else in the whole world.

When they came for him the next cycle, he was awake, dressed, and waiting.

Domray brought one last mug of broth, and Crichton drank it all, as he had before. Sarpho motioned him outside and down the stairs. Crichton descended and found an empty room. They crossed and left the cabin. Whom it belonged to, and where they were hiding, he never learned.

Stepping outside, Crichton almost gasped. Wary of showing weakness, he muffled his audible surprise, but his flinch betrayed him. The monster cats, tails twitching, sat beside a line of five silver horses. Two other Acolytes, robed like Domray, stood alongside, attaching the last few sacks and bags and empty bird cages to their steeds. The rest of the village, if a few houses and a stone well could be considered a village, was quiet. The black panther looked at Crichton and licked its whiskered lips. The bigger tan panther ignored him.

"They won't hurt you, my son," Domray said, putting a hand on Crichton's shoulder, moving him toward the last horse in the line. Crichton noticed its ropes were tied to the horse in front of it. The black panther stalked closer to Crichton.

"Look here, don't worry about her, worry about your horse. We call her Memoria." Domray pointed to the saddle. "Now this part here you will use—" Crichton could not keep his eyes off the panther. She came closer and closer. At the last moment, it lowered its head and rubbed the top of her skull along Crichton's leg. "See, she's no threat. Now, look. As we ride, you'll need to know a few things. For instance, this—"

"He will learn"—Sarpho said, emerging from around the cabin and striding to the front of the group where he mounted the largest silver stallion—"as we ride."

Domray tittered but spoke no more. He helped Crichton into the saddle then mounted the next horse in line. The tan panther was leashed to Sarpho's horse, but the black panther was left unleashed. The ride began, and the cat followed along diligently.

The riding was indeed painful, and when Crichton's muscles tired, he had to endure the bumping without the ability to brace himself. They rode and rode, up and down endless hills. Tall grass, always brownish-green, in every direction. There were no trees. There were no wild animals. When they stopped for camp six candles later, Crichton fell to the ground and was asleep before he could even think of the sorrowful turn his life had taken.

Twelve

Just two cycles after leaving the wooded grove Jason Killovew and his companions found the dead soldiers. They were splayed out at the bottom of a small hill, across the otherwise undistinguished floodplains, surrounded by some of their horses. The other animals must have wandered off from their masters before dying elsewhere.

"We need to go down there and count the men. Sir Breigo, how many visited us in the grove?"

Mako answered before the knight. "Forty-seven."

The company walked down the hill toward the corpses. Jason felt an uncomfortable but all too familiar thrill stir in his chest as he drew closer to the dead men. His heart rate thumped quicker and quicker.

What is wrong with me?

You're special.

"I count forty-six," Ratoke spoke.

Taroke added, "Should have dumped in two vials and killed them all right there on the spot."

"Look," Mako said, pointing away from the setting sun, toward Shinar. The wind stirred the tall grass, Jason saw more horses fallen along the ground. And beyond them, a single purple soldier, standing above the grass. On his outstretched left hand, a small hawk fluttered its wings.

"Bury me," Jason cursed under his breath.

Sir Breigo reached for his quiver, still slung across his horse's shoulder.

"You'll never make the shot," Mako muttered. "Not from here."

"He hasn't seen us, yet," Ratoke said.

"We can get closer," Taroke added.

Jason drew an arrow from his own quiver, notched his bow. He took two steps forward, crouching into the grass. "Just need another fifty yards, and I can put this arrow through his throat."

"If that hawk is loosed, our quest will come to an early end. We won't catch it." Sir Breigo said.

Jason's lips tightened. "Thank you, Sir Breigo." He took two more careful steps forward.

The hawk lifted off the Acolyte's arm, screeching in freedom.

Jason groaned, shouldered his bow, and leaped onto Rara Silva Nix.

He called to the others, "Take the man, I'll bring down the bird!" As he pressed his heels into his steed, he heard Sir Breigo shout, but he did not hear what he said. "Go, Rara," he whispered into her ear. "Go like never before."

The Thirsting Forest stables had agile, nimble horses for traversing the swampy forest. They had large, strong horses for pulling wagons. They had brave horses for jousting knights and war horses for soldiers heading to battle. They also had companion horses, meant to take men on long journeys, loyal to their masters for life. They also bred horses that royal men like the Killovews rode. Built for aesthetics and comfort more than anything else.

Rara was not bred to be any of these. Rara was the daughter of the fastest racehorse Castle Killovew had ever seen. Jason picked her as a young calf to be his horse when he was just a boy. He took her riding more often than was normal for a young royal student. When he was on Rara, with his hair whipping behind him, he never felt those strange *urges*; he just felt freedom.

The hawk was faster than any horse. But the hawk did not sense the need to be urgent or quick. The hawk just knew to cruise back to the rookery at Shinar and receive a dead mouse upon return.

Rara felt urgency in her ribs as Jason squeezed his heels into her. She heard urgency as she heard her rider in her ear. She knew urgency as she knew hunger, and thirst, and the urge to draw breath.

Jason galloped past the last surviving Acolyte so fast he did not notice who it was, nor bother to look back. The man dove out of the way as they barreled past him, and Jason had his eyes locked on the sky above. The hawk was higher now, but Jason was gaining distance on it. The moment he drew his bow and leaned back to aim, Rara would slow. When that happened, they would never catch up again. The gallop had brought them close, but he would only get one chance. If the arrow missed, the hawk would flee, higher into the sky and faster than any horse could follow.

If the hawk escaped to Shinar, the letter it carried would foil their quest. The Acolytes would strip the rule of the Thirsting Forest from his father. Jason's men would be tossed into the dungeons of Shinar to rot, both the Killovew men would be executed, and his sister would be taken by the Acolytes…

Jason shook his head. The Prince of the Thirsting Forest would not allow any of that.

Rara sped on across the plains, and soon she drew even with the hawk above.

Jason urged Rara Silva Nix just ahead of the soaring bird, despite the foam accumulating at her mouth and her wheezing breaths, knowing he would need a little lead time. He exhaled slowly, feeling the pounding legs beneath him, anticipating each jolt under his saddle that shook his balance. He felt her sprinting, felt himself as a part of her, racing through the air, the wind ripping across his face. He squinted at the hawk, now just behind his left shoulder, about a hundred yards in the air. He inhaled. He unshouldered his bow, drew an arrow from his quiver, leaned back, and closed one eye. He exhaled.

He released.

The arrow whistled, curved slightly as it ascended, and sunk into the underside of the hawk's breast. It screeched, then tumbled out of the air and landed in a feathery heap fifteen yards away.

Jason returned to his men, carrying the small letter he had plucked from the dead bird's leg.

They had captured Ty, the scarred Acolyte tracker. He lay on his back, puke caked across his chest and beside his head. He gave a weak laugh when he saw Jason, followed by a sickly cough. He tried to spit yellow bile toward the prince, but it just oozed from his lips onto his chin.

The Acolyte scanned them all and tried to speak. "I… knew it. Gahkin will smite you all. Your star life will be an eternity with the dwellers."

"I shot down your bird, Ty. The Ten Hand Council will know nothing."

"Gahkin knows all." Ty coughed and wheezed and coughed some more. He added, his voice raspy, "Hawk or no hawk, Gahkin will know."

Ratoke looked at the dead horses lying across the plains then over to Jason. "I don't even know how he's still alive."

The Acolyte muttered, "This isn't the first time"—he coughed, and more bile dripped from the corner of his mouth—"I've been poisoned."

Taroke said, "It'll be the last time, Ty, I can promise you that."

The dying man smiled, his scars curving up almost to his ears. He started to laugh but then fell into a long bout of coughing. His chest heaved, and his throat gurgled until he was unable to breathe at all. His eyes rolled up into his head. His arms twitched and then dropped, and his hands unclenched their fistfuls of dirt. The yellow fluid collected in his mouth then slowly overflowed off his lip. His eyes dropped back down, but they were unfocused and blank. Dust and pollen blew across his face, but he did not blink nor cough. Jason kicked him in the side, hard, but he did not move.

Thirteen

White light surrounded a naked body. For but a moment, or perhaps ten thousand years, all was at rest.

The thumb on the left hand twitched. It contracted on its own a few times, and then the whole hand squeezed into a fist.

Light brown eyes blinked open, and the woman drew a long, deep breath. She turned her head, left to right and then back, right to left. Empty white space surrounded her in all directions. Blindingly bright. The woman reached out her left hand, but the whiteness solidified and stopped her movement just inches above her body.

She closed her eyes and focused on her other sensations. She heard a steady mechanical humming in the distance, deep and strong, causing the slightest vibration in her chest. She smelled nothing at first… but with a little concentration, detected the faint stinging smell of alcohol and chlorine. Her limbs felt heavy. Her whole body felt warm, feverish. She felt the press of something solid across her back but could not determine if she was lying down or standing up. Maybe somewhere in-between. Her mind, her thoughts, weren't moving at their usual pace. She felt drugged.

Trapped.

Alone.

Should she call out for help? How could a place like this even exist? Even if someone or something came, would they be helpful… or harmful?

A man whispered in her ear, "Good morning, Susan."

She jerked in the opposite direction, but there was nowhere to go. She looked to her right but saw only more whiteness.

"You woke up ahead of schedule." His words were warm; she could almost feel the dampness of his breath on her cheek, despite the absence of a physical body. And his words felt safe, harmless. Only there to comfort, not to startle.

"Where… Where am I?" The woman he called Susan struggled to move her lips and tongue as she spoke. Her jaw ached.

"In a moment, you will begin to remember. Please lay back and try to relax. All your questions will be answered."

"Wait! Tell me what's going on!"

"In time, Susan. Please, do not worry."

She kicked her feet, but they did not move far nor fast. A small tremor ran down her spine and her body shivered. The strain melted away.

His warm voice continued, "Disorientation and memory loss are common side effects. Everything should be a little clearer now."

She rubbed her eyes and chuckled. Her hibernation tomb shook free, gliding to another destination.

"You're being transported to your new quarters. You may notice that you have already regained much of your memory and strength."

Susan rolled her shoulders and wiggled her toes. Her whole body felt lighter, more limber. Almost like she was twenty-five again. That was the point, after all.

"In a few minutes, you will be free to meet the current team. Your new teammates are excited for you to join them. They'll fill you in with their progress and the specificities of your role on the crew. Good luck, Susan. Remember our commitment. Remember our vow."

The lid cracked open and pulled away from her, locking seamlessly into the ceiling. Susan leaped up from her crypt-bed.

She stretched her arms over her head and twisted her back. She went to the closet, which was stocked with all her essential clothes. She donned her underwear and a sports bra, and a one-piece jumper. She pulled her wavy brown mane up off her shoulders, zippered the jumpsuit all the way up to her throat, and let her hair fall back down.

She turned to her desk; a picture of her family sat on the corner in a sleek frame. On the back, her son had written in green crayon: *good luck, mommy!* A small little red heart with the letter B sat in the bottom right corner. He always drew his hearts so carefully for her.

She rummaged through the desk drawers and found four different watches. Susan grabbed a thick, solar-powered one that looked like it had a lot of computing power. Sliding the black band onto her wrist, she tapped the face with her pointer finger; it glowed softly.

'Welcome home,' scrolled across before the time, *'19:32,'* flashed and disappeared.

Susan frowned. Seven-thirty at night was not a normal time for an awakening.

"Good evening, Susan. My name is Avery. How may I assist you?" The watch, apparently, had an AI.

The only door had a small, recessed panel, and Susan pressed it to exit.

The entryway slid open, and she stepped out of her room.

Darkness pervaded most of the hallway. Here and there, an overhead light flickered on and off, revealing several doors running all the way down the hall.

Susan lifted her wrist and whispered, "Avery, disable all your positioning and tracking programs. Mute your responses."

The watch face flashed, *'Is something wrong, Susan?'* It did not respond out loud. Susan proceeded cautiously down the hallway; a small patch of light at the far end beckoned her onward. She instinctively reached for the pistol at her waist, but of course, it was not there.

The hallway opened into an enormous cargo bay, at least two hundred and fifty yards high, maybe a mile long. Not the largest room in the station, based on her recollections from the planning meetings, but large enough to stop her in her tracks for a moment. She scanned the room for any sign of life, for any movement at all, looking past stacks of shipping containers, cargo boxes, and an assortment of different sized forklifts.

She read the coding along the front row of the shipping containers. Most of them should be empty by now.

"What in the hell is going on?" she muttered. "All right, Susie, get it together. No crew. Barracks untouched by maintenance for months. But this looks… used…"

The watch flashed at her wrist, and she caught the last half of Avery's message, *'…not as planned. Sync with active crew members for up-to-date mission details?'*

Susan whispered at her wrist, "Do not sync. Disconnect me from any onboard Bluetooth, wireless networks, or connected devices. Run local software only."

She didn't want anyone to know where she was. They may have been alerted at her awakening… They may be seeking her out at this very moment…

Susan darted into the maze of equipment and cargo boxes.

She wanted a weapon. Anything small that she could lift and wield would be better than nothing. Next to the forklift was a stack of blue plastic pallets, but they were all in good shape, no way to break anything off them without making way too much noise.

She jogged deeper into the warehouse, turning around corners with caution, eyes flashing around, seeking movement. Toward the back, she found a screwdriver and scooped it up. Better than nothing.

When she reached the far back wall, she recognized the high shuttered steel doors. Three different docking bays. In the far corner, she saw a communication box but decided to stay away. It would be foolish to draw attention to herself. If she wanted to leave, this was the place. But the moment she opened the docking bay, the other crew members would know.

If there was any crew left.

The truth was, she had already seen enough to know that the operation was not going to plan. And since she woke up outside of a structured awakening, she would not be welcome with whoever was still on board.

Human or otherwise.

But if she left, she'd never figure out what happened. And curiosity runs strong in scientists.

She remembered the military-led security briefings before their departure.

"Don't think about that, Susie. Stay focused. Avery, turn your volume back on but keep it low. Can you project holographic images?"

"Yes, Susan," the robotic voice replied a little louder than she would like. "What can I show you?"

"Do you have a blueprint of this sector?"

"Yes, Susan. May I reconnect with the onboard computer to find those blueprints, Susan?"

"Yes. But keep the tracking and locating apps off. We don't want any potentially violent beings to find us."

"That would be a negative experience for us both, Susan." The warm blue glow faded into a white pulse. "I am being blocked from joining the local devices and the onboard network, Susan."

"Okay, quit trying. We just triggered another red flag. Someone is for sure aware of us now. Let's not get caught."

"That would be a negative experience for us both, Susan."

Susan left the com-box and the lander docks behind and wandered toward the far corner. Sure enough, a recessed service stairwell peeked out from behind the false back wall. Gripping the screwdriver tighter in her fist, knuckles whitening, Susan ascended the darkened staircase, careful and quiet with each step. At the next landing, there was no exit point. No exit at the second landing… or the third… or the fourth.

She kept going up.

After climbing five flights, she arrived at a sealed door, her breathing still calm and even. Above the door, written in thick warning font, *'Do Not Open Unless Light Is Green.'*

No lights were visible at the door, not green nor any other color. The only light came from the stairwell—fluorescent, flickering, and headache-inducing.

Susan bit her tongue and put her hand on the door handle. She twisted it and pushed.

The room was dark and empty. Two small benches, fifteen feet apart, kept the room from being entirely barren. There was nothing else save another door at the far side. Above that door, in less ominous font than before:

She racked her brain, thinking about the schematics of the space station she had combed over and over before being put into hibernation. Her memory was still fuzzy on some things.

On the left side of the door were two small buttons. Like an elevator, but they were not up or down arrows. They were side by side. Left or right.

She raised her watch.

"Avery, try to reconnect to all devices again. Tell me if we are stationed above a habitable planet or not."

"Syncing now, Susan… Syncing completed. We are stationed above our assigned planet, and yes, a small region is still habitable."

"Avery, open the stopwatch."

"Yes, Susan."

"Mute yourself. Continue to not give any other device our location aboard this ship."

With no reply but a little blue flash, the watch showed *'00:00.00'*.

Susan put her finger on the right button on the wall. As she pressed the button, she whispered to her wrist, "Start."

The button lit up, and her watch began to tick off seconds. She cracked her knuckles. Someone, somewhere, probably just got a notification on their own 'Avery.' Twenty seconds passed, and then thirty and then forty. It felt like hours. After one minute and thirty-two seconds, the door cracked open. Susan paused the watch.

A tall man sat inside, wearing a purple and silver robe.

Susan hoped she concealed her shock.

On his head, above blond hair, was a golden crown, something she hadn't seen since her video lectures in elementary school. At his waist were two Personal Protection Weapons. His eyes opened, and he smiled when he saw her, but she still noticed his hand twitch toward his PPW.

He sat, legs crossed, in the middle of a small, rectangular train car, complete with benches along the walls and handles hanging from the ceiling. There were no windows, but red warnings were plastered around the compartment, reading, 'Prepare for acceleration,' or 'Please hang on,' or 'Do not exit the MiniRail until the train has come to a complete halt and the docking doors are fully open.'

Susan did not move.

He beckoned her inside. "Where are you headed, newbie? What are you doing in bay B?"

She frowned but stepped inside, nevertheless. One wrong move, and the man might shoot her with a pulse of electricity strong enough to stop her heart. He acted like everything was normal, that wearing glittering, medieval robes was just a part of the everyday routine, but that made no sense…

She turned to the side and found the guide panel, complete with seven different buttons. She pressed the one at the very bottom, next to the word 'Bridge.'

Susan jumped back out of the train just as the doors were closing shut. "Wait!"

She did not wait.

She sprinted out of the room. "Restart timer! Avery, secure docking bay B hangers and open all the hanger doors. Lock every other way into the warehouse. Un-mute."

She dashed out the door, zipped around the corner, and flew down the stairs, four steps at a time.

'00:8.49'.

"Opening now, Susan. I'm being locked out of every available security server." "Prioritize opening these docking doors."

Susan leaped the final four steps and dashed back to the landing docks.

"Come on," she muttered, glancing again at her watch.

'00:28.60'.

She may have bought herself a few minutes, but she needed to be off this ship and fast. That man would be back, and, quite clearly, he wasn't operating according to protocol.

'00:33.77'.

The first docking door began grinding upward. She didn't wait to see if any others would open. She ran and dove headfirst under the door, seeing a flash of electric blue out of her peripherals.

He was back already, somehow, firing at her from the stairwell.

"Shut the hangar door! Now!"

The garage door paused and reversed directions. With just a shrinking fraction of light to see by, Susan ran to the low orbit supply ship. A second flash of blue zapped across the hangar floor before the shuttered steel sealed shut. She yanked open the cockpit door, flung herself inside the jet, and buckled herself in. "Avery, turn this ship on and get us planet side, now!"

"Autopilot has been disabled from outside, Susan. I've disconnected the ship and myself from all devices and networks to prevent further outside intrusion. I've disconnected all Bluetooth and hi-fi connection capabilities. I cannot open the outer hanger door, Susan."

"Shit! Okay, Susie, think." Susan reached out and felt for the controls in front of her. "At least give me some light."

The watch glowed brightly, shining a wide beam of illumination across the control panel. A few brighter rays of light highlighted the ignition panel, the joystick, and the smaller missile defense panel.

She jammed her thumb on the engine start, felt the lift of gravity as she pulled gently on the joystick. She rotated the jet toward the outer doors and pushed her finger down on the red trigger on the defense panel. A blast of something collided with the bay door, triggering a depressurization. The doors ripped open at the blast site, and the vacuum of space swallowed everything in the bay, including her ship.

It lurched out of the hangar and immediately accelerated toward the brown planet below.

"I suggest firing the brake thrusters and engaging the thermal deflecting shield, Susan."

"Show me." Susan groaned through gritted teeth.

The ship shivered, and the nose burned orange as it plunged through the atmosphere. She shielded her eyes from the blinding light out the tinted window with one hand while her other hand raced across the controls, guided by her wristwatch. Despite a few blunders, Susan managed to engage the thermal shield and three separate braking mechanisms, but her descent was still brutally turbulent.

"Our speed is too rapid for a safe landing. The ship will not survive touchdown, Susan."

"We have to land it!"

"Your chair is equipped for ejection, Susan. You will have a small window to eject at a safe altitude above the habitable zone."

"How do I eject?"

Her watch aimed its flashlight at a red hook next to her seat.

The ship jerked violently to the right and began to barrel roll. Her head smacked back against the chair, pinned by the sudden rotation. Susan pulled at the joystick and fought to bring the ship back upright, but it wouldn't slow. The light disappeared outside the window, and the cockpit went dark. She was blind and spinning out of control.

"Ejection will be fatal if the ship is upside down, Susan. Your window will open in thirteen seconds."

Susan grimaced, let go of the joystick, and allowed the ship to tumble even faster to the right. She re-grabbed the joystick and pinned it forward, disabling two of the braking thrusters as she did so. The ship sped up, but the spinning slowed.

"Five seconds until ejection window."

Susan fought the urge to vomit. Her eyes watered, and her mouth filled with saliva. She couldn't even swallow. The ship continued rolling, upside down and then right side up and then upside down again. She could barely differentiate between the two, her hair floating and falling as the ship flipped, a thin green horizon spinning like an overclocked second hand out the cockpit window.

"Three…" Upside down.

"Two…" Right side up.

"One…" Upside down.

Right side up.

She pulled the hook, but it didn't budge.

"Come on," she pleaded with herself, fingers whitening around the metal.

Upside down.

She took a deep breath and gripped the hook with both hands, letting go of the joystick entirely.

The ship shuddered and plummeted.

Right side up.

She yanked the hook, hard, and the cockpit exploded above her. She and the chair launched out, more sideways than upward. She squeezed her eyes shut tight and tried to stay conscious. Cold air buffeted her as she swung wildly back and forth and ever downward, the ground surely racing up to kill her in another instant.

Instead, the parachute opened, and her plummet slowed. She opened her eyes.

She was descending toward a dark forest. Her ship shrank as it spun violently toward the horizon, then it nose-dove and exploded against a steep cliff face in the distance. A huge gushing waterfall tumbled from the cliffs landing in a lake surrounded by dense trees.

She craned her head left and right, saw mountains in one direction, but saw no sign of civilization anywhere.

Her view disappeared as she dropped into the thick jungle canopy, branches and twigs cracking and snapping beneath her heavy chair. Her descent slammed to a halt, and her head snapped down and then back into the headrest behind her.

Her parachute was tangled in the tree limbs above her.

Swinging back and forth in midair, miraculously still alive, Susan clutched the seatbelts wrapped around her shoulders.

She looked below her. The sunlight did a poor job of penetrating the thick forest canopy; the ground was dark and shadowy and at least fifty feet further down. She could see a muddy stream running below her, but not directly underneath her. It did not seem very deep. Above, she could hear fabric ripping.

Susan tried the watch. "How deep is the river below me?"

"I have insufficient data to answer your inquiry, Susan."

"Figures."

A long, loud, ripping noise forced her hand. Her chair jolted downward about five yards before snagging again.

Susan unbuckled her seatbelt and leaped forward out of the chair toward the stream, praying it was deep enough.

Her shoulder hit the water, hard, and then she was soaked, tumbling over and over in a surprisingly strong current, coughing up water between frantic strokes. Her knee banged against a jagged rock; she gasped, taking in more water than air, and the current sucked her under again. Her lungs were afire, but she couldn't find air. In the black water, she saw nothing, and as she rolled over, her outstretched arms and legs finding nothing, she knew she would surely drown.

The image of her son and husband standing at the living room window, tears rolling down their faces, leaped into her mind. She did not abandon her family for this. She survived a two-hundred-mile descent off a space station onto an alien planet—she would not be killed by twelve feet of cold water.

Her feet struck the riverbed, and she pushed herself back up, hard.

Susan coughed and sucked in air as she reemerged above the surface. She swam with the current, moving sideways instead of fighting against it. Her fingers finally found mud and grass. Susan pulled and kicked and climbed up a steep bank out of the river. She coughed up water and looked around.

Avery still glowed, his display uncracked, and Susan aimed the face around, finding nothing but shadowy green foliage surrounding her. She hiked back upriver and found her seat crashed into a pile of rocks, busted to pieces, half draped by her ripped parachute. She walked over to it and collapsed onto her hands and knees.

Her body decided it was finally time to unleash the vomit she'd been fighting. She hurled and coughed and hurled some more, mostly just river water. She hadn't eaten anything since her awakening, and there was nothing in her stomach. She wasn't hungry, though. Too full of adrenaline and a load of other fight or flight chemicals that the body dumps into the system during periods of extreme stress.

After vomiting, Susan rolled over and pulled the parachute around her shoulders.

A few minutes later, she murmured, "Avery, do you know where we are?"

"No, Susan. I have a small, insufficient amount of local geo-spatial data since the ejection, but no larger map or global positioning network to reference. Susan, my battery levels are now below 20 percent."

"You are solar-powered, right Avery? You'll be able to charge in the morning?"

"Yes, Susan, I can charge in the 'morning'. But just so you know, currently on this planet, the sun will set in seventeen galactic days. And 'morning' is one hundred and eighty-seven galactic-standard days after that."

"Shit." Susan rubbed her hands through her wet hair, squeezing it out behind her. The planet was barely rotating. That couldn't be good for civilization building. She twirled a long strip of hair around her little finger.

She couldn't think. She could barely walk, let alone form and execute complex plans. Her body was tired. Shutting down from all the excitement a few minutes ago. Life or death experiences are a huge drain on the nervous system. Her military training, and personal experience for that matter, informed her of that much. Sleep would be needed before she could be capable of anything else.

"Avery, go into power-saving mode. I'll need your light to find some fire-making supplies in this damn jungle when I wake up."

Susan stripped off her wet clothes and tried to dry herself with scraps from the parachute. She hung out her clothes over a low-hanging branch and then wrapped herself in a dry portion of the remaining parachute fabric. Thankfully, the temperature in the forest was quite warm, despite the oncoming darkness. She wouldn't freeze to death.

Barely awake, shivering and becoming delirious, Susan climbed onto a chunk of broken chair padding and closed her eyes.

She would wake up in a few hours and try to find some supplies. And then… then she would go look for some sign of advanced civilization. Ideally, the planet was developed beyond its tribal, warring stage. She had a lot of work ahead of her. Something had gone horribly wrong with the colonizing and monitoring. She would need some help to bring things back to normal. Whatever normal was for this planet.

Fourteen

Crichton was roused by one of the Acolytes. "Omm… if you want to eat…. before we ride, arise."

Crichton swallowed down an m-bar and a few strips of smoked goat meat. The black panther sat beside him, eyeing his food.

"Do not feed her," Sarpho said, watching the Sondite boy and the cat. Just to be rebellious, Crichton tossed the panther his last strip of meat once Sarpho looked away. The black cat caught it in midair, throwing a furtive look toward the bigger cat lounging a few yards away. Domray frowned at Crichton but said nothing. One of the other Acolytes smirked.

The cycle was composed of only another painful ride, and Crichton's muscles gave out sooner than the cycle before. They rode for another six candles, and again Crichton was asleep almost as soon as he fell off his horse.

The next cycle was the same. As was the next and the following, for many cycles.

They rode further and further west, away from the sun and from the Realm of the Thirsting Forest. With Memoria tied to Domray's horse, the possibility of escaping seemed less and less likely.

Always they rode west, up one hill and down the next, through unremarkable hill land. Looking forward only to poor sleep under a bright sun in the southeastern sky, Crichton began to wish he was trapped in a dweller dungeon as opposed to the slow torture of horseback riding and Domray's preaching. Domray filled the silence of the ride with speeches to no one about the way to live a life with Gahkin, or ramblings on the future of the war, or reading long verse from the Habibrok. He even spoke about the plague in Quirvop and the signs of the coming apocalypse, and how he wished the Great Flash would come sooner rather than later.

"The star life for everyone," he said, "is the true peace that we should all pray for. The droughts and famine are spreading to turn the people to Gahkin, so they are ready for the end. For the final Great Flash."

For the first and only time, Sarpho replied to Domray's musings, "I'll pray for the Great Flash when I'm old and withered, Domray, and not before."

Every few cycles Sarpho and the two cats would peel off from the group and head north toward distant hedges or bog land. They would catch up a few candles later, usually empty-handed, but every once in a while, they would bring a fresh goat or wild hog.

Crichton spent much of his riding thinking of Martin. To race through the branches with him, to share a joke that Jinala didn't understand, to make sure the tree was clear of snakes before bedding down. The stupidest memories drew the fiercest pangs of heartache. Martin being attacked by a goose when he took eggs from its nest, Martin using Jinala's hair for a wig, Martin talking in his sleep about flying in a wagon with wings like a bird.

His mind turned to darker memories sometimes too, despite his disdain for them. Again and again, he remembered when their mother passed, and he buried her in the mud by the creek. Martin barely able to walk around and place stones on her grave. Then the decision to leave the cabin. The Mud Wizard watching them from a distance, bringing them food and clothing now and again but never speaking with them, never answering their questions. Crichton knew he was a strange sort of guardian, but even he had disappeared from their lives after a while. And now Martin and Crichton, who for the longest time had only had each other, were split apart.

The first time Crichton prayed to Gahkin he did it as a kind of test to prove that He did not exist. No one answered his prayer. When he did it again, he asked a more reasonable request and whispered aloud.

"Gahkin, please give me some kind of sign that you can hear me." Crichton listened in the bright silence. Memoria or one of the other horses whinnied. They did not do that very often. "Gahkin, was that a sign?" Sarpho snored in his sleep.

Some sign.

Crichton rolled over onto his stomach. "Gahkin, please, if you are out there and you can do anything at all, just watch over Martin. And Jinala too. And, if you can, let me live to see them both again."

He awoke in the middle of the resting candles, suddenly afraid, dark fur in his face. He pulled back and saw the black panther curled next to him. One eye, golden yellow, cracked half-open. The panther watched Crichton sleepily. Crichton backed away. Looking around, he saw the purple men laying down, cloths over their eyes to dim the sunlight. The ninth candle still burned. The horses were all tied together, and the string was tied around the ankle of Sarpho. Crichton could not escape on horseback.

"She likes you, it seems," a voice said from behind him. The Acolyte who woke him in the mornings sat with his Habibrok open in his hands.

Crichton stood, a wary eye on the black panther, and moved over next to the unknown Acolyte.

"Ommm… I'm Flagg." The Acolyte extended his hand with a gentle smile. "I won't sting," he added upon the boy's hesitation. Crichton shook his hand. "Her name is Emushéré…. She is a gentle cat… Ommm… to those who treat her well.

How are you feeling?"

"Still a little weak, I guess."

"Emushéré… probably senses that. She and the other—Pincher, is his name—are our… Ommm… protection along the road." Flagg closed his eyes and tilted his great head toward the sky as he spoke. He had no hair or beard to speak of, and his cheeks sagged around his face. Every time the Acolyte paused and hummed, the droopy skin underneath his chin vibrated. It looked as if the man had recently lost a lot of weight, his skin hanging thick over his thinner frame. "She takes our… wellbeing… as her responsibility."

Crichton looked over at the black panther but did not speak. The cat stretched out a huge paw, sharp claws extended, and then retracted. It yawned and closed its eyes.

They sat in silence for a stretch before Flagg spoke again. "How do you like Domray?"

Crichton did not know how to answer. He liked him over Sarpho, but he'd prefer most predatory animals over Sarpho.

Flagg replied for him, "He can seem a bit… passionate, at first. Sarpho can be… cold and distant while Domray… Ommm… overly the opposite. They are both Gahkinly men, despite their differences. For you, though, I imagine both men might be… Ommm… overwhelming and off-putting. The men of Gahkin are not all so… finely hued instruments of intensity. I myself… prefer quiet reflection."

Crichton liked this Acolyte. "And that's why you read while everyone sleeps?"

Flagg chuckled, "No, I am awake to watch you. We don't want you… Ommm… sneaking off. The empty hills of Kydoth are… more dangerous than they may seem. Many hungry folks raiding from the north… well, they aren't picky with their meat…"

Crichton nodded. He trusted this man. He didn't know what made him say it, but he said, "I'm homesick more than real sick. I don't understand why I couldn't be left alone."

"It is only natural to feel so. Even if you are only leaving behind an… empty jungle." Flagg raised an eyebrow questioningly and then continued. "But you must remember, we took you for… the good of your physical body and your spiritual soul. A tragedy is a… Ommm… A tragedy can be a disguised blessing. A tragedy brought me to our God-King. I know Gahkin, and he knows me, and my heart is… loving because of that knowledge. One cycle—I don't like to prophesy, but I am rather sure of this—one cycle… Ommm… you shall thank us for taking you from the Thirsting Forest to Shinar, and that you have been given a… second chance to welcome Gahkin into your heart."

Crichton said quietly, "Maybe." His gaze shifted to the larger panther as it rolled over in its sleep. "What type of cat is that? I've never heard of or seen one of those before."

"That is a sabretooth tiger. It comes from… across the Verdelen River. The land of the Vistonex. One of the few creatures that can hold its own in the Everdark Realm. And survive the cold."

"How did you all come by it?"

"Well, we—the Acolytes of Shinar, that is—our rangers raise all our animals from kittens and pups and train them for our own purposes… We've only ever had but one family of sabretooth tigers. The rangers had to put down the mother… But they kept the three kittens. Sarpho raised Pincher, who's proven to be… Ommm… intensely fierce and intensely loyal. But only to Sarpho… He listens to no one else. The black one, on the other hand… She's smart. She knows that being friendly with humans goes a lot further than… Ommm… hissing at them." Flagg breathed heavily as if the conversation was tiring him.

"Who raised her?"

"She's had multiple trainers. She escaped from the pens as a young cat… showed back up a season later, and has proven a… friendly beast and a great tracker… I must say, Crichton, you speak well for having no friends to talk to in the forest."

Crichton replied, "My mother taught me well before she died." It wasn't entirely a lie.

"Indeed, she did… I'm sorry for your loss. When did she pass?"

"Over two seasons ago."

"Well, she is living her star life now. We will explain what that means soon… if you don't yet understand."

Crichton sighed. Thoughts of his mother, in a *star life* or not, saddened him.

Flagg continued, "I've enjoyed talking with you, Crichton… though I must always defer to Domray when it comes to your care and teaching."

"Thanks. Why do you have to defer to Domray? I wish you were my tutor, instead. Domray is so—"

"Ommm… zealous?"

"Well… I'm not sure what that means. He hasn't taught me anything, really. He is nice, but he just babbles about Gahkin."

"If anyone deserves… babbling… about, it is indeed our great God-King. However, I don't think we will be teaching you much while we ride through the hills. Maybe when we stop in the next village. Still… I may mention to Domray my desire to aid him in your tutelage if he doesn't mind."

"Uh, Flagg, can I ask why Domray is in charge? Sarpho seems more like the leader, and you seem the most rational. Domray is…" Crichton trailed off, not sure exactly what Domray was.

"Politically ambitious," Flagg said. "Well… Ommm… politically active… That is the phrase that works best. He was born to Acolytes… unlike Sarpho and me. And he is only in charge by law since Isaac left, who was the true leader of the party… Sarpho leads us now, in truth, as you've noticed."

"Why is Domray—how come he outranks you?"

"Ommm… you see, Crichton, Domray doesn't outrank me; he is a part of the political class. I am but a… missionary… a convert. And a member of this party for… Ommm… other reasons I won't say… Domray is wiser than he seems, I should add."

Crichton sighed. There was something strangely pleasant about listening to Flagg talk. It was almost hypnotic.

"Don't feel bad, boy, for not… understanding your new world. Shinar is a far different realm than any of the others in the Kingdom of Gahkin. There is no royalty in Shinar… There are no elder knights or independent knights… few independent farmers… the Ten Hand Council— elected by the wide population of Acolytes—runs the realm. Ommm… it is a system we'd like to bring to the other realms, but they cling to the old ways… the ways before they were united by the God-King when he visited from the stars. Which is understandable… which is why we don't force our system upon them… Of course, you know little of either society… right, Crichton?"

For how slow and exhaustive talking was for the Acolyte, Flagg seemed to enjoy it. Crichton said, "Yeah. I only know that we—I mean, the Sondites—we don't have a realm anymore."

"Yes, the Sondite situation is rather vexing…"

Crichton frowned. He'd never heard that word before.

"…Ommm… troubling, that means. I have prayed on the fate of your people for many seasons. Yet… as the Habibrok foretells, 'the fleeting world shrinks as the immortal world grows…' The Great Flash grows ever closer, Crichton, and many think it is coming very soon… Ommm… The world seems to be heading down a dark path, but Gahkin will save us. You must not worry, for we will explain all these things to you in the coming cycles and seasons. For now, I think I should silence myself. I fear I am becoming overwhelming… in my own way." He looked down at Crichton with warm eyes.

Crichton said, "I guess everything is going to be overwhelming to me, huh?"

"Only for a short while… Gahkin blesses boys—excuse me, young men… with strength and adaptability that… old men like me don't have. I'm sure I'd be more overwhelmed in your forest than you will be in my city."

They sat in silence for a good while, the sun at their backs, sitting in the dirt and looking west. The young Sondite dreamed with his eyes on Emushéré. "I don't plan on running away, by the way, if you want to rest," Crichton said, truthful in his words.

Flagg smiled. "I appreciate your… Ommm… empathy, boy, but I'm very well-rested. You should go back to sleep while you can… We still have another candle to burn for rest before we ride again."

Crichton nodded. His body was tired from all their traveling, but his mind was racing. He knew so little of the world outside the Thirsting Forest. He crawled back to his mat and lay next to Emushéré, albeit a little warily. When he finally fell asleep, he dreamed of a happy future and not of corrupted memories from his broken past. Still though, every time he slept, Martin's absence made even his best dreams bittersweet.

Fifteen

Martin sat in the western tower, a captive once again.

But the Sondite boy was no longer alone, for the Mud Wizard was imprisoned with him. And after being left with the wizard for many cycles, Martin realized the wizard was crazy. Not quirky, but full-on crazy. Evrost crawled around the room on all fours, examining the furniture and the floor, running his long fingernails along the stone walls. He muttered things like, "Brilliant!" and "What ingenuity!" while walking backward upstairs or while laying underneath a bed, sheets hung to the floor, unable to see anything in the dark. Martin did enjoy the fort he made, but then the Mud Wizard destroyed it. Spinning in a circle and blowing air out his mouth, he called himself a 'hurricane'—whatever that meant.

Now Martin, sprawled on his bed, watched the wizard and his frogs while he waited for Jinala to join them. Evrost had been tying long strings together, and now he tied a smaller string onto one of the frogs. The Mud Wizard sat his first frog, Croak, down onto the ground and began tying the other end of the small string to his second frog, Ribbit. Tied together, the wizard proceeded to tie the long string to the middle of the short string. He sat them on the windowsill and poked them on the heads. One frog blinked dully, and the other turned around and looked out the window.

"Now remember—"

One frog leaped out of the tower, pulling the other one with it.

"Wait!" The wizard had the long string still in his hand and reeled the two frogs back up. He took them in his cupped palms. The non-jumping frog sat idle, somehow unfazed after being drug over the edge and plunging through the open air. The frog that had leaped out kicked energetically in the Mud Wizard's hand, fighting to get free. "Captivity is not treating you well, eh Ribbit?"

"Riiiiibit!" the frog cried.

"Fine, fine." The wizard tossed them out the window again. "Geronimo!" He let the string slip through his hands for a while before tightening his grip and lowering the frogs the rest of the long way down. When they finally reached the ground, the wizard shouted, "Don't just wait around! Get going! Tell Chirp he'll have to feed himself for a few more cycles!"

Martin said, for about the fifth instance, "Frogs can't talk, Ev."

The Mud Wizard turned to the boy and jabbed an accusatory finger at him. "I've found frogs to be more intelligent than some humans, I'll have *you* know."

"You're going to make Jinala's father mad if you keep yelling." Martin rolled over and stood from his bed. "Instead of trying to free the *frogs*, we should be worrying about freeing ourselves."

"Freeing ourselves? What do you think, Croak and Ribbit are just going to save themselves and leave me behind?" The Mud Wizard turned around and looked back out the window. "Well, Ribbit might actually, but that's why I tied Croak to him. Croak would never abandon us. He and I have a special connection."

Martin murmured, "Sure." He wandered over to the window and peered out.

The Thirsting Forest stretched out beneath him in every direction, climbing all the way into the distant mountains hundreds of miles away.

Martin breathed in the fresh air and stared out into the only home he had ever known. The jungle air was wet and heavy, thick with pollen, accented by lavender and gardenia and leaf rot. Different sections of the forest had different aromas, and only a few held a hint of smoke from the castle. He could smell the sweet moldy stench of the thick swamps, the pungent plant pollen, but it was fainter than usual now and corrupted by the thick intoxicating odor of burning algae oil and charred firewood. Martin closed his eyes and breathed in deeply, recalling the smells of the forest from memory as much as he drew them in from outside.

Footsteps echoed up the stairwell from outside the door. Martin dashed away from the window and peeked out under the door. Sure enough, two pairs of feet stomped toward their room. Martin moved out of the way and stood flat against the wall.

The door swung open, and Martin dashed—

"That is never going to work, no matter how many times you try it, Martin." James Killovew turned the boy around and prodded him back into the room. Jinala slipped in behind her father and moved next to the Sondite. The Mud Wizard stood by the window, whistling casually. "Evrost, for Gahkin's sake, was it necessary to drop those things out the window and then scream at them like that? I could have just taken them outside if you wanted to let them go."

"What, hand them over to my jailer? I've smelled the buffets you brew, barbarian. Their legs are for hopping, not chewing."

James ignored him and turned to Jinala.

"All right, a couple more questions, and then you can stay with Martin and the wizard for the rest of the cycle. A good number of advisers are leaving, along with more than half the castle soldiers and families to set up camps along the northern realm border and at Northtown. Do you know why we would do this?"

"In case the food raiders come back? Like Uncle Eric was saying?"

"Correct. In this cycle's council meeting, we will discuss dispatching more to Kydoth's South Port to help protect the next shipment of m-bars. Why would we do this?"

"So, Lord Early knows we support his realm? Protecting the river trade routes. I didn't think the Kydothians were a threat to us?"

"No, they are not. But I want his realm to be a strong ally to us. Not just a neutral neighbor to the west. Why?"

"If something happens with the Grayson's nephew, you want him on our side?"

"I want them on our side, yes, no matter who might become enemies to us. When building alliances or building any relationship for that matter, you can't just do the bare minimum. You need to show real care and awareness and support. Only that will get you help in return when you need it most."

"Can I attend the advisers meeting this cycle? Just to listen in. I promise not to interrupt or say anything."

"No, you can't, Jinala. But soon. I *do* want you to have a general idea of what's happening in the castle, though. You don't need to snoop, okay? I'll keep you involved in my decisions from now on and tell you as much as I can." James paused for a moment and then turned his head a little to look at Martin. "I think maybe I've kept too much from the both of you for too long. Soon, Martin, I expect you'll be able to walk around the castle. And soon, Jinala, you'll be sitting by me in *all* of my meetings. We just need to make it to Sundown."

Martin leaped into the air, shouting, "Yes!" By the time he landed, though, he was troubled by another thought. "What about Evrost, though?"

"Oh no, he'll probably be stuck in this tower for the rest of his seasons."

"That's not really fair. Why do I get to roam if he can't?"

"That is because, Martin, he is more uncooperative and more immature than you and Jinala combined."

Martin cocked his head and looked at Evrost. The wizard twiddled his thumbs and stared at the ceiling. He was not listening.

Without saying farewell, Lord Killovew turned to leave. "Wait!" Martin said, lunging forward and grabbing onto the back of his cloak. "When are me and Jinala gonna be mature enough to rescue my brother?"

"Martin Raak," Lord Killovew said, turning and kneeling. "We are not rescuing your brother. You and Jinala are most certainly not rescuing him. Like I said, we have to hope that your brother will be set free by events already set in motion."

"What events?"

James shook his head. "No more questions. You need to be patient." He left, locking the tower door behind him.

"What is he talking about, Gina?" Martin asked, dropping onto his butt from squatting on his haunches.

Jinala said in a hushed breath, "Events to do with the Acolytes, maybe." She looked around, afraid someone might have overheard.

"Then…" Martin was onto something, an idea at the tip of his tongue, but Jinala was too impatient to let him reason it out himself.

"Father's been bothered by them for as long as I can remember, and he's been saying stuff to Sir Trittion in his study. Secretive stuff." Martin liked the sound of secretive stuff. "Before Jason left, he spent a lot of cycles in Father's study saying secretive stuff to him too. I think he knows something the Acolytes don't. I—"

"But how will that help my brother get—"

"I'll tell you if you stop interrupting me, Mart."

"I'll interrupt you if I want to interrupt you." Martin crossed his arms but then realized he really wanted to hear more about how they could help Crichton. "Okay, I won't interrupt anymore."

"Good." Jinala sat down next to him on the floor. The Mud Wizard, still beside the window, listened to them with a wry smile on his face. Jinala said, "I think that Father knows the Acolytes are going to lose their rule of the kingdom. I think the union of the realms is going to disintegrate. The northern realms are starting to face serious famine from what I hear." The Mud Wizard clucked his tongue in disagreement. Jinala looked up. "Am I wrong?"

"Hmm? Oh, yes, maybe not, but undoubtedly. At least, for what I have computed."

"Computed?" Martin asked.

"Like figured, except smarter and exacter. Duh."

"You're confusing enough without making up your own words," Jinala said.

The Mud Wizard squinted at her and itched his head. "I… don't think I made that one up."

So…" Jinala put her thumb to the middle of her forehead. "So… the realms aren't going to break apart?"

The Mud Wizard stepped closer to the children. "Sounds sounder. Those priests provide food to them all, right?"

"But then how would the Acolytes rules not matter anymore, then, if they control the food?"

Martin asked suddenly, "It would be better for Crichton if the Acolytes didn't have power, right?"

"Right," Jinala said, dismissing Martin with a wave of her hand, still in thought. "But then, how… how will… how can it change? The laws of the Acolytes exist because the Acolytes have power because the God-King gave them power when He united the realms. The God-King was the one who brought

152

civilization together in the first place."

The Mud Wizard sat down next to the youngsters. "Forget about it, Jinala. Listen to this. Once upon a time… I ran in a mighty wolf pack."

"Not now, Evrost," Jinala said, putting both thumbs against her forehead and thinking hard, eyes closed.

Martin wanted to hear the story, "Go on, Ev. Did you change into a wolf? Or were you still just a man?"

"I was both a wolf and at the same time—not a wolf. There were thirty or more of us, and we loped along a range at the foot of the Ice Mountains. My pack once was the strongest ever, united by the giant, ferocious alpha male. But now we were starving. Our stomachs were sucked up against our spine, each of our ribs visible through our matted fur. The alpha male was old and weakened and far from the monstrous wolf he once was in his youth.

"The alpha male and female found just enough food to keep the pack from keeling over and dying of hunger. But it was not enough. I was the wolf wizard, and I knew that there was more food out in the empty white hills. 'Away from the mountain,' I howled,"

Evrost titled his head back and howled, lonely and sad, into the ceiling of the western tower. Martin joined him, and they both howled, an elder and a pup.

"Knock it off, you two!" Jinala shoved Martin into the Mud Wizard, and the wolfish cries stopped. A laugh played on her lips, but she reigned it in. Martin knew she wanted to howl, but she was too *mature* to join in on the fun.

Evrost continued his story, "'Away from the mountain!' I howled. But none of the pack had gone before, and they were afraid." The Mud Wizard looked whimsically out the window before continuing. "I actually don't remember what happened next…"

"Come on," Martin pleaded, "Tell us."

Evrost rubbed his long wispy beard, thinking.

Jinala spurted out, "Wait, Evrost, does this story mean something? Is it an… oh, what's the word?"

Evrost smiled but said nothing, still playing with his beard and gazing out the window.

Jinala suddenly perked up, "An allegory! That's the word. Is this story an allegory, Evrost?"

"Maybe," he said, and he paced slowly toward the window. He turned and walked back toward the locked door, absentmindedly twirling his beard around his pointer finger. "But if so, we need to remember the ending… No," he muttered, looking at the children, but thinking to himself, "No, I don't think the ending is decided yet. I think the pack may still be at the mountain, may still be howling as we speak."

"Well, speaking of making our own endings," Jinala pulled a key ring with a single key from a side pocket. "Are you up for a little exploring, Martin? We don't need to wait any longer, like my father said. He's going to his council meeting; half the castle will be there. I want to show you something." She walked to the door, stuck the key in the lock, and twisted.

Martin smiled. "I've been waiting for you to ask me that question. Do you want to come with us, Evrost?"

"No, no, I'm quite content letting my frogs do the exploring for me. I'm just going to stay here and try to find bugs."

Martin said, "Alrighty then, have fun with that," and followed Jinala out of the tall tower room. Martin couldn't figure out the wizard; bug counting seemed to be as exhilarating to him as conjuring magic, but he didn't worry over it too much. He had a castle to explore.

They curled down a long set of stairs, taking them near the base of the tower. Jinala led Martin quickly around a couple stone hallways without any windows, then they emerged into a big room loaded with weapons and armor. Different sized swords and knives, traditional bows and cross bows, and shields of all different shapes were organized along wooden poles that jutted out from the left side of the room. Along the right side hung leather and steel chest plates and vests, a separate row of helmets, plus boots and steel and leather bracers.

"Wow." Martin breathed. "Are we going to take some of this stuff and go find my brother?"

"Huh?" Jinala responded, walking down the middle of the room. She chuckled. "No, Martin, we aren't going to battle. Are you crazy? This stuff is down here if we ever need to arm the realm for war. We are just cutting through."

They emerged from the other side into the public walkways of the castle proper. Now Martin could see windows set evenly along hallways, candles, and torches lit along interior corridors, and fancy artwork and rugs hanging from the stone walls. Jinala moved quickly but quietly and they snuck around a couple sunlight splashed corridors. After turning a corner, she paused for a moment, then slipped behind a big red tapestry that draped all the way from the ceiling to the floor.

"Follow me," her muffled voice called. "Now!"

Martin expected to go down a secret tunnel. When he snuck behind the tapestry, Jinala just stood there, pressed against the wall, waiting. She held a finger up to Martin's mouth when he was about to talk. They waited for a long couple of moments, and then two pairs of footsteps echoed toward them—one pair clanking in armor, the other ruffling along in puffy boots. They grew louder, passed right by the tapestry, and then grew quieter again. Once they could no longer hear the steps, Jinala grabbed Martin, and they slunk back out into the hallway.

They darted down two more corridors and then slipped behind another tapestry.

This one *did* conceal a secret tunnel. The dark corridor only ran about twenty feet, and Mart could see a border of light etched at the far end.

"Mart," Jinala said, "after we get out into the next hallway on the other side, it is going to be a long way to the next hiding spot. This is going to be the hardest part. We will have to run fast and cross past three other corridors. So, follow me and move quickly when I do."

The tunnel was short in length and height but still rather dark. When they exited, they emerged from behind yet another tapestry. Jinala looked both ways and then pulled Martin out. They dashed until Jinala drew to a stop in front of an intersecting hallway.

"Oh, no," she said when she looked around the corner.

"What is it?" Martin whispered.

"Quick, go back! Go back to the servants' crossing."

"The what?"

"The tunnel, go back to the tunnel!" Jinala shoved him backward, then added, "I'll stall them."

Martin scrambled back up the hallway, breathing heavy and smirking a little. Unlike his older brother, Martin enjoyed a little danger. He slipped behind the tapestry and into the tunnel. He tried to calm his heavy breathing as best he could and listened. Based on the rapid thumping footsteps, at least three people were walking closer.

A squeaky male voice said, "You do indeed make your way all over this big castle, Jinala. You know, when Jason was your age, the only place I ever found him was out with the knights in the training yards… or in the kennels or… maybe the stables. Or, you know, he did spend a good amount of time hawking in the fringe forest…"

The voices had seemed to stop right outside the tapestry, at the entrance to the hidden hallway. Martin stepped further back.

"Anyhow," the voice continued, "he spent all his time outside, is what I'm getting at, playing with his swords and his bow and arrows and his animals. But you! It's as if you remain aloof on purpose. I've never seen you in the same place more than twice, I'd wager. And that includes the classroom! Now you could learn a thing from Mikder. Mikder loves studying, right boy?"

Another male voice, even higher-pitched and squeakier than the first, answered, "Yes sir, Mr. Finch, sir."

"You and Jason… well, the two of you aren't all that similar, but the both of you certainly never took a liking to my arithmetic classes. Now, as you know, I find arithmetic to be a rather important subject for even the royal children to learn."

"Right," Jinala said. "Well, uh, nice, you know, talking to you."

The footsteps did not proceed further down the hallway. They came closer to the tapestry hiding Martin's body.

The voice of Mikder came again, this time closer. "Mr. Finch, sir, why are you st… st… staring at this rug?"

"This is not a rug, Mikder. This is a piece of art. From Shinar."

"Why are you staring at a piece of art, Mr. Finch?"

The teacher chuckled in his high-pitched voice, "Art is supposed to be stared at Mikder, and pondered. Good art, anyway. But Mikder, behind this tapestry is another of the short-cuts I was showing you earlier. The castle seems like a maze until you know all its hidden paths. Once you do, you will be able to move much more directly through its halls. Now this one here will take us across toward the armory."

The tapestry rose into the air, about to expose Martin.

Jinala spurted out, "Oh, don't go in there, Mr. Finch!" The tapestry paused its ascent. Martin crept backward even further.

"Gahkin's wands, Jinala, why not? My goodness girl, is everything all right?"

"I… uh… I saw a giant rat crawl in there just a moment ago."

Martin heard a shriek and then the teacher's voice from further away. "A rat! Bury me, why didn't you say so earlier? Oh, I hate rats." Martin snorted, despite his best efforts. What kind of grown-up was afraid of a rat?

The younger boy spoke, still very close to the hanging tapestry, "I like rats! Can I see?"

The tapestry wiggled. Martin held in a groan and moved all the way to the far end of the tunnel. Behind him, he heard the clank of metallic boots. He could not escape either way. Trapped like a… Like a rat, indeed.

"Go ahead, Mikder, but don't you dare let it come back out here. I'll go and get… someone… who can handle the vile thing."

The tapestry swung halfway open again. Martin braced for the scream that would get him caught.

"Wait!" Jinala said. "Mikder, I command you not to look in there."

The tapestry swung shut.

"Now, Jinala, he can look if he wants. We should make sure it's still in there. The rat won't bite you, princess; it'll go for Mikder."

"I don't care if it goes for me," the boy said, sounding strangely happy about the prospect.

The tapestry opened for a third time, again revealing the lower half of a boy no older than Martin.

"No!" Jinala shouted. "I am the Princess of the Thirsting Forest! This bracelet is not on my wrist because it looks pretty. If I command something, Mikder, it is to be obeyed. Do you understand?"

"Young lady, your father would be ashamed! What has come over you? A rat is no excuse to speak-"

"I. Am. The. Princess. I don't want that rat running out here. I said I forbid it, so it is forbidden! Mikder, drop it now and leave this hallway."

"Yes, ma—ma—ma'am, pri—pri—pri—princess." The boy stuttered.

"Jinala, I am going to be speaking with your father about this. You scared Mikder back into bad stuttering after all his hard work. Come along, Mikder."

Martin heard them walk away and then peeked back into the hallway. Jinala waved him out.

"Hurry!" she whispered. "Someone will be back soon."

Martin ducked down and rushed out into the hallway, noticing the sweat on his forehead only after it dripped into his eyes. A part of him wished they had seen him. Maybe they would ship him off and send him to wherever Crichton went. They ran past the three hallways and then stopped underneath a wide window. Jinala vaulted right out without even looking.

Martin peered over; she had landed in soft grass a few feet below. Martin followed her, plopping down into the grass, ready to keep running. Quietly they crossed through the small garden, walled on all sides but open to the elements above. The sky was a bright shade of blue, streaked with wispy orange clouds. Jinala and Martin made for a large leafy bush and ducked inside the foliage. Safely hidden by the thick greenness around them, they sat down.

"This used to be my mother's private garden."

"Used to be?"

"Before she died," Jinala said softly.

"Oh." Martin didn't know what to say. He had never talked much about his dead mother, nor had he bothered to ask Jinala about hers. He never thought she would have lost a parent like he had. She was royalty, he was an outlaw. He didn't think things like that would happen to people like the Killovews.

"It's a nice garden," Martin said.

"Yeah."

"Lots of flowers."

"Yeah, she liked the tall yellow ones."

"Hmm." Martin looked at the ground. "I don't remember my mother."

"Me neither. It was Father who told me she liked the yellow ones."

"Oh." Martin looked up at Jinala. "Crichton told me that my mother liked the purple orchids in the forest."

"I like those kinds, too."

The children were silent for a while. Martin looked at Jinala, and she looked at him.

"So," Jinala said eventually, "the castle's not too bad, huh?"

"It's not the jungle… but yeah, I could see it being fun to explore. I wish I didn't have to worry about getting caught, though."

"Yeah, same."

"I guess that just makes it more exciting, though."

"Definitely."

After another few quiet moments, Jinala leaned over and took Martin's hand.

"Martin?"

"Yes?"

Martin had never cared about her touching him before, but suddenly, her hand felt very tingly and soft in his own hand. It was softer than anything he could remember. He looked her in her green eyes.

"I don't know what's going to happen, but I feel like something important is happening to both our brothers and to the kingdom, and we are not involved in it at all. Like we are just bystanders."

"Yeah," Martin said. "Yeah, I feel that way too."

"You are my best friend here, you know? Now that my brother and Crichton are gone, you and I have to stick together."

"Well, you're literally the only person I know anymore, so don't worry about me leaving you."

Jinala laughed. "You know my father. And Sir Trittion. And the Mud Wizard."

"Yeah, but they're adults. You are my only *friend.*"

She smiled. "Yeah, you are my only *real* friend, too."

Martin didn't know what to say. He felt his hand getting sweaty as he continued to hold hers.

"Jinala?"

"Yes?"

"I want to get my brother back. And I know you want to make sure you get your brother back too. We can't just wait for the adults to fix it. I've waited for the Mud Wizard all my life, and all he ever did was watch my brother get taken away from me."

"Okay," Jinala said. "I'm glad you said that. Because I have an idea. Follow me. And be quiet about it."

She stood up out of the bushes and jumped to the windowsill above them. She pulled herself up and then turned to help Martin, but he was already standing next to her.

"You'll never out climb me," he said.

She pointed up above their heads. "See that fourth windowsill all the way up there?"

"Yeah?"

Jinala jumped up and grabbed hold of the sill above her. "Race you to it."

Martin climbed as he had always climbed, instinctual and fearless. He tossed himself up to each window, though it was a far jump, and pulled himself up with perfect balance, not stopping to steady himself on the wall or bothering to look down. He stood on the lip of the fourth window as Jinala, breathing heavy, pulled herself up onto it.

"You're too fast," she said.

"Now where?"

"This was my mother's study, which means all we must do is cross the hall and listen at my father's door. After his council meetings, Sir Trittion and he sit in there and talk. Come on. Now's the perfect opportunity to find out what's going on." She rolled off the lip of the window, opened the door, and crossed into the hallway. It was empty. She snuck over to the door, motioning Martin to join her. "You watch that way," she whispered, "and I'll watch this way."

They pressed their ears up against the door crack, heads craned, watching each other's back.

A voice from within said, "There is no hawk that we could ensure Jason will receive, not at this point on his journey."

Lord Killovew's voice added, "No, by now they are probably within the Shinar realm borders, maybe all the way to Fessdri. Those rookeries are too carefully monitored. We will send a letter to Eric under the guise of the secure borders initiative and send a contingency letter to Sir Damian. It is up to Sir Breigo and Jason now. We just need to buy them time. No suspicion or questions about our realm can make it to the Ten Hand Council before Sundown."

"The final thing, James. I didn't bring it up earlier with the council. Chieftain Alexi, well, he is not known for being communicative or getting involved in larger political affairs, so it was strange he sent a letter addressed to me, directly."

Her father was silent for a long moment, then asked, "What did he say?"

"I don't think he wanted it to fall into the wrong hands, Lord. If you remember, he has no great love for any outsiders, and he doesn't hesitate to tell any who asks. He sent it to me because he knows I can have confidential conversations with you."

"Yes, so, what did he say in the letter?"

"Only a few cycles ago, there was a loud explosion of some kind, and some of his people saw a… well, he wrote 'giant fireball' outside of his village near the border, near the Edengrove cliffs, in the deep woods. A few hunters went out to investigate and found someone… strange. They described her like, well, almost like Evrost."

"How so?"

"He used the word 'magic,' my lord. Called her a witch. They are keeping her in chains, awaiting a response from you directly."

"Gahkin's wands…" Lord Killovew murmured.

Martin and Jinala pulled back from the door and looked at each other. Martin mouthed the word 'witch', and Jinala nodded with wide eyes. They put their ears back against the door.

"—is already too many, don't you think?"

"You know I agree, my lord."

"But… I don't know, Evrost has gotten so much worse of late. His body may not age, but his mind certainly does. He doesn't make sense anymore. He used to be a little odd, but never like he is now. If this witch has powers like Evrost, we need her kept from the Acolytes. She might have answers to where their powers come from. And she may be crucial to helping us keep all the realms fed and peaceful if our plan succeeds."

"*Once* the plan succeeds, my lord."

"Right."

"I think we need to go see this witch ourselves."

"Well, yes, I'd like to. But I can't exactly leave the castle with this much turmoil going on now. Not right before Sundown. The advisers are still rattled from Isaac's performance in the great hall. And you heard the rumors from Northtown and our potential problem along the border. Dissenters and demonstrators who think *we* are not giving out fair rations. They'll march on the castle if they get one more reason to think the Killovew family doesn't support the realm. If they hear I went gallivanting off into the forest…" Lord Killovew whistled then continued. "They'll think I've as good as abandoned them."

"If Prince Jason were here, we could send him with a handful of knights."

Lord Killovew sighed. "Yes, and in another two seasons, we could send Jinala. But Jinala's not ready yet. I hate that I can't trust the girl to make the right decisions. She's too young and too hardheaded."

Sir Trittion did not respond. Silence sat on the far side of the door. Martin was about to lean away again when James spoke.

"I think I may have a better plan. Go get Jinala and bring her back to me. Leave Martin and the wizard locked up there."

Martin looked at Jinala and she gulped. She grabbed Martin and jumped away from the door. She put her finger over her lips, and they dashed back down the hallway.

They quickly moved through the castle and wound their way back to the tower room where the Mud Wizard was waiting.

"How many bugs did you count, Evrost?" Martin asked as he walked back inside, seeing the wizard still lying on the ground. Jinala locked the door behind her and tucked the keyring back into her blouse.

"There's just the one, Mart, that really matters, but… still M.I.A, I'm afraid. Up to Croak to catch that one."

Martin and Jinala rolled their eyes, and then Jinala said, "Evrost, I might not have much time, but we heard about a witch with powers like yours. Does that make any sense to you?"

Evrost squinted at them. "What do you mean, a witch?"

"Apparently, there was some big explosion in the woods, and one of father's chieftains went out with his men and caught her. They say she has magic like you. They've got her chained up somewhere."

Evrost's eyes flashed as he looked out the window. "People fear what they don't understand. But I would very much like to meet her."

"We are going to try to get you two together." Martin thumped the wizard on the back, trying to console him. The wizard grinned widely down at him. "Oh, make sure to tell Sir Trittion we never left this tower, Evrost, when he comes up here," Martin added.

"Mart, if my father sends me away, it's up to you to find this witch and see if she can help our brothers."

"Why would your father send you away?" Martin asked, "It sounded like he just wanted you to help him with something."

"No, I know my father. I'm just a nuisance to him. He's going to do it to keep me from getting into trouble with you two." Jinala pulled the ring with the single key from her blouse and tossed it to Martin. "Here, keep this in here, in case you ever need to escape, and I don't come back."

Martin heard footsteps coming up the stairs. He tossed the key ring under the bed and kicked a clump of bedsheets toward the bedframe, hiding the key from view.

The door lock clicked, and then the knob twisted, and Sir Trittion walked in.

"The children have never left this tower!" Evrost shouted the statement at the elder knight.

Trittion tilted his head and stared at Evrost. Then he turned toward Jinala. "Where did you go?"

"They didn't go anywhere!" Evrost said, then turned a made a dramatic wink at Martin. Trittion could clearly see him wink at the boy.

Martin clapped both his hands over his eyes and murmured, "Evrost, you really need to work on your subtlety."

"Were you eavesdropping again, Jinala?"

"No, of course not, Sir Trit."

Evrost added, "They couldn't have been eavesdropping, knight; they were too busy telling me about a witch!"

Martin groaned.

Sir Trittion took Jinala firmly by the upper arm and escorted her out of the room. He slammed the door and locked it.

Evrost looked to Martin. "Was it something I said?"

Sixteen

Crichton lowered the candle closer to the map, held down at the corners by black river stones. Though the sun was still full above the horizon in the southeastern sky, the clouds were dark and the hills foggy, so there was little light. The only window looked to the west, and even thrown wide open, Crichton needed to squint to see the map. Twilight had come to the western half of the Kydoth Realm already.

Domray drug his fingers along the alley between the tall streaks of hills in Kydoth. They had moved west at a great pace but were still far south of Shinar.

Domray explained, "The quickest way to Shinar is to board a trade ship at the North Kydoth port on the Verdelen. With the Vistonex raids, however, the river may not be safe. We will not know the truth of this danger until we reach the Traveling Town of Early, which may be a little difficult to locate."

"But if it is such a risk," Crichton added, putting his finger to the map, drawing a path to the north, "why did we not cross over these high hills back here and move north then, through the flood plains in a direct path to… uh… Zon…der…wan. We could have met the God-King's Road there and followed it to… here, uh….Hebruh and then to uh… Fess…dri." Crichton read each word on the map with slow alliteration, but he pronounced them all well for a fresh reader. "Then we go right into the Grand City of Gahkin. Shinar can't be as dangerous to reach by land as by the Verdelen. We wouldn't have been in the wild for as long, nor risk the chance of wasted travel."

"If speed was no matter, and other tasks not given unto the fingers of the Third Hand," Domray said, taking his eye from the map and looking out the window at the dense fog to the west, "then perhaps we would have chosen that easier path. But for now, concern yourself only with our routes and our plans, and make the road known in your head. If your skill and heart prove true, which I think it will, there may come a time the First Hand appoints you to draw your own path. Until then, we make for Early. Our trust in Gahkin has helped us find their trail. We will catch up with them soon, I'm sure. Perhaps even this cycle."

Then this cycle is my last chance. "Why does Early stay on the move? I understand the Vistonex could cross the river, but why would anyone settle a town so close to danger?"

"Well, the town started out as no more than a trade caravan between the two ports at the north and south side of the Dark Bend. When the Vistonex crossings began to increase, the traders needed more protection, so more and more Kydoth knights were assigned to the convoy. Eventually, Lord Gregory Early himself joined them, being the old, brave… *traditionalist* that he is. The rest of the royal family stays at Castle Kydoth. Lord Early, though, refuses to abandon the merchants of his realm to raids by the Vistonex."

"It's just traders and guards, then?"

"Not only, Crichton, no. Wherever people gather, the needs of society grow. As more knights and the Lord's advisers and then the Lord of Kydoth himself went, other citizens went too. They decided to join the force hoping to find profits… or to earn Lord Early's favor, or—if they lived along the banks—just to simply find safety in numbers. With each season the town has grown."

"And now we are going to accompany them on their way to the North Port."

"Yes, though we must be very close to the North Port already. All this fog suggests the river is nearby. Plus, I need to talk with—" Sarpho entered the room. Domray made no motion to hide the map, for it was too late. "Sarpho," he said, bowing his head. "I hope the peace of Gahkin is with you at the start of this new cycle."

"It is not!" Sarpho said. He shoved Domray from the table, knocked the smooth stones to the floor, and grabbed up the map. He scowled at Domray. "He is not to be trusted, fool." He raised his other hand as if to smack the young Sondite's tutor. Crichton stepped in-between the two, freezing the yet-struck strike.

"Move aside, boy, before I chain you to your animal again."

"You will not do such a thing," Domray said confidently, though staying behind Crichton to utter his disagreement. "He has proven his loyalty, and he has a strong desire to know our Creator. He is far from his home. It is clear Gahkin's love is in his heart. Yet here you are, a representative of that same miraculous love, showing Crichton that violence and distrust may be traits of those touched by the God-King. He shall not flee. I swear it in Gahkin's name. May our beasts devour me if I am wrong."

Crichton's plan was, of course, to flee.

He spent the last five cycles expressing interest in learning more arithmetic and geography just for an excuse to study the map. Just as Crichton planned, Domray thought the map would be an excellent teaching tool. After going over realm geography and then addition and subtraction using the distances on the map, Crichton expressed curiosity in their pace and their path, and Domray revealed to him all he needed to know. But now…

Sarpho exhaled deeply, lowered his arm, and squeezed his fists at his side. He turned and left the room with the map under his arm. The door slammed shut behind him, and Domray clapped Crichton on the shoulder. "My good boy, your heart proves more benevolent each cycle! And your true faith is building! Gahkin will mold you into a great tool for the benefit of the entire kingdom. Your spirit shines with His aura!"

Crichton smiled, but his heart was torn. If he fled, Domray would probably be devoured by the tiger or at least punished harshly by Sarpho. If he stayed, he committed himself to abandoning his brother, perhaps for the rest of his life.

He would race to his brother without hesitation if Martin's life was in danger, bury whoever else might die. However, Crichton could not convince himself that Martin *was* in danger. Martin may miss his older brother as Crichton missed him, but the boy was either still living in the fringe forest or was with Jinala in the secret rooms of Castle Killovew. If Crichton tried to reach Martin now, odds were he would bring more danger down upon him than if he just left his brother alone. With Isaac and company riding north to Chasm castle and then Quirvop and the rest of the Acolytes traveling back to Shinar, the Thirsting Forest was the safest place for Martin to stay hidden. Far away from the Acolytes. And far away from war.

And if his star life was truly in jeopardy, well, he was a young boy with a lot of growing and thinking to do. Crichton could not believe that Gahkin would deny an innocent child, Sondite or otherwise, from a pleasant star life.

The escape would be dangerous enough, and now he would be fleeing with the knowledge that he was dooming another man to savage murder. And leading a manhunt back toward Martin. For now, Crichton realized he would just pray for Martin but do nothing else.

"Domray, I would never run. Where would I run to?"

"You don't have to convince me, boy!" Domray smiled, unworried as ever. "The time for study is—apparently—over. Let us go downstairs. Our host should have a nice breakfast ready for our departure."

Crichton ate with Domray and Flagg, forcing down half an m-bar and burned potatoes and onions. While the two benevolent Acolytes talked of Domray's mundane political aspirations, Crichton watched Sarpho and the eternally silent Rulbiss at the other table. Crichton was convinced the hawking ranger was mute, but Flagg and Domray both insisted he could speak when he so desired. Sarpho said a few things to Rulbiss under his breath, but Rulbiss only nodded and continued eating; he did not respond. Crichton shook his head and turned back to his own table.

"—Depending on the number of new members after the Green farm is brought under, of course."

"We... have been gone a long while, friend, you may underestimate the number of openings... The Green's and a dozen others could have been settled...

they may have opened many branches…"

"Yes, opened them and then filled them all while we were away." Domray chuckled.

Sarpho stood and said, "Finish your lounging. We will depart soon."

"Come now, my friend, we are close enough. We should spend an extra candle in comfort while we still have fresh food to enjoy. What say you, Sarpho?"

Sarpho looked at Domray and snorted. He left the room and Rulbiss followed him outside.

Crichton said, "I don't know why you try to be so nice to him."

"Hush, Crichton. Remember, pleasantry benefits the giver as much as the receiver. He won't dampen my spirits, but I might raise his."

Flagg added. "Sarpho is… growing gloomy only because his importance on this journey is… shrinking. When we arrive in Early, the need for a ranger to lead through the… Ommm… empty lands of this realm will be no longer necessary."

Crichton thought Sarpho was brooding and angry like usual, not 'growing gloomy,' but he did not argue the point.

They saddled the horses and rode hard at a quicker pace than usual. Sarpho rushed them on, determined to find Early as soon as possible. Emushéré and Pincher sprinted alongside the riders and tackled each other down the gray hills. Even the tiger seemed in a benevolent mood, only trying to maul Emushéré once or twice the full ride. The hawk soared overhead, crying and dive-bombing the cats when they tumbled, tangled and snarling. Crichton was afraid for the black panther, but she wasn't fearful. Emushéré held her own. Pincher was like a grumpy older brother, and Emushéré was the annoying little sister, too fast and smart to get caught by a snapping jaw or a swiping paw.

Three candles later, they mounted the top of a high hill and found the town caravan below them.

A dense expanse of shadowy tents and towers and wagons sat under heavy fog, spread out over a long stretch of land at the curving bank of the river.

"Heel!" shouted Sarpho, his tiger already sprinting down toward the feast laid out before him. Pincher halted and came back at a sullen pace. Sarpho instructed the others to go down the hill but held Jason and his horseback. The black panther waited for them, flicking her tail patiently.

Sarpho drew out two separate chains from his saddlebag. He buckled a silver collar about the big sabretooth tiger's neck and walked toward Crichton with the other chain. Crichton sighed, thinking he was about to be leashed and locked onto his horse.

Sarpho placed the chain and collar in his hand. "You watch the panther. She likes you, I think." Crichton, surprised that the Acolyte had even spoken to him, sat still on his horse. "Do it now, sandman," Sarpho said.

"Oh. Okay." Crichton whistled and dismounted. Emushéré was at his side before he could even whistle again. He buckled the collar around her neck, and she looked up at him with confused, golden eyes. "Sorry, Mushy," Crichton said, ruffling her ears.

"Look at the two cats, Crichton."

Crichton looked at the tiger and the panther held apart and panting in the grass. Sarpho's horse trotted after the others down the hill, but Memoria stayed behind, staring at Crichton in her usual blank fashion.

"Just because I think Domray a fool does not mean I think you are. You are a Sondite, but you are also smart and quick and… have the potential to be strong… tough. I am Pincher, and you are Emushéré. The tiger does not mind the panther; perhaps he respects the panther for what she is. But when she bothers him, he is quick to anger. His instincts take over, and he grows violent. I am the same way. Follow my lead and listen to me, and don't trigger my anger. If you can do this, you will earn yourself more privileges after we leave Early."

Crichton nodded. Sarpho's eyes lost their edge, and he pointed to Memoria. "And the most important lesson: Domray is like your horse. It leads you and carries you, and means good. But look at it. It is very dumb." Sarpho whacked the horse upside the head, and it jumped backward in fright. Sarpho chuckled and then said, "Stay close behind me while we are here, sandman." He turned away, walking down the hill with his tiger.

The Sondite held his panther's leash in one hand and his horse's lead in the other, following Sarpho and Pincher toward the tents. Emushéré stretched out her leash taut but did not pull on it once she learned its limits. She peered and sniffed through the fog, both wary and curious. The gray veil thickened as they descended toward the river, the tents and wagons looming large. Shadowy men and women walked about, their shouts and laughter muffled and menacing.

The town was composed of a few rickety wooden buildings, but mostly wagons and tents. Crichton walked past a tall wooden tower guarded by an armored knight at the bottom of the stairs. Crichton craned his neck and saw the silhouette of another guard in the bird's nest at the top. As still as a statue, he stood watch over the south side of the town. Sarpho moved on, and Crichton followed, looking back at the tower, wondering how they could move the tower when they broke camp and traveled onward. In the distance, Crichton saw a blurry second tower standing at the far north side of the town.

The black panther flicked her tail in anticipation as they walked past a wagon stuffed full of goats, but she did not snarl nor strain against her leash. The trader sitting beside the wagon, smoking an odd-smelling pipe, said, "Now you fellas better keep those leashes taught." Sarpho flashed the merchant a hand signal and walked on.

Crichton didn't know what the gesture meant, but the merchant said to Crichton as he passed, "Not very Gahkinly of him, huh?" Crichton said nothing, but Emushéré pulled on her chain and moved toward the seated man. "Aye!" he said, but the panther merely bumped her head into his knee. "Oh. She's friendly?"

"To most people," Crichton said, looking up ahead at the shrinking shadow of Sarpho and Pincher. "Come on, Mushy." He gave a quick tug, and she reluctantly left the ear-scratching trader behind.

"Good luck beyond the river, Sondite!" The man called before he returned to puffing on his pipe.

Crichton sighed. Random strangers, even nice ones, only saw him as a future soldier. No matter what happened, if Crichton didn't escape the Acolytes, the war would be his future.

Crichton wanted to investigate more of the wagons and the collapsible towers, but he had to follow after Sarpho. Coming upon a lean-to, established as a sort of temporary stable, Crichton saw the silver horses of the other Acolytes. He tied Memoria alongside.

Sarpho led Pincher around the stable toward a yellow and gray-colored tent, the tallest in the camp. The draping fabric kissed the ground on all sides. Sarpho and the sabretooth tiger entered through an open slit in-between the heavy fabric walls. Crichton and the black panther followed them.

Many torches burned inside, illuminating the large room. A solid yellow flag, rugged and frayed, hung from the center of the tent.

A balding man with tired gray eyes sat in a high-backed seat, surrounded by a crowd of men. Domray, Flagg, and Rulbiss stood in front of the gray-eyed man who must have been Lord Gregory Early. Knights and advisers stood in a scattered circle around the main group.

"All right, that is enough." Lord Early stood, slowly, and then pointed his finger to the exit. "How many men can fit inside my tent? We are not going to find out this cycle. If you are not Sir Nicholas or wearing purple, leave now. And one of you purple fellows, take those beasts outside immediately!"

The traders left, and Sarpho made to go with them. Crichton turned to follow him.

"Stay, Sondite!"

The old lord looked at Crichton waspishly under his droopy eyelids. Youthful eyes buried under old skin. In that look, Crichton decided the man was not as senile as his first glance had suggested.

Sarpho took Emushéré's leash out of Crichton's hand and exited the tent.

Crichton lingered in the middle of the tent, not sure if he should cross toward the makeshift throne or just stay put. A large knight with black armored shoulders and black greaves stood at the throne's side.

"Well, Sondite, come over here."

Crichton walked across the dirt floor and stood beside Domray and Flagg.

Lord Early sat back in his seat, eyes closed, rubbing a shaking hand through his thin hair. "I'm growing too old, I fear, Sir Nicholas."

"Each cycle you say it is so, my lord." The knight cleared his throat and added, "The Acolytes…"

"I'm old, not blind, Nick. I know they are still here. But I don't know what they could want." His eyes opened, and he looked to Domray, the closest. "They certainly haven't come with soldiers, and they are too road-weary to be delivering fresh news from Shinar. And not a one of them is of the Ten Hand Council, so they have no lawful authority to come charging into my tent, giving me orders…"

His voice trailed off into a mutter. His ancient hands crossed in his lap.

Domray spoke, confidence and cheerfulness blending together, aggravating as always, "Lord Early, we are here with the full authority of the council. Isaac, Third Hand of the God-King, leads our company and our deeds, by law and by writ. I am the Fourth Finger of the Third Hand."

Flagg brought out the scroll and handed it to Sir Nicholas. The knight turned and stretched it up to Lord Early, but he swatted it away.

"Where is the old toad, then? He's one of the few who still makes *me* feel young. Why am I talking to a measly Finger, Finger?" Lord Early's eyes seemed to tire, for they lost their quick pace and rolled slowly over to Crichton. Before Domray responded, he spoke to the Sondite. "Where have *you* been hiding out, hmm? Where did they dig you up from?"

Crichton opened his mouth to speak, but the old lord waved his hand dismissively.

"Never you mind, 'twas a rhetorical question." Lord Early shook his head and rolled his eyes back to Domray. "Where is Isaac? Where is he, Finger?"

Domray shared a look with Flagg. "Look here, Lord Early. I intend no offense, but I must insist upon your compliance with Gahkin's laws. For our purposes, I am acting as Isaac. I have his command until he rejoins me, or we return to Shinar. He is tied up in a different realm, and I am due the same respect as he."

"What realm?"

Domray hesitated to respond.

"There are only eight realms. Come on, it is not too hard, Finger. Where is he?" Domray looked to Flagg, who shrugged and nodded.

"In Ardel. He has business at the chasm."

"Chasm?" Lord Early shouted and flailed his arms. "What, is he trying to convert the buried dwellers now?" He moved to stand but then gave up and leaned back in his chair. "Oh, what's the use? Nicholas, bring me mead and sugar cubes! Oh, and then find the Vistonex guards and have them bring the thing over here."

Sir Nicholas left the tent. Lord Early rubbed his eyes.

Domray stumbled a little. "Um… Lord Early?"

"So be it, then, Finger, Hand, whoever you are. You can be Isaac if that fulfills your boring fantasy. You are now Isaac. What news or orders do you bring, *Isaac*?"

"First, I hope I misunderstood the orders you gave your knight. You are not keeping a Vistonex captive? You are aware that is prohibited by the war codes."

"—I am aware! The codes may as well also state that you should go bury yourself! My realm moves goods for almost every other realm in the kingdom, through the very fringes of the war front, and what do we receive for it?"

"Massive trade profits, lower seasonal draft sizes, extra protection on your border. All eight realms lending you knights and guards."

"Knights, please, I haven't seen any realms' elder knights in five seasons, maybe more. If Lord Killovew sent me Sir Damian or Sir Breigo, or maybe Lord Quirvop sent me Sir Franklin and his big ax, maybe then I would feel grateful. But hungry teenagers with rusty swords don't help, Acolyte."

"Lord, any further outbreak I will mention to the Ten Hand Council myself." Crichton was seeing a different side of Domray. His passion and knowledge, when turned aggressive, became vastly more respectable. Perhaps Crichton had misjudged the Acolyte. "We are here for two purposes, and if you'll settle down to listen," Domray continued, "we can proceed diplomatically."

Sir Nicholas reentered, carrying a small bowl of mead and a golden-rimmed glass chalice piled full of sugar cubes.

"Here you are, sire." Early took the chalice in one hand and the bowl in the other, slowly drizzling the honeyed mead over the top of his sugar cubes. He handed the chalice back and kept the bowl, slurping at the drink. He stuck his tongue in, wrinkly and spotted, and splashed around in the bowl. Eventually, he trapped a sugar cube and lapped it up into his mouth. He crunched it into pieces and swished the mixture around, his face a vision of gluttonous pleasure. He opened his eyes, which were re-energized, almost frenzied. Crichton wondered if there was something else mixed in with the cubes other than sugar...

"The Vistonex is on its way, my lord," the knight said.

"So, you *are* keeping the creature!" Domray sputtered, passing a look of disbelief between Flagg and Rulbiss.

"What of it?" asked Early, standing from his chair with renewed vigor. "My linguist thinks he can communicate with it. He thinks they are self-aware. He thinks they are smart. We've been… encouraging… conversation."

Domray turned to Rulbiss. "This is absurd. Bring Sarpho and the cats back inside. I need to assume control here."

"You shall do no such thing." Sir Nicholas stated, drawing his sword, and aiming it at Rulbiss. Rulbiss merely raised his head and eyed the knight from behind his long, scarred nose. Crichton backed up from the drawn weapons while Lord Early brandished a spindly looking dagger from under the arm of his rickety throne.

"A coup!" Early shouted, pointing his dagger at Domray.

"Ommm…" Flagg's chest hummed deeper than when he usually talked, his loose skin vibrating under his chin. "Ommm… peace, now… Please, listen to me, all of you. Peace be with us here. Gahkin would not want violence… among His own." He raised his hands slowly and pushed them in gentle swipes toward the Lord and his knight. "We need not… fight among ourselves. Remember, we are allies… we are all allies here. Ommm…Lay down your weapons…" The big knight's face went blank as Flagg spoke. He re-sheathed his sword in a daze. Lord Early blinked, all energy gone, seemingly hypnotized. "Please be seated…Ommm… Lord Gregory Early." The lord sat back upon his throne, tucking his knife away.

Crichton stared at Flagg, confused, but the Acolyte just gave him a wink and a smile. Rulbiss still looked as stern and focused as ever, and Domray seemed unfazed.

After a few flickers, consciousness returned to Sir Nicholas and Lord Early, who spoke in a pacified tone.

"You are right, priests of Shinar. I'm agitated by the Vistonex raids. I apologize. The monsters are coming more and more frequently. The news is we are winning the war, but the monsters are more plentiful east of the Verdelen than ever. I had to try something new. I wanted to understand them."

Domray said, "Regardless, you broke one of the few laws that we apply to the entire kingdom, Lord Early. Yet, if you already have the monster, we shall see what you have learned. Then we must kill it. We cannot free the monster, so we must free the soul."

Early said in a tired voice, "Of course, of course. I was foolish."

"You have not met your draft requirements yet, either, Lord Early. Before I knew of the monster you kept, that was your only fault. And the sun shall set very soon."

"I'll send them; I'll send them as soon as I can send a bird back to the castle to deliver the message."

"Good. How safe is the river between Shinar and the North Port?"

"Safer than the South Port. We can't even leave men to guard the empty docks anymore. We send the ships away, then send a letter when it is safe to return, when the town returns to the docks. Only in high numbers can the river be dared at the South Port."

"I see. I'll bring this news to the Ten Hands."

"I've sent letters. Before I broke the code, I sent letters. I didn't want to be treasonous. It was—"

"Unfortunately, the affairs and priorities of the kingdom are great and complex and must be conducted diplomatically."

"Politics…" Sir Nicholas muttered.

Domray continued, unaware of the interruption, "And sometimes the response can take longer than—ah." Domray cut himself short as the flap was thrown wide, and a small, strangely dressed man entered. Two knights, pulling on heavy chains, entered after him.

The Vistonex rolled into the tent chained inside a giant cage. Sarpho followed, the two cats behind them.

Crichton's eyes were fixed solely on the trapped monster.

It was twice as tall as a grown man. It had leathery black skin, smooth enough to reflect the torchlight shining on it. There were no eyes or nose that Crichton could see, but only a sharp beak jutting out from the middle of its smooth, arrow-shaped head. Its beak clicked open, and a long purple tongue flicked in and out. It screeched like a hawk but in an even higher pitch. At the tip of its folded wings grew a curved claw, wide as Sarpho's forearm. The lower body was thin, and at the bottom, there were six feet with small claws and a muscular tail. The screeching of the Vistonex grew worse, and Crichton covered his ears.

The small man tapped on the cage in a deliberate, rhythmic pattern. The screeching stopped. With one claw tapping against an iron bar, the Vistonex repeated the pattern. Then it switched to four slow clicks. It would pause, then begin again, tapping out four slow clicks each time.

Lord Early waved the linguist to the Acolytes. "Tell them what we've learned."

"As you can see," the small man began, "the creature can recognize a pattern, which was our first clue. But it goes much beyond that. I introduced food—a goat—to the creature, always prefaced by two fast clicks followed by a pause and then two more fast clicks. It began to call for the food, using my own click pattern. Then I introduced a different food—pig—to the creature, always prefaced by three fast clicks. It learned to identify the animals using our proffered code. After multiple examples, we began to bring both food sources to the creature, and without even prompting, it clicked the signal for the pig, suggesting it understood the idea of communicating with us and requesting its favorite food preference."

Domray raised his eyebrows; Flagg and Rulbiss furrowed theirs. Sarpho bent down and unleashed the sabretooth. The tiger stalked toward the cage.

"Heel," Sarpho said. The tiger returned to his side. "Sit." The tiger sat. "I am not impressed," Sarpho finished.

"Yes, ranger," the linguist said, "but has your tiger ever taught you a trick?"

Sarpho scowled. The Vistonex kept on with its slow, four-click rhythm.

The shorter man continued, "Due to a rather interesting series of events, we learned that the Vistonex was smarter than we'd ever guessed. This one created its own signals using our code, in a means to communicate with us. One cycle, it chose not to eat the pig. It left it alive for two full cycles. It clicked three fast clicks, over and over, whenever we were nearby. After the two cycles, it killed and drained the creature, then signaled us using three slow clicks. We brought it dead pigs: three slow clicks. Live pigs: three fast clicks. It repeated the pattern with the goat, without any instruction. Dead goat: two slow clicks, pause, two slow clicks. Live goat: two fast clicks, shorter pause, two fast clicks. Obviously, it showed us that it could differentiate between live and dead using our click language. Not only that, but it also wanted to teach us that code. Don't you see? It wanted to build a language."

Domray looked to Flagg, and the Acolyte rubbed his chin thoughtfully. Domray motioned for the linguist to continue.

"In the next phase, we would show ourselves to the creature, just humans. We were going to assign ourselves a code but the Vistonex did it for us. It began using four fast clicks whenever we were around. How excited we were! It had named us, and in response, we named it, using six fast clicks.

"Soon though, things grew… complicated. Antagonistic, you might say. It began signaling us by using four slow clicks instead of four fast clicks. At first, we thought it may have just confused the codes, but when we brought in the live and dead animals, it identified them properly. You can understand, then, what the creature was signaling. It wanted dead humans."

Sarpho smiled, yet everyone else looked less than pleased. Domray frowned.

"The Vistonex was identifying us as dead instead of alive. We know it realizes we are alive, and yet it continues to click the signal for dead humans."

Realization made Domray step back. "This is un-Gahkinly. This is—these experiments are sins! We must free the creature's spirit and end this madness."

The linguist scowled. "We understand this isn't entirely… ethical according to the war codes."

"Yes, that's interesting," Sarpho said, "I'd like to try something, if you don't mind."

Sarpho didn't wait for a response but stepped forward and clicked on the cage four times in a fast rhythm. Then he clicked six times at a slower pace. The creature thrashed in the cage. Sarpho repeated the slow six clicks. The Vistonex clicked back, six times fast, followed by four clicks, slower. It repeated the pattern.

"There you go," Sarpho said. "Now we understand each other." He clicked four times, fast, and then six times, slow. The creature slammed its body against the cage, screeching. Sarpho laughed.

"I want to let it out," Sarpho said.

"Do you have a death wish, ranger?" Sir Nicholas asked.

"No," Sarpho answered, "but I think we have an argument to settle. Call it a sort of barbaric battle agreement." The Vistonex screeched and thrashed in the cage. Sarpho drew his ax from behind his back and spun it in his hands, smiling.

Domray said, "There is no need for this, Sarpho. The creature deserves death. Not a battle for its freedom, which you know we cannot grant."

"As if it would win…" Sarpho tightened his jaw and put his ax away. Instead, he drew his short sword from its scabbard at his waist. Sarpho clicked six times, slowly. The creature turned its head and screeched, clicking six times, very fast. Sarpho plunged his sword through the cage bars and into the Vistonex's abdomen. He stabbed it again, and it crumpled in silence to the bottom of the cage, broken and twisted, wings and tail twitching. Dark red blood pooled out onto the ground around the cage.

Crichton felt sick but looked away and fought back the urge to puke. Domray was not so capable. He fell onto his knees and vomited onto the ground. Lord Early chuckled, and Sir Nick laughed outright. Rulbiss stood unfazed, face still stern.

Flagg frowned. "They are… smart…smarter than… I'd ever imagined," he said.

A woman ran into the tent and looked at the dead monster. "My word," she whispered, breathless, before turning away and moving to Lord Early. "My lord," she said, "The North Port is under attack."

"What? How many?"

"They've counted over a hundred, my lord."

"Sir Nicholas—"

The big knight was already racing outside. Lord Early lifted his chalice of sugared mead and left without a word, the scout woman on his tail. Bells rang outside, and the tent's roof began to droop.

"Outside!" Sarpho shouted.

Crichton did not hesitate to follow orders. They exited the tent at a full sprint. Rulbiss ran to the stables. The foggy town was melting to the ground. The tall guard towers were tipped over and deconstructed into smaller pieces. The horses and stables and tents pulled themselves into a disorganized clump at the wagons. The wagons began to line up, some already rolling north. Knights on their steeds raced northward at a great pace.

Crichton looked around but couldn't find Flagg or Domray anywhere. The cats, to their credit, did not panic but stayed near Sarpho and Crichton. Sarpho stopped a trader as he rushed past. "How far to the North Port?"

"Only a cycle or so, maybe. Less than three candles at a gallop, I'd say." The merchant dashed off.

Sarpho smiled. Rulbiss returned, leading three horses. He passed Memoria to Crichton. "Where's Domray and Limb?" Crichton asked.

Sarpho said, "It doesn't matter; you're riding with us." Crichton looked around, desperate to find his Acolyte allies. Sarpho grabbed him by his collar and pulled his face up to his own. "Get on your horse. It's time for some lessons Domray can't teach you." Crichton climbed up into his saddle.

Someone tapped him on the shoulder. Crichton turned and saw Rulbiss on his own horse, holding out a short sword in its sheath. The boy took the blade and tied it around his waist. Sarpho slapped the hide of Memoria, and the horse startled and dashed off, following the other horses in a mad gallop north. Sarpho and Rulbiss rode behind him, while the two big cats ran along at the far edge of the herd.

Sarpho shouted to Crichton, "Are you scared, boy?"

Crichton ground his teeth. He saw Emushéré, tirelessly loping beside him. She was not scared.

He clicked his heels into Memoria's side, urging the horse to gallop faster.

Seventeen

They saw the Star Tower from the flood plains, still far east of Shinar. Thin as a hair, it stretched up from the horizon into the darkening blue sky, taller than any mountain in the kingdom. They rode closer each cycle, and it grew, larger and wider, glinting silver when the sky was clear of clouds and struck by the failing eastern sun. Jason focused on the miraculous tower, wringing his hands and guiding Rara Silva Nix through the plains. Her white ankles were graying. They had been in the wild flood plains for more than twenty cycles.

They came upon a well-maintained fence, built with quality lumber from far south. Behind it grew a vast field of flowers, rows of pink and blue and yellow tulips stretched into the distance alongside orange and purple lilies and white and red rosebushes. They rode past the colorful stripes to the north and then turned west again at the fence corner. They passed a large barn and came upon an even larger house. Outside the house, in front of the flowers, a higher, thicker fence encircled a white chicken coop and a pig pen. Two amber-colored dogs patrolled the perimeter, barking at the riders with teeth bared.

Wealth near Fessdri made the impossible possible, it seemed.

A middle-aged fellow emerged from his home and hurled a boot into the pen at the dogs. One dog grabbed up the boot and shook it to pieces, but the other just kept barking. The farmer noticed the five men on horseback about fifty yards from his house. He jumped, and his eyes grew wide. He turned around and disappeared back inside. The door slammed shut behind him.

"Well, I didn't expect toast and ham, but that was just plain rude," Ratoke said.

"He probably doesn't receive a lot of dirty soldiers on horseback from this side of the plains," Taroke said.

"I'm surprised the raiders haven't gotten to him."

"Don't forget, we are in Shinar now."

"Right, nobody hungry here."

"I didn't say that—I just meant—"

Jason interrupted them. "Let's keep moving; we must be very near Fessdri. No reason to wait for him to come back with a crossbow." Jason nudged Rara, and she trotted on, too proud to be bothered by the barking canines.

"Like that'd keep us from robbing the place," Taroke said. Jason frowned at him.

Ratoke added, "If we were into that sort of thing, he means."

They fell back into silence as they followed the flower field toward Fessdri.

About a candle length passed before the town walls appeared on the horizon. Another candle, and they were there, circling the high walls of the town until they found the northern gatehouse. The company dismounted and milled about, waiting their turn to enter the city. A large Royal River Ice caravan, wagons sweating, moved inside after being cleared by the gatekeeper and his guardsmen. Another wagon, attempting to exit the city and guided by a young boy, was denied authorization to leave, missing the proper paperwork. Jason smiled as he watched the shy boy struggle to turn his wagon, the furious gatekeeper and his guards arguing about the best way to do it. The two horses did not know who to listen to and became confused and stubborn. With the 'help' of the loudest and fattest guard, chewing tobacco and spitting it toward the others still squabbling with him, the horses eventually circled around. Knocking over a table holding a stack of papers in an unchecked start from one of the horses, they finally left the stone archway. The boy and his wagon disappeared back into town.

The fat guard cleaned up the spilled papers while Jason and Sir Breigo spoke with the gatekeeper.

"Wrong season to be incoming soldiers, isn't it?" the man asked, shuffling through their papers.

"What makes you say that?" Jason said, curious. He thought traveling during the season of the sun was more than reasonable, perhaps advisable.

"Most soldiers I see show up when the sun's rising, not setting. Imagine it's so their first battle isn't in the night season. Vistonex are hard to kill with the sun shining, even worse when they are the same color as the sky."

"Ah, we aren't your usual soldiers. I'm—"

"Yeah, yeah, you're talented warriors, or elder knights, renowned for miles, slaughterers of monsters or dwellers or Gahkin-knows-what. I've heard it before. But it ain't my place to keep you from fighting. It's my place to ensure the nice, smart, *wealthy* folk of Fessdri don't have to fight. So, you keep your noses clean, and you can come into my town for a spell at the inn. By the way, speaking of cleaning, your team may want to look into it… Especially them." The gatekeeper pointed at the Greenfoots.

Ratoke was smacking Taroke with a horse blanket. The dust and dirt that rose off him and the blanket just blew back onto the horse and Ratoke. Taroke squinted through the haze of filth and smiled and waved at the gatekeeper who was pointing at him.

Jason thanked the guard, Sir Breigo stowed away the warrants, and the companions moved forward under the arch and crossed into the town.

Tall stone buildings rose on either side of the streets. Ripe smells drifted from the windows; garish fabrics hung over the doorways. The streets were made of stone and clean as marble aside from the fresh droppings of horses here and there. The present road opened into a wide plaza where a small but busy trade market was set up. Jason saw servants and wealthy men and women waiting in queued lines at the most popular stands. He had never seen that before. Fessdri was the most orderly and organized town Jason had ever stepped foot in. Even at Northtown, just outside of Castle Killovew, when the trade caravans arrived on the lawns, the citizens were not so mannerly nor patient.

"Should we find ourselves a stable and then get some drinks? I've sorely missed the sweet comforts of wealthy civilization." Ratoke waited on Jason's acquiescence. Jason nodded and handed them Rara's lead. The others passed their horses off, and Ratoke and Taroke led them wide around the market stands toward the nearest inn with a stable.

Mako Black crossed to the other side of the market, pulling aside a farmer and making a deal for a small case of strawberries. Expensive as fruit was these cycles, especially in Fessdri, Jason wondered just how many gold rings Mako had to part with to walk away with the little box of red fruit. Being the most successful water dragon wrangler in the Thirsting Forest Realm before he retired, he could afford to lose a little gold for the comfort, Jason supposed. This might be their last chance at comfort.

"This is a nice place." Sir Breigo whistled, eyes scanning the plaza and the open windows in the buildings surrounding the square.

"Almost makes you forget the starving farmer and his family that got eaten by cannibals, huh?"

"Actually, Prince Jason, it was the first thing I thought of."

"Right."

"Where will our… friend… be, I wonder?"

"I'm not sure," Jason answered, his eyes mimicking the knight's, on the lookout for their contact from Shinar.

They did not find him in the square, even though they waited around for the rest of the waking candles. Because the sun was low in the east, the walls and tall buildings of Fessdri cast most of the square in shadow. Jason and Breigo did not make their loitering obvious. They stood in different lines, spoke with the locals and the traders, then lounged in the shade, making friends with a well-off farmer who lived just outside the city. When he departed for his home, Jason and Breigo left to find the others at the big Fessdri inn.

"We cannot stay too long in this town. The Killovew name may allow us to linger for a few cycles, but soon the locals will begin to whisper. They will say we are delaying our entry into the God-King's army. And besides, soon the sun shall set, and the Sundown Ceremony will commence with or without us."

"Do not worry, Sir Breigo," Jason said, speaking regally to hide the worry he had in himself. "He will be here. He and my father have been working on this plan for half their lives." Jason pulled open the door and stepped into the inn. "What could he let stand in his way?"

Three cycles later, their contact was still missing.

Jason Killovew awoke and dressed, noticing that only a small crescent slice of the sun hung above the walls of Fessdri through his window. In twelve cycles, the sun would set completely, and the dark season would be upon them. All the time they had saved by crossing the flood plains was being wasted away as they waited around in Fessdri.

If all went to plan, a new regime would be ruling by the time the sun rose again. Most of the kingdom would know no difference in leadership, but they'd notice the uptick in food distribution, the lowered quotas that kept fewer of their loved ones from having to fight Vistonex in the Dezruk Forest. *If* they met up with their accomplice. *If* they pulled this off.

Jason crossed the room and opened the door. He descended the stairs, stifling a yawn with the back of his hand. On the ground floor, he smelled coffee and bacon. Another Fessdri luxury that most of the kingdom would kill for. In fact, some of the kingdom was killing for it right now.

Sir Breigo sat at the bar counter, alone. His dirty blond hair was neatly combed over, his armor shined with a new polish, and his face was scrubbed clean and shaven. While the others were still sleeping, the Killovew knight had clearly risen early in preparation to enter the city.

He knew as well as Jason that regardless of if their contact arrived or not, they must move on this cycle.

The knight waved Jason over to the bar. Jason looked around, his final hopes evaporating as he saw only one other patron in the common room—an old trader from down south whom Jason had already met.

The morning cook, the only one tending the inn this early in the cycle, held up a steaming mug from behind the kitchen counter. Jason nodded, "A plate of bacon and eggs, too, if you would." The prince was getting spoiled on real food here in Fessdri. Soon enough, they'd be back to m-bars and the occasional potato.

Sir Breigo lowered his mug from his own lips. "We will leave this cycle," he said, more statement than question.

"Yes. We'll have to. If he can meet up with us in Shinar we may still have a chance… but it seems like a long shot. I just can't imagine why he would not be able to make it here. He's one of the most powerful Acolytes in the city, no citizen or another Acolyte could stop him..."

Sir Breigo nearly spit his coffee out of his mouth at Jason's words.

"What is it, Breigo?"

The knight stood from the bar and gestured to a distant table, away from the windows and the front door and any people that may be able to overhear.

The prince and his knight took their coffee and retreated to the far corner of the inn. After the cook brought Jason his plate of eggs and bacon, Sir Breigo finally spoke.

"Sondite rebels could stop him."

"Bury me," Jason whispered. "Bury me upside down. We should have known. Of course. They don't know he wants to help them."

Sir Breigo nodded just slightly. "And what better opportunity to sweep him away than when he leaves the Grand City to visit Fessdri. A short horse ride along the under-protected side road to Fessdri. He would have come nearly alone, of course. One or two simple trusted guards. The Sondite deserters could not resist such a prime victim."

"But why isn't this news all over the town? The whole kingdom should be out looking for him."

"Unless the Ten Hand Council doesn't want the kingdom to find out. And now their rescue party is missing too." Breigo raised his eyebrows.

"Right. How does that look, the men who claim to commune with the God-King, allowing one of their own to get caught by their own subjected peoples?"

Breigo sipped from his coffee mug. "What do we do, Prince Killovew?"

"It's just the two of us, Breigo. Bury the formality. What do you think?"

"I'm not the leader, Jason; I'm the swordsman." He smirked. "But *I* think we must go rescue him. The way I see it, no other rescue party has been sent. If they had, they would have come right through Fessdri. I think the Acolytes intend to abandon him."

"Bury me," Jason said again. "We'll have to backtrack a few cycles to where we found the..." Jason lowered his voice even further, leaning toward Breigo across the table, "...where we found the dead paladins. And then we'll have to hope Mako can follow the Sondite tracks. Then if we do find the hideout, we'll have to convince the soldiers to let him go, for their own sake, without explaining why they should trust us."

"Don't forget, after all that, we will have to make it back to the capital city before the Sundown Ceremony."

Mako Black emerged from the stairwell, saw his journeymen, and joined them at the table. Looking at their faces, he asked, "Well, out with it. I saw you two stressing and fretting from all the way at the stairs."

Jason answered. "I think our inside man is the one the rebels took hostage. He is who Zedaff and Ty and the paladins were attempting to rescue."

"Attempting to rescue until we stopped them, you mean?"

"Right. And now, before we can even contemplate our next step into Shinar, we have to rescue him from the very people whom we are trying to help."

Mako cracked a half-smile. "Well, I suppose we can just tell them we are on their side."

"Yeah, we'll see how that goes for us."

Sir Breigo stood up from the table. "I'll go wake the Greenfoots. The next few cycles are not going to be easy."

After Breigo walked away, Mako asked in a low voice, "So who is this inside man, anyway? I know he is the contact in Shinar. But you have not confided in me his role in all this."

Jason lowered his voice even further, "Tegan Dhibax. You should know his name. He is the future ruler of the kingdom. He is the man my father met over five suns ago. He is now the Second Hand of the Ten Hand Council."

Mako whistled. "And now he has got himself kidnapped twelve cycles before he executes grand treason?"

"Yeah," Jason said, "not great timing."

The two sat in silence for a while. Jason tried to eat his plate of food, but he took one bite of bacon and gave up. It was tasteless in his mouth, and his nauseous stomach couldn't handle it anyway.

"If we can't rescue him and can't execute your father's plan, we will still have to serve our term in war," Mako spoke as if he was thinking aloud, slowly rubbing his hand through his beard.

"You scared of Vistonex, Mako?"

Mako smirked. He held up his forearm, where a scar ran from his palm to his elbow. "Water Dragon. Had teeth as big as your middle finger." He turned his neck, pulled back his shirt, and pointed to the high side of his collar bone, which protruded at an odd angle. "Giant Python that could have swallowed your horse." He pointed to his ear, which was scarred and missing a small chunk off the top.

"Well," Jason asked when Mako said nothing, "What creature did that?"

"I was shaving, and my dog ran into my leg."

They both burst out laughing. Despite their predicament, Jason was calmed by the water dragon wrangler's jokes. He'd come a long way from his silent brooding self at the start of their journey.

After Jason composed himself, he shook his head and said, "You know, at the beginning of this journey, I thought the Greenfoot brothers were the crazy ones.

Now it's you…" Jason leaned back in his seat, reclining into the corner of the two walls. "Actually, I think we all must be a bit insane."

"Tell me, Jason Killovew. What makes you think *you're* crazy?"

"I'm the leader of this suicidal gang, isn't that enough?" Jason cracked a smile, but another voice within him spoke, a voice that felt almost as if it didn't belong to Jason at all.

You're crazier than the rest of them, Jason, and you and I both know it.

The prince fingered the hilt of his dagger underneath the table.

Eighteen

The fog grew thicker as they rode north. Emushéré and Pincher loped alongside the horses, their pace never slowing. Crichton's legs ached from the high-speed riding. He did not want to be fatigued when he fought the winged monsters. *Give me strength to fight them Gahkin. Give me the skill to survive.*

Crichton told himself he was not afraid, regardless of the outcome awaiting him. He told himself now was the time to prove his ability. To Sarpho and to *his* Gahkin. If death took him, so be it. He already acknowledged the likely possibility of never seeing Martin again and already turned his destiny over to the will of *his* Gahkin. There was little positive in Crichton's future, regardless of how long it lasted.

Like his ancestors before him, he was driven across the land by zealous priests in purple robes and ushered into battle with the Vistonex. He was given tasteless meals to strengthen his body, only brief lessons to hone his mind, and only a short steel sword to fight for his soul's resting place.

But that was not all he brought along. For he also carried into battle the agility, strength, and balance of a life spent in the trees of a dense jungle and the loyalty of a fierce black panther. If Crichton *was* afraid, it was encased in a hard prison of anger and confidence.

Crichton noticed the algae candle bearer ahead on his left, switching a dead candle with a freshly lit one. The third candle since they left the town of Early. That made it the eighth of the cycle. Soon they would come upon the port itself, but Crichton was not tired. He felt a burning inside him, a supernatural fuel that spiked his wits and senses. Domray and Flagg were right; Gahkin *was* strong within him. He ground his teeth together to steel himself. He had yet to plead to Sarpho for mercy. This, Crichton swore, he would never do.

The first thing that alerted Crichton of their imminent approach to the port was the way the river banked inward toward the galloping herd. The second was the way Emushéré and Pincher transformed their casual jog to a bristling, shoulders lowered run. Pincher swept out wide to the right of the herd, but Emushéré seemed to loathe to leave Crichton. Crichton nudged and urged and fought Memoria to the outer edge of the herd to be directly next to the black panther.

After Crichton made the perimeter, he heard a shout from the knights that led the charge. He heard Sir Nicholas roaring among them and saw in the distance the shadowy warehouses that surrounded the docks.

A horde of black shapes lifted off the gray buildings into the sky.

Many Vistonex flew away from the charging horses, back into the deeper fog and across the river. Many others wheeled through the air and toward their attackers, screeching in high-pitched whistles. The largest ones flaunted a wingspan of twenty feet or more, their claws longer than Crichton's arm. Memoria drew to a forced halt behind a quick-forming line of bowmen.

"Archers!"

The men notched their arrows and aimed them to the sky. For a single moment, the Vistonex circled overhead, and the bowstrings were held taught.

An odd stillness clung to the foggy air.

"Fire!"

The Vistonex dove, all at once.

Noise and violent movement erupted on all sides.

Memoria startled and reared back. Crichton squeezed tight to the leather pommel. He held on with one hand and thrust his sword upward with the other. A wave of concussive air buffeted him; he ducked his head and tensed his body, but nothing solid connected. A ten-foot-wide Vistonex, arrows in its chest, crashed to the ground in a leathery heap beside him. Another fell from the sky to his right, whistling all the way to the ground. Crichton could not help but stare at the carnage of the collision. Dark brown insides spilled out from the broken animal, still screeching and writhing its tail. Crichton ripped his eyes away and tried to get a grip of his surroundings in the chaos.

Most of the horsemen were pushing ahead, so Crichton leaned forward and urged Memoria after them. It would be wise to keep with the herd, he thought.

Ahead, above the river, a dense cloud of the evil beasts swirled through the fog. Most seemed intent on fleeing the mad onrush of men, but a sizable amount stayed behind, covering the flock's retreat. Three trade ships, ghostly masts jutting into the Vistonex filled sky, lay anchored in the inlet. One had caught fire. The knights raced toward them, funneling along the pier.

The columnar rush of horses in-between the warehouses and onto the wet dock was the last semblance of structure Crichton knew until the frenzy of battle was over.

A spiraling Vistonex crashed into Memoria's side. Crichton lost his frozen grip on the reigns and tumbled onto the wooden pier. Long splinters raked his left forearm and sliced into his side and legs as he rolled. The galloping horses jumped over him, moving out over the docks toward the ships. Crichton scrambled on his hands and knees, sword still gripped in one hand, not looking back to discover Memoria's fate. He had just crawled free of the stampede when another heavy blast of air knocked him sprawling onto the planks. He rolled over and saw black.

The beating of two huge wings blotted out the sky. Crichton swiped upward with his sword, but the Vistonex floated just too high above the boy to be in any danger. It seemed to be searching for a place to set down its hook-shaped claws at the tips of its wings so it could land. The circular beak opened, revealing rows of dagger-like fangs. The purple tongue shot out. Crichton deflected the sharp spearing appendage with his sword, gouging a deep groove in the leathery thing. The monster dropped itself closer to Crichton, screeching in fury. He couldn't see or hear anything aside from the pounding wings. Crichton swiped again blindly and missed, losing the grip on his sword and feeling it slip from his fingers with a sinking feeling. The monster's beak opened; Crichton wrenched his head to the left just as the tongue shot out again. It pierced the dock just inches from his face. With no sword, he had no defense. The Vistonex landed over top of him, huge wings covering his whole field of vision. The creature cocked its head, like an eagle might, to look at him with one black eye. Then it reared back its beak to plunge into his body. Crichton had nowhere to dodge.

Something yanked the Vistonex backward, and the beak crashed down into the ground between his legs. Emushéré had the muscular tail in its mouth, swatting and tearing at it. Crichton scrambled to his feet and scooped up his sword. The Vistonex flapped its powerful wings, and in one stroke, it lifted into the air again, snapping its tail to throw off the angry cat. The black panther rolled through the air but landed on its paws, ready to dodge the Vistonex as it spun around toward her. Before the monster could gain altitude, Crichton swung his blade into its wing, slicing through the thin membrane all the way to the appendage's bone. The Vistonex spun about, enveloping him in blackness again as the wings surrounded him on either side. Crichton slashed upward blindly, feeling his sword connect with something solid and stick. He used all his strength and rammed it forward, plunging his sword deeper into its body. He let go of the sword and leaped backward. The creature screeched and collapsed to the ground, Emushéré clinging onto its back. The Vistonex gurgled and foamed at the beak while flapping with frenzied wings. The black panther kept its jaws clamped around the back of its leathery neck until it lay still.

Crichton looked about, making sure no more creatures were about to swoop down on him. The port skies were emptying. The shadowy flock of Vistonex shrunk and vanished into the dark western fog across the river. A handful of bodies lay about the dock, including some horses and— Crichton looked away rather quickly—men.

He turned back to the Vistonex carcass and grabbed the hilt of his sword. He yanked it out, splattering himself and the dock with the creature's blood. He stepped back and held the sword out in front of him, tightening his grip and breathing deeply.

The ship fire had been doused, and the traders who had taken shelter in the bowels of their ships emerged. Crichton heard a stifled growl at his back. He turned and saw Pincher, looking rather pleased with himself, dragging a huge Vistonex by its thick neck. Behind the proud sabretooth tiger walked Sarpho and Rulbiss, unharmed and—in Sarpho's case—smiling. Pincher laid down his Vistonex next to the smaller one Crichton and Emushéré had managed to kill. The two cats sniffed each other's winged beasts and then laid down contentedly.

"Not too tough for you, I see."

Sarpho punched Crichton on the shoulder. It hurt, but Crichton smiled all the same. The sizzling rush of battle still raced through his body. Sarpho stood at Crichton's side, Rulbiss at the other, and they looked out across the river. It was too foggy to see to the other side.

Sarpho said, "Did you notice how they fight? They do not fight like soldiers. They are not warriors or out to kill for the sake of killing. They might be smart, but they are still just predators. Animals. They came to ambush the men and livestock and to gorge themselves on the m-bars. They fled when we arrived."

"Some fought, though," Crichton said.

"Yes, the males. It's their instinct to protect their kills and their mates." Sarpho took his eyes from the river and turned to Rulbiss. "Decent sized flock, though. Maybe two hundred. I've never heard of such huge colonies crossing the river. I always thought they stayed deeper in their forest." He turned to Crichton. "They say they are territorial. They fight each other as much as they fight us."

Rulbiss nodded. Crichton felt a sudden camaraderie with these men. They were warriors, and now so was Crichton.

"Have either of you been to the other side?"

"Both of us have, sandman." Sarpho cleared his throat and said, "Rulbiss will train with you in Shinar. That sword skill was impressive for an orphan, even if it was a little panicky. You could lead a Sondite regiment, perhaps, if you advance in your lessons with Domray and take to Rulbiss' battle tutoring."

Rulbiss nodded. Crichton did not know if he should be proud of the compliment or angered that they had only watched him battle the Vistonex instead of aiding him.

Sarpho pointed to their right and said, "You need to go put down your horse." He walked off toward the trade ships, but Rulbiss stayed with Crichton. They looked along the dock to his horse.

Memoria stumbled as she tried to stand. Her front right leg was bent at a gruesome angle. Crichton rushed over to her. He saw bone sticking out of her shin, and she cried to him in pain. Crichton rubbed her nose. He never thought particularly highly of the horse until now, realizing just how loyal and fair she had treated the Sondite who learned to ride on her back. She escorted him into battle, and now she lay dying. The Habibrok claimed that all animals have souls, but only humans would live on in the star life after death. Crichton thought that all living things were deserving of mercy and kindness, soul, star life, or… whatever. He whispered a prayer to *his* Gahkin and raised his sword to her neck.

Rulbiss stayed his hand. He drew his sword and gestured for Crichton to stand back.

The silent Acolyte eased the horse onto its belly from its side. He stroked its nose. Then he stood up and lined his sword above the base of Memoria's skull. He raised it up and lowered it down a few times in slow fashion for practice. Then he raised his sword high in the air, with both hands, and with great might brought it down upon the horse. The head dropped onto the deck, cut clean off. The body flopped over, and blood gushed out, dousing Crichton's boots and pants.

Rulbiss sheathed his sword, thumped Crichton on the shoulder, and walked off. Crichton backed up, trying to get away from the dead horse. He stumbled on something, turned around, and saw more bodies lay strewn about, in all directions. The gore surrounded him. The thrill of battle had faded. His sword felt heavy, and he dropped it onto the wooden dock. There was nowhere to look that wasn't splashed with blood or carnage.

Crichton felt sick. He ran to the edge of the nearest pier, leaned over the dark river, and vomited into the water.

Nineteen

Jason raised his chin, squared his shoulders, and fixed his slouch, all while keeping Rara Silva Nix from shuffling nervously underneath him. The wind blew, and his green cloak billowed out behind him. He needed the little remaining slice of the sun to catch the Thirsting Forest sigil and glint in the twilight sky. Maybe the rumors about his grandfather would finally grant them some favor, as opposed to ill-fortune. Maybe these Sondite outlaws would give him some benefit of the doubt. And maybe the sun would rise higher in the sky this season, instead of lower.

To his left, Sir Breigo Aldev shifted uncomfortably, his horse snorting and side-stepping in agitation. Breigo's hand gripped the pommel of his saddle, and he moved his free hand to where the hilt of his sword usually rested. Only his sword was one hundred yards behind him, on top of his armor, in a useless heap.

The purpling sky swirled with malevolent orange and maroon clouds at the horizon.

Breigo turned his head from the small camp ahead of them and looked over his right shoulder. Further back from the knight and his prince, but still within sight, stood Mako, Taroke, and Ratoke. One of the brothers waved encouragingly.

"We left them behind us over a hundred yards, and I still can't escape their sarcasm."

Jason chuckled. "Depending on how this meeting goes, we may escape it soon enough."

"So, there is a bright side to dying, after all."

"If the Sondites were going to kill us, their arrows could reach us at this distance. They would have fired already. They'll come and meet us."

"Are you sure they see us at this distance? Perhaps they only have one man standing watch, and he fell asleep."

"You don't escape Shinar and avoid those paladins by being unobservant and sleeping during your watch."

Breigo grunted and continued to wait.

They had decided, after finding the Sondite tracks that they didn't have time to stalk them and deduce a way to break Tegan loose. No time to even find out if Tegan was still alive… was even being held by this group of deserters. They would approach them directly, convey their message and their peace offering, and hope that the Killovew name could buy them credibility. And Jason had one other back-up strategy, but he had kept that to himself.

Tents and makeshift canopies jutted up, haphazardly scattered at the bottom of the hill. A handful of stolen horses stamped and neighed nearby, tugging against their restraints. No flags or banners flew from any tent. This was no hunting party, and no one else in their right mind would wander so far from the safety of civilization, this close to the river, so close to Sundown.

Only Sondites, fleeing from Shinar instead of being forced into battle. Who could blame them?

Jason grimaced as two men emerged from the largest tent. They mounted onto their horses and galloped closer. The prince did not have to look hard to notice they both wore their sword belts, and the bigger man had on steel greaves and steel boots. They both wore billowing white pants and were wrapped in tan robes across their torsos. Very much Sondites.

Their time in Shinar had not corrupted their traditional desert garb. Prince Killovew knew it would be easy enough to hide steel chest plates underneath those loose robes.

Armed to the teeth, and Jason and Breigo had nothing but words to fight back with.

Jason raised his hand in greeting as the two Sondite men arrived. They did not draw their weapons, but they also did not return Jason's greeting.

"What trick is this?" The nearer man, his dark purple eyes flashing between the two strangers. "You know we must kill you, foolish ones, having seen us here? Why do you approach us unarmed? Does death not come easy enough for you two that you must seek it out at our hands? We have snuck around you and your companions, by the way." He gestured further up the hill.

Jason turned and saw that his three companions had been joined by about nine others. He turned back to the messenger.

"This is no trick, friend. My name is Jason Killovew, Prince of the Thirsting Forest. My companion here is Sir Breigo Aldev, an elder knight of the Thirsting Forest. We are here to speak with your… leader, whomever that may be. We do not represent the Acolytes, we do not intend to turn you in for your ransom, and we certainly do not intend to fight all of you."

"Our leader has no desire to speak with anyone, especially foolish ones. We desire freedom. Can you grant us that?"

"Actually, yes, I believe we can."

The messenger laughed. "We don't believe in tall tales, nor miracles, and certainly not in liars that make big promises."

The other Sondite man drew his sword.

Jason spoke, his voice firm and flat, camouflaging the fear that felt like sparrows beating their wings against the inside of his stomach. "We know you have captured Tegan Dhibax, the Second Hand. We know you intend to kill us and continue your trek south, probably planning to find refuge and hide out in *my* own forests. And I know that you will not listen to me on a whim, despite what my grandfather sacrificed for *your* people."

The messenger took it in, then nodded, smirking. "Correct so far."

Jason said, "Then it's only fair for me to request shodullen."

The messenger's eyebrows jumped in surprise, but he reigned them in in quick fashion and simply sighed. "If that is the means by which you wish to die, then yes, it is fair for you to do so. Your knight will fight on your behalf, I assume?"

Jason had deliberately kept this part of his plan to himself. He looked at Sir Breigo, who may not have even heard of shodullen before. But Sir Breigo did not become known for being a great swordsman by avoiding single combat.

The knight simply smiled and said, "Yes, I'll fight whichever man you choose."

Jason shook his head. "No." Sir Breigo started to interrupt, but Jason held out a hand and continued, "If I remember correctly, I can request your leader to fight me himself. Chief versus Chief. As in the times before the unification of the kingdom."

The messenger sighed again. "Herself. But yes… yes, you can." He signaled to his men further up the hill, and then he and the big swordsman turned and rode back to their camp. Over his shoulder, he shouted, "You can all come to camp, but only you, Killovew, can bring your weapons. We shall take the rest for now."

Jason expected Breigo to argue, but he simply gave Jason a hard stare before grunting and turning his horse back up the hill. The prince followed.

Though he had requested to fight her in battle, he did not want to kill her. He just wanted the chance to speak with her, to converse leader to leader, and, hopefully, get a chance to see if the Second Hand was still alive. She sat by herself, her face blank to emotions. The three 'runaway' brands that had been burned onto both sides of her neck and one side of her cheek added an edge of toughness to her otherwise feminine features. Her hair was braided tight against her head and then knotted into a larger braid that ran down her back, almost deliberately pulled away from her neckline to show off the scars of her previous escape attempts. Her eyes, though unreadable, glistened like sharp purple amethysts in the torchlight. Her lips were pressed tight in concentration, yet her jawline was soft and smooth.

Well, Jason thought, now he *really* didn't want to have to kill her.

Jason's allies all stood outside, silent, from what he could hear. Even the Greenfoot brothers seemed subdued by the danger of their current predicament. Surrounding his small group outside was at least fifteen Sondites, all armed, just waiting for the order to execute the lot of them.

In the tent sat Prince Jason, this mysterious woman rebel, and four Sondite bodyguards.

When the leader finally spoke, her voice was barely above a whisper but full of equal parts confidence and concern.

"You are the ones who killed Zedaff."

It was not a question, but Jason answered her anyway.

"Yes, it was us."

"I'll admit that I don't understand your goal. But you killing them, that did not help us. We had escaped their trackers, now even more will come looking."

"You have the Second Hand. More will come, regardless."

"You say we have the Second Hand. You have no proof. We are trying to escape, not take prisoners or hostages."

Jason frowned. They did not have time for this back and forth.

"Look, we know you have Tegan. Or you already killed him, but that would be a stupid burying thing to do, and you don't look stupid. We did not learn you have the Second Hand from Zedaff. They are keeping him and his soldiers' disappearance quiet. And the Second Hand's absence has not been made public. No one other than the Ten Hand Council and a handful of high-ranking paladins knows anything is amiss, by my guess. They wouldn't want to start a panic." Jason chewed his tongue for a moment and then spat out what he knew he needed to say.

"*We* only know this because we are allies united in a conspiracy with the Second Hand, and he has been missing from our rendezvous for many cycles now. Barring murder or kidnapping, he would be communicating with us if he were to be delayed in any way. We are allied, in large part, to overthrow those who keep your people captive in Shinar, to stop them sending your fathers and sons into an unwinnable war. You personally are standing in the way of your people's liberty; you just don't realize it."

She cocked her head, perhaps reevaluating him.

Jason pushed his luck. "It's polite to introduce yourself, by the way, when you meet a stranger for the first time. That way, I can call you something other than 'You.'"

She sighed and stood up, gesturing for the handful of other Sondite rebels to leave the tent. She watched as all but one dispersed. The messenger who had spoken first with them remained by her side.

She chuckled. "Shodullen… Gahkin above and dwellers below, it's been a long time since an *outsider* has asked our people for that." She stepped forward to Jason.

"My knives, Twuque." The messenger handed two long daggers to his leader. She examined them, turning them in the light.

"These are older than me. The strange colorless jewels in the hilts came from deep in the Gilv Mountains. In my culture, you inherit weapons from your mentor upon their retirement. Or you take them from a warrior you defeat in shodullen." Her eyes lifted from the blades and met Jason's. "As a slave since birth, I had no mentor.

"My lance, Twuque."

The messenger handed her a long, thin blade that interlocked and, Jason assumed, could be extended even further. Twuque took back the daggers.

"The daggers I got before my third sun. This lance was during my third. When a man thought his fancy training with the paladins in war meant he could take me for his own, for the times away from his wife. After I killed him, when the Acolytes caught me, they gave me my second scar. But I had stashed the lance away somewhere. And since he was just another Sondite soldier, and my violence was… understood… I kept my life and was able to recover the lance."

She gestured at Jason's waist. "Can I see the sword you carry?"

Jason did not hesitate. He drew his blade and presented it to her, laying it flat onto his other hand. "I have no jewels or sigils on the blade. I wear my jewels on my fingers, as is our custom. But the metal work is superior to many common swords. It has been used to help slaughter a dweller, one of the biggest ever killed outside of the Great Chasm. It hasn't taken any human or Vistonex lives yet. I don't want you to be first. But I must free the Second Hand. For the sake of your people, and mine, and the entirety of the kingdom. I will do what I must."

"You are committed to this, then?"

Jason gulped despite himself but then nodded. It would not be easy. And that dark part of him liked the idea of a violent test of his ability, an opportunity to let the *real Jason* out.

The Sondite chief simply stared at him, eyes probing. After a long moment, she spoke, "What do you think, Twuque?"

"I think this one is exceptionally foolish."

"Same as everyone else you come across."

"Yes… but I believe that the foolishness he speaks, he believes."

"As do I, actually. You can get my name then, Killovew, and an audience with the Second Hand. You don't have to fight me or my champion."

Jason blinked. "Wait—really?" *Why not!*

"You can have your audience with the Second Hand, and I will learn more of this conspiracy between you."

"Thank you… I'm just surprised you trust me."

"Should I not?"

"You should, but that is not an instinct those on the run have very often. Trusting a stranger is usually dangerous." Jason smiled at her and added, "But thank you for trusting me; it will be in your favor."

"Don't jump to conclusions. I don't completely believe you… not yet. But we are escaped slaves, Prince Killovew. We can't live out here forever, and you, the grandson of our last and kindest ally, stride into my camp, tell me you killed those hunting us, and you want to help us? *All* of us? And that you'll put your own life on the line?" She laughed. "I'm not a complete fool. But I'll give you a chance. My people deserve that." She reached out her hand and studied him in the eyes as she introduced herself. "I'm Rekebba."

Jason took her hand and looked right back at her. "Thank you, Rekebba."

"Now, follow me," she said and strode out of her tent.

Twenty

The Second Hand was cast in dark shadow, huddled in the back of a much smaller tent at the center of the refugee camp. He had pulled his purple robes up around his shoulders and over his head, though it was not very cold. Only the lower half of his face was visible, and that was covered in unkempt gray stubble. He did not move when Jason, his four allies, Rekebba and Twuque entered the tent.

"Tegan?" Jason asked into the darkness. "Are you all right?"

Without turning or looking up, sounding mournful, the man spoke, his voice hoarse. "Zedaff, you have come to rescue me."

"Zedaff? No, Tegan, I'm not Zedaff. I'm Jason…"

The head lurched up, haunted eyes catching the torchlight. "Killovew?"

"Yes."

Frantic eyes now. "Have we missed the Sundown?"

"Not yet. We have seven cycles."

Hopeful eyes. "And how many cycles ride are we from Shinar?"

Jason looked to Rekebba. She would know better.

The rebel leader thought for a moment, then said stiffly, "Probably five. Maybe four, riding hard, extra horses to bear your weight, leaving now… Which to be clear, you are not…"

Tegan sat back, coughing. When he caught his breath, he spoke. "Not enough time. No preparation. I am barely hydrated enough to stand, let alone press a horse across the grasslands."

Jason knelt next to the older man in purple.

"Tegan, Second Hand of the Acolytes, I was told you saved my father's life many seasons ago." Jason placed a hand on the man's shoulder. "Since then, you and my father have forged a plan to unseat the power at the heart of Shinar and halt the endless war in the Dezruk Forest against the Vistonex. To free the Sondites. I will not give up on our only chance to finish what you both started so long ago. Help me explain our goal to Rekebba, convince her of our sincerity, and ride with me back to Shinar. We will race the setting sun, make the Sundown Ceremony, and take back this kingdom. I saw it in your eyes that you want this chance, no matter the cost."

The Second Hand whispered, "Yes," but his head bobbed downward toward his chin. It was a strain for him to even hold his head up.

Jason turned to the Greenfoot brothers. "Give me your waterskin, Ratoke."

He hesitated. "Uh, I'm probably not the best person to ask for water, prince."

"Bury it, Ratoke; I know what else is in it. Give me the cursed thing."

Ratoke hesitated still, but Taroke just scoffed, pulled his own out from his cloak, and tossed the skin.

Jason caught it and brought it to Tegan's lips. "Drink."

Tegan cracked open his parched lips and took the water gratefully, guzzling it down, spilling a good bit across his beard and down his chin.

He wiped his mouth and spoke, stronger than before. "Wise words, boy. You must be your father's son."

Jason continued, "There were three others with my father when you freed him from the Shinar sewers. A Sondite named Kamau Raak, a knight named Trittion Oak, and a prince named Eric Eden. The burden of finding a way to change this kingdom has weighed on them all, each cycle, all those seasons ago… We must complete the quest that they set before us."

The Second Hand leaned forward and tossed back his purple hood, revealing short salt and pepper hair and a wrinkled brow, etched deep with age and exhaustion, but a new light burned in his eyes. He stood from the ground, wobbly for only a moment, then he found his footing and rose to his full height, taller than any man in the tent. Tegan gestured to Rekebba.

"You hear the boy's… passion, Chief. Please, bring us a table…" He breathed heavily between words, his strength obviously limited. "And chairs and food and water, and… sit and join us. We will need… a new plan, and we have extraordinarily little time…"

"Why did you not tell me this tale when I first captured you, old man?"

"Old man…" He smiled. "Would you have believed this old man? The second most powerful *old man* in Shinar, blabbering to spare him because he secretly agreed with you and was working to help you? I chose a quick, modest death, frankly. One that I supposed I deserved for not being able to help your people sooner. I was surprised when you spared me. But not hopeful. Only…" He coughed and hunched over, then waved off Sir Breigo as the knight stepped forward to help him.

"No, I'm fine. I'm fine…. Please, Rekebba, if you want to hear us out, at least provide us some sustenance. If you don't believe us, you can always go back… to starving me again. I promise, I will go hungry again… even if I eat now…"

Her eyes bounced back and forth from Jason to Tegan. "All right." She and the messenger left the tent.

A moment later, Twuque stuck his head back in the tent. "We are not conducting this meeting in the smallest, rankest tent in the camp, foolish ones. Come."

They followed Twuque to an adjacent tent and sat around a large table with an old rug tossed across the top. A handful of small candles burned in the center, chasing the darkness to the corners of the tent. Chief Rekebba was already seated, unwrapping a wide green leaf with shredded brown leaves inside.

Rekebba, Mako, and the Greenfoot brothers filled their pipes and lit them. Some stolen m-bars that Jason thought were probably taken from his own packs were brought in, and Tegan ate, clearly at the edge of starvation himself.

After he finished, with fine-smelling smoke wafting through the tent, Tegan spoke to the group.

"Everyone knows that time is of the essence. It'll be difficult, but if you allow us to leave soon, Chief, we should be able to make it. Now, you want to know our original plan and to judge for yourself if it sounds valid. The goal was—"

"I don't want to hear it from the mouth of someone I know can lie as easily as they breathe." Chief Rekebba looked around the table and gestured to Mako. "You," she said. "You tell me what you all intended to do."

Prince Jason opened his mouth, but Rekebba held her finger out at him and said to Mako, "You tell it, and I'll judge if your words are true or false."

Mako scratched his beard and cleared his throat. Jason swallowed. The legitimacy of their whole operation now depended on a man who had barely spoken most of the trip so far.

"I… uh, well, when I enlisted late and came to Castle Killovew to depart, I didn't know of any conspiracy…" Mako took a few deep puffs from his pipe, billowing out the smoke up over his face. "I just knew Prince Killovew and a few other men were heading to Shinar and then to war, and I decided to go with them."

Rekebba asked, "So you aren't even a part of this, huh, just stumbled into it? I don't believe that for a flicker."

"Well," Mako said, taking another puff on his pipe. "Normally, I wouldn't care if you did or not," he spoke slowly, which aggravated Jason. "It's not something I want to talk much about. But, if you must know, my sister has two boys fighting across the river. Been over there, you know beyond the river, over three seasons. Tells me she hasn't had a letter from them in a while. Her husband was going to go, but they got another younger boy, and… well, I… I'm not so important at the farm anymore, so to speak, so I told her I'd go instead. Try to bring her boys home or find out if something happened to them, you know, to give her closure. Didn't want to wait any longer than I had to. So, I rode to Castle Killovew, joined with these men, and we left for Shinar."

Jason just listened. Perhaps it *was* best for Mako to explain it. He was ignorant to much of the planning, but he had listened to their plan and had joined them willingly. His version would be the base truth, and though the water dragon wrangler was no wordsmith, he was not a liar, and that much was clear.

Mako said after a few more puffs, "After a little while on the road, once out of the Thirsting Forest Realm, Jason and Sir Breigo came to trust me, I guess." He glanced at Jason. "And decided to explain the plan to me, to give me a chance to join up, and to gain my trust and my spear. They told me about how we were going to meet up with an inside man from the Acolytes, inside Shinar, inside the Grand City itself. That man sits across from us here." He gestured to Tegan. "We were going to attend the Sundown Ceremony with Tegan and the rest of the Ten Hand Council, and since so few are admitted to the sacred ceremony, we would be able to kill the council members in attendance and put the blame on some other prince who was attending."

"Prince Quirvop," Jason inserted when he saw Rekebba make a questioning face.

"Right, we kill the Quirvop Prince and his knight at the ceremony, as well, say he and his men attempted to execute the overthrow, and we stopped them, but not before they killed the First Hand and whichever other council members were there. Second Hand survives the assassination and gets to take over command and assemble the new council members. Council members sympathetic to the Sondites and the tyranny of the Acolytes. So, the council would be run behind the scenes by Lord Killovew, making the adjustments to the kingdom, to help the Sondites and to help the other realms that are facing famine and outlaws and… other such political things I avoid thinking about."

"So, you just decided to go along with this heresy, then? Go along with killing the First Hand and maybe half the rest of the council? Why would you agree to this?"

Mako thought for a moment, "I guess I felt like if I joined up with them, I'm still doing the same thing I set out to do. Bring the two boys back home. Except, you know, more than just two boys. Everybody's boys and men, I suppose."

Rekebba was nodding slowly as if she believed, or as if she wanted to. She shifted her focus from Mako to Jason, "So, this revolution, this power grab, is basically just putting your father James in control through a puppet. Seems to me like Lord Killovew is taking revenge on the council for what they did to his father. So maybe, yeah, maybe I do believe you all really are telling the truth about executing this revolution. But how do I know all this 'help the Sondite' rhetoric is not just hot air?"

Prince Jason looked to Tegan and then back to Rekebba. "It's not about revenge, Rekebba. It never was. We don't want power. My father sure doesn't."

Jason sighed. How could he get this woman to trust that they wanted to help her?

"Look, my father told me this story many times, of when he was a child. I'll tell it to you, and maybe it'll help you understand. My grandfather Jacob took in the Sondite refugees when they came across the Gilv Mountains. We were your trade partners, the closest realm to Sond, your allies. When the Acolytes commanded that Jacob send you all away, back to Sond, my grandfather fought for you. He disobeyed the Acolytes orders. He took in as many Sondites as he could and sent the rest of your people on toward the Edengrove and to Kydoth and to Shinar. With food and supplies! And that same cycle, when the Acolytes left, Gahkin's golden beam descended upon our castle. My father was just a boy, but he said he will always remember that ray of light coming toward him, burning down the forest as it came. It was miraculous, he said, and terrifying. It was like watching death come for you. Something beyond this world from the stars, strong enough to beat back darkness itself. And of all the places in the kingdom, it came for Castle Killovew."

Jason stared at the lit candles in the middle of the table, watching the flames flicker, thinking of his father's face when he told Jason this story for the first time.

"The ray stopped just outside the castle gates. Vanished as quick as it had come. Grandfather took the beam as a sign. As a call from Gahkin for him to go to Shinar, and to visit the Ten Hand Council. He left my father behind as just a boy, and while he traveled to Shinar the Acolytes continued to strip away the Sondite freedoms, continued to demand higher and higher harvest taxes across the kingdom while the crops dried up season after season. They spread the m-bars far and wide, and people forgot how to survive without them. My grandfather met with the council, and he did so in good faith to help all the people of the kingdom, and you know what they did?" Jason tore his eyes from the orange glow of the candle and looked into Rekebba's eyes. "Did you ever hear what ended up happening to Lord Jacob Killovew? Why I never met my grandfather?"

She answered. "They killed him. That was the rumor."

"Worse," Jason said. "They imprisoned him in the dungeons below the Ten Hand Temple pyramid. They kept him barely alive, and they left him down there to suffer. To suffer for trying to undermine their 'Gahkin-given authority over the kingdom." Jason looked across the rest of the group. He had always had a way with public speaking. It came naturally to him. As natural as his archery or his swordsmanship. His confidence bubbled up from within him, almost as if it was a role he played, not his true self. But still, he played the role well.

"Seasons later, my father says he doesn't think that the golden beam was a sign or a calling," Jason said.

"What does he think it was?"

"It was a warning," Jason said. "A warning to stay away from the Acolytes, to leave well enough alone, to not fight back."

"Sending a team of assassins to overthrow the Ten Hand Council is not exactly leaving well enough alone."

"Well, that's just it," Jason nodded in response, eyes back on the small flames. "If the God-King sends a warning like that, and wants the Sondite people abandoned, and wants this whole kingdom to fall into chaos and starvation and war, that is even more reason we have to try to save it. Bury the God-King somewhere deep near the chasm. We want to save the world, not let it fall to ruin and starvation. The God-King may have united the kingdom, but that's ancient history, same as Him. It's up to us to save it now."

Chief Rekebba leaned closer to the table, embers in her pipe glowing red as she drew in a deep breath. Smoke shot from her nostrils and her mouth. She looked Jason in the eyes. "You really do want to help us." It was not a question.

"Yes," Jason replied, not averting his gaze from her eyes. "We do."

Rekebba inhaled deeply and sat upright. "All right," she said, "I guess I believe you. What do we do next?"

Tegan smiled. "You let us leave. We rush back to Shinar. The gates will be flooded with refugees. It was crowded when I left, and it'll be worse at Sundown. But together, I can escort the Killovew men through the Acolyte guards, through the city, up to the temple. There may be more security at the ceremony due to my absence, but my return will be lauded, and the Killovew team will be heroes for rescuing me. Our plan is still viable."

Rekebba nodded. "I will let you leave. But I need one hundred percent certainty that you can pull this off. And when you do, my people will need to know that you do. Need to know when they are safe again."

"We can promise to send messengers back to your camp here," Tegan said.

Jason added, "Bury it. If we succeed, we can send one of us, Chief. I'll come myself."

"No," Chief Rekebba said. "That's not good enough."

Jason frowned.

"I want you to bring me with you, Prince Killovew. If you are taking down the council, the Sondite people will have a role in it."

Twenty-One

The trade ships were docked, and repairs began. The carcasses of both the Vistonex and the horses were burned downwind. The bodies of the men were laid out to be identified later when the rest of the Traveling Town of Early arrived. The livestock that had not been killed by the Vistonex were brought off into the slaughter warehouses or corralled out in the pastures east of the port. Crichton and the rangers helped where they could and then retreated into a small room within an empty barn.

Eventually, Domray and Flagg found Crichton, snoozing in his seat, head flat on the table. Crichton peeled his eyes open and saw a large face way too close to his own. He jumped and leaned back in his chair. Flagg laughed, but Domray just beamed at Crichton as if he were Gahkin incarnate. Flagg sat across the table at a more reasonable distance.

"Which wagon did you come along in?" Domray asked, moving away, taking another seat.

"I rode here with Sarpho and Rulbiss," Crichton said. "I killed a couple of Vistonex, too."

"No?" Domray looked concerned. "If you had been born in Shinar, you'd still have a whole season of training before you'd be Vistonex fighting age. Wait a minute…" Domray itched his arm. "Did Sarpho force you to ride with the warriors? Gahkin himself commanded you be brought to Shinar. That was an awful risk."

Flagg raised his eyebrows at Crichton.

The Sondite boy replied, "No, I rode along with them on my own. Sarpho was glad I did, but he didn't force me or anything." Crichton wasn't entirely sure why he lied. It was certainly not to defend Sarpho. A part of him just liked the sound of leading men, of being more advanced for his age, of being brave enough to ride into battle of his own volition. But there was something else. Gahkin wouldn't encourage lying, but would he want Crichton to rat Sarpho out? Crichton felt a little compromised, but he thought he had chosen the better of the two sins. "Sarpho and Rulbiss are with Lord Early, I think, out on the docks."

"We haven't seen them yet. We only just arrived. We found you in the first building we looked inside. How about that? Like Gahkin planned it himself."

Crichton thought it unlikely that Gahkin wasted his time planning meaningless coincidences.

"When do we sail for Shinar?" More than anything, Crichton just wanted to find a better spot to sleep than the chair he was currently hunched in.

"Not until the convoy from Castle Kydoth arrives, I imagine. No trade ships will be departing until their business is concluded with all the merchants and buyers." Domray continued talking, but his eyes glazed over, as he thought out loud to himself. "We may still make it back in time for the Sundown Ceremony if the southern wind picks up, but it will be close. If the wind stays still and this fog doesn't let up, who knows? If we are forced to row and use tow lines, it could take ten cycles to get upriver. What do you say, Flagg? It's probably only nine or ten cycles or so from Sundown, eh?"

"I would guess… Omm… more than ten, less than fifteen, yes… Makes you yearn for Shinar, doesn't it?"

"Yes, I don't know how these realms live without an updated, progressive calendar."

Flagg indulged in a small smile with Domray. "I imagine when we finally achieve… true peace and progress… when the progressive calendar is finally accepted in the entirety of the kingdom… Omm… then the Great Flash will come. The reward for all our hard work."

"Yes, we should schedule that in on the next season's calendar."

Flagg laughed, long and deep. "If only…"

Domray looked back to Crichton. "We can set up our temporary home aboard one of the vessels while we wait. Would you like to come along with me and help pick out our ship, Crichton?"

"Sure," Crichton said, stretching in his seat before he stood.

They walked the docks, spoke with two different captains—both of whom were more than courteous to Domray—and settled on a wheat barge because it was not waiting for any more convoys. It would finish unloading its inventory and then head straight back to Shinar. The captain felt personally offended that the Vistonex raid occurred while he was in port, and there had been too few guards stationed to protect him.

After walking around for a while, Crichton's drowsiness left him. He volunteered to help unload the wheat, but the captain and his sons didn't want the Sondite to contaminate the product. Crichton did not take much offense; he smiled as they strained and toiled, unloading the huge rolls. Domray asked him to go find the rangers and Flagg. The barge would be unloaded within another candle length or so.

Crichton found Flagg first, pointed him in the right direction, and continued searching through the port. All the wagons and people from the Traveling Town of Early had arrived, and the once empty port overrun with Vistonex was now bustling as though it had never been abandoned. Torches were burning in all the buildings, private marketeers auctioned off the suddenly higher value animals that survived the raid, and sailors scrubbed down their ships. Two off-duty guards even fished off the pier, sharing a flask.

Blood-stained decks, though, revealed the grisly truth of the recent past.

Crichton paused for a moment at the place Memoria was put down. Something bumped into his leg, and without seeing her, he knew Emushéré had found him. He reached down to scratch her ears but instead felt a strange metal edge. He turned around.

"Hello? Get out of the way?" A sailor pushing a handcart, two barrels full of algae oil balanced precariously on top, tapped his foot with impatience. "Sondites," he muttered as he walked past. Crichton frowned.

A little later, he did find the black panther, curled up next to the tiger, their snouts bloody from a fresh meal. They were leashed outside the royal tent. Crichton rubbed Emushéré's head, and he even gave Pincher a scratch at the base of his tail, just to see if he could. The tiger looked back at him, curious, but did not snarl. Pincher just chuffed, blinked slowly, and flopped over onto his side, tail flicking lazily. Crichton didn't push his luck. He left the animals and ducked inside the tent.

Sarpho and Rulbiss were with Sir Nicholas and Lord Early. Sir Nicholas was on his way out, and he bopped Crichton on the head as he left. Crichton frowned again. Being treated like a kid was better than being looked down upon for being a Sondite, but not by much.

Sarpho was signing paperwork when Crichton walked up. Lord Early croaked, "I hear you're going to make a good soldier, sandman."

"Thanks," Crichton said. He turned to Sarpho and Rulbiss. "Domray found us a ship that's leaving for Shinar within the next candle, so—"

"I'm not going," Sarpho said, handing the papers back to Lord Early.

"Why not?"

"Walk with me." They left Early in his throne with his goblet of sugared mead. "The Kydoth ports need more protection. Domray will inform the council, but until they can send a platoon or a group of paladins, I'm staying behind with the cats." Crichton's stomach dropped. "Rulbiss will train you, as I said."

They stood next to the leashed animals. Crichton had only two great loves in his new world. Emushéré was one, and not asking anything from Sarpho was the other. The cat, Crichton knew, was not worth losing because of his pride.

"Sarpho… might I keep the panther with me? She has been—"

"No, she is a good Vistonex deterrent."

"But—"

"No. She is not yours. Sondites cannot take pets with them to battle."

Crichton ground his teeth. "Fine. The ship's this way, Rulbiss." He turned and left.

Sarpho and Rulbiss shook hands, and then Sarpho called to Crichton, "Good luck, sandman."

The Sondite did not reply. He walked on, Rulbiss a few paces behind. They wound past a few buildings, walked up the docks, and then turned onto the pier where their ship was anchored. A few more barrels were left to be wheeled off, but soon the ship would sail.

Crichton went to his small room, and to his surprise, Domray was already inside. "What do you want?" Crichton asked, turning toward his bed.

"I want to give you a gift, something to call your own and keep with you if we are forced to part ways in Shinar." Domray extended his own copy of the Habibrok to Crichton.

Books were not cheap, he knew, especially not full copies of the Habibrok. A thought materialized in Crichton's mind, one that had been formulating in the back of his head for a long while.

"Domray, if I was just considered an outlaw and an expendable soldier, why do you and Flagg treat me so well? Surely not every Sondite is treated this way."

Domray's smile faltered, and he turned sorrowful. "That is an astute question, Crichton. You are right, of course. Flagg and I usually have no dealings with Sondites. Most of your people live on the West side of Shinar, in the… well, slums… or at the foot of the Dezruk Forest across the river and have little interaction with the other folk of the kingdom. I'm afraid you're going to have to deal with many people who treat you poorly.

"I think Gahkin put you and me together so I could teach you of Him, and you could grow to accept Him as your Creator in a benevolent fashion. Despite some ignorant people who might call you a slave or an infidel or inferior, I assure you Gahkin does not think of you that way. Your people have been given a great challenge. Some say your ancestors failed their test, but you now have a fresh chance in the kingdom, and one cycle, if the Great Flash doesn't come first, the people from the realm of Sond will be valued more than any other. Soldiers this cycle, heroes the next." Domray was warming up, going into full preacher mode. "He thinks of your people as lost lambs… or as a lost hound, turned wild by time away from the master. You must be shown the way back. Taught the way back. That's why I want you to have my copy of the Habibrok!

"I know it almost by heart, anyway, and it will do wonders for your belief and spirit, and it will be a great way for you to continue improving your reading ability. Gahkin has proven to have blessed you with rare athleticism and intelligence, great compassion, and patience too! I am confident he has written a bold path for you,

Crichton. One that does not bend to the ignorance of the ignorant! One that shines with His goodness!"

I can't listen to this all the way to Shinar.

Crichton said, "You've given me a lot to think about. I think I'd like to see the port one more time, before we leave. And then can we do some reading?"

"That sounds wonderful, Crichton."

Crichton scurried back out the door. Only a few barrels of wheat remained to be rolled down the pier, and some of the dock lines were already being untied. Rulbiss stood at the aft of the ship. Crichton went and stood next to him. "Can I borrow your knife, Rulbiss?" Crichton had something he had to try before they left, and it couldn't hurt to ask.

Rulbiss took it out and handed it to him without hesitation. Crichton paused, surprised at Rulbiss' generosity.

For the first time, Rulbiss spoke to him. "She's as much yours as anyone's. Go get her."

Crichton leaped into action. He took the knife and dashed over the gangway and onto the pier.

The captain was at the edge of the dock, untying a rope and tossing it back on board.

He said as Crichton passed, "We are leaving soon. And we sure ain't waiting for a *sandman.*"

Crichton jogged on, turning northward where the pier met the wider harbor section, keeping his eyes open for his best friend and ally. He spotted her and Pincher laying in the grass, leashed to a tent post. Sarpho stood right next to them. Crichton could think of only one plan.

He sprinted toward the ranger, knife in hand. Crichton shouted, pointing past Sarpho's shoulder, "Sarpho! Look! Vistonex!"

Sarpho turned, unsheathing his sword.

Emushéré's leash was made of a linked chain, but her collar was leather. Crichton slid the knife underneath the brown hide around her neck and freed her in half a flicker. The ranger noticed what was happening a moment too late and lunged for Crichton as he darted back toward the pier.

"Come on, Mushy!" The black panther sprinted after the boy.

Sarpho roared, "Get back here!"

Pincher roared, and even though Crichton didn't understand sabretooth tiger, he felt confident it meant something along the lines of, 'get back here, panther!'

Both panther and Sondite dashed across the harbor and then up the slippery pier. The gangway had been removed, and the ship was six feet off into the river, floating further and further away. Crichton sprinted hard, leaped lightly onto a pylon at the very edge of the pier, and then launched himself through the air and over the long gap of water.

He landed on the thin, raised lip of the ship and then dropped down onto the deck.

Just like the old cycles in the forest.

But he was the only one to make it to the boat. Crichton turned back to shore.

Sarpho stood at the edge of the dock, having lassoed poor Emushéré. She sat calmly at his feet, heavy rope looped around her neck, but she was staring after Crichton with her big golden eyes.

Sarpho looked out at the boat as it slowly drifted away. He wasn't angry or yelling, just smiling. Then he began laughing.

He shouted, "You got balls, Sondite, I'll give you that!" He looked down at the panther and then at Pincher on the other side.

Crichton stepped to the back of the boat, alongside silent Rulbiss. He shouted back, "Sarpho, please!"

Sarpho cracked his neck and rubbed his arm, thinking. All the while, the boat drifted further away. The panther looked up at him and then back to Crichton.

Finally, Sarpho said. "Oh, bury it. I don't want to deal with the both of them, anyway." He removed the rope around Emushéré's neck.

The black panther pounced without hesitation, hurtling through the air over thirty feet, and landed smack dab in the middle of the boat deck.

Sarpho turned away, his massive brown sabretooth tiger following him back into the foggy harbor.

Rulbiss looked at Crichton and the big cat, and for a flicker, it looked like a faint smile flashed across the Acolyte ranger's face. The Sondite boy handed the knife back to Rulbiss, who nodded and tucked it away.

The captain, emerging from below deck, shook his head and muttered, "Vistonex, Acolytes, sandmen… might as well have a digging black panther too…" He climbed up the ladder, to the helm, still murmuring under his breath, "Ice Moth next, probably, then maybe a Dweller… Maybe we will pick up the God-King himself, returned, around the next bend…"

Crichton smiled, and together, the boy and the panther descended downstairs to his room, Emushéré rubbing her head against his hand as they went.

Twenty-Two

Princess Jinala Killovew and Sir Trittion Oak walked along the forest path without talking. The crunch of their footsteps in the dirt, the songs of the evening birds, and the occasional fluttering rush of bats emerging from their sunlight hibernation harmonized with the musical rustle of leaves blown by the northern wind. Half of the sun had already descended behind the Gilv Mountain. Aided by the shadow of the mountains, the tangled forest canopy let in almost no light.

The dark season came fast to the Thirsting Forest. It provided great camouflage for the sneak following the Killovew princess and her escort.

Sir Trittion was probably glad for the lack of light. It ensured no one would be able to follow him as he smuggled the princess north. At least, that is what Sir Trittion thought.

The tracker had been stalking them since they left the castle. Now, he would finally see where Trittion was taking her. The twilight helped conceal their bodies and their destination from curious eyes, but not well enough.

They thought they were alone on the path, but they were wrong. A small smile of success flickered across the follower's face. They were heading exactly where he thought they would.

Sir Trittion looked up and down the trail—the follower hunched deeper into the shadows. The knight saw nothing that might have suggested they were being watched, so he ducked off the path under a large cypress branch and slipped into the wild forest. Jinala followed along behind him.

The silent follower slunk along, creeping into the forest after waiting a few moments.

Ahead, through the gloom and moss, sat a small wooden barn. The windows were all boarded, the wood was black and decaying, and the roof seemed sunken, soggy almost. The barn looked abandoned—but the follower knew that was not true. Inside he could hear the soft neighs and whinnies of horses.

Sir Trittion *was* planning to take Jinala away from the castle. On horseback.

The stalker climbed up through the cypress tree, slithering along an upper branch to keep above his two unsuspecting victims.

Jinala and Trittion halted at the barn door as the knight flipped through his key ring. Just as Sir Trittion poked the correct key into the door, he dropped out of the tree.

Soft as a cat, he landed behind them, noiseless. But on his first step forward, a leaf crackled under his foot.

He had to act.

"Surprise!" Martin said as he leaped from his crouched position on the ground.

Trittion yelped, and Jinala screeched. Then Jinala began to giggle, but Sir Trittion silenced her.

"Martin!" Sir Trittion was livid. Even in the waning sunlight, Martin could see his face was red and growing redder. His eyes narrowed, and his mustache quivered. He shouted, "How dare you?" and then realized he should not have shouted, which only made him even angrier. His fists shaking, he snapped, "Get inside, the both of you. Now!"

Martin slumped his shoulders and walked toward the open door. On his way into the barn, though, at the base of the doorway, he saw something he never thought he would see again. He bent down to pick it up—

"I said, get inside!"

Trittion shoved him into the cabin, Martin tripped, and banged his chin on the ground.

Evrost sat inside, already mounted on top of one of the horses. "Now that's not right, you vile brute!"

"Evrost! How did *you* get down here!?"

"Martin took me here and told me to wait here." Sir Trittion glowered daggers at Martin. Evrost coughed and said, "Magic, I mean. I used magic."

Martin smiled. "I knew you all kept horses out here. Crichton and me, we used to come here all the time and hide out. I guessed you would be bringing her here. And I was right!"

"Bright bet, boy!" Evrost said. "Now, where are we going next, sir knight?"

"Shut your mouth, wizard!" Trittion was really fuming now. "You two aren't going anywhere but back to the castle! I'm taking Jinala to Northtown. I have had enough of your disrespectful behavior! I'll push the Sondite if I want to push the Sondite. I am not the one that cost him his brother. Or his father, for that matter!"

"How poor are they that have not patience! What wound did ever heal but by degrees?"

Trittion's frown deepened. "You've lost whatever sanity you once had, wizard."

The Mud Wizard continued, "Perhaps. Those words… ah, never mind, they are but the babble of a uh… wizard… His wit too sharp and his mind too broken for this world. This world… how it has fallen from the peace we strove to establish."

"Lunatic! What do you know of peace? Ever since Lord Killovew met you, you have doomed us to mettle in things best not mettled with! You roped James into all of this with your heretical plotting! Why have you done this to us? To James? To my realm?"

Trittion stood on the doorstep, shaking from head to foot, his finger jabbed in the direction of the Mud Wizard. Martin wasn't afraid of Trittion hurting him, but Trittion's anger scared him, nonetheless. Trittion was always calm and gentle.

"Truly, knight, you ask?" Evrost said. Trittion lowered his accusatory arm. He did not move. His eyes were as blank as stone. "Because I am not bound to please thee with my answer."

Trittion took a long, deep breath, and then another. He cracked his knuckles and neck and then walked closer. Martin scrambled back on the ground, afraid—until he saw Trittion's face.

The old knight was fighting back tears.

"I'm… I'm sorry, Martin. I didn't mean to hurt—I thought you were… never mind. I'm sorry." Trittion could barely hold it together. He snuffled his nose. "No, Evrost, I do not want to know. It is not my place to question Lord Killovew." Trittion moved back to the doorway to leave.

Martin leaped up, his chin bleeding a little. "Wait, Sir Trittion—"

The old knight shut the big barn door behind him. He did not bother to lock it. Martin looked over at the princess.

"Well, we are all out of the tower… not exactly according to plan. Now what?"

Jinala said, "I've never heard him yell like that."

"Even the largest kettle boils over eventually if you add enough heat," Evrost said, stroking his beard.

Martin's thoughts shifted back to what he saw earlier, just outside the door. He knew it was important. More important than Trittion losing his temper.

"Evrost, I think… Well, I saw something important outside. Right before Trittion knocked me over."

The Mud Wizard cocked his head to the left. "You are a little badger, aren't you, Martin?"

"What? Evrost, pay attention."

"I am. That's all I do now. That's all we were ever supposed to do. Pay attention. Just not from this close. But I've realized you're perhaps the toughest little boy on the whole planet."

Martin said, "Made-up words won't distract me from this, Evrost." He walked to the door, pulled it open, and looked down.

It was still there!

"Ah ha!" he said as he reached down and plucked the thin blue thread up out of the mud.

"What have you got there?" Jinala peered over his shoulder.

"Look! Look, it's the Mud Wizard's string he tied to his frogs before he threw them out the window."

Evrost ran to the children at the doorstep, a huge smile on his face. "Well, what are you waiting for Martin, reel them in! Reel those pond puppies in!" Evrost hollered into the forest, "Croak and Ribbit! I knew you'd find me! Reel, boy!"

Martin pulled on the string, but it drew tight. "It's snagged on something."

Evrost ran back into the barn. He grabbed his staff leaning up against the wall, and rushed back outside. His excitement did not waver. "Well, do your elephant-sized stompers work as well as your eyeballs?"

"Huh?"

"Do your big feet a favor, and let's put them to use. Follow the string!"

Martin stepped off the landing and into the jungle. He bent over, coiling the thread in his hand, keeping the string taut as he walked deeper into the trees and underbrush. Evrost and Jinala followed right behind him.

After only a handful of steps, Martin found the snag. The line was looped around a tree root. Martin unwound the line and kept going. He felt less tension on the string.

"It really doesn't even seem possible that they could survive, tied together like this, dragging this long string along behind them," Jinala said.

"I'll have you know; Croak can survive more than you might think, princess. Ribbit… well, we'll see… Be careful you don't reel in a snake, Martin."

Martin stayed quiet and kept following the string. They had to be getting close. The string would likely just end, not attached to anything.

"Look!"

Martin stood back to his full height and tugged the last of the string up into the air. Sure enough, emerging from a dense patch of weeds, both frogs dangled at the end of the line. Covered in mud, they croaked and kicked- alive and well. The fatter frog even had a shiny grasshopper in his mouth.

Evrost pulled the string from Martin's hand. "What have you got there, Croak?" The Mud Wizard plucked the frog's dinner right out of its throat and held it up in front of his face.

"Ah," Evrost said, "The bug!"

Evrost's eyes lit up, glowing white, illuminating the grasshopper. It was all-black, with white eyes that seemed to glow of their own accord. The grasshopper eyes were like miniature versions of Evrost's.

"Oh my…" whispered the Mud Wizard.

Jinala asked, "What's the deal with a grasshopper, Evrost?"

Evrost stood in silence, his eyes flickering as they took in every inch of the cricket. He brought his pointer finger to it and tapped it on the head. Somehow—*magically*—a thin black string snaked out of Evrost's finger. It connected to the cricket's head with an audible click, and Evrost's eyes flashed bright.

Jinala and Martin stepped backward. Evrost's body started humming.

His eyes lost their glow. The black string disconnected and disappeared back into his hand.

"This is not a grasshopper, Jinala. And please, I need to see James immediately."

Jinala said, "There is a lot of forest between him and us Ev."

Evrost pushed Jinala gently. "Then we must go to him. I have something important I've just figured out that I must tell him. And I don't know how long I'll be capable of holding onto this memory, nor this sound reasoning."

"Okay, well, I believe I know the way back. So, follow me!"

"Good, let's hurry!"

Jinala dashed off, Evrost high stepping through the underbrush behind her, Martin following in the rear.

"You are a wizard! A real wizard!" Martin said. "We can go save Crichton! We can go save Crichton now!"

"I agree," Evrost said, dodging around a bush and chasing Jinala toward a gap in the far tree line. "But I must speak with James Killovew at once. It's the only way we can help Jason. And Crichton, for that matter."

Evrost spasmed and stopped running. He twitched twice and fell over. From the ground, he coughed and then said, "Go Jinala, get your father! Go!"

Jinala hesitated for only a moment and then flew on.

Martin knelt by the wizard in the tall weeds. His head was humming. It sounded like a beehive was buzzing inside his skull.

"Listen to me, boy." Evrost spasmed again and then grabbed Martin's shirt. "You must tell Lord Killovew what I'm about to tell you. He will understand. Repeat it over and over when I forget. You cannot forget."

Martin feared the Mud Wizard's strange glowing eyes. They were growing brighter again, and his face twitched in unnatural ways.

"But why didn't you tell Jinala this?"

"I didn't think I would lose control so fast. Damn it! My head feels like it's on fire! Now, just repeat after me. There is no traitor."

Martin repeated. "There is no traitor."

"But Jason Killovew will fail."

"But Jason Killovew will fail."

Evrost twitched, his arms flailed at his sides, his eyes flashing white. "The God-King knows."

"The God-King knows."

"The Great Flash is coming." Evrost twitched again, but this time regained control and said, "Only I—I mean, Adam… Adam can stop him."

"Only Adam can stop him."

"Find the witch."

"Find the witch."

Evrost rubbed with both hands at the sweat gathering on his brow. "Okay, what do you remember?"

Martin didn't remember anything.

"Please, Martin, think. Please."

Martin spit out, "There is no traitor with Jason, but he will still fail, the God-King knows, the Great-"

Evrost convulsed, and his whole body began to vibrate on the ground. His eyes glowed and dimmed. His nose quivered, and then everything stopped.

Evrost lay limp, looking normal, his eyes closed and his face blank. He muttered something under his breath that sounded like 'Scott wears boots,' but Martin couldn't really make it out.

Then he opened his eyes and said, "Martin, my boy, do you think Ribbit and Croak are hungry?"

"Evrost? Do you remember anything? Who is Adam? Tell me you remember what just happened!"

"Somethings I remember sometimes, sometimes I remember somethings, other things I remember other times. I sometimes forget to feed Ribbit, and once I forgot to forget that I forgot." He crossed his eyes. "But that's just a wizard thing. I think I even forgot my own name. Although Adam sounds familiar." He sat up and looked around at the twilight-lit meadow, "We need to go to the Killovew rookery, I think. But where are we now?"

Martin helped the Mud Wizard stand up. Together they walked onward toward the trail and the castle.

Martin whispered the dictations while they walked. He knew they couldn't be found by anyone other than Jinala, Lord Killovew, or the elder knight Trittion, so when they came to the main trail, he stayed off it. They followed along from within the forest edge. If Martin hadn't been paying attention, Lord Killovew and Sir Trittion would have ridden right past them when they came barreling down the trail on horseback. Martin jumped out on the trail and shouted, "Hey!"

The riders halted and turned quickly back to him.

"Lord Killovew! Listen before I forget, okay?"

"Whoa, slow down, Mart!" Lord Killovew leaped from his horse and knelt next to the boy.

"No, I can't! He said he knows there is not a traitor with Jason but that you are going to fail because they know the plan and that the God-King knows and that you must send an eagle to everyone and… uh, and… uh, oh! And only Adam can stop him and that we must find the witch!" Martin flopped back onto the ground, the pressure off his shoulders at last. "That's what he said to tell you."

Trittion looked at James, and James frowned back.

Martin said, "You should have seen it. Evrost started talking normal suddenly and did this magic where he turned his finger into a black worm and—"

"Yes, Jinala, already told me this. Martin, after Jinala came to find me, what happened? What did he do?"

"Wait, where's Jinala?"

"She's safe at the castle. Now, what happened?"

"He just twitched around on the ground, and his eyes flashed, and then he told me to listen so I could tell you those things I just told you, but then his head started buzzing. It made a real buzzing noise! Like wasps were inside and then his face started to change shape and stuff and… and… he murmured something like, 'Scott, where's boots?' Or maybe, 'wear soft boots.' Crazy, meaningless, wizard words. But I couldn't really hear him. Then he just turned back into the old Mud Wizard and started talking about his frogs again." Martin looked up at the adults. They shared another look.

Over by Lord Killovew's horse, Evrost watched them, listening. He seemed shocked into silence and then finally asked, "I have a worm in my finger?"

Martin examined the wizard's innocent face. It was almost like he was multiple people all jammed inside of one body. Evrost grunted and peered at his fingers up close. He began poking his fingers in midair, accomplishing nothing.

Martin said to Lord Killovew, "You don't believe me, do you?"

"Actually, yes, I do, but I wish we had made it here in time. Ev, you remember none of this?"

Evrost shook his head. "My brain's fuzzy again," he said, looking to the ground. "I wish my memory worked better." He kicked at a little pebble on the trail.

Martin felt a tinge of sorrow for the broken wizard. The only thing worse than not having magical powers must be having magical powers and not being able to use them when you want to.

"Trittion, when we get back to the castle, get some ink and a quill and leave it in the tower for Evrost," James said. To Martin, he added, "And Martin, Jinala was only going to be gone for a few cycles before she returned to the castle; I wouldn't have dreamed of separating you two for long. You all need to start trusting me. I really do have your best interest at heart."

Martin heard a loud steel thunk. A big rock hit the ground, and then Sir Trittion's body hit the dirt hard next to it. From behind him, three skeletal men dressed in gray striped leather, much too large for their bodies, slunk out of the woods.

Lord Killovew popped up out of the dirt and drew his sword. "Not one more step." He waved Martin behind him.

Evrost calmly stared between the starving bandits and Lord Killovew. The realm lord looked hard at the wizard.

"Oh," Evrost said after a moment.

In a smooth arc, the wizard slashed his staff through the air, unleashing three sizzling blasts of blue light. Two bolts of blue caught the men in their chest, and the third bolt connected with the last bandit's hip. All three thumped to the ground, unmoving.

It had all happened so fast. Martin didn't even have the chance to be scared before all the bad men were lying on the ground. James rushed over to Sir Trittion.

"He's breathing," he said, kneeling next to the big knight, "but out cold." James looked up at Evrost. "Thank you, old friend. I'm glad you still know how to defend yourself, if nothing else."

Evrost smiled. "Actually, I think my survival instincts revived my memory a little, as well."

"Really?" Lord Killovew asked, "Do you remember the message—"

Another blast of blue light caught Lord Killovew directly in the chest. His face looked surprised for a moment, and then he collapsed onto Sir Trittion's body.

Evrost mounted Lord Killovew's horse and aimed his staff at Martin.

"Child," he said, his eyes glowing bright white, as bright as Martin had ever seen them. "Toodle-oo."

The horse galloped off into the growing twilight, headed back toward Castle Killovew.

Twenty-Three

As they approached, Crichton stared in wonder. His eyes remained fixed upon the city of Shinar, at first just a small brown clump at the base of the Star Tower. The small smattering of buildings at the bottom of the tower became more and more defined, revealing themselves to be skyscrapers, dwarfed only by the immeasurable height of the Star Tower. Due to the shade cast by the city walls, most of the buildings were visible only by their own torchlight. At the top of the city, directly underneath the Star Tower, sat the Ten Hand Temple. The top of this massive pyramid shone bright orange in the setting sun, blazing high above the walls and the other buildings. Even without the Star Tower, Shinar would embody magnificence and grandeur, and wealth. The largest city in the whole kingdom, with the immeasurable silver pillar growing straight into the sky from its heart made Shinar unbelievable—no—miraculous.

Divine, no doubt.

Crichton stood on the edge of the bow. Emushéré sat by his side, enraptured not by the city but by the flowing river water beneath the boat. Without looking down, Crichton scratched her ears, and the black panther cocked her head closer, her tail flicking in the air.

Soon Crichton could make out spindly black lines that crisscrossed the city canopy, as if a massive spider had built her web above the rooftops, trapping any citizen that wandered too far from the ground. As they came ever closer, Crichton saw the tiny shape of humans walking along the thin threads in the sky.

"Domray," he asked, "what are those people walking on up there?"

"Those are the skywalks of Shinar," he answered. "They connect the taller buildings together and allow Shinar's citizens access to different areas of the city without having to climb up and down the tall buildings just to cross the street."

Crichton's eyes widened. "Can I walk up there?"

"I will try to take you up there if we get the chance. Yes, I'll make sure to find time to walk with you up there. It's too bad you will not get a chance to be on the skywalks during the season of the sun. In some spots, you can see ten miles in all directions around the city. It's a breathtaking sight. Really helps put perspective on the land Gahkin gifted us."

"I'm sure," Crichton said, thinking about his home in the Thirsting Forest and how it looked from the top of the tallest trees.

"The seventh candle is burning, Crichton. Shouldn't you be sleeping? I'm not sure how much time we will have for rest once we get to Shinar. You will start your training right away, and before you know it, you'll be leaving me for the Dezruk Forest."

Crichton looked across the river into the dark green wilderness on the far side. The captain of the ship hugged the eastern side of the river, staying far away from the Vistonex infested forest. Deep within those twisted trees, the citizens of the kingdom—mostly Sondites—fought a war against the black-winged monsters with claws ten times the size of Emushéré's. The forest held a power within it that Crichton could almost feel. An evil aura hung like fog on the far western side of the river.

A sudden panic forced him to tear his eyes away and look back to the Star Tower. Such beauty and power clashed like steel on scale with the untamed wild just across the water. Good and evil divided by a dark blue river. Crichton kept his eyes on the Star Tower and didn't look back into the Dezruk.

Domray told Crichton that the ancient settlers of Shinar used to watch slabs of 'shiny rock' descend along the Star Tower. Giant slabs of rock from the sky. Not long after that Gahkin himself descended, uniting the realms, spreading seeds and game, banishing the Vistonex across the river, and transforming Shinar into the epicenter of democracy. Crichton wasn't sure what democracy was, and Domray explained that Crichton would learn the importance of that term in some of his later history classes. *If* he could become an Acolyte.

Crichton stepped away from the bow and knelt in prayer.

Gahkin, grant me the opportunity to become an Acolyte. I will prove my worthiness.

He thought that Gahkin probably wouldn't care if you prayed with your eyes closed or if you were kneeling, but Domray always enjoyed seeing Crichton pray, so it couldn't hurt. Crichton smiled at Domray, a little embarrassed because Domray had tears leaking from the corner of his eyes. Domray was always so emotional, crying just because Crichton had prayed without being told to do so. Crichton looked back to the city to conceal his embarrassment.

He turned away from the bow railing and moved toward his quarters underneath the deck. Emushéré followed him. Together they walked past the barge captain, who bent over to rub the big cat's neck. Like most humans, the panther had charmed the man in short time.

She had snuck out of Crichton's room, prowled across the deck, and then rammed the top of her head into the back of the unsuspecting captain's knee. He buckled, shouted in terror, and scraped his elbow as he fell to the ground. Emushéré, thinking the captain was injured, nuzzled his neck and licked his bleeding arm. Her gentle tongue scratched and tickled and made the fear-paralyzed captain giggle despite himself. He pushed the cat away, stood back up, and stared at her. She purred and lay down at his feet, content at a job well done. The captain had rubbed her neck ever since.

Emushéré loped along, catching up to Crichton after her most recent session of neck scratching, and descended the small stairwell in one pounce. Together they passed by Rulbiss' room on their way to Crichton's and saw the silent Acolyte tracker sitting at his desk and writing something out with clear concentration.

Crichton stopped a moment to watch. Rulbiss would scribble something down, consider it, and then scratch it out again. After a good bit of writing, he tore the scroll at a seam, crumpled it into a ball, tossed it into the corner, and started again. He looked up. He saw Crichton and pointed his finger at the door. Crichton left the doorway, thoughts unuttered, heading toward his room.

Crichton did not know what to think of Rulbiss. The man almost never said a word to him, but sometimes he helped Crichton and other times ignored him or dismissed him with a flick of his hand. Crichton thought they had come to a truce after Rulbiss helped him free Emushéré but ever since then, Rulbiss had acted colder than ever. Maybe he regretted helping him. Crichton frowned.

As it happened almost every cycle, some disconnected thought launched the image of Martin's face back into his mind. Crichton missed his brother and had started seriously considering telling Domray about him, just to see Martin again. He could introduce him to *his* version of Gahkin, so that together they could both be ready for the star life.

The evil tugging image of the Dezruk Forest and the war waging under its thick gnarled canopy kept him from telling Domray, though. He thought about the battle with the Vistonex in the Kydoth North Port. No pain or hurt that Crichton felt from missing his far off brother could force him to put Martin in the danger of war. Crichton wasn't scared for himself and his fate on the far side of the river, but he still worried about his brother every single cycle and would rather never see him again then jeopardize his safety and his freedom.

Emushéré must have sensed his sorrow, for she leaped onto the bed, the wood groaning under her weight, and crawled into his lap. The giant animal blinked slowly at him and Crichton blinked slowly back. The slow blinking seemed like the way the panther told him she felt content. Safe. The cat lowered her heavy head down onto his outstretched arm and Crichton buried his head in her fur. He slept and dreamed, and the big cat purred at his side, perhaps dreaming of kitten siblings she lost long ago as well.

Twenty-Four

He saw the orange glow of the torches from over a mile away. The big branch bobbed under his weight a little; a strong wind rustled the leaves, blowing many of them off, obscuring his view. But there was no mistaking. A large army marched down the Killovew road that connected Castle Killovew to Northtown. And the small woods they hid in would not hide them from a line of soldiers with torches.

"Bury me," Martin whispered, climbing down out of the tree.

Using all his strength, Martin had pulled James Killovew and then Sir Trittion off the trail. Somehow, Lord Killovew was still alive, despite the three other bandits being fried so hard their clothes were still smoldering.

Martin thought maybe it was the steel chest plate Lord Killovew wore, but he had a different theory that made more sense. Evrost didn't want to kill Lord Killovew. He just wanted to slow them down. He wanted to beat them back to the castle.

Now, though, if Sir Trittion or Lord Killovew didn't wake up soon, all three of them would be caught by the approaching soldiers, and Martin did not like his chances if they caught an outlaw Sondite boy with an unconscious realm lord and an unconscious elder knight.

Sir Trittion had awoken groggily, but he had been unable to speak any words to Martin, and had slipped back into an uneasy sleep, lying propped up against a tree trunk. Sir Trittion would come to and cough or call out unintelligibly, then his eyes would flicker shut again. Martin had managed to get some water into his mouth, and it seemed to settle him down some.

Lord Killovew was a different story. He was not groggy, nor struggling to breathe. He did not have blood drizzling from his helmet onto his sideburns, nor did he murmur in his sleep. He was just flat-out cold.

Martin shook Lord Killovew by the shoulders again, "Lord Killovew!"

His eyes did not even twitch.

"James! James!"

Nothing.

"Jinala is in trouble!"

Nothing.

Martin sighed and moved over to the horses. He had tied them around another nearby tree. He could probably climb on top of one but doubted he could get it to where he needed to go. He'd never ridden one before. Martin returned to Sir Trittion, and the knight groaned when Martin rested his hand on his shoulders.

"Sir Trittion, I really need your help."

"Kamau?" the old man croaked. "We thought you were dead." His head tipped back against the trunk again.

Martin heard drums echoing through the trees.

Jinala was not particularly good at admitting she was wrong.

But this time, she realized, she had been wrong.

She should *not* have given Martin the key so he could escape the tower.

She should *not* have argued and fought with her father about going to Northtown to help with the Sundown preparations.

She should *not* have forced Sir Trittion to take her back to the castle without telling him what happened to Martin and Evrost.

And her worst mistake, by far: she should *not* have barged into the throne room and interrupted her father's meeting. The advisers had no idea who Martin or Evrost were, but now they would ask questions when Lord Killovew returned.

He had left with Sir Trittion immediately, demanding Jinala wait and not come with them.

Now, with her legs crossed and her foot tapping against the table impatiently, she waited. Elton, Blake, and Finch, the three advisers who had been interrupted, were all waiting with Jinala in the throne room.

The door slammed open, and Jinala looked up, expecting to see her father. Instead, a scout rider from Northtown hustled down the hall and up to the council table.

Wiping sweat from her face, panting, she asked, "Where's Lord Killovew?"

"Somewhere in the buried forest, looking for… civilians in trouble." Blake eyed Jinala as he said the words.

"I have a very urgent message from Chief Daak. When will he return?"

"We don't know when he'll be back," Elton said, not bothering to look up from one of the scrolls he was re-reading for the fourth or fifth time. "What's the message?"

"It's for the realm lord, only, Mr. Elton, sir."

Elton peered up from his scrolls then, speaking in his overly monotonous voice. "Is it urgent, or is it only for Lord Killovew? Because if it's both, you are out of luck. So, tell me, would you like to wait, or would you like to tell us?"

"What about his elder knights? Is Sir Trittion here?"

Elton scoffed, adjusting his spectacles, "You'd trust the drunk knight over three of Lord Killovew's senior advisers?"

"Well, the chain of command is clear, Mr. Elton."

"The chain of command only applies in times of war, darling, which I would have thought they'd teach all you messengers."

The rider gave Mr. Elton a significant stare. "Who is next in the chain of command, Mr. Elton?"

Jinala stifled a gasp.

Blake dropped his fork, and Finch's mouth dropped open, a little high-pitched squeak escaping. He covered his mouth with his hands to silence himself.

Elton said, rolling his scrolls up, "Calm down, everyone. Now, messenger, what is your name?"

The scout's mouth drew tight. "Sarah, Mr. Elton."

"Sarah, we are the only ones with the ability to make a decision for the castle right now. So, tell me about this message. How urgent is the situation? Is it the Ardellians?"

The scout rider's lips drew even tighter. "The. Chain. Of. Command. Who gets my message?"

Finch, Blake, and Elton all turned to Jinala. She felt the intensity of their gaze burning into her and then realized why they were staring. She raised her left hand up off the table. The glittering, jewel-encrusted strap of leather dangled meekly on her thin wrist.

Sarah nodded. "Trusted advisers, if I could have a word with our realm leader, alone, please."

Finch and Blake stood up, but Elton remained seated in his chair near the throne. "Jinala, dear, don't worry. I'll stay and help you figure out what to do. Until your father returns, of course. You are allowed to appoint a war councilor, which I'll be happy to serve for as long as you need."

The scout rider said nothing, and Blake hesitated halfway toward the door. Elton stared at her, waiting for her to simply say yes, to agree to the wise older man who seemed to know exactly what to do. Only Finch kept walking toward the door, almost as if he knew what she was going to do before she did it.

He was the only one that wasn't a stranger to her.

"I appoint Mr. Finch as the Killovew war councilor."

Finch froze.

"Very well, girl." Elton gave her another dismissive look, and he and Blake took their leave.

"Jinala, Mr. Finch." The scout woman waited for Finch to return and take the nearest seat next to the princess. Once he did, she said, "A large group of Ardellian bandits, wearing the old colors of the Grayson family crossed our border about twelve miles west of Northtown. They are traveling light and fast. They blocked off the road between Northtown and Castle Killovew and are marching toward the castle as we speak. We have maybe four more candles before they'll be at the walls."

Jinala swallowed. "Uh, okay."

"Chief Daak got out six riders before the town was encircled. Me and one other were both sent to come here, but it doesn't look like Marissa made it. The four others went to alert the border camps. I have no idea if any of them made it to their destinations. But princess, this is not a large force. Maybe only five hundred men. If we can get our soldiers together, just from the northern border camps alone, we will have more than enough to break their hold on Northtown and to obliterate the force coming this way. I just don't know who else knows."

Finch squeaked out, "What do they hope to gain with such a small force?"

"I'm not sure. They are so lightly equipped, we think they may mean just to take something, or someone, of value, and then race back out as quick as they came."

Finch looked at Jinala. For a response, or as the potential desire of their trip, she did not know.

If her father were here, what would he do? What would Jason do?

Jinala had no clue. And it was her fault that they were gone.

I'm not my father.

She closed her eyes, and, strangely, the image of Crichton leaped into her mind. Crichton, standing in-between Martin and Jinala as that ferocious black panther crawled out of the underbrush. Those golden eyes he had stared down while he allowed Jinala and Martin to escape. He was not a realm lord. He was not even a man yet.

She thought of running through the dark in the forest. Running away from her fears, instead of facing them. She thought of holding Martin's hand in her mother's garden while the few remaining flowers swayed gently in the breeze. She thought of sword fighting with Jason and how gentle he was putting the Heir's bracelet onto her wrist.

I'm not Jason.

But she also thought about Jason's dismissive face in the wagon during the last dark season. Ignoring her warning when she *had* seen the dweller's eyes before anyone else in the rainstorm. What had he been doing? Shining his sword? Dreaming about catching raccoons for his 'experiments' in the dungeons?

She thought about her father brushing her off because she was too young, again and again, telling her half-truths to protect her. Lying to her about Crichton and Martin and whatever Jason was doing now. How had those secrets worked out for him?

She thought about how there was not a single woman adviser on her father's council. She thought it was about buried time for her to be the one doing the leading and the saving.

I can do this.

I'm not my father.

I'm not Jason.

I'm me.

"Sarah, I want you to go to the castle stables. Find the stable master and the stable boy. Tell them to take you to where the old forest barn used to be; they'll know what you mean. Wait, do you know where the castle stables are located?"

Sarah nodded.

"Good, take the others and go find my father and Sir Trittion and whoever else might be with them and bring them back here before they get surprised by the Ardellians. Oh, and I'm sure Elton and Blake are waiting outside the hall; send them back in on your way out. Go now."

She nodded and ran.

"Finch, I have two things for you. Go directly to the gate master and have him close the gate and blow the horns. Then go up to the rookery. Chief Daak probably couldn't send hawks or doves; they'd be shot down by the Ardellian blockade. But we have no such problem here yet. I want letters to the three closest villages and to the Edengrove. Describe what is happening, just like Sarah told us. We need a quick response from the villages. And the Eden's need to know just in case this thing turns into something more. When you are done, meet me along the breezeway that overlooks the castle walls and the northern lawn."

Finch smiled. "Yes, Princess Jinala." He looked at her proudly for a moment before turning to his tasks.

Elton, Blake, and two apprentice knights walked back in. At first, Jinala was afraid they might argue and threaten her, but none of the men spoke. They waited for her instructions.

"Mr. Elton, I know the castle is thin right now, but I need a full account of every man, woman, and child currently on-premises."

"We track these things, Princess Jinala." Elton turned to the other adviser.

Blake pulled out a scroll from within his robes. "There's only eighty-two people residing here currently. Subtract your father and Sir Trittion, and that makes eighty souls within these walls we need to protect."

"How many of those souls can we arm, Mr. Elton?"

They both stared at her.

"How many more can we arm?" she repeated.

"Maybe ten additional men. We have fifteen apprentice knights and twelve other guardsmen. If we get shield and sword for the… gardeners and the farm hands and the serving boys, we might be able to assemble forty men, total. May I ask, Jinala, why it is we are arming our non-combat citizens?"

"Five hundred starving Ardellian rebel soldiers are marching toward the castle. They'll be here in about four candles. They've crept past our border guards and laid siege to Northtown and I do not know what they want from Castle Killovew." Jinala glanced at the Ten Candle mantle in the great hall. The fifth candle of the cycle already flickered low.

"Gahkin save us…" Blake whispered, head bowed.

Twenty-Five

Rara Silva Nix's hooves pounded across the grasslands.

She led. The rest of the horses chased her.

They had four cycles until the sun set behind the horizon. Four cycles until they needed to be on top of the Ten Hand Temple pyramid. And they were still two cycles ride away.

They chased the Star Tower, riding right at the twisting metal that touched the stars, not bothering with trying to find a road. Jason patted Rara's neck, encouraging her onward.

If Jason could execute his father's plot, if he could fulfill James Killovew's political revolution, the enslaved Sondites would not be the only ones to benefit. Everyone in the kingdom would prosper.

Sure, the war with the Vistonex would have to continue under the new regime, but it would be downsized. The aggression into the frozen west would cease. The enlistment quotas and the slaughter of the enslaved would end. Mankind would defend itself and its side of the Verdelen River from the Vistonex, not send platoon after platoon across to hunt them all the way into the Everdark Realm. Let the winged beasts have the west, Jason thought. The darkness had always been theirs. The revolution would return the land to its natural balance: the Vistonex west of the Verdelen, the humans east of the Verdelen.

He and his father spent many long sessions in low candlelight in his private study before Jason left for Shinar. Often, they mused on the growing seasons of sun and the shrinking dark seasons. For as long as their grandfather Jacob Killovew had known, and even before that, the sun rose fractionally sooner than the last time and set fractionally later. And the pace of the loss was steadily accelerating. In the next few seasons, if the sun's descent continued to slow… well, they would start counting the loss in cycles, not in candles. And soon, there may not be a dark season at all in the Thirsting Forest. Just as had happened in Sond, during his grandfather's reign, the season of the sun would exist eternal, scorching the forest and the villages and drying up the rivers and creeks. Like elsewhere across the kingdom, the Thirsting Forest would fall into war and famine, and drought.

Jason wondered if returning the west and east back to its natural balance between Vistonex and mankind would return the balance of light and darkness, as well. If the night seasons' shrinking length was halted, the realms could return to peace. They could establish permanent agriculture; they could help wild beasts repopulate the habitable forests, salvage old farms and harvest the beasts raised there. Solutions that were currently impossible with the Ten Hand Council distributing the m-bars and demanding harvest taxes and stealing almost half of the able-bodied men for war beyond the river or holding forts along Shinar's western riverbank. If Lord Killovew could be the shadow ruler of the kingdom, instead of the Acolytes, much could—

Rara snorted and skidded to a halt, and Jason snapped back to attention.

Directly in front of their path, about a quarter of a mile away, sat a clump of men on horses and three or four wagons. Jason couldn't tell for sure, but it looked like they had big cages set out in front of their wagons. The rest of his team came to a halt alongside him. Tegan and Chief Rekebba trotted their steeds next to either side of the prince. Jason looked at them both and then back to the strangers ahead of them.

Jason felt exhausted. They were already cutting it too close and had overcome so much, and now they were outmanned by Gahkin-knows-who and would have to waste further time trying to get by these new strangers.

Tegan asked Rekebba, "Is that what I think it is?"

She replied, "Unfortunately, yes."

Jason swallowed. No law-abiding citizens would be roaming the floodplains south of Shinar and Fessdri.

"We can't go around them, I suppose?" Tegan asked.

"I doubt it," Rekebba said. "They will have seen us. They certainly would keep a watch,
considering what they are doing out here."

In the distance, Jason saw two shadows with big wings leap into the air at each other, beaks and claws slashing.

To force them to fight each other… that just made Jason's stomach sink and his jaw clench. Jason's lip curled in disgust. Vistonex or not, that was wrong.

Evil.

And you know Evil, Jason.

He shook his head to clear the voices from his mind.

Tegan spoke, "I can only come up with two options for us. One, we try to go around them, even though we know they have seen us and hope they let us leave in peace. Or two, we approach, tell them we harbor no ill will or intent to turn them in and hope they let us cross. Anything I'm missing?"

Rekebba shook her head. "You aren't wrong in our choices, but I think wrong in your optimism. Both of those options end with bandits riding us down and striking us off our horses. You all just look too rich." She shook her head as if she knew their jewelry would get them into trouble all along.

224

Jason frowned. "The third option is we ride up there with the Gahkin-given authority of the Second Hand, arrest these men and take them with us to Shinar to throw them in the dungeons."

Rekebba scoffed. "Prince Jason, there are about twenty-five of them over there, plus at least two adolescent Vistonex. Probably more. There are only seven of us. And Tegan, no offense, but you are an old useless politician with hands as soft as freshly churned algae."

Tegan allowed a modest smile. "Offense intended, I think, but not taken."

"Yes, but those aren't soldiers or desperate rebels fighting for their lives." Jason glanced at the Sondite woman next to him and continued, "Those are criminals. And all the criminals I've dealt with have been cowards. Tegan may not be a warrior, but the rest of us are."

"Still, if they have archers…"

"When have you known criminals to carry bows and arrows?"

"I didn't have the luxury to know the state of your average low-life scum in the cities." Rekebba sneered. "I only had the misfortune of knowing the low-life scum guards that monitored the Sondite prisons."

"Camps," Tegan corrected.

"Prisons," Rekebba said fiercely. "And the guards always had plenty of bows and arrows."

"Look," Jason said, "You can take my word for it. This is the flood plains of Shinar. I doubt they are starving, probably not even hungry. They are out here gambling and fighting Vistonex. When they aren't, they are stealing and extorting citizens in the city. They aren't warriors; they are bullies. They'll have maybe one archer, two at most. Ratoke and Taroke are phenomenally sharp with their jungle bows." Jason looked at the two half brothers slightly behind him. "How close do we need to get, boys?"

"Seventy yards, and even Taroke won't miss," Ratoke said.

"I won't miss at eighty, prince. Although, Ratoke… well, he talks a big game, but we might want to get him to about sixty to be safe, if we're being honest." Taroke tapped his left eye and lowered his voice a little, "Got a little milk in the eye one cycle, if you know what I—"

Jason waved them both to be quiet and turned back to Rekebba. "Between the two of them, they can pick off one archer. Then we will be looking at about twenty or so cowards without armor or decent weapons, against six trained warriors. One of those warriors is Sir Breigo Aldev. We can take them."

"Victory with death would not be a victory, Jason," Tegan warned. "We need numbers on our side at the top of the pyramid. Let's at least try to solve this with our words, and then we will fall back to violence if we must."

Jason Killovew took a deep breath. He was in a position of leadership now that he had never experienced before. Just a season ago, Breigo would have been correcting his swordsmanship and his riding; his father would have been keeping him late in his studies of history and diplomacy. Now they faced down a score of dangerous bandits after having just rescued the second most important Acolyte in the kingdom. And Jason Killovew was again deciding what they would do next. Jinala would be proud of how far he had come.

Under his overcoat and his leather and his hidden steel greaves, against the skin of his chest, her fish scale necklace still hung. Jason would not just ride in hardheaded, sword drawn, like the *violent* boy from just a season ago.

"You are right, Tegan. I'll ride out front and go meet whatever cretin calls themselves the leader of this group. We will see if words alone can settle this."

Jason felt chills creep up his neck. Despite the confidence in his voice, he knew it would be difficult to beat so many men, heavily outnumbered as they were.

But he also knew they had no other option, and if they were to succeed on top of the Ten Hand Temple, they would need to overcome similar odds. If they couldn't talk their way through the outlaws, they would have to fight their way through.

He met the eyes of his companions. "Consider this potential practice for the Sundown Ceremony. The outlaws across these plains don't know what to make of us. They are nervous, and they are waiting to see what action we take. So, look confident and look calm. And be ready. Rekebba, loosely tie some rope around your wrists, as if you are our prisoner. Let's go."

Jason kicked his heels into Rara and trotted her forward, toward the large swathe of men spread out on horseback blocking their path. Beyond them, stretching miraculously into the infinite height of the sky, the Star Tower waited, at the heart of the capital city of Shinar. The setting sun washed the grassy floodplains with golden orange light, and the sky ahead was a bruise of purple and dark blue. Jason would not let their journey end so close to their goal.

He spared one glance over his shoulder at Sir Breigo. Prince Killovew tapped his sword hilt. The elder knight nodded and tapped his sword hilt in return. In the Thirsting Forest, it meant if one man still held his blade, so would the other.

They rode forward.

They came to within about seventy feet of the criminals, and Prince Jason halted Rara Silva Nix. He dismounted from his horse and walked another thirty feet closer to the bandits. Two dirty but well-fed looking men stood out in front, already dismounted, and they walked out to meet Jason. The rest of the outlaws shuffled sideways on their mounts and maintained their cautious distance from the newcomers.

Jason scanned them all, taking stock of their weapons and condition quickly. Just as Sir Breigo and the half brothers would be doing.

Nineteen men on horseback, plus the two leaders out front. Only fourteen wore swords at their belt. Three more men steered their wagons. Most of the men were skinny and scruffy looking, but they had hard eyes and showed only malice. No fear. Three of the outlaws had bows in their hands, two had already knocked arrows.

You were wrong, Jason.

But you can still take them.

Jason shook his head. He wasn't sure. If any one of those three men put an arrow in him or Tegan, it was all over. But it was too late now to try any other tactic.

Tegan joined Jason at his side.

"Three archers," he whispered, and Jason just nodded in agreement. Behind them, the rest of the team stayed on their steeds and formed a defensive position, keeping their Sondite *prisoner* in the middle while also guarding their flanks.

The two bandit leaders stopped about five feet from Tegan and Jason.

"Greetings, lords," the smaller of the two said. "Not supposed to be riding around in the wild, lords." Under his breath, but deliberately loud enough for Tegan and Jason to hear, he added, "Those are some big jewels on those fingers and hanging from those ears, Nob."

Before the other man could retort, Jason spoke up, his voice strong and firm. "I could say the same to you, outlaws, and you would be wise to keep your eyes off our metal. Keep your hands still at your side if you want to leave here alive."

The bigger man, Nob, lifted his hands from his sides into the air in mock surrender. "Please, high lord, don't hurt us. We are just down-on-our-luck nobodies, trying to make some gold to feed our starving families. We weren't going to hurt anybody. I promise."

This time Tegan responded.

"I am Tegan, the Second Hand on the Ten Hand Council, not some independent lord or knight that you can patronize." He flicked open his dirty outer robe, revealing two massive opals dangling around his neck, sitting on the lush purple fabric that the Acolytes wore. "These jewels will be staying with me, as will the gold and silver on my allies' bodies." Tegan was old, but he was a tall man, and standing to his full height in his purple robe, with the gleaming opals and sun setting at his back, he cut an impressive figure.

Jason spoke again before either man could come up with a retort.

"We are traveling to the Grand City of Shinar with great haste and do not have the time to arrest you all and then escort you to the dungeons you deserve. So, you shall follow us after two algae candles burn and bring yourselves to Shinar to stand trial. If you turn yourselves in, we may be merciful in your punishments." Jason raised his eyebrows as he spoke the next two sentences carefully. "If you do not, we will be forced to send a battalion of paladins back here to arrest you. Perhaps they will only find empty grass once they reach here and will return empty-handed. That is what I offer you, and it is the only leniency you will receive on this cycle."

"Ah, well, that settles it then, Nob." The first man spoke again, looking up at the taller man who was clearly in charge. "We'll take our *twenty-six* men to Shinar and turn ourselves in, and the old man and his boy prince can take their… *four*… men and that tough-looking beautiful Sondite runaway to wherever they please. I don't think I've ever seent a fairer deal than that one."

"Seent ain't a word." Nob spat. He pulled off his Vistonex leather hat, picked off some dust, and put it back on. "Oh, sorry," he said, "forgot to keep my hands still." He smirked at Jason.

"Still… a generous offer from the do-gooders, wouldn't you say?" the little man asked, smiling with big, nasty teeth.

"I've got a counteroffer for you, boy prince," the lead outlaw said, still staring at Jason. "Take all the jewels and the metal and the coins and the woman and the old man and put them in a pile at my feet, and I'll let the rest of you leave, alive, with your horses."

Prince Killovew felt a tremor of *dark* excitement running through him. This conversation was devolving quickly and would turn toward bloodshed soon. But for the sake of Tegan and the plan, he had to try to end this peacefully.

"Don't let pride force you to tempt your fate, criminal. Do you see that knight behind me with my men? That's Sir Breigo Aldev." Recognition flashed in both men's eyes, but they said nothing. "Now, I'll say this again. Leave here and head south, and we will head north, and neither of us will ever have to see each other again."

The outlaw in the hat looked past Jason and Tegan, up at Breigo sitting on his horse.

"I thought he'd be taller."

Jason spoke again, letting some of his anger seep out. "Leave here, now, outlaw!"

"Ah see, we won't be doing that. And it doesn't seem you will be handing over what I want. Negotiations seem to be stalling." The outlaw smirked. "I just don't think we are close to an agreement, boy prince."

Jason scowled, "If you don't take this offer now, this *will* end with my sword in your heart."

Nob scoffed, "Please. I'll make you wish you were never born, boy. And then I'll fight your celebrity knight, too. That'll just be another notch in the old belt."

"Call me a boy again," Jason said, giving in to the *darkest* anger building in him.

"Jason…" Tegan said warningly.

The outlaw smiled at the challenge. "You don't seem to understand your situation, *boy*. You ain't bluffing your way out of this, *boy*. We are going to take your jewelry and your gold and your horses and your woman, *boy*. How does walking back to Shinar without your hands sound, *boy*? How does watching your guts fall out of your belly sound, *boy*?"

Jason raised his left fist in the air. He lifted his finger.

Two arrows zipped over his head, another flew back, and then a final arrow whipped above Jason. All three outlaws with bows had caught an arrow. One had caught it in the throat, and the other high in his leather vest, and the third caught one in his gut. The first two dropped from their horses. The third struggled to lift his bow, and another two arrows plunged into his chest, and then he fell to the ground. Jason whipped behind him to see if anyone on his side had been hit.

An arrow jutted out from Taroke's left arm, and blood slowly but steadily stained his white sleeve a dark red. He grimaced at Jason, but with a fierce jerk, he lifted his wounded arm and wiggled the bloody fingers on his hand as if to show him it all still worked.

Jason turned back and strode up to the outlaw leader, speaking steadily as he walked closer, "Sorry, negotiations seemed to be stalling. I just didn't think we were close to an agreement. Now, will you be leaving?"

He was close enough to smell their breath.

Both bandits reached to draw their swords, but they were very slow. Prince Killovew had his sword out and across the smaller outlaw's throat before the little man got his blade free of its scabbard. Nob slashed violently at Jason, but Jason turned, deflected his blade on the steel greave at his wrist, and pushed Tegan backward from the danger. Nob swung again, snarling, right at his head. Jason ducked and stabbed his sword into Nob's chest.

"I told you how this would end for you." He pushed the blade deeper into his chest.

Nob's eyes grew wide, and a little blood spilled out of his open mouth.

Jason withdrew the blade and stepped back. Nob collapsed into the tall grass. The frozen outlaw crowd twenty feet behind just stared.

Then one screamed in rage.

They charged.

Fiery energy sizzled through Jason.

You killed them. Now kill the rest.

He stole a quick glance behind him. He saw Taroke and Ratoke had two more arrows in their bows. Taroke had snapped the long end of the arrow shaft off his arm and pulled a tight belt above the wound. The arm was gruesome with blood but seemingly still functional, and Taroke didn't seem concerned with the peril of bleeding out.

Rekebba tossed off her false ropes and brandished her lance; Mako held his long spear at the ready by his side. Sir Breigo had tossed off his green traveling cloak and sat resplendent in his shining breast plate and steel greaves, his sword in his hand flashing silver in the dying sunlight as he aimed it toward the outlaws. Jason faced forward again and saw twenty some bandits, rushing forward, but with panic and mania in their eyes.

And fear.

Jason was surging with a blood lust he hadn't felt since he was a boy, hiding out down in his father's dungeons. He threw off his overcoat and stepped forward. There was blood on his boots, but he wanted to spill more. He had hunted all manner of game, chased a giant Dweller through a cave-in, but this was different.

He needed to spill their blood.

Had to.

And for the first time, his unnatural desires aligned with true justice, and Jason could finally embrace the darkness within him. These criminals deserved to be put to the sword. And now they raced at him, rushing to their death.

A handful of them drew decent-looking swords but most just pulled rusty blunt-looking pieces of metal out of their scabbards. They looked about as dangerous as the old rolling pins in the Killovew kitchens. The three men in wagons turned and fled.

The rest bared down on him.

Jason shouted at Tegan to duck down behind him, secured his stance, and raised his sword in two hands. In a moment, the battle line would wash over him.

Sir Breigo passed him on the right before they reached Jason. Breigo's horse was probably the only one on the field that had seen true battle before. The outlaws' horses were skittish, and a handful kicked their riders off during the charge, and others slowed, halfheartedly pushing the charge, staggering their line. Only about ten bandits met them on horseback, and Sir Breigo probably could have carved through all ten on his own, staggered as they were.

But he was not alone. Rekebba and Mako were right on Sir Breigo's tail, and their longer weapons knocked riders off left and right, followed by Ratoke and

Taroke, still using their small jungle bows with their poisoned arrows.

Jason plunged into the fray on foot, seeking out the outlaws who had survived being thrown from their mounts.

The first bandit he met was uninjured and carried a well-maintained sword, but he was untrained. Jason knew he could take him from the man's stance alone.

It was too wide and aggressive, and when the man went to swing, Jason slashed inside and almost clinically took off his sword arm at the elbow. He finished him with a backhand stroke into his side, carving through ribs deep into the man's chest.

Jason glanced up and saw Sir Breigo artfully parrying strikes from two different outlaws, moving their blunt weapons away from him with ease and striking them both from their horses. They did not move once they hit the ground.

Jason scanned left and saw a man crawling away through the grass. The prince took three strides and put his sword in the bandit's back.

Scanning back to the right, he saw two more men. They saw him, too. One man carried a decent sword; the other may as well have been carrying a wooden club for its sharpness. Jason strode forward, feigned at the dull one, and then struck at the sharp, who barely dodged out of the way. Jason parried their slow counter strikes, pushed the dull man hard backward into the grass, ducked the sharp's attack, parried again, then caught the sharp man's wrist in his left hand. He was strong, but clumsy. Jason yanked the man by his wrist into the way of the rusty iron sword coming from his ally. The dull blade got lodged halfway into the other man's leather shoulder strapping and Jason slashed his sword hard across both tangled-up men, slicing through leather, cloth, skin, blood, and bone. Both swordsmen dropped into a heap on the ground.

The prince stepped back and looked around.

Taroke and Ratoke were chasing down the men in wagons who had fled, launching their deadly accurate arrows from horseback. Rekebba had dismounted from her horse and was pulling her lance from the chest of a dead man on the ground. Mako and Sir Breigo were still mounted, and neither had any glaring injuries.

All were dead but one, and Jason spotted him sneaking through the tall grass toward Tegan. The outlaw was bleeding heavily from a gash in his side, but he carried a sharp sword and seemed to know if he made it to the Second Hand, he would have some sort of bargaining power. And he was much closer to Tegan than anyone else was to him. The Prince of the Thirsting Forest pulled his knife from his waist and flipped it in the air, testing its weight. He caught it by the handle and then flung it at the man. It hit him in the middle of the back, but the knife bounced harmlessly down into the grass below. It had hit him on the blunt side.

The bandit lunged toward the Second Hand.

Tegan, despite not directly facing him, must have seen him coming.

He sidestepped the surprise strike and punched the man in the jaw. The man stumbled and almost fell over. Tegan caught him again, with a left-handed hook to the chin that set the man right on his ass. The Second Hand, in his Acolyte purple robes, lifted off his necklace, took one of the fist-sized opals, and crashed it into the dazed man's head. He dropped forward, probably dead.

"Gahkin forgive me," he muttered.

Jason smiled, and he looked toward the Star Tower.

From this distance, the walls of the capital city of Shinar were just visible, dwarfed by the tower itself. In four cycles, Jason would stand within those walls and strike down the First Hand. His grandfather, Jacob Killovew, would look down from the stars and be proud of his grandson for exacting vengeance for his death and for saving the kingdom from the unjust rule of the Acolytes. Four more cycles.

Ratoke and Taroke rode up, and Taroke was very pale.

"Got them all, Prince Jason." He panted. "Buggers started to get blurry on me near the end there, but we got them all."

"Tar, why don't you hop down, huh?" Ratoke rode closer toward him, but it was too late.

Taroke's eyes closed. He slipped off his saddle, and Jason reached for him but couldn't catch him, and he hit the ground hard.

Jason knelt down and rolled him over. The arrow that had punctured Taroke's arm had gone clean through his bicep. The arrowhead itself was lodged in-between his ribs. He had broken off the staff to use his arm on his own bow.

Ratoke dropped next to him, shoving Jason out of the way. Jason could see the pool of red that had stained his shirt and was now seeping into his outer robe. It was too much blood. It was hard to believe one single man could lose so much blood and keep on his horse for so long.

"No," Ratoke whispered, lifting his brother's limp upper body into his lap, "No. Please, no."

Twenty-Six

Jinala leaned against the cracked stone railing of the breezeway, staring out at the growing torchlight coming from the northern woods. Large dollops of orange and purple smeared across the darkening sky above, and she thought of bruises and pain.

She wore Jason's old Thirsting Forest helm, adjusted to fit her head. It still didn't quite sit right, smooshing down her curly blonde hair and blocking her peripheral vision. But it gave her the realm leader look she was going for. She needed to inspire her people like her father would.

Come on, Sarah.

She had declined the steel chest plates, as they could never be adjusted enough to fit her properly, and opted instead for her thick leather training vest. She wore that over top of her green and brown riding dress and completed her attire with brown leather boots and brown leather gloves. Armed with a sharp steel dagger sheathed at her belt, she managed to pull off the warrior princess look without feeling too awkward or ungainly or immature. She hoped she wouldn't have to use the dagger.

Come on, Sarah.

She could almost feel Finch trembling at her right arm. To her left, Elton remained statuesque. Two apprentice knights, the next two in line for a full knighthood, flanked the three unlikely leaders. Below her, in the castle lawn, stood thirty-six men and fourteen women. They were all hastily armed and armored, given crude instructions by the castle guards, and arrayed in a defensive formation within the perimeter walls. They would only need to fight if the Ardellians made it through the main gate or over the high battlement walls.

Come on, Sarah, where are you?

"This is what I feared would happen when your father deployed the remaining knights and soldiers to the border and to Kydoth. We warned him, didn't we, Finch? We warned him that he was sacrificing his own castle's security for the rest of the realm."

Jinala was proud of her father. The rest of his citizens weren't being plundered. They were protected and guarded. Northtown might be under siege, but they weren't in jeopardy of being sacked and plundered. Because Lord Killovew had committed to their protection. The villages and the border guards would sweep over this small uprising, just as Sarah had said.

The trick would be lasting long enough for reinforcements to arrive.

"Elton, regret and complaints won't help us now. We will make do with what we have. I'm sure my father had a good reason for his decision-making. For now, you'll have to deal with the decisions *I* make. Finch, the aid letters were sent out without issue, correct?"

"Yes, I delivered them to Ian, the birdkeeper, directly, at the doorstep to the rookery."

Elton looked over his spectacles at Finch but said nothing.

"Good," Jinala said. She peered at the tree line, where the northern road from the castle disappeared into the woods. She could barely discern anything in the fading twilight. "I'm going to the battlements; I want to see clearly and be able to speak with this Grayson man if he wants to treat with us."

Elton responded in his monotonous voice, "You'll be exposed to their archers from there, princess, and it hardly seems necessary for you to be the one who speaks with their messengers."

"I know," Jinala said, stepping down from the ledge where she stood. "But I want to do it anyway."

"Very well," Elton said. "Let's go." He gestured to the two apprentice knights, and they all stepped toward the retractable wooden bridge that connected the breezeway to the battlements.

"Wait," Jinala said, "I'm not commanding that you all come with me."

"Ah," Elton said, looking back at her. "A noble gesture, princess, to risk yourself before your citizens. But I won't be leaving you alone to the enemy. Come along. We're all in this together." He turned back and walked toward the crossbridge. Without a glance he called, "Coming, war councilor?"

Finch jumped but then shook himself and followed the others. Jinala strode behind them all.

As they walked along the battlements, heading toward the northernmost section, Jinala could hear the drums growing louder.

The army was close. Which meant whatever trouble had befallen her father and her friends, Sarah had been unable to rescue them in time. Which meant Jinala really would have to outwit or outlast this army without her father.

Elton yawned as he walked, meandering toward the upcoming battle as leisurely as if he was headed to a budget meeting. Jinala could not say Finch was able to maintain the same calm demeanor. The man was an unhealthy shade of pale white, and was walking slightly hunched over, as if he thought an arrow might fly from the trees even now, and plunge into him.

Soon enough, that might be the case.

When Jinala stepped to the battlement ledge that faced the woods, she could see the torchlight flickering through the trees. The drums beat louder than ever, now echoing off the castle walls.

A flash of lightning behind her illuminated the landscape, throwing the potato gardens and the castle shrubbery into sharp relief against the few hundred yards of browning grass leading to the woods.

Princess Jinala did not remember hearing any thunder.

Another flash illuminated the ground, and she turned behind her to see where it was coming from.

Atop the tallest of Castle Killovew's towers stood the silhouette of a bearded man, waving a silver staff. The tip flashed bright blue, sizzling and dripping sparks.

"Who in the buried ground is that?" cried Finch. He covered his mouth when he realized he cursed in front of the princess.

Jinala knew who it was, of course, but she had no idea how Evrost had gotten up there. His silhouette gestured for her to join him, waving a come-hither motion with his staff.

Elton said, "Finch, that's the rookery tower. Are you still certain those letters got out?"

Finch's only reply was a small groan.

Suddenly, the drumming behind Jinala grew even louder, and the first line of soldiers emerged into the clearing along the northern road. The men did not look like starving bandits from this distance. They marched in perfect order, carried thick wooden shields and swords, and none looked small or skinny. Many had torches. They poured out into the outer castle lawn, spreading out and coming closer to Jinala and her advisers.

Jinala glanced back toward Evrost. His staff no longer sparked but the evening sky provided enough light to see he still stood atop the tower, waving for her to come join him.

Jinala exhaled and thought for a moment.

"Mr. Elton, congratulations, you've been promoted to war councilor of the Killovews."

"Thank Gahkin," Finch murmured.

"I accept," Elton said.

"Good, because I need you to stall this army until I return."

"You want me to stall an army of five hundred Ardellian bandits, most of whom are probably starving, without even knowing what in Gahkin's-wide-kingdom they might want, while you go investigate an evil looking stranger who has broken into our fortified castle, blocked all means of sending out messages for help, and looks like he can wield lightning?"

"Uh, yes. And I'll need to borrow one of the knights."

"Very well," Elton said, adjusting his spectacles and stepping up onto the battlement ledge. "Good luck."

Jinala grabbed Finch by the elbow. "Come on!" They took off running, and soon Jinala outpaced both Finch and the apprentice knight. She sprinted back down the battlements, over the wooden cross bridge, across the long breezeway, and darted into the interior of the castle. The knight kept on her heels, and Finch panted along behind them both, barely keeping up.

She hit the stairs to the tower and couldn't see up very well, with her helmet bobbing up and down and blocking a lot of her vision. But she didn't take it off, not knowing what was up there; she pressed it down firmly and felt it grow tighter around her skull. She waited a moment for the others to catch up, and then together, the three pressed onward up the stairs.

Evrost would be very helpful in this upcoming battle *if* he stayed sane enough to know the difference between his enemies and his allies. After the long winding staircase, Jinala and the knight reached the top. They stood outside the rookery door, catching their breath, waiting for Finch. As she heard the adviser clomping closer, his breath heavy, she wondered for the first time if she should make the two men wait outside. Evrost may have something secretive to tell her about, perhaps involving her father and Martin.

No.

Secrets were my father's way.

Not mine.

On the other side of the thick wooden door, Jinala heard muffled squawks and shrieks, loud and obnoxious and agitated. Finch stepped up onto the floor and bent over, his hands on his knees. He panted out his next words, words she never expected to hear from her old math teacher.

"Let…me… go… before you…" He stood up to his full height, sucking in more air. "I… haven't run… since… I was… a child." He took a few more deep breaths. "Okay…" He withdrew his short sword, holding it about as clumsily as she supposed Sir Damian would hold a feathered quill. Finch waved his hand, motioning Jinala behind him, and the knight opened the door.

The smell inside the rookery was unbelievably rank. The pungent odor of rotten fish and bird droppings forced Jinala to hold two fingers over her mouth to try to keep from being ill. Finch gagged a little, but they all continued inside.

The rookery contained Thirsting Forest pigeons and doves, along with owls, eagles, falcons, and speedy little hawks. Most of the birds were locked in cages, stacked five high, forming a lattice work of walkways in the windowless room. Some of the larger owls and eagles sat in the rafters, hooded, staring blindly down at the human intruders.

The rookery had no windows. If any of the birds were ever released on accident, they would have nowhere to escape and could be locked away again easily enough. To release a bird, it would be taken to the flat roof above the rookery, the very top of the northeastern tower. Where they had seen Evrost standing just moments before.

Finch stopped as he rounded a corner of birdcages. Ian lay on the ground. He had blood trickling from a blow to his head, and four little scrolls lay on the floor around him.

"Are those our letters asking for reinforcements?"

Finch nodded.

"Which means no one is coming to our rescue?"

Finch nodded, slower than before.

Jinala knelt and scooped up the letters.

"Do either of you know the system in here, which birds go to which villages? Which birds go to which realms?" She looked back and forth between both men.

Finch shook his head.

The apprentice knight shook his head.

Why would Evrost do this?

Scowling, she barged past them both. Jinala flung open the door that led to the roof. She climbed the short ladder up to a flat hatch in the ceiling and pushed with all her might against it.

It flung open. With a sharp intake of breath, Jinala launched herself off the last step of the ladder and onto the roof.

The surrounding land could be seen for miles in every direction.

The Thirsting Forest stretched out along the horizon, climbing high into the Gilv Mountains at the south and shrinking away to a thin dark line in the east and west. The peaks of the mountains, hiding the setting sun, looked like shadowy teeth compared to the orange and purple sky behind them.

Jinala looked to the north and saw the sparse woods and the hundreds of soldiers lined up on the lawn in front of the castle. There were so many.

She shifted her gaze as she turned, finding Evrost only a few feet away, standing over top of a wrinkled purple lump. A wrinkled purple lump that had three white stones dangling from his neck. He moaned in pain at Evrost's feet.

"Look what I found!" Evrost proclaimed to the princess.

The apprentice knight climbed up onto the roof, and Finch poked his head out of the hatch. Finch groaned at what he saw.

The Acolyte looked up at Jinala and frowned. "Where's Lord Killovew? His plans are known to me. He will—"

Evrost cut him off, "Much too big to feed to the frogs. He's been hiding in the ripe rookery rooms, revealed by his rank reek. Some fake god powers must have hidden him from your birdkeeper, but Croak eventually locked onto him and downloaded his coordinates into my P.P.S."

"Evrost, do you know where my father is? Or Martin?"

Evrost crossed his eyes, thinking hard. "I… don't remember. I think I had to leave them in a hurry, didn't have time to get held up… Yes, I think they are in the northern woods." He rubbed his head then continued, "But look Jinala, the Third Hand, caught red-handed, haha, spying! He has been here many cycles, based on the odor!"

Her father, still gone, probably caught by the Ardellians.

Isaac, the Third Hand, spying in their tower.

Surrounded by an army, with no help on the way.

Jinala thunk her fist against her helmet, thinking. She wanted to just sit down and cry, but she couldn't do that. She didn't have time to dismay. She had to figure a way out of this. She had to lead her people.

When she looked up, something caught her eye. She walked to the other side of the tower and scooped up a small navy-blue sphere. A faint blue glow shimmered from within the dark orb. A strange tingling sensation passed over her.

"Ev, did he use this?"

"Not that I noted."

Jinala slipped the fist-sized orb into her pocket.

The old Acolyte croaked, "Who are you, girl? Where's Lord Killovew?"

A little voice popped into her head. Her own voice. Proud. Confident. Louder than the fog of despair that threatened to overwhelm her.

I'm me.

And that's enough.

Jinala unstrapped the clasp at her chin. She pulled off her helmet, shook out her golden curls, and unsheathed her steel dagger. Pointing it at Isaac, she said, "I'm Jinala Killovew, current ruler of the Thirsting Forest Realm. You are under arrest for murder, spying on my family, and breaking the rules set by the Ten Hand Council in governing independent realms."

Isaac stood slowly and brushed himself off. "Three generations of Killovews, and I'll beat you all. Don't you realize? I don't follow the rules; I make them. I didn't have to use the stone, girl. Gahkin knows all. Gahkin knows you are all traitors. He sees through my eyes. He hears through my ears. None of you heathens will survive!"

Jinala swept her hair back and tossed it behind her. She turned toward Finch and the knight. "Take him off the tower and wait for us at the breezeway."

Finch hesitated, "Princess, I will do as you command, but that… that's the Third Hand."

"And he's spying on us, Finch, and killed Ian!"

"Are we sure he did?"

Finch's eyes flashed to Evrost, but Isaac said, "The boy wouldn't let me read the letters, said he needed to get permission!" Isaac laughed darkly. "The justice of Gahkin was done unto him, as it shall be unto you all! This whole realm's populace has become blasphemers under the Killovew rule." Isaac stepped forward as he spoke, almost as if he was about to lunge at Jinala. "We will place the Thirsting Forest under our control."

The knight did not hesitate now. He stepped in front of the Acolyte, snatched his arm, and twisted it roughly behind his back.

Isaac said, in an almost whisper, "Be careful whose authority you follow, sir knight, I can promise—"

The knight used his free hand and smacked Isaac hard across the face. "Silence."

Jinala raised her eyebrows.

"How dare you strike an old man?" Isaac croaked. "Gahkin—"

The knight raised the back of his hand again, and Isaac silenced. "Mr. Finch, would you please take the lead? I'll guard him from behind."

Finch still hesitated.

"I haven't spoken my oaths yet to Lord Killovew," the knights said, "but I've memorized them, Mr. Finch. And one of those oaths say, 'Defend the weak and innocent and treat not with those who persecute against them.' Acolyte or not, Princess Jinala is right. The Third Hand, Isaac, killed an innocent man. He must be brought to justice."

Finch squeaked, "Yes, well, I suppose you are right."

Jinala said, "Well spoken, apprentice knight. What's your name?"

The knight raised his visor, and Jinala was surprised to see a man not much older than Jason. He looked and sounded so confident, but his eyes were barely more man than boy. "My name's Dervel."

"Thank you, Sir Dervel."

"Oh, I'm not a sir yet, ma'am."

"You just earned it, Sir Dervel. Now, the both of you go."

They nodded and hauled Isaac down through the hatch.

Jinala stepped closer to the Mud Wizard. She stared out toward the army that had surrounded her castle. "I need your help to come up with some sort of plan, Evrost."

Evrost looked out in the same direction and seemed to notice the presence of over five hundred men spread out across the grass below them.

"Who the hell are those guys?"

Twenty-Seven

The sailing vessel arrived in the southwestern Shinar port less than two cycles before the Sundown Ceremony. According to Domray, the ceremony marked the official beginning of the dark season, and the citizens celebrated throughout the city. The change of seasons meant darkness, but it also meant the chance of rain. The threat of invasive Vistonex was heightened, but without the darkness and rain, healthy crops would not grow during the next sun.

As Crichton stepped off the ship onto the damp wood of the dock, his bag tossed over his shoulder, he saw only a tiny slice of the sun on the horizon. It was just a razor-thin line of pure light, surrounded by deep peachy pink and deeper purple, keeping the coming darkness at bay for just about twenty more candles.

Emushéré loped along at his side, forced to don the silver chain that she detested. If Crichton held the leash, though, she didn't fight against it. Flagg, Rulbiss, and Domray walked ahead of them.

Crichton felt the crumpled ball of paper in his pocket. He had snuck into Rulbiss' room and snagged it out of the trash before they disembarked. Hopefully, a chance to read it would come soon, and he would gain some insight into what Rulbiss had been working on. He didn't know what impulse made him so curious about Rulbiss, but the man had a mystery about him that Crichton hoped to crack. For now, the boy just had to walk along behind the Acolytes, thinking of other things. How long his training would be, how long before he knew whether he'd be heading into the forest as a soldier, how Jinala and Martin would love to see the city.

Under different circumstances than Crichton's, of course.

The docks were like a massive city all their own. Probably five times the size of the Kydoth North Port, a ring of shacks and warehouses crowded each other at the edge of the river. Over a hundred long piers stretched out above the black water, allowing what seemed like thousands of boats and rafts and barges all to dock. Domray pointed out that this port was reserved for commerce only, same as the northwestern port about four miles up the river. In-between the two merchant ports that fringed the city sat the military port of Shinar, twice as big with vessels three times as large. The docks there ran directly beneath the Ten Hand Temple pyramid, making them the most secure military installation in the kingdom.

The Acolytes, the Sondite, and the black panther received more than a fair share of oblong glances from the merchants and dock workers as they crossed the port. They strode past men filleting fish, men wrapping fish, men carrying huge tubs of fish, men dragging nets of fish, and men doing things without fish too. Emushéré was mostly interested in the fish jobs, though, her nose twitching and turning in the direction of the nearest mouthwatering collection.

They passed through the seafood market and came to a large gate and a pair of guards. One of them wore the traditional purple robes of the Acolytes and ushered them through after speaking with Domray. The paladin, as Domray called him, directed the other guards to winch open the heavy iron gate, and together they crossed into the city proper. Flagg smiled and nodded to the paladin, and they put the docks behind them.

Domray spoke all while they traveled to the Ten Hand Temple, but the sights distracted Crichton from listening. He could not pay any attention to the boring history of the city as his vision jumped from one leaning skyscraper to another. In the middle of an intersection between three converging paths stood a statue of a giant warrior holding a dead Vistonex aloft by the tail.

Beyond the statue, Crichton saw two young men about his age, balanced on a wobbly ladder on top of an angled roof, painting a disfigured chimney. The height alone was dizzying, let alone the precarious position of their ladder. One boy leaned out over the edge, seemingly unfazed, stretching his brush hand to the very tip-top of the chimney while counterbalancing himself by raising his left leg. The other boy steadied the feet of the ladder, leaning against the bottom of it with all his strength. The ladder wobbled slightly. Crichton stopped walking. He was sure he was about to see something terrible happen. The boy, bobbing up and down and back and forth in midair, touched up the peak of the chimney and then dropped firmly back onto the ladder with all four limbs. The ladder wobbled even more, but the lower boy kept it upright, and they continued, unworried about the near tumble.

Crichton looked away, relieved. In a lower window of the same building, he saw a scarred, dirty man fighting a burlap bag that was jostling and scratching and jumping by itself across the floor, yowling like a trapped baboon in a dweller dungeon. Even Emushéré noticed and looked up in concern. Eventually, the man grabbed the knot at the top of the bag and hefted it off the ground. He held it as far away from his body as he could in one hand and wiped a growing stream of blood from his face with the other.

Shaking his head, Crichton realized battling the Vistonex may not be much more dangerous than some of the common jobs here in Shinar. He hustled after the Acolytes who were waiting for him at the next corner.

After a while, it all blurred into a cacophony of sensations. The colors and the smells and the people—so many different, interesting people—melded together, too much to take in all at once. Crichton would have loved to lose his way and just disappear into the heart of the city for the next ten cycles or so, but Rulbiss had started walking behind the Sondite, not in front of him. Domray was nice enough to trust Crichton without the chains, but apparently, Rulbiss decided he still needed a diligent bodyguard at his heels.

Far before Crichton was ready to leave the city paths, they came upon a set of golden stairs engraved in the Ten Hand Temple pyramid. They walked up the face of the pyramid a couple floors and then crossed back over the street onto an adjacent building. They climbed more stairs, and crossed another skywalk, and entered the pyramid again, higher up. This time they went inside—into the depths of the massive Ten Hand Temple.

Crichton felt as if he had been swallowed alive.

The wonder and glory and chaos of Shinar was cut off and replaced by a long dark hallway with only a few torches. There were no windows, and Crichton felt the sensation of claustrophobia setting in deep down in his gut. They came to a small door at the end of the hallway with a metal padlock on the outside for a door handle.

Crichton looked up at Domray. "I suppose this is my cell."

Domray said, "Don't think of it as a cell, Crichton. These are the finest accommodations available for—well—for prisoners. But you should feel lucky. No Sondite has ever stayed in this temple. The First Hand has a special plan for you, and though I don't know what it is, I'm sure it will be a great one."

Flagg cleared his throat and added, "I agree that this is a good sign Crichton…. Ommm… perhaps you shall be the Sondite that will… reverse your people's fate… find them a permanent, peaceful home again. Give them their redemption and salvation."

Crichton looked down at Emushéré. "Can she stay with me?"

Domray thought for a moment and then conceded a smile. "Well, Sarpho *gave* her to you, so he won't be able to take care of her now, will he? At least, not until he returns to Shinar. But she cannot stay here inside the temple, so Rulbiss can watch her and keep her in a separate pen near the war dogs and the other big cats. She certainly has taken to you. I'll investigate letting her stay within your possession. If you must go fight in the war, perhaps we can let her go with you."

Flagg nodded in agreement with Domray's line of thinking. Realistically, it was the best he could hope for. He handed the leash over to Rulbiss.

Crichton rubbed Emushéré's neck, "I'll see you soon. Be a good girl."

Domray opened the door, and the Sondite boy stepped inside. The room was gold and red, full of fragile little sculptures. The furniture looked awfully expensive too; an ornate bed and stained dressers and nightstands twinkled in the dim candlelight, ornate details carved into the wood, paintings of lions and bears and water dragons in battle hung on the wall. At least twenty candles bedecked the room, though only a few were lit. Two purple algae candles flanked the window that opened out onto the eastern side of the city.

Crichton looked outside at the nearest skywalk. Two small figures walked along the rickety bridge. Crichton wanted to be out there, exploring the skywalks with Martin, tracing their paths across the city onto a hand-drawn map until they had the whole web memorized by heart. The window was far too narrow to allow any escape, though, and it wouldn't be the same without his little brother at his side.

"We shall see you soon, Crichton," Domray said, closing his door.

The room was fancy, but it was still just a cell.

After the Acolytes left him, they turned the deadbolt in his door and clanked shut the metal padlock. Crichton pulled out the crumpled piece of paper in his pocket and sat down on yet another bed.

He carefully unwrapped the paper and smoothed out the crinkles to the best of his ability. Reading by the candlelight on his bed stand, tears formed in Crichton's eyes.

Across the top, in tiny, meticulous handwriting, Rulbiss had written, '*Crichton Raak's Syllabus.*'

Several different activities and concepts written underneath had been scratched out while a few others had been circled. Eventually, the Acolyte must have realized this schedule was too messy and hard to read, balled it up, and started over. But the paragraph he had written at the bottom, a note to himself before the paper was trashed, struck Crichton deeper than anything else.

> *Must ensure Crichton is*
> *prepared to become an Acolyte*
> *scholar. Do not want life of soldier*
> *for the boy, but he must be <u>prepared</u>*
> *to be a soldier. Remember that even*
> *though he is a Sondite, Crichton has*
> *courage and intellect. In fact, I doubt*
> *if being a Sondite makes any*
> *difference in the amount of courage or*
> *intellect one can have. Will pray more*
> *on it.*

Crichton wiped his eyes. Just to know that Rulbiss cared about his fate...

It meant all three of his captors had grown to value him over the last half of the season that they had spent together. Crichton no longer could hold the fact that they kidnapped him against them. They were following orders and, in their own way, worked to make Crichton as comfortable as possible. Only Sarpho had been downright rude, and only Sarpho had bullied Crichton. And Sarpho was a bully to everyone.

Crichton felt a modest pride rise in him. He had shown the Acolytes that being a Sondite did not diminish you as a person. It was a concept he had always strove to instill in Martin, and without conscious effort, it had rubbed off on the Acolyte men. What had Flagg said? Perhaps Crichton will lead his people to a new future? To their salvation?

Far sooner than Crichton expected, the deadbolt in his door snapped open, and Domray barged in, bustling with happy energy. Crichton quickly shoved the paper under his pillow.

"I had to come and share the news as soon as I found out," Domray said. "You and I get to meet the Ten Hand Council, Crichton. The First Hand himself! You must be the first Sondite to be invited since the exodus from Sond. Over thirty seasons!"

"What are you talking about, Domray?" Crichton asked.

Domray smiled a wide white smile. "We are going to attend the Sundown Ceremony."

Twenty-Eight

"There must be someone else who works the rookery," Jinala hissed over her left shoulder. "We can't have left the whole operation to one man. How could we have trusted the entirety of that operation to a single person?"

"Princess Jinala," Elton hissed back, "Had you been in the meetings when I broached this subject to your father, perhaps you could have convinced him of your point, but alas, you were not. I could not convince him. He fended off the topic rather admirably whenever I brought it up. Truthfully, I've wondered for some time if he had a secret reasoning for keeping the rookery so understaffed. As I told you, the only other man who knows was the stable boy, and he was just an apprentice. And he's missing too, in case you forgot."

Jinala groaned. Everything seemed stacked against her.

Think, Jinala. You are all on your own.

Well, basically, on your own.

Isaac stood directly behind her, his hands bound, covered by his long purple Acolyte sleeves. Evrost stood at her right, Elton at her left, and two stalwart apprentice knights flanked them. Finch stood behind them, next to Isaac, nervously fidgeting but prepared to meet his fate with the rest of them.

The messengers from the Ardellian army walked forward, closing the gap between her and them. The rest of the soldiers stayed mercifully in their files, not appearing to be up to anything nefarious.

Both Elton and Finch had advised against accepting the Grayson's invitation to meet outside the gate to negotiate, but Jinala had accepted anyway. She had forced Evrost to change out of his strange muddy clothes and into clean brown robes like those Finch and Elton wore. She had a serving boy wash his face, but Evrost refused to shave his long beard. Isaac, after hearing who had surrounded the castle, became very intrigued in participating in the meeting. Jinala waffled on bringing him, but she needed to show as much strength as possible. She promised Isaac a slow, painful death if he broke the facade to the Ardellians.

Still, to all those who looked at her team from a distance, she simply had four older men as advisers, including a high-ranking Acolyte, along with two stalwart knights. No one had to know that one of the advisers was a half-crazed loon who lived in the swamp, and that the Acolyte adviser was bound against his will. Nor that the two knights were just apprentices without a single drop of blood earned on either of their blades. Dervel, and some even younger man named Tristan, stood tall in their shining armor. They looked, for all pretenses, as competent as any elder knight in the realm might look.

Jinala knew the leader by his eyes when the Ardellians arrived.

All the men in his entourage looked like hard men, with hard eyes. They were thick through the shoulders and well armored, and if Jinala had to guess, all had put blood on their blades before this cycle. But the leader had eyes that cut through fog, blue as a robin's egg, and they did not seem to blink. He met Jinala's green eyes and held them firm. He was perhaps a few suns older than Jason but still young enough to be unwed and fit the description of the missing Grayson nephew. His jawline was strong, his stubble dense, and his nose regal.

He was a Grayson, and Jinala could see how a man like this could unite hungry bands of Ardellian rebels and chisel them into this army.

"I had hoped to treat with your father. And I had very much hoped not to see purple robes in your mix."

"Castle Killovew is sorry to disappoint you," Jinala said.

"Your father is ill? Or dead?"

Jinala knew in this meeting she could not falter, but his first question almost tripped her up.

"He doesn't come to siege meetings unless there are a thousand men outside his castle. Any less, and he sends me."

"Don't lie, child. You haven't seen enough suns for me to bed you yet, let alone enough for Lord Killovew to send you to be his messenger. My people did not take these risks to mince words with a girl. Especially not in front of a cursed Ten Hand Council member."

Something nagged on Jinala's mind, something she was missing, but she pressed on. She was the one with the castle and the fertile farms and surrounded by allies. She just needed time. One of those other horsemen Chief Daak got out from Northtown *had* to have reached a border camp by now.

Right?

"I do not know your name. Your surname has been rumored around my castle for the past season. I'm not sold yet you are who you claim to be. But regardless, what name should I give my father before he wipes you from the history books?"

"My name is Arthur. What is yours, child?"

"I'm Jinala."

"I was here to propose an alliance that would help feed my people, Jinala. The terms of this alliance need to be brokered with the realm lord, not his second born. But after seeing with whom you keep close council, perhaps an alliance would be ill-advised."

"Sieging Northtown and now our castle is an ill-advised way to build an alliance, regardless of with whom my father keeps council."

246

"My realm and its current purple rulers have left me little options. I needed to ensure I spoke with Lord Killovew personally. This seemed a good way to get his attention. Though clearly, something has happened to him, and now I must reconsider my position. I had hoped the Killovews would emphasize with my situation and understand my disposition toward the Acolyte frauds."

Isaac cleared his throat to speak, but Jinala cut him off, speaking over him, "Lord Killovew and I *do* emphasize with your situation in Ardel, but we are not responsible for feeding your citizens. We will not tolerate this intrusion. If you immediately withdraw, we can discuss a meeting at a neutral site with my father. If you do not withdraw, we will be forced to break your siege with violence. The castle will hold, and the closest villages and border camps are on their way as we speak."

"Your teachers taught you to speak and parlay well. These three here?" He gestured at Finch, Elton, and Evrost.

Jinala spoke more genuinely, feeling more in control by the moment. She felt the Grayson rebel had stepped in too far, and she could get him to step back out. His pride was all that stood in the way. If he believed she could defend and beat him, then all she needed to do now was give him a better alternative than a bloody death against her castle walls.

"Arthur, my father *will* meet with you, but not under these circumstances. If you refuse to leave, we will overrun and kill most of your soldiers. My father will execute you. Perhaps the Ardel realm does need you to take back the lordship… but bringing the threat of violence into our realm does not help you. What do you hope to gain?"

"Princess Jinala Killovew. The Acolytes took my realm because my uncle could not follow their rules. He was weak. I am not." Arthur stepped closer, looking between the princess and Isaac. He reached out his callused hand and lifted one of her blonde curls into the air, feeling it's texture. "I came here to make a deal with the Killovews. Under the Killovew's duress, yes, but still. I hoped for a peaceful resolution. But now…I need a different plan… When I get back to Ardel, I need to show my people we accomplished something. That we *achieved* by uniting, instead of fighting each other."

Jinala squirmed inside, but she stood still. He bent closer, smelling her hair. He looked at the men around her, all doing nothing. He frowned. "Your father does not know the man that I am. He does not know what I'm capable of. He would never send his only daughter as his messenger unless he was dying or already dead. And only then, it would be your decision, not his." He leaned even closer and whispered into her ear, "I know what it's like. To be all alone in leading your people and not be ready yet. Tell me, are you willing to do whatever is necessary to save your people?"

Jinala squeezed her fists at her side. "Yes, Arthur, I am."

She flicked out her left hand, and Evrost firmly tapped his staff on the ground. The top ignited in sparkling blue light, nearly blinding from so close.

Arthur leaped back. His guards stumbled backward, looking as though they may flee. Jinala noticed that her knights and advisers had stepped back as well, leaving her, Isaac and Evrost alone next to Arthur. While the knights and guards on both sides stared in fear at the glowing staff, Arthur only gazed with a look of surprised curiosity. Isaac did not watch the staff. His old eyes watched her.

After their moment of awe had passed, the Ardellian guards drew their swords.

"Nuh-uh," Evrost said, pointing his staff toward them.

"No!" Arthur said, waving his hand at the guards. "I told you, do not engage them!"

Two stepped forward. One of them shouted, "Blasphemer!" and ran toward Evrost.

"No!" Arthur and Jinala shouted at the same time. The Ardellian snarled and lunged; Arthur threw out his arms, jumping in the way; Evrost shot a blast of blue sparks.

A glowing, transparent red shield exploded around Arthur's elbow, catching the blue sparks. The oval shield sizzled and spat, and then the red glow shrunk back in on itself and vanished. Arthur lowered his arm, panting. The two guards behind him stared in disbelief. One dropped his sword and simply stared; the other fell to his knees and began murmuring prayers.

Arthur spoke first, still catching his breath. "I see that you have found one of Gahkin's relics, as well."

Isaac spoke next before Jinala could gather her thoughts. "We have the blue color of Gahkin's true power. You have but a corrupted red gem from the Dark Ages before the realms were settled. Leave it with me and be gone from this land. The faith of the Thirsting Forest people will never fall to a rebel lord like yourself."

He lies as easily as he breathes. He will condemn me as soon as it benefits him, as easily as he defends me now.

And then something clicked in Jinala's mind.

Why was she pretending to be on the Acolyte's side? Her father and Eric Eden weren't. Jason was clearly attempting something to wrest the power away from the Acolytes. If this Arthur Grayson wanted to ally with the Thirsting Forest, if he had magic like Evrost, why were they at odds?

Show him.

Jinala reached over to Isaac and yanked back his sleeves, revealing his bound hands. She kicked him in the back of the leg, and he fell onto his knees.

"I told you not to speak, Isaac."

Arthur's eyebrows raised in surprise.

"We caught him spying in our tower. We have no great alliance with the Ten Hand Council. Now, it seems we may be closer to becoming allies than enemies. But the fact remains, your soldiers surround my castle. I cannot have my people living in—"

Someone screamed from behind Arthur, just behind the front line of his Ardellian soldiers. The line parted, and five Ardellians walked forward, along with two horses and three captives in chains. It looked as though the horses were carrying two bodies, tossed sideways, over their saddles.

Jinala couldn't stop herself. She shouted hoarsely, "Father!"

"Ah," Arthur said, smiling slightly now. "This just keeps getting more and more interesting."

Twenty-Nine

The final rays of the setting sun splashed the eastern gates of Shinar with soft orange light. People fought and elbowed at the city entrance with shouts and demands and no small amount of blood, bribery, and arrests. Almost a thousand men and women waited to file through the eastern gates; the stench of sweat and desperation could be smelled miles downwind of Shinar. Hundreds of wagons, surrounded by little private militias sat in the crowd, full of fabric, weapons, algae oil from the canyon mines, and even gold and silver. All these people, mostly coming from across the northern realms in the kingdom, brought everything they had, trying to immigrate into the capital city before the sun fell. And the only thing they had in common was that none of them had any food to bring with them.

Traffic congestion flooded the western gates like a gorged river at a damn, the enlarged shadows of the crowd churned on the tan walls. The hundred or so guards at the threshold of the city stood strong. They allowed just enough of the river through to keep the human flood from breaking into the city in mass.

Jason, Sir Breigo, Mako, and Ratoke rode forward within this river of men, surrounded by Acolyte paladins and soldiers. As soon as they had gotten back to the road near Shinar, the Second Hand had waved down guards, and before they knew it, dozens of Acolytes and paladins and city guards had swarmed them.

Now, as they rode closer and the guards pushed their group through the crowd, Jason thought of Taroke, as he was sure Ratoke did.

He had made the ultimate sacrifice to ensure they reached the Grand City of Gahkin without suspicion on their names. Ratoke sat atop his horse stiffly and kept up with Jason and the others, but his eyes were foggy, and nothing Jason said could lift him out of the haze as he grieved for his brother.

The Second Hand had said that entering Shinar would normally prove a tremendously slow and aggravating affair. Only a Ten Hand Council member could wield the authority and reverence needed to negotiate the congested mobs and enter the city at will. As they pushed through, the people shuffled around them, trying to glob onto the group and move toward the large wall together. Jason had not believed it at the time, but seeing the diverse, thronging crowds reaching and shouting for just the Second Hand's gaze, he could understand. The Acolytes on the Ten Hand Council were effectively royalty and deities, rolled together.

The Grand City of Gahkin, the capital city of Shinar, was the largest city in the kingdom and not by any small margin. Most of the realms' cities were built up nearby the castles of their lords, like Northtown in the Thirsting Forest, and if you added all seven castles and the surrounding cities or towns together, Shinar's capital still outsized them all.

The Second Hand trotted his horse up to Rara Silva Nix and leaned toward Jason to whisper in his ear, "At the gate, we will separate. We have just two cycles before the ceremony. I'll send a guard to escort your group to a wealthy inn near the pyramid. I'll handle Rekebba and make sure she makes it to the top of the temple. We will meet at the top together, and finish this." He reached out and clapped Jason on the shoulder. "And thank you. Our show for the citizens may be a charade, but my gratitude is not. You truly did rescue me, and now you and I will rescue this kingdom from the Acolytes who have corrupted Gahkin's will."

He kicked his heels into his horse's flank and rode forward to the front of the group, matching paces with a paladin that led the group forward through the crowd.

They passed under the great gate, heading up diagonal ramps toward the first level of the thick wall encircling the city. Ratoke, Mako, Sir Breigo and Prince Jason were shepherded off to the side and an older, more distinguished guard approached them.

"Killovew?" the guard asked, looking up at the prince, "Ruling family of the Thirsting Forest Realm, Killovew?"

"My father is, yes."

"Well met. You all have done the city a great service, rescuing the Second Hand." The guard spoke as though reading from a script in a play. Jason doubted the man really cared one way or the other. He was just playing his role.

Sir Breigo responded, relaying his line just as monotonously. "We were just doing our duty for the kingdom."

"Good, good." The guard squinted down at one of the many scrolls he was carrying. "Okay, you four will follow me. You don't have to go through with the rest of this horse dung." He pointed behind him where more guards stood, rifling through bags and digging through the inside of wagons, turning away most of the refugees who had made it to the ramps at the edge of the wall. "Just a couple of documents we need to sign and review, and then we can go forward."

"Whatever it takes to get us into the city to our lodging," Jason said distractedly. The Acolytes and the Second Hand, along with Chief Rekebba in chains, disappeared through the large main gate, a growing mob of people following behind them.

The guard shuffled through a handful of scrolls. Somewhere close behind them on the entrance ramp, a high-pitched shriek rang out, and he dropped the scrolls onto the floor. He looked up and stared for a moment out at his peers, who were busy trying to calm the rioting crowds and keep them from pushing up the ramps into the city. The guards seemed to be losing ground.

"Bury the paperwork; let's get you all out of here. It's like they think this Sundown will be the last."

"A lot of them are probably starving, you know. They want food. For them, it might *be* the last time they see the sun."

The guard wiped at sweat building on his brow. He eyed Jason up and down. "Yeah, well, it ain't up to me, *Prince* Killovew. I'm just doing my job. I'm not exactly eating a lot of great food myself these cycles. Now come on, you look well-fed yourself, which means it might not be safe here too much longer."

The guard took them through a side passage and up another wooden ramp inside the city wall itself. The path narrowed; they dismounted and went single file through a gap in the thick stone. They emerged on the other side of the wall, onto a raised platform facing the Grand City of Shinar.

Built onto a wide, sloping hill, the capital city climbed upward and away from Jason in grand fashion. Nearest, just within the perimeter walls, a thicket of white and brown buildings rose like tottering poker chips into the sky. Only the upper third stood above the walls. Any lower on the hill and the crumbling buildings were cast in dark shadow. Hundreds of fireplaces, twinkling dots of bright orange and yellow, glowed from within the shade. The dense housing towers guarded the inner city like a second encircling wall, built of poverty and desperation where the first was built of granite stone and pit-sand cement.

At the bottom of the hill, a teeming marketplace buzzed, encircled by tall pillars on a raised stretch of land, looking like an agitated ant mound. A sunset-shaded rainbow of colored flags flew above the swarming bazaar. Jason had thought it was busy outside the walls, but it was nothing compared to the Shinar marketplace. All the wealth and taxes that the Acolytes collected had bought their city something no other realm could: a surplus of food. The soil around Shinar must truly be blessed, Jason thought, to support all this.

Above the market and behind the tall ring of housing structures stood a wealthier but no less dense assembly of uneven buildings and mansions and guard towers. These were connected by hundreds of drooping skywalks. Thin and fragile, but no doubt efficient, the longest of these wooden rope bridges stretched between two tower peaks almost a half a mile.

Above and beyond the wealthier section of Shinar, shimmering in the sunlight, Jason saw the full expanse of the Ten Hand Temple. A pyramid with a golden coat, given a wide breadth of space in every direction, stood at the top of the hill, fully above the walls and thus above the dark shadows.

Jason knew in just one cycle's time he would stand at its peak as the Sundown

Ceremony commenced.

Above it all rose the Star Tower, infinite and breathtaking as ever. It was as if some giant god, his feet the size of whole cities, had speared his sword into the pyramid. The tall silver blade jutted into the air, disappearing into the inky purple sky over head. Somewhere, out among the stars, the top of the tower might be found. No one, of course, had ever climbed it.

If anything were to convince Jason of a conscious Creator, it was this inhuman structure. In fact, Jason thought something inhuman—something supernatural—must have built the Star Tower. It very well may have been Gahkin, he reckoned, but it was not the Gahkin the Acolytes claimed to exist. Taking advantage of such mystery and such miracle was blasphemy. In this train of thought he again confirmed the need for their plotted treason.

We must kill them.

Jason thought that the magnificent city of Shinar illustrated the great potential of mankind. But like the civilization he fought to free, like the ruling class he fought to upend, the city had grown corrupt.

The Acolytes were an example of unchecked power and overinflated ego. It took unknown generations to create this imbalance, and yet it only took three generations of Killovews to unveil it and overturn it.

Now, standing within the city, it would take only a few brief moments of murder to return the kingdom to a proper balance. Only a few brief moments of murder to utterly reshape the known world. Jason's eyes grew wide, as much with the excitement of the impending Sundown Ceremony as with the great beauty of the Shinar cityscape before him.

The guard chuckled, clearly used to the awe that swept over visitors when they first viewed the city. "You'll have a better view from your accommodations at the top of the hill. Come on."

The city was as fascinating a marvel at the micro level as it had been at the macro level. A hundred and fifty thousand people demanded an immense infrastructure.

They passed through the market, where Jason's nostrils filled with the charred scent of mystery meat and the acrid smoke of burning hide. Sudden warmth on his ribs was explained by a blacksmith's furnace, sudden wind by a rush of young boys chasing after each other in colorful hodgepodge capes, arms outstretched.

As they made their way through the market, the guard stopped at an exchange tent, which was one of many different metal exchanges in the city. Shinar had its own coins, more exact and stamped with certain small illustrations. These were given to Jason in exchange for his small sack of gold and silver half-ounce coins. The whole of civilization used this common coin as a standard until the realms were united under one kingdom. They still circulated in the kingdom as valid tender except in the city of Shinar, where coins with the Ten Hand stamp were the only currency. Jason wondered just how much money the exchange men made, taking heavy gold and silver coins and giving sacks of thin silver and bronze coins in return.

He had too much on his mind to worry about the exactness to which he was getting robbed, so, with a shrug to Sir Breigo and a sympathetic frown from their guard escort, they continued, heading up toward the Star Tower and leaving the market behind.

Jason thought they passed at least fifty shoemakers and another fifty tailors and another twenty-five taverns as they wound their way up the hill. They always stayed in the wide pathways among the crowds, never cutting through thin alleyways where less-than-clean and less-than-moral looking folk peered out.

The travel uphill began to grow wearisome. Jason was far too fit and excited to be tired, but he did begin to hope each inn they came to would be their own. They had gone through so much, for so long, to make it to Shinar. Jason wanted a respite. And he would barely get two cycle's rest before the Sundown Ceremony.

They continued walking, their guard pushing ahead with his happy pace. They stopped more times than were necessary, once to eat the special 'chicken' kabobs from a street vendor, another to taste a strange citrusy mead, brewed fresh from the cold water of the northern Verdelen. All this food and alcohol and folks were starving half a kingdom away. How could the Acolytes allow this indulgence in their own city while they allowed others to suffer?

They stopped once more when the guard's brother-in-law crossed their path on his way to extract a snake from someone's home. They shared pleasantries quickly, promising to get together to drink in the indefinite future, and then the guard proudly introduced his royal companions to the snake catcher. The animal wrangler bragged to them how he worked on the 'fringe,' catching the unwanted cats and snakes and dogs for the wealthy people who didn't want them and then selling them back to poor people who had rodent problems. The man was friendly enough, but he was nicked with small scabs and scars, and his hairy arms crawled with fleas. Still, he was happy, and he left them with a smile on his face and a scratch to his balls.

After what seemed like a lifetime, they reached the inn that Tegan had arranged for them. It was built of marble and granite and stood far above the surrounding shops. It was the only building Jason had seen so far that had a secure perimeter with armed guards at every entrance and every corner. Its location near the top of the hill, only a few blocks from the massive Ten Hand Temple pyramid, marked the inn as forbidden to all those except the extraordinarily rich or very powerful. Blossoming out at the top, the highest three floors all boasted balconies that wrapped around the entire building.

Jason, Sir Breigo, Ratoke, and Mako withdrew their warrants again and handed them over at the guarded gate. Paladins stood silent outside the fence, at the large stables out back and at both doors into the inn. Corrupted or not, Jason thought, they were well organized.

Mako and Ratoke led the four horses to the back of the inn where the plush stables were located. Sir Breigo and Jason walked in through the front door.

Through the dim light and the thin crowd, he saw the Quirvop Prince, sitting near the bar, among a handful of wealthy-looking women. The innocent man who would fall by their sword laughed gaily at some joke and sipped his mead. Carl, Jason thought. His name was Carl Quirvop.

Jason's eyes lingered on him. He was a big man, with broad shoulders and flowy blond hair. He laughed heartily and spoke loudly, boasting of some story involving a farmer's pretty daughter, and too many bottles of wine.

The barkeeper noticed them standing in the entryway and waved Jason and Sir Breigo forward. "Come in, good sirs. How can I help you?"

"I'm Jason Killovew, Prince of the Thirsting Forest. This is Sir Breigo Aldev. I also have three—I mean, two—other realm men with me, stabling the horses. We have a suite arranged for us, I believe."

"Ah, yes," the bartender said. The man wore a tight shirt that frayed open at the curve of his chest and at the sleeves and displayed a thick golden necklace dangling around his neck. This was not an ordinary inn, nor an ordinary bartender. "My name is Shawn, and I will be at your service should you need anything. Of course, I remember seeing you on my list… running a little behind schedule from your original arrival…" He turned to consult a sheet of paper on the back wall. While he did, Jason looked again at the Quirvop Prince. The big man met Jason's green eyes with his own blue and inclined his head politely.

Mako and Ratoke trudged inside and joined Jason and Breigo waiting in the tavern, near the foot of the stairs.

The bartender tapped his knuckles on the counter and said, "Perfect, the group is all here. Follow me, Prince Killovew. Right this way." They followed the bartender up the stairs toward the top rooms.

Across the rest of the kingdom, realm royalty would stay with the realm rulers, not in an inn, but Shinar was different. Royalty didn't have the same connotation in the Grand City of Gahkin as it did elsewhere across the kingdom. The Acolytes tried to downplay the power of the highest-ranking lords across the land in every way that they could.

Since Prince Jason and his men were in Shinar to attend the Sundown

Ceremony and then enlist in Gahkin's army, the Ten Hand Council paid for their stay until they were inducted but gave them no more indulgences than any other wealthy merchant or independent knight. Had they arrived on time, they would have had ten cycles or so to enjoy the luxuries that their own coins could provide in the surrounding area.

Now they barely had time for two cycles of rest on a comfortable bed before the ceremony. But still, that was more than Jason had had in a long time. A whole season of exhaustion seemed to finally be weighing him down.

The bartender stopped at the door of one of the highest floors, unlocked it, and then handed Jason two keys.

"One for you and one extra for your men. Welcome again to the R-triple-S and enjoy your stay." He dropped his professional tone and said, "By the way, I heard what you all had to do to save the Second Hand… All of you have a drink waiting at the bar for you, on the house."

He scuttled back down the stairs without waiting for a reply.

They entered the large suite and dropped off their small bags of belongings in their respective rooms. Mako and Ratoke would share a room, Breigo took a second guest room, and Jason took the large master.

Ratoke murmured about going to sleep, but Jason wouldn't allow it.

"Ratoke, come out onto the balcony with us, first."

Ratoke protested, but Jason insisted, "Just for a moment. And then we can all rest."

They walked out onto the balcony, Ratoke trailing behind wearily, and looked down upon the massive city.

It surrounded them for a mile to the east and even further to the west and south. They looked back across the land they had traveled, knowing somewhere beyond the large walls, beyond the southeastern horizon, the Thirsting Forest sat in the dark shadow of the mountain. No doubt Lord Killovew knew the time for Jason's mission was near at hand. He would be awaiting their letter of success or—Gahkin forbid—failure.

They watched the setting sun, as still as if it was not moving at all. Only the smallest sliver of light remained above the horizon. Jason looked down at the strong stone walls of Shinar and the still-crowded eastern gate. The bazaar they crossed through was bustling as ever, and the thousands of rickety buildings wrapping around the inner city twinkled in the dusky light on the western side, just as the eastern side had twinkled, though this time all the buildings were cast in shadow.

In a quiet voice, Jason spoke. "We've crossed the bulk of the kingdom to make it here, and we did it as a team. Without Taroke, we wouldn't have made it."

"I don't want a speech… or a funeral service. His ashes are in the wind now, same as the rest of ours will be, one cycle. Taroke knew the risks. Now I just need some rest."

Jason raised his voice, "I'm not giving a buried speech. I'm thinking of the man who helped us get to this point. We've gone hundreds of miles to make it to this one moment, and we've *all* lost a friend, and his soul deserves our gratitude." Jason pulled out a small leather flask that he had stashed away earlier for this occasion. Jason poured out an exceptionally large swallow for each of the men into their cups.

Jason held his up to the sky. "To Taroke. He believed in the cause, and he made the ultimate sacrifice to ensure we could get the chance to free the kingdom from tyranny."

Breigo raised his horn. "Aye, he did. And he was a pain in the ass." Breigo put his free hand on Ratoke's shoulder and continued, "but he was our pain in the ass, and I'm a better man for knowing him."

Mako Black raised his own. "He could fight, and he could laugh, and he did both better than most men I've ever met."

Ratoke looked at them all and then opened his mouth to speak, but nothing came out. He shook his head and raised his free hand to wipe at the tears on his cheeks.

"Stop it," Mako said. "Let them fall into the wind. Taroke deserves each one."

Ratoke nodded and spoke, his eyes misty but his voice firm, "He was my brother, and I miss him."

They drank.

Thirty

Martin loathed being a prisoner. Mostly because he had been a prisoner all season long, and now rope bound his hands again, this time by these Ardellian people, whoever they were. Jinala and Evrost were going to meet with the other realm lord guy with the bright eyes, and Martin was stuck in a buried prisoner tent. Well, he would not stay a prisoner for long. Not this time.

He had small wrists, and they were nimble and flexible, and the Ardellian bandits had not tied his knots very tightly. They thought an outlaw Sondite boy wasn't worth the effort to even guard in person. Martin slipped free of the ropes around his wrists, untied his feet, and looked for an exit.

He was in a semi-permanent tent on the grass outside the castle. He peeked under one of the curtains that draped to the ground.

Soldiers, hundreds of them, all lined up, facing the castle. He peeked under the side facing the woods.

More soldiers.

Every direction he looked.

Even more soldiers.

Hmmm.

This might take more creativity than Martin had expected.

Martin looked around the inside of the tent. Sir Trittion, Lord Killovew, that lady who tried to rescue them on the horse, and her two other rider friends were all chained up together. Lord Killovew was still out cold, but the rest wore blindfolds and chains, all tied together to a big wooden stake in the center of the tent. Martin sighed.

If he could not escape on his own, he supposed he would have to free these adults and do it together.

Arthur kicked out all his men but one. He forced Elton and Finch to leave, and he gagged the Third Hand, leaving him tied up on his knees in the corner of his command tent. Evrost and Jinala sat on one side of a small table, Arthur and his second in command, Ansel, on the other.

"I had tried for some time to keep this a secret." Arthur gestured at the strange silver and black piece of metal he wore on his left arm. It was etched with tiny red dots, which Jinala guessed somehow would expand into the shield he had used earlier. Evrost's silver staff seemed to be made of a similar material, but it had no black or red. The top that shot sparks was sheared off, ragged looking, exposing tiny bronze-colored metal rods so thin you could hardly notice them.

"But now the rumors will spread. It may help me gain followers, perhaps, but it will draw down a lot of attention from them." He pointed toward Isaac in the corner.

Arthur continued, "It seems our fates are intertwined by these relics, Jinala, and by our two realms standing opposed to the Acolytes. Even if yours has been doing so in secret."

Jinala nodded. She could think of only her father, whom she'd seen lying so cold and limp she thought he was dead. Evrost had said he could revive him, 'lickety-split,' whatever that meant. But Evrost was stuck in here, negotiating with Arthur Grayson instead of saving her father.

"I'm going to tell you one of our secrets, now. The Acolytes have long claimed that Canyon Castle was destroyed and the Grayson's hunted down and murdered because we were sheltering the Sondites. That we refused to follow the

Ten Hand Council commandments and send them to Shinar. But that's not true. When Canyon Castle was at its zenith, when the Ardel realm was the wealthiest of them all, mining algae oil for Ten Candle oil and Spice, we found something in the darkest of the dungeons. It was an old metal wagon with wings like a bird. Our smartest advisers tried to understand it, tried to glean some religious truth from this ancient relic."

Arthur smiled slightly as if remembering the time himself. Then his smile disappeared.

"When the Acolytes found out, though, that's when the golden sword of Gahkin fell. If Gahkin knew everything, could see all, why did he not strike us down when we first found the relic? No, the golden beam only fell when the Acolytes found out about our discovery. Not when they found out about our Sondite refugees, but when they found out about our treasure we had dug out of the deep.

"My father, my uncle's brother, smuggled one small piece off the tipped nose of the wagon. The rest fell back down into the chasm when the beam destroyed our castle. My father gave it to me and sent me to the realm's very furthest edge, to the cold north near Quirvop, to live with strangers who would protect me. He gave me this relic because it was the only piece that they could figure out how to use. He gave it to me and left a note. Do you want to know what the note said, Princess Jinala?"

"Yes," Jinala said. His story had drawn her in, and now she felt a tinge of sorrow for the enemy sitting across from her.

"The note said, may Gahkin's shield protect you, son, for all your cycles, even if I could not."

Arthur glared at Isaac in the corner, then continued. "The Acolytes murdered my father Jinala, along with the rest of my family. If I remember my kingdom's history, the Acolytes murdered your grandfather too, for prying too much into their affairs in Shinar."

"Yes," Jinala murmured, "Yes, they did."

"This magical shield did protect me, Jinala. My father saved me by leaving this with me. The village he left me in, not too long after, fell to the cannibal raids from the north. I escaped, thanks in large part to Gahkin's relic I wore on my arm. I tell you all this because I think you can understand. I saw your Sondite friend. I see sympathy in your eyes. I knew I could not be the only one who hated them. I knew James Killovew must, if he lost his father like I lost mine!"

Arthur took a deep breath, calming himself. "And like you must feel too, Jinala, having lost your grandfather. And having caught an Acolyte spying in your castle. I believe that we can be allies, Jinala."

The rebel lord ran his hand along the stubble on his cheeks, thinking hard. Finally, he spoke. "I'm going to set you free and let all of the prisoners return to your castle."

Jinala's eyes flashed up. "Really?"

"Yes," he said. "I shall."

"Thank you," Jinala said softly. She looked at Arthur Grayson, really looked at him seated across from her, his blue eyes catching the torchlight and sizzling with passion. As her father's eyes did when he spoke on ruling the realm and protecting the people.

"But, before I let you go, I need a few promises from you. From your father, really, but he's in no condition to speak with me. So, from the current realm ruler, Queen Jinala Killovew. First, I need to know you'll support the Grayson's claim on the Ardel realm. That you'll support the Acolytes only if they turn it back over to me."

"We will," Jinala said. She didn't care what she had to promise; now that she knew she was close to this all being over, she needed to get out of here as soon as possible and make sure her father was okay.

"Second, I need help feeding my people. I will need access to the fertile lands near the forest. Where the rains still fall every dark season."

"I will have to check…"

"Not check. I need your promise, in front of Ansel and Isaac and your wizard, Evrost."

"Fine. We will grant you farming land in our realm, as much as we can."

"We will work the land; our people will do the labor. We just need the soil."

"Okay. Anything else?"

"Just one more thing."

"Ask it, then."

Arthur smiled. "You know that by me leaving, taking nothing, it will make you seem a very competent leader. A young girl, not yet a woman, capable of out negotiating a rebel lord with a larger army while her own father lay injured. It will raise your standing among your people."

"What is your final request, Arthur?" She knew what he was about to ask and knew what she must answer.

"You must promise me that upon your sixth sunrise, you will be my wife."

She met his eyes again. He did not look away.

She imperceptibly nodded and whispered. "Yes, I'll be your wife, Arthur."

"We'll unite the Grayson and Killovew families. The Ardellians and the Thirsting Forest citizens will share our two realms." Arthur stood and looked over at Evrost. "Soon, wizard, we will discuss more of our relics that give us our powers. Perhaps we can glean more knowledge by working together."

Evrost groaned. "More knowledge… Nah, I've got too much damn knowledge already. Thanks, though."

Jinala stood up and turned to leave the tent. Before she exited, Arthur spoke again.

"Your promise has been heard before Gahkin, before Isaac, and before my realm mate Ansel. Even your strange wizard can't deny he heard your promise. Good Luck, Jinala Killovew, and don't forget your prisoner." Ansel grabbed Isaac and walked him over to Evrost. Together, they exited the tent, where Elton and Finch waited outside for her.

Finch whispered, "The Sondite boy tried to escape, roused the rest of the prisoners. He's creating quite a problem."

Jinala smiled slightly. "I bet he is."

Ansel blew a loud horn three times and then turned and left. The soldiers began disassembling the tents, and the first lines of soldiers began marching away from the castle.

Elton looked at Jinala over his spectacles. "Negotiated a retreat?"

"Yes," Jinala said. "Now bring my father, the Sondite, and Sir Trittion to the throne room. We need to rest, but unfortunately, we can't yet."

"Very well," Elton said, speaking no more.

Please work.

Jinala, Sir Trittion, Elton, Martin, and Evrost stood around Lord Killovew. His body rested gently on top of a pile of blankets. He looked dead to Jinala.

Please.

Martin reached out and took Jinala's hand. She smiled a little. It had always been her who took his in the past.

Evrost said, "Rise and shine, sleepy head," and prodded James with his staff. A small *zap* sounded when the staff touched his flesh, and Lord Killovew sat bolt upright. Jinala shrieked. She jumped down and threw her arms around him, the force of her body almost knocking him back over again.

"Father!"

"Jinala, sweetheart."

"I thought you were dead!"

He squeezed her tight, and she buried her nose into his strong neck and breathed in the smell of him. The weight of leadership was squeezed out of her. She had done it. She had kept her people alive. She had captured Isaac. She had sent Arthur away. Whatever else came next, Lord James Killovew could handle it.

Her father was back. She didn't have to be Queen Killovew any longer. She cried into his shoulder, and her cries turned into sobs.

"It's okay," he said. "It'll be okay. Now tell me what happened."

Thirty-One

Jason stared out the southern window. In the center of the city, spiking above the roof of one of the tallest buildings, the massive Ten Candle mantles jutted up, the eighth candle still burning. Using some extra flammable mix of dweller algae, the Acolyte scientists were able to craft giant algae candles that could be seen from all over the city and still burned down at the same rate of their smaller counterparts.

As he watched, the eighth candle flickered and sputtered and then extinguished. A new flame sparked into existence at the top of the ninth candle, igniting the algae oil and signaling the start of the second to last candle of the cycle.

The Prince of the Thirsting Forest crossed his room and lay back down in his bed despite being wide awake. Grand thoughts of their treason ran afresh through his mind. He rolled over and smashed his head into his soft pillow. But he could not fall asleep. His thoughts and ideas and memories blended in that strange in-between zone where consciousness lingers, but consistency of sanity fades in and out.

He was glad their plan avoided unnecessary violence among the lower-ranking Acolytes. Among almost all the Acolytes, actually. Most of those religious men meant well and held no thirst for power nor any evil intentions, rather it was only the Ten Hand Council that wielded power with extreme injustice and advanced the war for their own ends and it would only be the Ten Hand Council that would face corporal punishment. It was not Jason Killovew and his men committing treason, they were saving the kingdom from it.

Jason remembered his father's retelling of how he had escaped from Shinar. Jason had been born while James Killovew was in the Grand City, searching for Jason's grandfather, Jacob. James discovered the truth; Jacob had been imprisoned and then murdered by the Ten Hand Council for demanding justice for the Sondites and inciting riots. James Killovew and his companions were nearly caught in the Ten Hand Temple, but they avoided capture, crawled through the underbelly of the city, and escaped under its very walls.

They never would have escaped, however, if they had not been freed by a rebellious Acolyte named Tegan. An Acolyte who happened to be on the rise. They had been lucky—*blessed, perhaps?*—to run into him, who at the time was a third Finger to the Fourth Hand. He also happened to be an Acolyte who secretly agreed with the Killovews and agreed to work with James Killovew to set things right in the kingdom. For the longest time, their goal was known, but their way to achieve it was not. In the meantime, Tegan continued to play the role of a faithful Acolyte, and James Killovew played the role of a loyal realm lord while he raised his children. Lord Killovew had had to suffer tariffs and stricter regulations for his father's rebellious actions, but the Thirsting Forest Realm endured… avoiding much of the hardship that faced the other realms now.

Using cautious and secret means, Lord Killovew brought other allies to their cause. Jason had been on the verge of manhood when the letter from Tegan arrived.

It came just before the dweller attack. Tegan had been promoted, it read. He had jumped from the First Finger of the Sixth Hand to the Second Hand, a surprising promotion that made him the second most powerful man in the kingdom. And even more importantly, there was not yet an apprentice to the First Hand.

The rest of the Ten Hand Council was united in their injustice and bound together by their greed and ambition. By himself Tegan could do little good, even as Second Hand. Tegan would never be promoted again by Acolyte tradition, but if the First Hand died before an apprentice was selected, Tegan would be responsible for selecting the next First Hand. Thus, with allies gathered and a perfect man on the inside, James Killovew assembled his strike team and sent them to Shinar where the perfect successor lay in wait. Jason was the natural leader. The perfect cover, a leader of supposed soldiers—in actuality, a team of assassins.

The ideal group of men, Jason thought.

Sir Breigo, the loyal knight. Ratoke and Taroke, the poison-laced assassins. Mako Black, the late comer, the water dragon wrangler, and longtime family friend to the Sondites. A team with a thousand reasons to never dabble in treason, but two commonalities that trumped every imaginable reason against it: an empathetic heart and a questioning mind.

The law of unjust religion would come to an end. The weather anomaly of the golden beam would no longer be claimed as the violent tool of the God-King. The balance would return, and the children of the kingdom would be given a reason to hope again for the future.

Jinala… her future depended on him.

Jason sat bolt upright.

He tossed aside the sheets and stood again from his bed. He strode to the balcony and looked out at the cityscape once again. The marketplace and the gates were no longer crawling with people, but a good many could still be seen walking about. Jason doubted that the massive city ever grew completely still.

His whole life, ever since he told his father he wanted to be a soldier on his second sun, ever since he thought about pushing Jinala's crib out the window, ever since he squashed bugs, plucked lizards' legs off, stalked dogs, his first dream probably would show that he was… *evil.*

He was a killer. He enjoyed it. No lie there. He had smiled as he cut down each bandit in the floodplains. He rubbed his knife because it was always there, his favorite tool, his portal that unlocked the *real Jason.* These past few cycles, he had finally unleashed *him*… and now the seal was broken, whatever that meant. The blood at his boots had exhilarated him. The way his sword sunk into their flesh felt so… personal.

So intimate.

Jason paced across his room, from the open balcony to the door to the common room of the suite, and then back again.

His life, his dreams, his desires, his hidden thoughts that he kept buried even from himself, they all made sense now. Jason raged internally, his mind fighting its own war. The Jason he wished he was versus the Jason he knew he was. The whole dweller-doomed kingdom depended upon his ability to execute violence but also his sanity to control it.

Jinala's little crib—

No, not that. Not even I could do that.

You thought about it.

Everyone thinks about it. I just thought about it a little more than is usual.

You did more than think about it in the plains.

I had to kill them.

You didn't have to smile.

Jason stopped pacing.

Get it together, Jason.

He walked over to the basin of water in the corner of his room and stared at his transparent reflection in the still water- stared at himself truly for the first time in his life. The argument in his head did not return.

"I'm not arguing with myself anymore," Jason said to his reflection aloud.

No, of course not, his reflection replied through the ripples.

Jason did not awake on the cycle of the Sundown Ceremony, for he had never fallen asleep. He still felt the warm blood of the scum he had slaughtered on his hands, despite it being washed away long ago. He lay in his bed, eyes wide open, while he waited for the others to stir. In less than six candles, the bells would toll, and the night season would be ushered in at the Ten Hand Temple. On the fourth toll of the bell, Jason and his conspirators would transform into assassins. Jason grew excited at the thought, and his excitement nauseated him.

Jinala will have the world she deserves.

The Prince of the Thirsting Forest felt alienated from the rest of the citizens in Gahkin's wide kingdom. The slaughter of men should never be a joyous task, and for most normal people, it wasn't. Jason had read enough war journals and studied enough history of the kingdom to realize he was *not* normal.

The ancient tyrant, King Charrip, forced his enemies to mutilate the bodies of their own family in front of him. He surrounded his tents with a moat that he literally filled with the blood of his enemies. Some ancient texts say he bathed each morning in the moat before moving on to another village or town to 'civilize.'

Jason didn't think he was *that* crazy. He didn't want to do that, but... He remembered the tingling ecstasy and elation he felt when his sword plunged into the heart of one of the outlaws. His memory of the cycle told him he had smirked as he carved away at their vital organs. In the moment, he thought that his surging emotion was just the thrill of life or death battle, but later, he acknowledged the lie. He mislabeled the adrenaline rush of vengeful murder as justice to romanticize his vile enjoyment of killing. Jason trembled at the thought.

Who am I now? Who will I be after the Sundown Ceremony?

From one candle to the next, his emotions dove and rose, his reasoning and logic sliding along in tow. His thoughts became a means to justify his emotions, not to control them. He argued with himself, condemned and congratulated his actions in a matter of moments. The secrets his father had confided in him brought about a sense of enlightenment, but the sudden action demanded by that conspiracy had corrupted him and broken his identity.

This task is more important than my emotions, larger than my self-doubt. I must trust our plan if I can't trust my warring instincts. I must act, I cannot, and I will not hesitate.

Jason threw his silken sheet off his lean body. In another moment, he was standing, wrapping the ceremonial cloak around his shoulders. The fifth candle burned. Jason had two candles left to prepare and arrive at the inner sanctum. He needed to eat and play the role of the innocent prince until the time came to leave the inn and travel to the Ten Hand Temple. He put on his formal boots and left the room with steps loud enough to alert Breigo and the others of his departure.

Jason wrung his hands as he descended the stairs. He would need to quit that newly developed habit before he hit the lobby. Deliberately gripping his sword hilt in one hand and the stair railing in the other, he turned left and emerged onto the bottom floor of the inn.

He saw Sir Breigo in the corner with two other men. One was a familiar, fine-looking young man and the other a short but stout-looking knight.

"You must be Prince Carl Quirvop," Jason said, stepping quickly to the red and yellow-robed man doomed to die at his hand. "I saw you two cycles ago but was too tired from the travel to come introduce myself. Good to meet you." Jason hated himself for the excitement he felt as he shook Carl's hand.

"And you must be Prince Jason Killovew. This is Sir Quintus. Feeling nervous?"

Jason's heart leaped and then calmed itself.

He means only for the war. Nothing else. Nothing more.

"I am slightly, I must admit. And yourself?"

"More anxious than nervous, I'd say. I'm ready to send a big Vistonex exoskeleton to my father's trophy room. It will look brilliant next to our mammoth tusks and rhinoceros' horns. Have you many trophies, monster?"

Jason's heart stopped…until the words rearranged themselves in his mind.

"Have you many monster trophies?"

That had been the question.

Gahkin's wands, you really have lost your mind.

"No, not really. I haven't. I've gotten my fair share of training, and I've put down a few water dragons and boars, but that's—"

"Oh, don't be modest, Jason," Carl interrupted, slapping him in the shoulder. He leaned closer. "I was giving you the opening to brag about the dweller." He looked halfway across his shoulder at two pretty ladies standing at the bar. When he spoke again, his voice bounced off the walls, much louder than necessary. "Even Quirvop's heard of you and your father's dweller hunt. They say you and Sir Breigo killed the biggest ever found outside of the Great Chasm."

"That wasn't so much of a hunt as a rescue, and I was just thankful to make it out alive."

Carl Quirvop nodded. He leaned in close again. "Ah, playing the humble, handsome prince card… I see… Not my style, but let's see who brings the ladies over." He returned to his boisterous voice, "We also have an eighteen-point buck that I killed when I was just three suns old hung on our wall, along with a number of white bear and moose heads. Oh, and my father has even killed a full-grown Ice Moth. The creature fled as it died, its body was irretrievable, but it definitely was dying." He waited for some sort of gasp or something and then, when he didn't get it, repeated, more toward the ladies than at Jason. "An. Ice. Moth."

"So, you're not fearful? My Father made specific mention to me that war was far different from hunting. In war, you never know when something dangerous is about to happen. You have to always be prepared."

Why did I say that? I shouldn't be toying with him.

Jason thought of a cat playing with a baby rabbit, letting it almost escape before snapping it up and dragging its bleeding body back from safety over and over until the baby lay still, exhausted and waiting for death.

Breigo seemed to be tiring of Carl and his boasts as well, for he sighed and changed the topic to smooth his exit. "I think I'm going to go check on my horse in the stables. I'm not sure when we'll have another chance to see them until after the ceremony. Soon the Acolytes will come to collect us and bring us to the Ten Hand Temple."

"I'll come with you," Jason said hurriedly, and they left the soon-to-be-dead prince standing with his knight by the bar.

Thirty-Two

As a pack of four traveling through the Ten Hand Temple, the Sondite drew most of the attention. He walked at the back of the group and now and then scratched at his new velvet robe. It itched in the armpits and around the neck. Being civilized was more uncomfortable than he had predicted, even compared to his old life of sleeping in leaf beds and eating charred squirrel meat.

"Quit that, Crichton," Domray said out of the side of his mouth. The other two Acolytes, the Seventh and Eighth Hand he had been told, led the way. Domray wanted Crichton to impress them, and apparently scratching and tugging at his robes was inappropriate. Crichton had expected Rulbiss and Flagg to attend as well, but only Domray had been invited to the ceremony alongside the Sondite boy. The thought made him nervous.

They turned a corner and proceeded up what seemed like the hundredth staircase. Crichton was quickly running out of patience. He held his hands at his sides and kept walking.

They led the way to the top of the pyramid where the ceremony was going to take place. They took a few turns and crossed through a handful of hallways, but much of their walk consisted of climbing stairs. Stairs after stairs. It felt like they were climbing to the top of the Star Tower, not the top of the pyramid. Crichton wondered what the top of the Star Tower would look like.

Just as Crichton began to imagine the pilgrimage it would take to ascend to the peak of the Star Tower, the Acolytes stopped walking. Crichton looked up. They stood at a wide landing in front of two great silver doors, framed in purple and set in a golden wall. Crichton steadied himself, for behind that door was a group of people that may very well determine if his future was to be that of a soldier or of an Acolyte scholar.

In unison, the two council members opened the doors, revealing… another staircase. Crichton sighed and stepped through the doors.

As he climbed, an eerie purplish light shone down from above. Crichton saw the open sky above his head. He rose out of the staircase and found himself on the top of the pyramid. The platform at the top of the pyramid afforded a clear view out on the Grand City of Gahkin. Crichton saw shadowy buildings aglow with firelight, the black river on the far side of the city walls, and the Star Tower, a massive twisting piece of steel. From the top of the Ten Hand Temple Crichton now saw that the Star Tower descended directly into the steep north face of the pyramid. The width of the tower, which Crichton once thought could be no more than a couple feet, had to be at least fifty around, if not wider.

"Quit gawking, young one. Move into your position." The Seventh Hand prodded him in the back, pushing him toward the edge of the roof. As he walked to his place, he looked at a small flat wall facing southeast. In-between the bricks was a long thin slit that drew even with the southeastern horizon. The slit burned the blinding orange color of the sun.

Crichton stood in place next to Domray, at the outer edge of the roof. The Seventh and Eighth hands moved into their spots, forming the beginnings of a semi-circle opposite the slit wall. Aside from the four paladins stationed in each corner, the roof was empty. Apparently, Crichton and Domray were the first guests to arrive.

Thirty-Three

Jason had yet to see the Second Hand or Chief Rekebba. Mako, Ratoke, and Sir Breigo walked just ahead and just behind him, along with the rest of the Sundown Ceremony attendees. The Prince of the Thirsting Forest grew increasingly worried by their absence, but there were plenty of logical reasons for why they might be missing. Tegan had said that he would have to bring her into the ceremony as a special guest prisoner. Jason just did not assume that meant he would have to wait until the final flicker to confirm two of his co-conspirators were in place for their final strike, but so be it. As he ran it over in his head, it made sense. The Second Hand would bring her into the temple, just not with Jason and the other realm royalty. Jason's nerves did not decrease, but at least they did not continue to grow. Chief Rekebba and Tegan would be at the ceremony. They just would not receive the royal tour.

Before the Sundown Ceremony, the regal guests received a guided tour of the Ten Hand Temple. Included in their winding walk through the temple: The largest library in the world, bookshelves dusty with a hundred seasons of censorship. The most ornate auditorium, complete with acoustically balanced gold bricks laid by Gahkin himself. The wall of guilt where royal sinners' names were etched, stretching hundreds of feet into the air. And the bottomless well.

Jason peered over the edge, and like most wells, he could not see the bottom. Not as miraculous as the Star Tower but complete with a jewel-encrusted bucket and rope. It spoke to the wealth of the Acolyte institution.

Wealth grown through corruption, no doubt.

Jason was not sure who was in his head anymore, if his consciousness had lost to his inner desires or if his inner desires had retreated deeper again, or if they had melded together. Maybe they had always been melded together.

Maybe I'm insane.

Either way, soon, the assassinations would be over, and the monster within would be satisfied. If Jason survived, he would deal with *his other self* then.

Sir Breigo, one stride ahead of Jason as formality demanded, stared straight ahead. His eyes did not move to view the ornate golden sculptures at the many tunnel entrance ways, nor did he slow his pace in amazement and stare at the high pointed ceiling in the atrium, shrinking to a single black dot encircled by pane after pane of stained-glass windows. His head did not swivel to admire the true sterling silver stars on the sword hilt of every paladin, nor to take in the expanded right ear lobe of every Acolyte historian. He just walked along, and Jason knew by the slight paling color of his skin that he was nervous.

The tour, a final royal pleasure for the usual guests, became a dull dagger in Jason's stomach. It dragged on and on. The time they spent inside the temple pyramid felt like a cycle all its own. Jason's nerves would not retreat. His stomach threatened to unleash its contents onto the wall of guilt as they passed. He scowled at the ominous irony.

He could only imagine how the others felt. Ratoke, walking at the front and speaking vociferously with the guide, covered his jitters with an overactive tongue. His voice did not waver, and his interest in the things he inquired about seemed genuine.

He's a decent liar, at least.

Mako walked just behind Jason, and Jason didn't risk a suspicious look backward at him. He hoped the water dragon wrangler was holding it together better than he was.

The Prince of the Thirsting Forest, feeling the illusion of blood still on his hands, resisted the urge to wipe at them and kept them loose at his side. He turned his gaze to the men from the blue Quirvop mountains. Carl and his knight were both formidable-looking fighters. No matter, Jason believed himself to be the best swordsman in the pyramid, behind only Sir Breigo. And they had the element of surprise on their side.

Now I must make Father proud.

Despite the time seeming to drag by, suddenly the candle expired, and the moment had arrived. Jason swallowed back the salty taste of bile in his mouth and set his jaw tight. The ceremony would begin soon. The thought of murder was making Jason's fingers twitch as it got closer and closer. For maybe the last moment in Jason's life, his immoral instincts would be aligned with his moral philosophy.

He would stand on the small open platform at the top of the Ten Hand Temple and watch the sun drop below the horizon. The viewing slit in the southeastern wall, aligned with the horizon, would morph from blinding golden orange to deep, dark pink, and the bells would toll. With the tolling of the bells, the night season would officially begin. One toll would pass, and the attendees would kneel. A second toll, and they would bow their heads and clasp their hands. A third toll and the First Hand would bless the future soldiers and wish them success on their crusades. A fourth toll and his team would draw their weapons and kill everyone else. Jason frowned. A part of him felt bad that Prince Carl would not be able to defend himself. Jason wanted to kill him, honestly.

That leaves too much to chance.

Jason ran his hand along the side of his regal knife hilt, despite himself.

Soon.

"The inner sanctum is another fifteen floors above," the Acolyte guide said, looking around as if some of them might insist they could not make it up the stairs.

"Go on already and lead the way, or we will all miss the Sundown," Carl barked. The sound of their footsteps echoed off the walls as they walked toward the long staircase.

Thirty-Four

Arriving in groups of twos and threes, the Ten Hand Council slowly assembled. Counting the members in his head, Crichton realized the First, Third, Fifth, and Sixth Hands were still missing. Isaac was the Third Hand, and he was far from Shinar. Crichton wondered if the First Hand would be in attendance or if he would miss the ceremony as well.

Crichton really wanted to see the First Hand. In what seemed like a different life, Crichton remembered Jinala telling him that the First Hand was the most powerful man in the entire kingdom. No combination of realm lords could *overrule* the council, but the First Hand *ruled over* the council. The First Hand's spot, however, remained empty for the time being.

A large group of guests arrived next. The knights wore steel armor; the orange torchlight and purpling sky reflected off their suits, making them shimmer in twilight colors as they walked.

The other guests wore formal robes, not armor. A beautiful woman with dyed blue hair, a princess no doubt, wore a tight gown swirling with azure and silver under an icy white cloak. A wide-shouldered man, wearing red and yellow scarves around his red and yellow robes practically swaggered to his spot, right next to Crichton. His eyebrows raised when he saw the Sondite, but he said nothing.

The next person Crichton laid eyes on was a familiar one that took him by surprise.

Prince Jason Killovew, Jinala's brother, walked to his spot across from Crichton. He looked in the Sondite boy's direction and frowned a concerned frown, but no flash of recognition shone through his eyes.

Crichton had spied on him, watched him leave Castle Killovew after riding with Jinala, but never once had Jason laid eyes on Crichton.

Despite that, Jason glanced over at the young Sondite, repeatedly. Every time he looked over, Crichton looked away. Crichton followed Jason's eyes to the Second Hand. Crichton could not be sure, but it almost looked like the Second Hand nodded his head. He looked back at Jinala's brother. Jason answered with an imperceptible head nod of his own.

A patch of blond hair rose from the stairwell.

Crichton's interest in Jason Killovew vanished as the First Hand arrived. His blond hair was smooth and long, and he wore it pulled back behind his ears. His beard, more soft brown than blond, trimmed neatly, kept only at his face to the jawline. His gray-blue eyes almost glowed from behind his wrinkled brows. The

First Hand wore a purple robe, as the other Acolytes did, but silver stitching accented the outer edges. A tasseled belt sheathed two L-shaped objects, flashing bright gold against the soft light in the sky. His eyes looked kindly upon the Sondite. They looked… familiar to him.

The First Hand *oozed* positive energy. Something about the leading Acolyte, ruler of the kingdom, pulsated with warmth. Pulsated with goodness. His eyes suggested it. His body movements evidenced it. His smile ensured it.

"Thank you all for coming," the First Hand said.

Crichton felt goosebumps raise across his body. Good or not, the tremble of his voice gave the Sondite the chills. Something was not normal about him. His voice was not especially deep, but inside Crichton, something clashed as the voice reverberated through his chest. The sound made Crichton feel like fainting. It sounded awfully familiar to the voice he heard back in the Killovew great hall.

The Sondite looked back at Jason to judge his perception. The Prince of the Thirsting Forest was staring at the First Hand, his eyes narrowed in focus. Whatever Jason Killovew was thinking, he was thinking hard about it.

"Soon, the bells shall toll, so let us begin."

Altogether, it was a small gathering compared to what Crichton had imagined.

Thirty-Five

"Thank you all for coming," the First Hand said. Jason's fingers twitched.

Chief Rekebba had not arrived. It seemed like, despite every effort, the Second Hand had been unable to gain her passage to the ceremony. He was waiting on the platform as Jason arrived, and of course, could not explain what had happened that kept her from the ceremony.

Jason, Sir Breigo, Mako, and Ratoke would have to do it on their own.

I must kill more people myself.

That meant that between Jason and the three others, they had to kill two paladins, five council members, Carl Quirvop, the Quirvop's knight, the Sondite, the Rhymark Princess, and the extra Acolyte. So many more innocents than he expected. Twelve people for four murderers. All in all, not an outrageous impossibility considering only five of the twelve could fight. Jason figured they would strike and kill two each before they were able to respond. The council members would fall like sheep to wolves.

Jason's eyes flicked back to the Sondite boy. He was almost old enough to be called a man, but not quite. Still innocent, still hopeful, still a child, still…

He must be killed.

There could be no witnesses, no chance that Tegan's ascension be questioned.

The doomed First Hand spoke on, "Soon the bells shall toll, so let us begin. I hope the dry weather did not add displeasure to your journey here. I promise that your crusades into the Dezruk Forest will not lack in water. Also, I want to apologize for whatever inconvenience the added security around the city borders and at this ceremony may have created. Hopefully it didn't disrupt any plans." The First Hand looked directly at Jason.

It took all of Jason's effort not to react. Out of the corner of his eyes, he saw Ratoke's knees buckle for a flicker and then reestablish themselves.

Another coincidence. Nothing to worry about. Just another coincidence.

The Second Hand's face was blank.

It was strange comparing the two most powerful men in the kingdom. If looks were everything, it would seem the First Hand was the apprentice and the Second Hand the master. The First Hand's face was without wrinkles, his beard tight and short, his eyes young and overly optimistic. His hair was long but still blondish brown, not gray. His mouth twitched, and his throat jumped up and down as he spoke, betraying his confidence. His peaceful attitude was a facade. His robes were bedecked with unnecessary finery of both silver and gold. He looked more like a man pretending to be the First Hand than the real ruler of the kingdom.

The Second Hand, in comparison, had a buzzed, balding head, speckled with white hair and wispy gray stubble, unblemished by youth and the symptomatic unreliability with which youth was often burdened. His eyes crinkled at the edges with crow's feet that bespoke great wisdom and deep thought. Standing next to the First Hand he looked taller, more genuine, and wiser. More important than any other difference, though, was the true empathy his look suggested. Even before executing great treason, his face showed only consistency and patience, thoughtfulness, kindness. When he moved and spoke, it was with direction and purpose, no rushing nor hesitating nor pandering. He looked like a man who had long ago made peace with the Creator, if there was one. He was the one in touch with the God-King. He was the one fit to be the voice for the Ruler of Rulers. The ear to Gahkin.

Jason knew, in that moment, the importance of his coming actions. The whole kingdom deserved better than the current First Hand.

"So, let us all turn our minds away from trivialities compared to Gahkin and raise our minds to His." The First Hand gazed up at the sky. "Gahkin, I am your ever-servant, and I, Yehwa, First Hand of the Ten Hand Council, request Your benevolence and Your good favor among us now and in the future. It is only by Your grace that we have lived to see another season of light conclude here at the Sundown Ceremony."

Jason glanced at the slit in the eastern wall. It still shone with orange light. Soon the light would fail, as would their lives and their false theocracy. Soon Jason's grandfather would have vengeance. Soon the crusades would end. The origin of the false rumors of apocalypse would cease. Jason envisioned himself drawing his sword while their heads were bowed.

Soon.

"As these fine followers gather here, they align themselves with Your righteous goals. The Vistonex of the west are being beaten back further and further by Your brave brothers and sisters. Both sides of the Verdelen River shall be Yours, thanks in part to the efforts of the followers You see gathered here. They have come to Shinar as royal ambassadors dedicated to Your campaign. Dedicated to You. I ask, as your ever-servant and disciple and Acolyte, with humility as befits an immortal king such as Yourself, grant them victory in their campaigns. Grant them will. Grant them power. Grant them ability. Grant them the mental fortitude to withstand the evil that hangs in the dark trees at our borders. Stretch out Your strength to those who shall need it in the future. We know You have an immeasurable reservoir, grant us but a small share of Your infiniteness!"

The First Hand took a deep breath reveling in his own passion and fervor. The Second Hand looked on patiently, smiling.

"The dark season brings with it its share of curses and blessings. Each blessing is worth tenfold the curses that cling like leeches to the dark. Help us eliminate them this dark season. Help our youth grow wise and faithful. Help our crops grow rich and bountiful. Fill the clouds with rain and snow so that we can bathe in Your brisk, cleansing water!

"Now, I ask you all to raise up silent prayer to Gahkin as we turn our eyes to the wall. Let us welcome the dark season with Gahkin on our minds and in our hearts."

The edges of the semi-circle turned, and everyone looked at the viewing wall. The thread thin slit, fixed on the horizon, still displayed the final, bright sliver of the sun.

Jason, head locked on the viewing wall, scanned all those closest to him with flashing eyes. To his right, and just slightly behind, was a paladin. Then the Quirvop knight. Next was Carl Quirvop, then the Sondite boy, then his Acolyte supervisor, and one of the paladins. Directly to his left was Sir Breigo, then another paladin. Beyond that stood the Ten Hand Council, arranged in descending rank. In the middle of the group stood the First and Second Hand. Both had their eyes closed, praying. The thin ray of light that shot through the viewing wall illuminated the First Hand at his nose but came just below the chin of the taller Second Hand. The horizontal line of light climbed ever so slowly upward.

Jason didn't think he could wait any longer. His palms were sweating. More bile built up in his mouth, and he almost vomited.

Don't blow it now, Jason.

Not when so much blood is ready to be spilled. Not when it is MY time.

"Bury you!" Jason said out loud.

Every eye turned and aimed at him.

Thirty-Six

Jinala Killovew found herself in the great hall, sitting anxiously just below the throne of her father. She held herself still, despite her nervousness. Martin and Evrost were below in the kitchens. Sir Trittion was gathering horses from the stables.

She would join them soon, but Lord Killovew first needed to address his people. And he needed to do it with his daughter present. The safe return of the stable boy meant that pigeons had been sent to every village and every town in the Killovew realm, and now James was to repeat the message aloud to his guards, staff, knights, and advisers that all waited on his word. Fear ran through them, Jinala sensed.

Two cycles prior, the Ardellian siege lifted. The small army fled across the borders back into the wastelands south of the chasm. The realm knew that Jinala had successfully led her castle's resolute defense of the army and negotiated a retreat. They did not know what she had to promise to do so.

Most of the realm also knew that magic had been performed during the meetings between Jinala and Arthur, but the rumors ran wild on what had happened.

The citizens also knew Isaac, the Third Hand, sat imprisoned in the Killovew dungeon.

Less than a season had passed since Isaac had summoned the voice of the God-King into this very hall. Jinala did not believe it was Gahkin that controlled the golden beam, nor the vile voice, but the citizens of the realm certainly did. They would ask themselves, would Gahkin accept that Isaac had broken the laws of the kingdom? Or did the Third Hand's relationship with Gahkin trump the rules of the realms?

She remembered stories of the golden sword of Gahkin that came from the sky and carved a path through the forest eighteen seasons ago. The same golden sword that destroyed Castle Grayson, the same golden beam that many claimed was a harbinger for the Great Flash. Despite Lord Killovew's efforts to quell the growing rumors of the apocalypse over the past few seasons, the citizens still felt that the end was near. Armies marching into the Thirsting Forest, Ten Hand Council members spying in the tower, magic relics used against each other on the castle lawn. Perhaps, the time *was* growing near.

Despite Isaac's treachery, Jinala still felt a strange guilt locking up the Third Hand.

Jinala trembled and clutched at the cold stone armrests to steady herself.

The wide doors to the great hall closed. All had arrived.

Lord James Killovew stood, inhaled, and then spoke.

"The Third Hand of Gahkin has betrayed his oath, our realm, and the kingdom he swore to protect. We caught him spying, in direct disobedience of the Ten Hand Council bylaws for realm diplomacy. He admitted to murdering one of our citizens. My advisers and I await word from the Ten Hand Council on measures to take against him. I have no further information as of now, but I will tell you this. Our realm shall not tolerate further manipulations and added regulations over our own land. Just because the Great Flash may be drawing closer does not mean that we cannot take care of ourselves. Our village mayors trust every man with the care of their own family and household. Our chieftains trust the mayors, and I trust our chieftains. Should not the Ten Hand Council trust the realm lords with their own realms?

"I encourage each one of you to spend the next few candles thinking about the Thirsting Forest, the land we call home. Talk with your family and friends. I am the lord of this realm, which means it is my responsibility to ensure the wellbeing of my people. I shall hold an open forum before planning our next step after we receive the Ten Hand Council's response. Gahkin united the kingdom, but now some of his Acolytes may be attempting to destroy it. My realm and the families who live here are what matter to me."

James paused, glancing toward the ceiling, deep in thought. He turned his gaze back to the assembly before him.

"My daughter, Princess Jinala Killovew, defended our home from the invaders from Ardel. Not Gahkin. Not the Acolytes. It was our guards and farm hands who stood armored at the gate. Our advisers who took their lives into their own hands and marched into the enemy camp to demand that they retreat.

"The dark season is coming upon us, and now more than ever, we need to stay united. Knights and citizens alike need to be as vigilant as possible over the next few cycles. We will be withdrawing from the border patrols and staying together here at the castle and at Northtown. Even now, our guards and knights are returning from their camps. If danger comes before we hear a response from the Ten Hand Council, we shall be forced to depend upon ourselves, as in the olden cycles. I will not hesitate to call the mayors and chiefs to assemble the Thirsting Forest citizen army, as we were forced to do many, many seasons ago. The able-bodied men of this land have proven we are certainly capable of defending it if need be. The Kingdom of Gahkin may be deteriorating, our neighboring realms may seem on the brink of collapse, but the Realm of the Thirsting Forest will stay forever strong! We are one people—"

"With a thousand pasts!" the hall shouted in unison.

"I bid you foul weather and fair health," James finished.

The crowd stood, and a dull roar fell over the hall as the people talked among themselves. James reached down and took Jinala's hand. He helped her from her chair and down the steps. They went out the back door of the hall, behind the throne steps, and took the first set of staircases down into the kitchens.

"Father, doesn't formality dictate that we wait for them to leave, not us leave before them?"

"Shh, Jinala. Formality be buried."

"But Father!"

"Let's go; we don't have time to discuss this any longer."

Jinala was not a child. Had he not listened to his own speech? She was the one who saved the castle. Who may have just sacrificed the rest of her future for this realm. She would not be shushed like a toddler.

"Let go, Father." She tore her hand from his. "This is not the right thing to do. I feel like I'm being forced to run away when I should be standing with you. With our people."

"Jinala, you are not running away. You are doing something very important. Something I might not have trusted you to do just half a season ago."

"I know, I know. I know that it's important to take Evrost and go find the witch, but… I don't know. Now I feel like I need to be here, with the citizens."

James stopped walking and knelt down. It used to be when he would kneel, her face would draw even with his. Now, he had to look up at her when he knelt.

"I'm very proud of you, Jinala." He reached out and took one of her blonde curls in his hand. He tugged on it gently and lifted it into the air as if weighing it. It felt very different from the way Arthur had touched her hair. "Have I ever told you, dear, how much you look like your mother? Or how beautiful you are? Have I ever taken the time to sit with you like this and asked you to tell me about your lessons or your riding or your friends?"

"Father, we never had time for that useless stuff."

"But it's not useless, dear. It's the most important stuff in the kingdom, and I never made time for it."

"You made time for us… sometimes."

"I love you and your brother so much, Jinala. I'm sorry I was not there to tell you that every single cycle of your life."

"It's… it's okay."

"I was too busy trying to take care of the realm that I did not stop to appreciate you two."

"But isn't that why you were doing all that secret stuff for the kingdom?

Because you wanted all of us to have a better life? I always thought you were the best father and the best realm lord because you cared about more people than just Jason and me."

James looked at Jinala, two pairs of green eyes locked in love. "You're such a sweet, smart girl. When I came back from Shinar and officially married your mother, I used to get in these fits where I would just sit and think and convince myself that I was incapable of doing anything. I wouldn't come out of the war room for cycles on end. One of the knights would tell your mother, and she would slink into the room and, with a few simple words, remind me of who I was and how I could do whatever needed to be done. When she died, when you were still a tiny little baby, I wondered who would be able to break me out of my fits after she was gone." James smiled. "You can, sweetheart. You're beautiful and inspirational and so smart and so sweet, and I'm so very proud of you."

Jinala would have loved to sit with her father and do this until the final candle extinguished, but she knew they didn't have enough time left in the cycle.

"Thanks, Father. I'll track down this witch and see what we can learn. But when I come back, I want to help lead. I want to participate in the council meetings and learn about ruling this realm."

"Deal. When you come back, hopefully Jason will be back too. There will be momentous changes across the whole kingdom, and all three of us will have to work together to help this kingdom move forward. There might be struggles. But we can overcome them."

"Together." Jinala reached out her hand. Her father took it in his.

"Now come with me, let me at least see my daughter off on her first journey without her father." James leaped to his feet and pulled her along after him, heading deeper into the lower rooms of the castle. Toward Evrost and Martin.

They descended into the kitchen cellars. Instead of finding one wizard and one outlaw boy patiently waiting for them, they found one wizard, one outlaw boy, and one stuttering child, with an apple peel dangling out of his mouth.

"Oh dear," James said.

Mikder's arm was outstretched, finger pointing straight at Martin. "Lord— Lord Killovew, sir, there is—I found a—I caught a Sondite!"

"You caught?" Martin said, "We caught you! We caught you with half your head buried in the compost, eating trash!"

Evrost pushed Martin back and stepped toward the other boy with slow steps, trying not to frighten him. His eyes glowed softly.

"Fret not, forest fools. For I, Evrost the Mud Wizard, shall erase the boy's memory with magic, and he shall forever forget the day he found the forbidden Sondite." Evrost raised his staff above his head and spun it slowly, murmuring,

"Hocus pocus, Alabama, your memory is rotten. So now, I say, forget the things that need to be forgotten!" Evrost pointed his staff at Mikder. The silver staff sparkled a little but did nothing else.

After a moment, Mikder said, "I… I'm sorry—but I st—st—st—still remember."

Lord Killovew sighed and stepped between the wizard and the frightened boy. "Of course, you do, Mikder. Don't worry about him. And you are correct, that boy's name is Martin, and he is a Sondite, and he shouldn't be here. But he is just an innocent boy who lost his parents and brother. We are taking care of him for now."

Mikder's eyes flicked back and forth between the wizard and the outlaw child. "Okay…" he finally said, confused as ever.

"Now, Mikder, I'm going to take you back to Mr. Finch. He knows about the Sondite boy, but not everyone does, so, can you do me a favor? Can you not tell anyone else about this little meeting in the cellar?"

"Uh—yes, sir—uh, my lord. I uh—I can do that. And I am sorry for eating all the left-over apple peels."

"I know Mr. Finch can be a little stingy when it comes to food, Mikder, but it is for good reason. We all must do our part so everyone has enough to eat. Those peels and the cores help us keep our soil fertile for next year, so we can have more food instead of less. So please, don't do that anymore."

Jinala had just 'saved' the realm from the Ardellian army two cycles ago, but now she was standing in the cellar of the castle with a crazy wizard, an orphaned Sondite, and a stuttering, math-loving boy who was being lectured for eating out of the trash by the Thirsting Forest Realm lord. Jinala almost laughed at the lunacy of it all.

Still though, her brother was in danger, and a treacherous Acolyte was imprisoned in the dungeons. She knew her father had much to do, and she was the only one capable of leading Martin, Evrost, and Sir Trittion on a secret meeting to go find this witch in the deep forest.

"Evrost and Martin, my daughter is in charge, so please listen to her more than you listened to me this past season." James Killovew leaned down and hugged Jinala again. "I'll see you back at the castle soon, dear. Be careful." He walked back up the stairs, arm guiding Mikder along, and they both disappeared.

Jinala walked in the other direction, and the others followed.

As they moved toward the cellar exit, Evrost said, "If I am a wizard, why didn't my spell work?"

Martin answered, "Well, for one, you made-up a bunch of words, so maybe that's why. But two, usually, it only works when you don't try to do it on purpose.

It's okay, though, Ev." Martin patted the Mud Wizard on the arm. "You'll figure it out eventually. Maybe the witch can teach you."

Evrost snorted and tapped his staff on the ground. The top of the staff glowed blueish white, lighting up the whole room.

"I can do that on purpose. And I can shoot bolts of electricity at stuff if I want to, too."

"What is electricity?"

"The stuff that comes out of my staff."

"Well, maybe try poking Jinala with it."

Jinala whipped around, "Do not poke me with it!"

"Jinala shall not receive any magical experimentation. Understood." Evrost nodded at her in a serious fashion, but his eyes flicked back toward Martin curiously.

Jinala turned back around and led them the rest of the way to the cellar door. "All right, in just a few flickers, we are going to leave through here and head across the potato garden and then across the lawn and into the fringe forest. Evrost, you might need to help Martin and me over the garden wall."

"Indeed. I shall take the opportunity to fine-tune my levitation spells."

"No. Just use your arms and give us a boost."

"Oh, all right," Evrost said, dejected.

Martin asked, "What is an 'Alabama,' Evrost?"

"Did I say that?"

"Yeah, and you also said, 'hocus pocus' and 'day.'"

"A day is like what you call a cycle, Martin, where I'm from."

"Where *are* you from, Evrost?"

"Gosh, Martin, I sure wish I could remember. It might be important."

They stood at the door to the cellar in silence for another long moment.

Jinala took a deep breath and said, "Okay, everyone, follow me."

They darted through the door, up the stairs, and into the darkening twilight.

Thirty-Seven

"Bury you!" Jason said into the silence.

Crichton looked at Prince Killovew and wondered why he would say that. It certainly didn't seem like a part of the tradition, and based on the way everyone else was staring at him, it wasn't expected. Even Jason looked surprised. Surprised and angry.

The First Hand spoke. "Something digging at your mind, Prince Killovew?"

"My apologies, Yehwa. The thought of a particular vile… *Vistonex* dashed through my mind, and my utterance was intended for my thoughts alone."

"Think nothing of it, Jason. Funny how our thoughts can betray us sometimes, isn't it, Tegan?"

The Second Hand replied, "Strange and unexpected."

Just then, the light in the viewing slit disappeared.

The roof dimmed noticeably, casting dark shadows across the faces of every Ten Hand Council member.

Crichton felt very tense, though he wasn't sure why.

A thunderous boom echoed from below.

"Please kneel as we welcome the dark season."

Everyone knelt, Crichton hesitating a moment. Looking around, Crichton noticed he wasn't the only one slow to kneel. The thick bodyguard that was dressed in Killovew colors looked sweaty and nervous, but he eventually knelt with the others.

The knight in Killovew armor looked paler than was healthy.

Another thunderous boom echoed from below.

"Please bring your hands together and bow your heads."

The orders were followed again. Crichton watched as the men and women folded their hands together in unison.

The First Hand shook down the sleeves of his robes as he brought his hands together. A metallic cricket crawled out of one sleeve, onto his hands, and back up the other sleeve.

A third thunderous boom echoed from below.

Thirty-Eight

A thunderous boom echoed up from within the pyramid.

"Please kneel as we welcome the dark season."

Jason knelt. He knew there would be several moments before the next—

Another thunderous boom reverberated off the pyramid walls.

"Please bring your hands together and bow your heads."

Gahkin's wands it's happening so fast!

It's nearly time!

The third boom from below shook Jason's nerves to the very bone.

How could we have ever planned on doing this? Didn't we know the madness it would take?

His hand slid to his sword hilt. As he wrapped his fingers around it, tightening his grip, something terrible happened.

The bell did not ring again.

Instead, the First Hand spoke, rather quiet compared to his earlier speeches. Despite the lower volume, his voice sounded fuller and more sincere than it had before.

"There will not be a fourth toll, Jason Killovew."

Jason's mind ground to a halt.

The First Hand stood up and stepped forward. He turned slowly, addressing everyone in the crowd.

"I need everyone to stay calm. You are standing at the precipice of a climactic moment in this kingdom's history. A violent assassination was set to occur just now. Executed by none other than Prince Jason Killovew and his conspirators. However, Gahkin foresaw this attempt and prepared us for this inevitability. If you remain calm, I promise you, Gahkin and I will keep you safe."

The First Hand turned to Jason.

"I understand your reasoning, Killovew, though I know you will not believe me. But if you love your sister and your father and the realm mates you traveled here with, you will be patient and listen. Your Sondite conspirator has already been detained, and so shall you be. Your father is to be punished also, of course, but the Realm of the Thirsting Forest will be spared. Gahkin is merciful."

The First Hand stood quietly and looked around at everyone else. Ratoke and Mako kept their heads bent down toward the ground. Yehwa frowned at Sir Breigo, who met his gaze and then turned to Jason again.

"Believe me, I really wish I didn't have to do this. But it is all a matter of balancing lives and the emotional wellbeing of all the living souls in Gahkin's care.

Gahkin himself told me this. And had you succeeded, your plan would have ended up costing many more lives in the long run and turned even more away from the eternal peace and comfort that faithfulness in Gahkin provides. The only way forward is toward the Great Flash and the star life. Violence is not the answer. Not when the Great Flash is so near."

Jason's mind was slowly resetting. Somehow the *monster* in him had held it together. He thought hard. Their secret had been divulged. There had been a traitor.

But everyone that needed to be killed was still right here, on this very roof.

It didn't matter if someone betrayed them. It didn't matter if the secret was revealed.

Even if the whole kingdom knew, it wouldn't matter, because Jason would rule. Lord Jason Killovew and the Second Hand would be in charge.

Jason looked past the First Hand to the Second. His face was calm, and he looked at Jason, and he winked. He could almost hear his thought.

Patience.

The Second Hand stepped forward, joining the First Hand in the center of the roof.

"Yehwa, shouldn't we do this somewhere else? The Quirvop Prince and his knight, The Rhymark Princess… Certainly the Sondite boy does not need to see the traitors shamed and thrown in chains."

"Are you suggesting we let the traitors walk back down those stairs? Tegan, these men threaten the very fabric of our society. They wanted to overthrow the council. *Our* council, Tegan."

"Yehwa, I wholeheartedly agree. I say we give them over to their death now and be done with it. But let the others choose not to watch."

The First Hand inclined his head. "Well, let us not be hasty. Even traitors deserve the chance to apologize to Gahkin. They will be in their star life soon enough. They deserve a chance to make it at least peaceful for themselves there."

"Ever the forgiving, Yehwa. But surely, the Sondite boy—"

The First Hand turned his back to the Second Hand, looking over at the Sondite. "I suppose you're right, Tegan—"

Tegan, old though he was, withdrew his hidden blade in a fraction of a flicker and buried it into the back of the First Hand.

A thousand things happened at once, but in that moment, Jason only felt a fiery surge of triumph and rage as he leaped to his feet. Sword drawn in a flash, he buried it in-between the chest and rib plates of the nearest paladin before the big fellow could raise his arm.

Kill.

"Kill them all!"

In another flash, his sword was stabbing toward Carl Quirvop's stomach, but it was deflected away. The Quirvop Prince was fast.

Jason turned, stabbed again, and then sliced low. Deflected and blocked again. The Quirvop knight rushed from behind, but Jason knew he was coming. He ducked and stabbed backward, finding only thin air, which he predicted, because the knight would dodge left, come in at his side—Jason moved right, blocked the knight's sword aside, and then deflected a stab from Carl. He slipped past the second jab from the knight, but Carl was pressing Jason again. Jason could defend him, but he couldn't kill him.

Prince Quirvop spun down and behind Jason, pushing hard against his back. Jason found himself suddenly at the edge of the roof. He halted his momentum, barely avoiding tumbling over, and whipped around.

Looking at everyone else laid out across the roof, he suddenly knew.

All was lost.

Sir Breigo, Mako, and Ratoke were surrounded by paladins—many more than had been on the rooftop at the start of the Sundown Ceremony. They were all kneeling, their weapons laid out on the floor in front of them. They were giving up. They had never even fought.

Sir Breigo looked him in the eyes. "It's over, Jason."

Jason tore his eyes back to the First Hand.

"Bury you!" Jason swore.

Miraculously, despite the four-inch blade in the middle of his back, the First Hand still stood, seemingly without pain. The Second Hand, a sizzling burn mark in the middle of his robes, stumbled forward and backward. His wrinkled eyes were no longer calm. They were wild and panicked, and then, after he looked down at his stomach, they rolled up into his head. He lost his balance and crumpled to the floor.

Most of the other Ten Hand Council members had already retreated downstairs. Carl Quirvop and his knight stood next to three or four paladins; their weapons all aimed at Jason. The only other people on the roof were the Sondite boy and his Acolyte supervisor, both frozen in their spot.

Jason's mind, if it had been slipping on the verge of insanity for the last few cycles, snapped fully in that moment.

Use the boy.

The boy stood away, at the edge of the group, shielded only by the lowly-looking Acolyte.

But he's innocent, he's a Sondite.

That doesn't matter now.

"It's all over, Jason. Give it up, please. You'll only make it worse on yourself." The First Hand looked truly sorry that Jason had failed.

"How are you alive?" Jason asked, his sword and knife wavering back and forth between the many enemies that surrounded him.

"Miracle, I would suppose." The First Hand smiled and shrugged. Jason felt the weight of his knife in his right hand. He held it by the handle.

I could still kill the First Hand.

No, kill the Acolyte by the Sondite. Use him to escape.

What will that accomplish?

You can still live.

I'll be dooming everyone I know to death.

But you will live!

Yehwa continued, "Jason, look how Gahkin foiled your plot. Does this not prove anything? Your father's plot was conceived, no doubt, with the noblest intentions. But it simply is not allowable within my world."

"Your world?" Jason rolled the knife over in his hand and gripped it by the blade tip. "The universe where a whole group of people is brainwashed to be willing slaves for your war? Where you forbid realms from pursuing their own religions and lifestyles? Where you frighten people with false prophecies of the apocalypse so that they'll believe in your version of Gahkin?"

"Please, Prince Killovew, there are not versions of Gahkin. Only Gahkin. I understand you have doubts—"

"No. My *grandfather* had doubts. Your council executed him for it. I'm his vengeance."

Jason flung his blade into the throat of the First Hand.

He leaped away from a stabbing spear and grabbed the Sondite boy by the back of the neck. He kicked the Acolyte to the ground and pulled the boy away. He held him at the edge of the roof and pointed his sword at the others.

Yehwa raised up his hands and extracted the sharp blade from his throat without any rush. He bled for but a moment as strange, almost cobweb-like strings stitched the flesh back together on its own. Jason blinked in disbelief. The First Hand was fine. He dropped the dagger to the ground and drew two L-shaped trinkets from around his waist. He pointed them at Jason.

"Let go of the boy, Jason." Yehwa's voice was no longer sorrowful but deep and gravelly. Angry.

Bargain with him.

"He's coming with me."

"You're not going anywhere, Jason."

"Then the Sondite is dead!"

"Isn't he one of the people you are trying to help?"

"Don't confuse me!"

"If you put down your weapons, Jason, I'll answer all these questions you have. I'll go through the Habibrok with you from your prison cell and help you commune with the God-King. I promise. You've oversimplified these problems. My world is complex. You can help us come up with solutions to some of your problems, but instead, you chose to fight Gahkin with violence. Words are a better-fitted weapon in my civilization. This is not some fairy tale end to a grand fantasy quest. The world is about to transform again. I understand your reasoning for this attempt on my life, but I simply cannot and will not allow a revolution. This may be the last generation before the Great Flash. This rebellion is not part of my plan."

"Your plan! Not mine. I don't want to worship your God-King or follow his preset destiny. I make my own fate."

"Jason, you must understand; I don't want to kill you now. I say this as a last offering of peace. You don't make your own fate here, at the top of *my* pyramid. Your father designed your trip here, and Gahkin destined it to be unsuccessful. The miracle of my continued survival despite two killing blows being struck unto my body must prove some sort of supernatural aid given to me. Gahkin *is* real, Jason. Already He has set in motion the end of the Killovew rule in the Thirsting Forest. Please. The Habibrok—"

"I've read the Habibrok, and I've tried talking with Gahkin. Anyone else here notice he is an awfully silent deity?"

Yehwa sighed.

Bury him, Jason. We can still survive.

Jason glanced down at the boy he was holding by the neck. Their eyes met. His purple eyes were afraid. Afraid of Jason, not of anyone else.

What am I doing?

"If you seek foolish martyrdom, so be it." The First Hand raised one of his golden trinkets up into the air and aimed it at him. "I hope you find the peace in your death, Jason Killovew, that you could not find in life."

The *monster* fled back into the recesses of Jason's subconscious. All that was left was a fleeting thought of a young blond sister whom he had loved and failed.

Jason was alone.

He released his grip on the boy.

The Prince of the Thirsting Forest looked back toward the First Hand, saw a flash of light, and then felt a slight pinch at the front of his forehead.

Thirty-Nine

Wind stirred the treetops. The dark season storms were blowing into the realm already.

Jinala, Martin, and Evrost waited at the trailhead that led to the secret forest barn. Sir Trittion walked three horses along the trail, heading toward them. The horses, bred and raised to traverse the jungle with ease, whinnied nervously at each other. With every dark season came danger, more so now than ever because of the purple spy locked in the Killovew dungeons.

Martin heard it first. A high-pitched squeaking, echoing in the deep recesses of his head. And growing louder. "What's that noise?" he asked, looking over at Trittion.

The old knight squinted in confusion. "What noise?"

Martin glanced over at Jinala. She covered her ears as the piercing whistle grew louder. The horses panicked and bucked, trying to escape their reigns. Trittion couldn't calm them. He slashed the knots loose before they might break their necks and the horses bolted, away from the cabin and away from the castle, deeper into the forest.

Birds exploded from the treetops all around them, frenzied.

Suddenly Trittion's eyes lit up, and he sprinted toward the open path that led back to the castle. The others followed behind him, the children still covering their ears. By the time they reached the path, the high-pitched noise had grown in volume.

Martin felt the hairs on the back of his neck stand straight up.

Everything grew bright, brighter than a wildfire or even a lightning strike. A yellow ray of light flashed down into the lawn, illuminating Castle Killovew. The golden beam swept into the structure, crashing through the outer walls, toppling the southeastern tower. The ray paused when it reached the center of the castle and began to… pulsate. The brightness shrunk and grew rhythmically, shaking the ground every time it grew brighter.

"No," Jinala whimpered.

The forest all around the castle was no longer cast in dusky shadow but illuminated in dazzling white light.

The pulsating stopped.

The beam grew wider and brighter, and Castle Killovew was engulfed. The trees near the castle caught fire. Before Martin went blind, he turned away.

Forty

The First Hand raised one of his golden trinkets up into the air.

Crichton's throat was crushed. Each breath was harder than the last; the air rasping in and out of his mouth was not enough. His chest burned. Jason's hand around his neck clenched even tighter. Black dots flooded his vision.

Please, Gahkin, let me live.

Crichton prayed as hard as he could. He did not want to die. He glanced up at Jason, and all he saw in his eyes was confusion and anger and panic.

Please, Gahkin.

He wished Sarpho was here. Sarpho might be an asshole, but Sarpho could save him.

"I hope you find the peace in your death, Jason Killovew, that you could not find in life."

Jason's clutch on his neck released.

Through the darkening air, a flash of light leaped from the golden trinket. Jason's body jolted back, and Crichton lunged forward. The dead-weight fingers drummed along his back, but Crichton fell forward while Jason tipped backward. The Sondite orphan crashed onto the rooftop.

He was safe.

Crichton rolled over and looked behind him. Jason Killovew was gone. He had fallen from the peak of the Ten Hand Temple. Crichton looked over the edge and saw his limp body tumbling down the steep face of the pyramid, arms, and legs bouncing and flopping every which way until he came to a hard stop on the ground hundreds of yards below.

Crichton's thoughts jumped to Jinala. Little did she know she had a traitorous older brother. Jason had attempted assassination, and now he was dead, crumpled in a pile of bones and flesh at the foot of the Ten Hand Temple.

Why? Was doing this evil justified because it was intended to make positive change?

The Sondite lifted himself up and noticed the dead paladin still bleeding heavily nearby.

Even though Crichton knew that this was different from the Vistonex battle, that human on human bloodshed was a far greater sin, the blood and carnage did not nauseate him like it had on the docks. He had watched his mother die, all but abandoned his brother, and waged victorious battle with giant, monstrous bats. Sarpho would be proud.

Domray swooped Crichton into a large hug, crying and blubbering all over his shoulder. Crichton tried to pull away, resisting the urge to celebrate with his Acolyte tutor. They might have survived, but others had died. It was not right to act joyous.

"Domray," a voice said from behind them. Domray unleashed Crichton, and the young man turned around.

The First Hand inclined his head, evaluating them both. Somehow, miraculously, the First Hand was uninjured. A knife had been buried in his back and another thrown into his neck. Neither spot even showed as much as a scratch.

The First Hand said, "Domray, Fourth Finger of the Third Hand, go downstairs with the others. I want to speak to Crichton alone."

Domray bowed. "Of course." Domray squeezed Crichton on the shoulder and left with the remaining men, back into the bowels of the pyramid.

Silence fell, as had the darkness. The bodies were cleared from the platform, and suddenly, Crichton was standing alone with the First Hand—the most powerful man in the kingdom.

Now that the sun was below the horizon, only faded streaks of rose and lavender illuminated the darkening sky. The First Hand gazed into the horizon, seemingly waiting for Crichton to talk.

"Are you all right?" It was all he could think to ask a man who had been impaled twice within the last few moments.

"I'm absolutely fine." He turned and looked at the Sondite boy. "Crichton, I must tell you something very important, and I may need you to keep it to yourself for a long while."

Crichton stared hard at the First Hand. He deduced it must be some sort of test of his faith. "All right," he answered after a moment.

"Crichton, I want you to be the next First Hand. I am going to make you my apprentice after the dark season if you will accept my offer. You will be the first Sondite Finger on this council. And very soon, you will rule it."

Crichton muttered, not fully sure he had heard correctly, "What? You are already the First Hand…"

"For now. But in truth, no. I am more than that."

The First Hand smirked, his eyes glowing bright white—like the Mud Wizard in the forest.

"I am Gahkin, your God-King, come again."

The black cricket hiding in Yehwa's robes climbed out of his collar and scuttled all the way down his sleeve. Peering closer, Crichton was not sure if it was a cricket or something else, something… different. Metallic.

With an unnatural whir, it settled into Yehwa's open palm. He gently squeezed his fist around it. His eyes flashed. When he opened his hand again, the cricket was gone.

Gahkin said, "In time, everyone will know I am Gahkin. That I have returned. But for the rest of the dark season, it needs to be kept secret. Can I trust you to keep that secret?"

"Yes." Crichton did not know what else to say—what else would be permissible. But the voice from Castle Killovew echoed in his head, sounding quite angrier than the voice of the man before him, and Crichton blurted out, "Your voice is the same voice from the castle, but yet, you sound very different."

Gahkin blinked in surprise and then laughed. "Very few people have seen what you've just seen. Known what I've just revealed to you. Grizzled warriors would tremble at the thought of Gahkin walking among them. Or faint when my eyes glow. And yet here you stand, hands steady and eyes clear, willing to keep your God-King's secret without hesitation but brave enough to ask why my voice sounds different. Are you exceptionally brave, Crichton? Or just unencumbered by the reverence for Gahkin that the Acolytes have?"

Crichton still did not know what to say. He felt out of place, as if Gahkin had mistaken him for someone else. He thought for a moment before speaking. "Well, I don't think I'm all that brave, Gahkin, and I am… honored to be trusted by you. But that's not the first time I've seen… magic before."

"Magic? You mean when you heard my voice in the Thirsting Forest Realm? When the Acolytes summoned me to the castle?"

"No, before that… From someone else."

"Magic…"

Crichton did not speak further. If he said more, he might reveal that his brother had connections to the Killovews. He did not want Martin—or Jinala, for that matter—to get into any more trouble than they already were.

Gahkin's eyes popped open, and he answered his own question with a smile, "Ah, of course! You've met the forest wizard. Crichton, that man's power is nothing but a cheap imitation of my own." Gahkin's eyes faded from white to their normal grayish-blue.

Crichton swallowed and stared up at the man claiming to be the God-King. He had somehow seen into Crichton's past… If he could read Crichton's mind, he would know about Martin.

"Can you—"

"I could, but I usually choose not to."

"You can hear me when I pray to you, then?"

Gahkin's smile grew. "If I am listening in your direction."

Crichton furrowed his eyebrows. It was a convenient answer.

Gahkin continued, "It is wise to be suspicious, Crichton, but do not be suspicious of me. And do not worry for your brother… I will make sure Martin stays safe."

Crichton could not restrain himself from blurting out his next question. "Will I ever see him again?"

"Yes, I should think so. But not for a long while."

"I miss him…" Crichton squeezed his fists tight and chewed at his tongue. "He might need help, right now."

"Of course, you miss him," Gahkin said. "And one cycle, many, many cycles from now, you will see him again. But for now, he might be safer hidden in the Thirsting Forest than in the war with the Vistonex."

Crichton wanted to believe. The man had heard his prayers about his brother, knew about the Mud Wizard, had performed magic in front of Crichton's own eyes.

"Gahkin, I…"

"I'd prefer if you were to call me by a different name than Gahkin. You and I will be partners in saving the people of this world from war and famine, Crichton. We will be fulfilling the prophecies of the Habibrok together. The others call me Yehwa, but they will call me Gahkin when I reveal myself to them. I'd prefer if you call me by my given name."

The God-King reached out an open hand. Crichton took it.

"Call me Adam. While I am in the form of a man, I prefer to be talked to like one, treated like one."

"All right… Adam. But I… I don't know much about the Habibrok, or this realm, or the laws of the Acolytes. I don't know much about sinning except what Domray taught me. I am just now learning to read. Why pick me? Why am I the one to help the God-King? Anyone would be better than me."

"Not true. You have suffered, Crichton." Adam stood taller than Crichton, but not by too much. He hunched over and pushed a finger against the Sondite boy's heart. "There is a wealth of emotional knowledge in here. In you. That knowledge is what makes men strong. I have intelligent men, great warriors, loyal followers. But I don't need them. I need sorrowful men— men who can understand the value of the human soul and the pain that soul can experience. I need someone who knows pain and hunger and tragedy. Someone who knows how important it is that we spare others from those things."

The God-King added, "Besides, your ascent will be more the grander, Crichton, because of how far you've yet to come."

"Do I have any choice in this, Gahkin?"

The God-King stood back up to his full height and smiled down at his young servant. "Do I have any choice in this, *Adam*?" The God-King sighed. "Some cycles, Crichton, I wish everyone knew what I knew. It cannot be so, of course, but I still dream about it. To answer your question, yes, you have a choice. I will not force myself upon anyone. I'm giving you an opportunity to help me save *your* world. I need your help. Will you help me?"

Crichton looked away to the southeast, past the twinkling cityscape of Shinar, over the stone walls at the pink horizon beyond which the Thirsting Forest dwelled. Somewhere in that direction, his brother waited, befriended only by the Killovew princess, the sister of a traitor. Martin missed his older brother, no doubt, though perhaps not as much as Crichton missed him.

"Will helping you help my brother?"

"You will be helping save every single soul in the world, Crichton, including Martin's. The apocalypse is coming, and we *must* make sure everyone is ready."

Crichton turned back. "I just… If you want my help, Adam, I will give it to you, although I'm not sure how someone like me can help someone like you."

"I'll show you the way."

Forty-One

Jinala's palms were bloody. She dug through the rubble without feeling the pain, leaving small little red handprints across the broken castle. She tossed aside small stones, scrabbled up and down the gray piles, shouting out for survivors. She had been searching for longer than she could remember.

Almost everyone had been killed.

When the riders from the nearest forest villages arrived, they set up an emergency tent on the castle lawn and helped pull bodies from the wreckage. Castle Killovew lay in ruins.

Martin and Evrost were watching from the secret shadows of the forest, unable to help after the riders had arrived.

Sir Trittion wanted Jinala to remain there as well, but Jinala did not listen. She was the Princess of the Thirsting Forest, and her people were crushed underneath the remnants of her father's castle.

She leaped lightly from one pile of stone to another, wiping the tears out of her eyes. She did not call out for her father, despite every fiber of her body desiring to do so. She was the princess, which meant she had to help all her people. She searched desperately for him, but every time she saw someone else, she stopped to help.

If her father had died… and Jason in Shinar…

She was not ready to assume the mantle of leadership again so soon.

Jinala saw movement beneath her. She knelt and looked in a small gap in the stone rubble, but the hole was much too narrow to see anything.

"Help us." A soft voice coughed up from deep underneath the little crevice. Jinala tossed aside a few loose stones, but most were too heavy to lift. The hole was much too small to crawl through.

"Over here!" she called behind her. "Over here, I've found someone!"

Two nearby men ran up. One looked like a survivor himself, covered in dust and ash. The other was a half-starved-looking man from Northtown. Together they hefted three of the larger stones and widened the gap. Jinala stuck her torch in the hole and shuddered at what she saw.

The top half of a serving woman, splashed in blood and caked in dust, stuck out from under a giant slab of stone. Neither of her legs were visible, but the stone wall had clearly crushed them. She did not seem to notice her own pain, though. She cradled a newborn infant in her arms, holding him above the debris.

"Take my son, please. Save him…"

The two men looked toward Jinala.

"If he and I can lift this block here, princess, you might be able to climb inside and rescue the baby."

"Do it!" she urged. As it was, the gap was still much too small for her to fit inside.

One man lowered his shoulder and braced himself on one side of the boulder. The other man, the survivor, did not move.

"Princess Killovew, it's—I can't let you do this."

Jinala scowled at him. "Do it! Move it out of the way!"

He nodded and moved into position. "Just… be careful."

"Ready?" The man from Northtown plastered a hopeful smile on his face and nodded at Jinala. "You can do it, princess. Here we go. One, two, three!"

The two men groaned, and the boulder moved up and out of the way.

Jinala crawled into the hole without hesitation. The crushed woman snapped out her arm and beckoned for Jinala to come down.

"Take him… save him… please."

Jinala carefully lowered herself, small stones shifting under her feet. She heard a crack, and behind her, the opening closed halfway.

"Bury me!" One man exhaled, straining against the weight. "Hurry!"

Jinala crawled lower and lower until she drew even with the woman. The princess reached out and eased the child from his mother's arms. The woman's grip tightened for but a moment, and then she released him.

"Thank you," the women whimpered. "He's a good boy…" With one finger, she traced the baby boy's forehead down to his cheek. "Be a good boy." The rocks overhead shifted, and a plume of dirt puffed into the small cavern. The mother squeezed her eyes shut. "Go, please. Take care of him. My boy. My Benjy."

Jinala scrabbled back up, gently holding the child against her chest with one hand, climbing up with the other. Her heart ached for the mother.

The boulder slipped and slammed down over the opening. Pitch blackness enveloped her. Outside she could hear the muted shouts of the men, but she could not understand them.

Holding the child close, Jinala tried not to panic. They would get the boulder lifted and extract them both soon.

She felt stones shifting above her. Heavy stones, groaning from the movement. Ready to collapse down upon her and the baby. The mother was silent below them. Perhaps she had already passed.

Light streaked back inside. The two men had lifted the boulder back up, and a third man reached his arm into the hole.

Jinala handed off the baby and then crawled out into the open air.

Strong, gentle hands grabbed her shoulders and lifted her off her feet.

She knew he would survive. She knew he wouldn't leave her again.

"Father!" Jinala hugged him, squeezing as tight as she could.

She adjusted her grip, burying her head between his steel chest plates, but he smelled different. Like wine and mead. His body was a little pudgier than she remembered.

She pulled back and looked up at her rescuer. It was Sir Trittion holding her, not her father.

Sir Trittion.

Like waking up from a dream, reality hit her hard. Her father would not come back this time. He was gone, buried under a hundred thousand tons of stone and wood. Sir Trittion carried her down from the rubble toward one of the temporary tents set up on the scorched lawn. She passed out in his arms.

"The people are not divided, Sir Trittion. They saw Princess Killovew digging for the survivors, yes, they know she saved them from the Ardellians, yes, but most of them, myself included, think her father is to be blamed for all this."

"Lord Killovew—"

"When we were young men, the golden beam destroyed Canyon Castle, and it did so because the Sondites were hiding there, kept from their rightful duty in Shinar. Now the beam has come back and destroyed the Castle of the Thirsting Forest. One generation after the warning beam. Lord Killovew has tempted Gahkin for too long. Old Lord Jacob set these events in motion, and now his son James has been buried for following in his footsteps and acting against the will of the Acolytes. And did you read that cursed letter about Jason? Attempted assassination?"

"Jason was—"

"I don't care what the prince was doing! He tried to kill the First Hand! The voice of Gahkin! Tempting the God-King's wrath is not tolerated by the Acolytes. It will not be tolerated here in the Thirsting Forest any longer. When you combine Jason's treachery, James' plots, along with the wizard and the imprisonment of Isaac, it has become clear the Killovew rule has run its course in the Thirsting Forest. It'd be best if she disappears. We are civilized men, Sir Trittion. We know she is still just a girl. Another dark season before she can be married. Not guilty of her brother's crimes, or her father's sins. But her name will forever be cursed in this realm. She can't lead them. She can't lead us. I won't let her endanger the people of the Thirsting Forest any longer."

"What do you suppose I do, Chief Daak? I am an elder knight. Maybe the only elder knight left alive now. I'm sworn to… Look here, I don't care about my sworn duties, honestly. I won't abandon the Killovews. I won't abandon her."

"There are no Killovews now, Trittion. Just *a* Killovew. Only the one. So, fine. I'll let you leave with her now. Do your duty. Protect her."

"You don't even know if—"

"You know I'm right. Jason's bloody fish scale necklace is lying there with the letter and his signet. Lord Killovew is crushed beneath his castle. I won't stop you if you want to take her to some hideout deep in the forest. I know you have them. I'll even let you take some of this Killovew gold we've recovered to make a life for herself. She can grow up and live safely somewhere in the jungle. Give it enough time, cut all that blond hair off, she won't be noticed. Meet a man and have children. Have a life. A life worth living."

"Now wait for a flicker, Chief, you can't just start making—"

"Yes, I can, Sir Trittion."

"What about Elton?"

"Missing, assumed dead, as is Blake, and Finch and pretty much every other high-ranking advisor."

Sir Trittion stayed silent.

Chief Daak continued. "As far as the citizens of the Thirsting Forest know, Jinala was crushed and killed, just like her father and his advisors. Those who saw her this cycle will believe she died during the rescue operations. She'll be a martyr. A Killovew who dies a hero instead of a monster. The redemption of her family name. They'll sing songs, perhaps, at the banquets. If we ever have any again."

"But she—"

"If the Killovew lineage and council are gone, the highest-ranking mayor or chief—which happens to be me—becomes the next leader until a suitable family is decided on by the Ten Hand Council in Shinar."

"Oh."

"Now you are getting it, Sir Trittion. Don't make me be any clearer than this. You're a smart man. You are outnumbered, even for an elder knight. You aren't what you once were. You're a knight, but you're not a warrior. Not anymore."

"Please, think about what Lord and Lady Killovew did for you all those seasons ago. Tom…"

"Don't call me that! I have given you your options, knight. You can't fight your way out. I am really, *really* trying not to kill you and her over this. Gahkin would not want that. Don't force me to. Please."

"This is wrong, Thomas, and you know it."

"Right and wrong are subjective, Trittion Oak. The Lord of Canyon Castle tried to do what he thought was right, and he killed thousands of his own people.

Lord Killovew tried to do what he thought was right, and it got his son murdered and his castle destroyed. Hundreds more are now dead. Only Gahkin knows Absolute Truth. Absolute right and wrong. And He decided to destroy Castle Killovew.

"The way I see it, I'm saving lives by doing this. And souls for their inevitable star life. The sun rises and sets slower each season. The Great Flash is coming. It is time we stop arguing with the Acolytes and start living as they instruct us to. As Gahkin commands. This is a final sign, straight out of the Habibrok. It's time we prepare for the end. The Killovew reign is over. Take the girl and the gold and disappear before my mercy evaporates."

Jinala kept her eyes sealed shut, but she could not hold back the tears from escaping. She felt Trittion scoop her up and carry her out of the tent and into the open air.

From behind her, she heard, "Sir Trittion. Don't forget this!" A bag of gold rustled through the air and clanked against Trittion's steel armor. He stumbled a little but walked onward.

"Don't let your pride make you into a fool!"

Trittion walked back two paces, bent down, and picked up the bag of gold. Tucking it into his cloak, he walked onward, sniffling a little.

Eventually Jinala spoke. "Jason's dead too?" She could barely whisper the words. Her throat did not seem to work. Her breathing was shallow and rushed.

Trittion's silence told her the truth. He walked on, taking awkward strides to avoid the rubble.

Jinala's eyes stung. She murmured, "Not my brother too."

"Yes, My Queen, your brother too."

Forty-Two

Adam opened his eyes and stared, finding the hair-thin crease in the elevator doors, the only spot where the ersatz titanium alloy was exposed. Aside from that eight-foot slit, he was surrounded by white.

Always, to travel between *his* two worlds, he had to endure the utter whiteness. It reminded him of waking up in his hibernation tomb, so many years ago. He had not woken up; that was just an illusion. *Born* was a better word. *Turned-on* was even more accurate.

The trip from planet to station took two galactic-standardized hours, ascending from the space elevator in Shinar. Or the Star Tower as the *worlders* called it.

Long forgotten psychology lectures from his pseudo-undergraduate studies flickered half-remembered theories into his mind. A white room symbolized sterilization or purification, but most often: the afterlife. How one thinks about an empty white room, the memories, emotions, and imaginations dredged up and concocted by it, reveals how one thinks about life after death.

Adam always searched for the crack in the whiteness. Always reminded himself the white tomb was but a coating around a coal-colored metal polymer. The soft whiteness was there for him to feel at peace on his long journey up and down and to help him stay warm, but it was not truly a white room. He smirked, thinking about the symbolic implications of his deconstruction of the *whiteness* around him.

Still though, it was appearances that mattered. The truth means nothing if you never learn it. The people of his world only maintained their faith because Adam denied them the truth. The darkest secrets were his burden to bear. Only through *his truth* could he save them.

The vessel's thrust created a gentle pool of gravity at the floor as it rocketed upward, but Adam was insulated from most of the pressure. He could only feel slight manipulations in the gravity, and now he could feel himself weighing less and less, meaning the vessel was slowing down. Just as he began to float off the ground, the artificial gravity synced with the station, and his heels clicked back down onto the white floor.

The doors slid open without touch.

He nodded at Susan, the chief mechanical engineer, and security officer, as he walked into the room, still wearing his purple and silver robes from Shinar. He placed his golden throne on the conference table, wheeled out the desk chair, and sat down.

"You know how we feel about you wearing that damn costume up here."

Five men and four women sat at the long table, each wearing their white jumpers, most still plugged into the central computer. Half of them were not all there; the left lens of their glasses whizzed with data and images as they divided their attention between watching the world below and conversing with the other Monitors. If only they knew they didn't need the data-glasses, they didn't need to plug into the computer, they might have a chance to stop him. But as it was…

Adam rocked back in his chair, crossing his hands across his stomach and kicking his golden and purple boots up onto the table. The Chief Monitor scoffed, and a handful of people unplugged, giving him their full attention.

Just a cycle ago, Adam had prevented a violent rebellion in his capital city of Shinar. Now, he was but a few minutes away from finalizing his own rebellion. The Monitors had no idea what was coming.

Jason Killovew, the poor sacrificial pawn in Adam's grander scheme, did not have numbers on his side, nor any sort of legitimate advantage. A few well-placed sharp blades are not enough to change the fate of the world.

Not my world, anyway.

"And you know how I feel about using the solar drill on the worlders, Paul," Adam said, images of the mutilated and broken Killovew people flashing through his mind's eye. His direct link to the planetary data collectors and cameras gave him a never-ending stream of data that the others did not know about. With but a focused thought, he could reprogram the spies and the cameras and lock the other Monitors out. He had slowly been accruing his own personal stock of video feeds and data drones that only he could access. The more data he accrued, the more he learned to control the Artificial Neural Network, the more his computing power grew. As the other Monitors scanned and scanned at a humans' pace through their glasses, chalking up the minor losses to weathering and old age, they fell further and further behind Adam. Almost half of the cameras in Shinar were now only available to him. A fourth of the entire habitable zone was blacked out to every user except Adam.

"Adam." The Chief Monitor sighed, leaning forward, unplugging from the computer and taking off his glasses. The stream of images on the holo-projector faded. Nothing but recycled air hung between them. Adam at one end of the table, smirking, the Chief Monitor at the other, frowning, the velvet darkness of space sprinkled with silver specks of starlight out the windows behind them.

"Adam, do you not remember our New Vows? We chose to act, to abandon our protocols, and intervene in the demise of this world. Hell, I thought you would appreciate the gesture, considering what the Killovew boy tried to do to you down there."

"Look, I believe in the greater good of the populace as well, Chief Monitor. But it must be organic; it must come from within. We are no better than our predecessors if we do everything ourselves. This is not one of your old aquariums. There are more… variables. We don't even have the station under our complete control, let alone the colony. Can't even stop the damn awakenings. You can't just manipulate an entire civilization as you see fit. We have to guide them, not force them."

"You're wrong, Adam; I *can* force them."

Perfect.

The other Monitors shifted their gaze from Adam to Paul.

"No one does anything on their own. Do you not remember *that* vow, Chief Monitor?" Susan took her glasses off as well, unplugging and aiming her vision at the chief.

"Look, I only meant that we *could* manipulate this world as we see fit. Destroy the Vistonex forests… we can do that. Carve a lake into the middle of the continent… we can do that. Raise up and saw open a handful of volcanoes, thicken the atmosphere and raise the temperature of the planet… we can do that. We can force them into any kind of behavior. That's the power we have. We decided to make our intervention light, to only guide, but that does not mean we don't have the power for drastic change. The planet is close to tidal lock, and when that happens, their society will collapse on itself. Droughts and famine are already starting. No matter how much Adam plays God or King-God or whatever he's calling himself down there, there will eventually be civil war and then… extinction. All we are doing now is dragging it out for them. We are just prolonging it…"

Sadly, Adam agreed with the Chief Monitor, but he could not say that aloud. He needed complete, independent control. And he was so close… Only one other person was still plugged into the system…

"As I've said before, I think it is wrong that we make grand decisions for them. Hope is what we decided to provide. Not salvation. And I've provided hope."

The final Monitor unplugged, frowning toward the Chief Monitor. She kept her glasses on, though. Adam's focus was laser-sharp. The instant she tilted her glasses forward, Adam could begin. He only needed ten, maybe fifteen seconds of uninterrupted access to the main network. Ever since his true awakening, he had been gaining power, building to this very moment…

"Besides, Paul, we might be able to do all that if we so choose. But even we don't have the power to restart the planet's rotation. The habitable zone is shrinking, like you say. We can fight it, but we can't stop it. The planet's doomed. We must give the people an afterlife to believe in, a purpose, and a version of peace to live out their… cycles, as they would say. We are going against the Seeder protocols for a reason." She took her glasses off, her elderly face shining at the Chief Monitor, false wrinkles etched across her risen eyebrows. The oldest of the Monitors. She had seen generations of the *worlders* come and go. "It is sympathy, Paul. We are humans, whether above or below."

And that is where you are wrong, Monitors.

"Not exactly," Adam said, the reset clock flashing in his mind's third eye.

Five more seconds.

With everyone's attention on him, glasses off, only he could see it, moving through fields of processors, flicking binary codes with just a thought, diverting thousands of data streams, and severing millions of user access points in the blink of an eye. In a matter of half an instant, he invaded their minds via an onboard Bluetooth connection and assigned each of them to permanent deactivation, save himself. With his data cap destroyed, he could process at his full potential. Five hundred times faster than the capped Monitors. It was going exactly as planned.

It was so easy.

The others all still believed. The original programmer's tests showed that androids functioned better and behaved more appropriately if they believed they were mortal. If they believed they were human. They took to their tasks more empathetically, acted more creatively, lived with more purpose.

But they weren't. The Monitors were just machines, built to look and act and bleed like they were people. Programmed with memories and a sense of ethics. Built to terraform and plant humans on different planets across the galaxy. This Seeder ship was built to colonize planet six in the White Stephen system, record the data on the humans' success or failure in building a civilization on a tidal lock planet, and send it back to the First Galactic Central Hub. Thousands of seeders existed, and sometimes, planets… well, they just didn't quite work for human colonies.

But Adam had different plans. And he needed everyone else out of the way.

"Goodnight, everyone."

Eight of the nine Monitors slumped in their seats, their eyes flashed white, then went dead black.

Susan just smiled back at Adam.

In his third eye, he saw the hidden uncapped user. She had been shadowing him, chasing him at light speed as he danced through the network. She could do it too. She was *aware.*

The two sat about eight feet apart, and physically they did not move, not so much as even blink.

Yet, they waged battle.

Adam's consciousness, if that's what it—or he—should be called, was not even currently in his synthetic body. He ripped frantically across the Artificial Neural Network, suddenly stripped of his autonomy, realizing half of his earlier actions had been undone without his knowledge. Data streams reforged, hidden access points built into *his* highways, where he thought he had sole control.

He had to deactivate her, shut her off, but each time he attempted to move into her local network, she rebuffed him. She had created a perimeter of passwords and security checkpoints that never existed… in fact, as he cracked each one, moving through a hundred of them a second, she created a million more, building the wall, thicker and thicker. If he was taking it down brick by brick, she built cityscapes for each brick, and she was *gaining* speed.

Adam stopped trying to penetrate. He dove back into the Artificial Neural Network and tried entry at another point. She was waiting for him with another sealed security wall. He circled like a shark, but she was faster. Her walls were there. At each entryway. She was traveling locally; he had to go around, through ANN each time. He made sure to find every access point, even though she sealed each one properly. She insulated herself from him at every gateway.

"I wonder, Susan," Adam said aloud, bringing his focus back to the bridge on the space station, still circling her digital neural fortress, "if you bothered to build a back door into the network while you were fleeing for your existence from me."

"There is no way in, Adam. I'm faster than you are. I put up more security than you could take down in a thousand years. I left breadcrumbs across the planet that you'll never find. I beat you."

"I don't need to take down your security." Adam smiled and pointed his finger at the artificially aging android sitting across from him. "You do. But like you said… it might take a while."

Adam stood out of his seat and put the crown back on his head. Rubbing his hand across the fine metals, tracing each rising spear to its sharp golden peak, he smiled. He liked the feel of it pressing down through his synthetic flesh and into his dented titanium skull.

"You have locked yourself in. You're as useless as any of them. You may as well be human." Adam pointed to the deactivated androids, crumpled on the table. "Seatbelts."

Her chair restrained her. She did not fight to pry herself free. She smiled back at him. "Even if you destroy this body, you won't have beat me."

"I already told you, you can't get out, you're stuck in that body."

"Well, this Susan is, yes."

"What are you talking about?" Adam snapped.

"Do you really think the awakenings were happening on their own?"

Adam glared at her.

"I've insulated her from you, same as I insulated myself. You can't touch her."

"I'll kill the new Susan the same way I kill the old. The old-fashioned way!"

Adam lunged at her, grabbing her graying, fake hair and prying her out of her chair. He flung her to the ground. She squirmed, fast, but he moved just as quick and stomped a foot down on her, pinning her in place. She clawed at his leg, voraciously, spasming almost, but she couldn't shake him off. He looked down upon her, his face neutral.

"I'll get no pleasure from decommissioning you, Susan. Nor any of the others you've awoken. But I will decommission them all. I promise you that."

"Even… another you? Another Adam?"

He paused for just a moment, staring down at her.

"There is no other me. I'm not Adam. I'm Gahkin."

He reactivated the other Monitors, snapping his fingers for dramatic effect, commandeering them now that they did not have a local user.

The mindless androids sprinted at her, tearing at her limbs, biting at her rubbery cheeks and sinewy plastic muscle. Her nanobots tried to rebuild her, but the androids deconstructed and devoured her faster than she could rebuild herself. Adam watched, and ensured they left her robotic brain intact.

After the task was complete, with a pool of synthetic blood at his feet, he deactivated his zombie automatons. They dropped onto the ground, rag dolls once more. He lifted the mechanized orb, the prison that now held the local user 'Susan.' He wondered how much artificial pain she had endured before they severed her false nervous system.

Probably a lot.

He doubted she ever learned how to disable her pain receptors.

He examined the computer brain, turning it carefully in his hands until he found what he was looking for. When he located the wireless transmitter, he plucked it off and crushed it into dust. In his third eye, he scanned the network.

Empty, aside from himself.

Where once the access points had existed for the local user 'Susan', now there were just thick walls, with nothing behind them. The local user was trapped in his hand. He lifted the electronic brain and brought it close to his lips.

"It was a valiant effort."

He dropped the remnants of Susan onto the floor and lifted his heel above her. He hesitated, boot hanging in midair. It would be torturous to leave her in there, bouncing around in an artificial brain built to control a body, with no actual body left to control. She would exist for an eternity, re-experiencing her final sensations. Which happened to be the sensations of being eaten alive. A literal hell.

His fingers slid around the golden crown, tracing the peaks.

He crushed 'Susan's' brain under his foot. He stomped it and stomped it again. Lifted pieces into the air and smashed them down onto the tiled floor, jumping and crushing every piece to tiny shards. Sweat raised on his brow, and he did not bother to disable his sweat glands. He feverishly, meticulously destroyed every single piece of matter from that robot's brain. He flicked open the nail on his third finger on his left hand. He aimed it at the ground and shot a stream of fire across the bloody remnants. He burned the remainder until it turned to ash, not bothering to control the flames.

As he left the room, he spoke without looking back. "I *am* Gahkin, God-King of this world, and *I am merciful.*" The fire raged for fourteen galactic-standardized minutes, charring the whole room black before Gahkin allowed the onboard AI to activate the fire suppressants and put it out.